PEONY
STREET

PEONY STREET

Pamela Grandstaff

Books by Pamela Grandstaff:

Rose Hill Mystery Series:

Rose Hill

Morning Glory Circle

Iris Avenue

Peony Street

Daisy Lane

Lilac Avenue

Hollyhock Ridge

Sunflower Street

Viola Avenue

Pumpkin Ridge

ISBN-10: 146101509X
ISBN-13: 978-1461015093
ASIN: B005UDQ2NG

For My Dad

Chapter One - Friday

You! You with the towels. Don't look at me, don't speak to me, and don't touch anything. Stay right where you are. Tuppy! Why is no one monitoring who comes in the door? Where is security?"

A shudder ran through Chance Farthington "Tuppy" Tupworth's body as the shriek of the diva preceded her noon-time appearance in the doorway to his hotel suite, where he was organizing her day. She had a plush towel wrapped around her head, and a peony-patterned silk kimono floated around her whippet-thin body. Her muscles were so tightly stretched and defined they looked as if they might snap and roll up at any moment. Soft terry spa slippers with miniature padded straps between each freshly painted toenail cushioned her tiny, manicured feet.

She glared at Tuppy and then, distracted by a noise, pointed at someone further down the hallway.

"You! What's your name? Speak up! I pay you people a fortune; why can't you just for once do what I hired you to do? Why am I surrounded by idiots? You're supposed to keep these people away from me. Get her out of here and make sure it doesn't happen again or you're fired."

Her perfectly motionless, exquisite face, the one so often displayed on film posters, in fashion magazines, and on tabloid covers, suggested twenty-nine. Every ropy vein in her arms and hands admitted thirty-nine, which was closer to the truth. The lack of any discernable emotion in her facial expression could lead one to assume all was calm behind her sea-green eyes. Tuppy hadn't made that assumption in a long while.

"Tuppy," Sloan said. "Where's Claire? This is royalty we're dealing with; I want everything to be perfect."

"Teeny's styling and Juanita's doing makeup," Tuppy said calmly. "Alexander McQueen sent a selection of couture with accessories, someone from Tiffany's will bring the jewelry this afternoon, Teeny has procured a selection of Christian Louboutin shoes, and Andrew Barton is sending a team to do your hair."

"I don't want a team. I want Claire."

"She's not returning my calls," Tuppy replied in a reasonable tone. "I've left voicemails, texts, and email messages."

"Then why are you just sitting there, you moron," she huffed. "Go find her."

"What would you like me to do when I find her, Sloan? Rough her up? Kidnap her?"

"I don't care how you do it, just get her here. Tell her I'll double her salary."

"You've tried that."

"Tell her I'll have Juanita deported."

"You've tried that as well," Tuppy said. "You might as well accept it, Sloan; that bird has flown."

"It's not over until I say it's over," Sloan said. "Claire just needs to be made to understand. If Stanley were here, he'd take care of it, and I wouldn't have all this horrible stress."

Sloan moved across the room to closely examine her face in a mirror on the wall as if searching for the detrimental effects of the horrible stress. Tuppy realized he was holding his breath and quietly let it out, willing himself to calm down and not let her provoke him. He recalled what Claire always said to him: "Remember to breathe, Tuppy. She won't kill you and eat you; she doesn't eat red meat."

Tuppy was glad Sloan's attorney wasn't with them on this trip. The man dressed like a mobster smiled like a shark and didn't miss a thing. Tuppy tended to stutter and drop things when Stanley was around, and the attorney enjoyed the effect he had on the members of Sloan's staff. Claire was the exception; she just rolled her eyes at everything he said, and for some reason Sloan let her get away with it.

"Why are you just sitting there?" Sloan asked as she continued her facial inspection. "Did I not make myself clear?"

"Claire quit," Tuppy said. "She gave a month's notice. We had a lovely party for her yesterday evening, which you didn't attend, and now she's free to leave."

Tuppy bit his lip; he hadn't meant to let that last bit slip out.

"What do you mean, she's leaving?" Sloan said, turning away from the mirror to look at him. "Where's she going?"

"I haven't the faintest," Tuppy replied. "I don't know, and I don't care. Life stories of the poor and witless bore me to tears."

Sloan tightened the belt of her robe as she came toward him and then stood way too close to him. He struggled not to choke on her strong perfume as she pointed a beautifully manicured nail in his face.

"I don't care what bores you; I don't pay you to have opinions. If you'd like to join Claire on the unemployment line, I can arrange that."

"I'm so sorry," Tuppy said. "I forgot my place. It won't happen again."

"You still have her personal information, don't you? Cancel her credit cards. Cancel her plane tickets. Report her as a terrorist. Do whatever it takes, but don't let her leave this country."

"Yes, Sloan," he said, "right away."

"Was that sarcasm?" she asked him.

"No, Sloan," Tuppy said. "I have your orders, and I'm on top of it."

"You'd better be," she said. "Tell her if she doesn't sign a new contract you'll be fired because you will be."

"Yes, Sloan."

Sloan looked around the beautifully appointed lounge of one of the most luxurious accommodations available in a five star London hotel.

"Is this the biggest apartment they have?"

"It's apartment one, Milestone Hotel," Tuppy said. "It's 1178 square feet."

"I know everything on this island is small, but this is ridiculous."

"I did suggest we take a whole floor in the main building."

"At least in here there aren't so many flowers and stripes," she said. "It's like Laura Ashley threw up all over my bedroom."

"Would you like to move?"

"No," she said. "This is supposed to be the best."

"They have agreed to secure sole use of the resistance pool for you every day at five a.m."

"Good," she said. "I want security to escort me, and not this idiot out here; get me someone competent."

"It's all taken care of."

"Where's my lunch?"

"Three steamed asparagus spears and half of a poached chicken breast will be delivered precisely at one o'clock."

"And spring water, the French one."

"I'll bring it myself."

"The most important thing for you to do today is getting Claire back."

"I'll deliver her in plenty of time for you to get ready."

Tuppy could see she was looking for more things to criticize to provoke him into raising his voice or defending himself. She loved to nick his self-confidence first thing in the morning and then pick at the scab all day.

Tuppy put on his headset, picked up his phone and pretended to make a call, hoping she would leave the room. As she went down the hallway, she screamed for Teeny and

Juanita. Doors slammed, people scurried, and another tension- and drama-filled day with Sloan Merryweather entered its seventh hour. Unfortunately, there were at least fourteen more to go.

Tuppy had worked for the award-winning film actress for eighteen months. He didn't know how Claire had lasted twenty years. Claire knew Sloan better than anyone, and she was able to advise the best course of action in every difficult situation, of which there were many. Fresh out of grad school and new to the personal assistant game, Tuppy had needed someone to steer him through the shark-infested show business waters until he could navigate on his own. Claire had done that. He owed her.

Claire was kind of a ditz, and the way she let Sloan walk all over her made him dislike them both, but she didn't deserve what Sloan had just instructed him to do. So instead of ruining Claire's life, Tuppy prepared to honor the reservation he had made for himself on the same flight Claire was taking. At 2:45 p.m. GMT Tuppy ordered car service to take him to Heathrow and retrieved his luggage from where he had it hidden behind the sofa.

When Claire didn't show up for their flight and didn't answer her phone, Tuppy was perplexed. Had she actually taken a different flight, he wondered, leaving the original reservation in place as a decoy? That seemed awfully clever for someone he considered so simple-minded. He left her a voicemail message and sent her a text while waiting at the gate. He continued to ignore all the calls from Sloan, which were now coming every thirty seconds.

At just before 5:00 p.m. GMT Tuppy's phone tweedled again as they called for first class passengers. He didn't recognize the number, so he answered, hoping it was Claire.

"Where are you?" Juanita asked in an urgent whisper.

Tuppy could hear Sloan screeching in the background.

"I'm on my way," he said. "I just have to pick up Claire, and we'll be there in twenty minutes, depending on traffic. Tell her everything's under control. Tell her I'm bringing the spring water and her nicotine gum."

"She doesn't like any of the dresses they sent," Juanita said. "She won't let anyone touch her hair; she says she's not leaving her room until Claire's here."

"Not to worry," Tuppy said. "Tell her Claire and I will take care of everything as soon as we get there."

His first-class seat was in the front row, left the side, by the window. It was Sloan's favorite seat, the one over which she would throw a colossal fit if she didn't get. As soon as he was settled Tuppy turned off his phone. He was done living in reactive anxiety over Sloan's rapidly changing emotional temperature. He was done trying to anticipate her every need and desire only to be jerked this way and that by her whims of iron. He was through being berated and belittled at every turn, until he agonized over every decision no matter how small, sure it would somehow turn out to be wrong. He was done with that part of his life and ready for the next part, the part where he would be the one making demands.

He ordered a vodka gimlet and took a sleeping pill. As he drifted off to sleep, somewhere over the Atlantic, he imagined the scene at the hotel, wondering how long it would take Sloan to realize he wasn't coming. If she had to cancel her appearance at the royal engagement party, she would be looking forward to firing Tuppy in revenge. As soon as she read the resignation letter he had arranged for the concierge to deliver to her at precisely 1:00 a.m. GMT (by which time he would have safely landed in DC) she would call Stanley, her attorney, who would conference the call with Angus, her agent, and Ayelet, her publicist. Damage control, revenge scenarios, and ass coverage would all be quickly and efficiently organized by the various parties involved.

'To no avail,' Tuppy thought to himself. 'I've seen to that.'

He fell asleep smiling.

At the baggage claim in D.C. Tuppy turned on his phone, which tweedled to inform him he had texts and voicemails waiting. He adjusted the time back to Eastern Standard Time, which meant it was just after 8:00 p.m. The phone's calls-received list was full of the various phone numbers belonging to Sloan and her fame preservation league, and his voice mailbox was full, but there was nothing from Claire. The same was true of the long list of texts he'd received. On impulse, he deleted "all previous" in each category.

Afterword, as he stood in line for a rental car his phone tweedled again. This text was from Sloan.

"Yr as gd as ded"

Despite his earlier bravado, Tuppy felt a knot of apprehension clench in his solar plexus. When he rented the car, he listed his destination as New York, NY. Thinking Sloan might have the authorities track him down through his personal credit card, and having no doubt reported him as having stolen her jewelry or something equally heinous, he impulsively decided to drive to Claire's hometown (where despite his protestations otherwise he knew very well she was going) in order to meet her and discuss the situation in person. She must be warned, and he needed somewhere to lie low until his appointment in Manhattan on Monday. What better place to hide than in Lower Podunk, USA?

He sent Claire a text, left her a voicemail, and then used his phone to map the route from Reagan Airport to Rose Hill.

After surveying the driving directions and accompanying map, he decided not to worry about that last thin, squiggly black line until he came to it. It seemed to represent a two-lane road that left a four-lane highway in southern Pennsylvania, wandered south along the Little Bear River, crossed over into West Virginia, and eventually meandered down to a tiny dot labeled Rose Hill. The next furthest dot encouraged him with the news that there was a ski resort nearby. Armed with the largest espresso-based beverage eight dollars could buy, he claimed his rental car and proceeded to rediscover the seventh level of hell, also known as the Capital Beltway.

It took him four hours to reach the start of the squiggly black line, which he quickly decided should be called "the nauseating trail of random wildlife crossing blacktop alternating with sudden fog pockets." On the bright side, fear of a life-limiting car crash joined caffeine in keeping him wide awake.

At one-fifty-five a.m. he arrived in Rose Hill, which the tiny dot on the map had completely oversold in terms of size. His arms and hands were rigid with tension from gripping the steering wheel. A song began to play in his mind, and he smiled as he remembered from whence it originated.

Tuppy was still humming a tune from Brigadoon as he parked the car on the main street and got out to stretch. The weather was exactly like that he'd recently endured for several weeks in Scotland. A bone-chilling misty rain fell, and much of the town was obscured by a low-hanging fog bank. The map on his phone stubbornly insisted on ending at the dot, even though he'd put in Claire's parents' full address. When he zoomed in for a street view of Rose Hill, he was only shown a field of gray with the black Co. Rte. 1/1 squiggle and the aforementioned dot. Beyond the dot, the squiggle took a sharp left and Co. Rte. 2/1 squiggled over to a town named Glencora, where the ski resort was alleged to be located.

There were very few cars parked on the street, and no cars passed through. The only sign of life, a light from the window of a bar on the corner, illuminated his parked car. He could hear what sounded like Irish fiddle music playing inside.

"The Rose and Thorn," he read on the window.

He thought about going inside to ask for directions, estimated the likelihood that he would be welcomed with open arms by the local rednecks, and decided against it. The town wasn't that big, after all. He could probably find it on his own.

The absence of traffic noise and the moisture in the air amplified every sound. He could hear the drip, drip, drip of water from every surface, and the tang, tang, tang as it struck hundred-year-old tin roofs above the brick storefronts that lined the street. There was a steady low roar from the nearby river, with which he'd become so intimate during his journey, having crossed it twice. A street sign informed him that he was parked at the corner of Rose Hill Avenue and Peony Street. He recalled Claire mentioning that every street in Rose Hill was named for a flower.

"How quaint," he'd said at the time, in a tone that indicated it was anything but.

Claire's parents lived on Iris Avenue, so logically he surmised that if the avenues and streets formed a grid if he stayed on Peony Street, he would eventually cross Iris Avenue. He popped the collar and tightened the belt on his Burberry trench and wished he'd thought to pack an umbrella. After a moment's consideration, he crossed the deserted street and walked east, which in Rose Hill meant up a steep hill.

The town was built on a hillside with the Little Bear River at the foot. Tuppy noticed that as he ascended Peony Street, the homes were bigger, were spread farther apart, and the properties were better kept. He crossed Lilac and Magnolia Avenues and ended up at Morning Glory Avenue, where the homes were quite grand, and the architecture was classic Victorian, Edwardian, and Gothic.

He turned and looked down the hill toward the river, where the main street was blanketed in fog. He had yet to see a person. All the homes looked tucked in for the night, with plumes of smoke curling from chimneys and a few windows lit by dim lamps behind sheer curtains. Tuppy had the strange sensation that he had somehow wandered into an Appalachian wormhole and gone back in time. When he returned to his rental car, he noticed the Irish fiddle music had ceased, and the Rose and Thorn was dark inside. He sent Claire a text.

Tuppy walked down Peony Street beyond the bar and the alley behind it and was gratified to see the first avenue on his left was Iris. Claire's parents' house was the third one on the right. The flickering blue light of a television seemed to indicate someone was still awake. Tuppy hoped it was Claire, having taken an earlier flight and suffering from insomnia after crossing time zones.

A large, elderly man answered his knock. He had on a stained sweatshirt, flannel pajama pants, and corduroy slippers. His eyebrows were wild, and he needed a haircut. He was frowning, but there was also an unfocused, fuzzy look in his eyes; Tuppy apologized for waking him.

"I wasn't asleep," the man said gruffly.

Tuppy explained who he was and that he was looking for Claire. This seemed to agitate the man.

"Claire's in California," he said. "She and Pip live in Los Angeles."

Tuppy knew that Pip was Claire's ex-husband, whom she hadn't seen in many years. Then the penny dropped.

Claire had mentioned multiple strokes, memory problems. Tuppy felt ashamed of how bored he'd been by the subject, and how poorly he'd listened.

"I won't keep you," Tuppy said. "Claire's coming here to see you this week. Please give her this."

"What is it?" the older man asked.

"A book," Tuppy said. "Will you make sure she gets it?"

"My memory isn't too good," Claire's father said.

"Tell her it's from Tuppy."

"What in the heck kinda name is that?"

"A family name," Tuppy said.

"I probably won't remember it. My memory isn't what it used to be."

"I'm sorry I disturbed you," Tuppy said. "It was nice to meet you."

"You could come in," the older man said. "You want me to get Delia?"

"No, please don't wake her. I've got to go. Goodbye."

Tuppy walked halfway down the block toward Peony Street and then turned to look back. Claire's father had shut the door. His phone tweedled that he had a text; it was from Sloan

"I no whr u r cmn 4 u."

It may have been a combination of fatigue, worry, and the freezing rain falling in this creepy fog-covered town that time forgot, but Tuppy suddenly had the urge to get the hell out of Rose Hill as soon as possible. Sloan's attorney Stanley had sleazy contacts everywhere and enough money to arrange any dirty deed. They must know where he'd gone; the rental car company could have tracked him through the GPS. Someone may have followed him at a distance.

Tuppy called Claire, left a voicemail, and then sent her a text. He had just pressed send when he heard raised voices nearby. A car started up with a roar and tires squealed. Then there were footsteps on the wet pavement behind him, running in his direction. The fog was so thick he couldn't see farther than a few yards in front of him.

Fear raced through his nervous system and adrenaline surged through his veins. He took off, running as fast as he had ever run in his life, only to trip over the curb and fall headlong into the middle of Peony Street. He was just picking himself up off the ground when headlights illuminated him, blinded him. The car roared toward him, and the impact flung him up over the hood of the car into the windshield, rolled him over the roof, across the trunk, and then dropped him back on the street.

Tuppy's head hit the pavement as he landed and a sharp pain radiated throughout his entire body. His ears rang, and a buzzing sound bloomed in his head. He felt so dizzy he became nauseated.

'This is so inconvenient,' he thought. 'I have the most important meeting of my life on Monday.'

Then he could no longer feel the hard, wet pavement, and the pain disappeared. He could see his motionless body on the street beneath him as he floated above it, but he only felt a benign sort of attachment to it. He felt confused, but not worried.

'This is interesting,' he thought.

The dark night evaporated, leaving everything shrouded in gray fog, but lit from above. It was like being on a plane as it ascended through a cloud, just before it rises into the bright sunshine of a blue sky. He realized he wasn't floating up; he was being drawn up.

'I must be in a coma,' he thought.

He heard music; it started out far away and faint, but soon gained strength.

It was "Rhapsody in Blue" by George Gershwin.

In his youth, Tuppy had been a dreamy, sensitive boy who lived mostly in his head, watched black and white classic movies, and listened to songs by Cole Porter and George Gershwin. His mother, who adored him, took him to

Broadway musicals and plays, and always encouraged his creative side. His father, who didn't have a creative bone in his body, ignored Tuppy to the point where the boy sometimes wondered if his father cared if he lived or died.

The music became louder as he rose higher. The piano chords had a curious vibration that overwhelmed him and infused his body with invigorating energy. This energy filled him up and expanded his sense of himself until he felt huge, vast, and couldn't tell where he ended and the music began. As he emerged into what looked and felt like bright, warm sunshine in a brilliant blue sky, the music rang out with raucous, almost unbearable joy.

In the distance, a tableau appeared against a backdrop of brilliant white light. Tuppy felt drawn to this apparition, whatever it was, and as soon as he had the thought that he wanted to get closer, he instantly found himself there.

He was standing on a street corner in midtown Manhattan. The street signs indicated he was at the intersection of 7th Avenue and West 58th Street. The blaring of vehicle horns and throngs of people hurrying every which way was familiar to him if their mode of transportation and dress were not.

The cars were huge, with all the edges rounded; their headlights looked like the popped eyes of cartoon characters. All the men wore suits and hats. If it hadn't seemed so real, Tuppy would've imagined he was on a 40s-themed movie set. When he looked down, he saw that he was dressed just like everyone else, and he could feel the hat on his head. He took it off and stared at the snappy gray felt fedora.

A traffic cop blew a whistle that startled him.

"Are ya crossin' or ain't ya?" he bellowed.

Tuppy hurried to the other side of the street.

"Tupworth, where the hell have you been?" a man said as he approached Tuppy and wrung his hand with enthusiasm. "We've got auditions in fifteen minutes at the New Century, and you're walking in the wrong direction!"

"I'm sorry, do I know you?"

"Does he know me? It's Sam, Sam Spewack. We've only known each other ten years. Did someone drop you on your head or something?"

Tuppy allowed himself to be turned and hurriedly ushered in the opposite direction, while his companion talked fifty miles an hour.

"Don't let the big man intimidate you," he said. "He might bust your chops, but Bella says he's the real McCoy."

"What should I do?" Tuppy asked him.

"What should you do?" the man laughed. "What should I do, he says. How about you do your job, pal, and make us all look good."

Sam led the way into the New Century Theater. There in the lobby stood a slightly-built, middle-aged, well-dressed man who was looking at his watch while leaning on a cane.

"I know, I know," Sam said as approached him. "Is Bella here?"

The man gestured to the theater doors, and Sam went on through. The older man looked Tuppy up and down.

With an arched eyebrow, he asked, "What took you so long?"

"I'm sorry," Tuppy said.

"Never mind," the man said. "You're here now."

He handed Tuppy a librettist's loose-leaf book with the title "Kiss Me Kate" typed on the cover page.

"What's this?" Tuppy asked.

He then looked more closely at the man and finally recognized him.

"That's the baby," Cole Porter said. "Let's hope it grows legs."

Tuppy was overcome; he couldn't speak.

This was heaven.

Chapter Two - Saturday

Claire Fitzpatrick flipped the rental car's high beams on and off. The fog from the Little Bear River kept appearing in dense patches along the curvy two-lane road, making it hard to see very far ahead. It was four in the morning, and Claire had been awake for over twenty-four hours. Her eyes burned with exhaustion, but she was almost home, almost to Rose Hill.

She sighed with relief as she passed the "Welcome to Rose Hill" sign. She passed the farmer's market, the city hall, the fire department, the police station, and then turned right on Peony Street. The pub on the opposite corner, called the Rose and Thorn, was owned by her family, but at this time of the night, it was locked up tight. She just had to go one block, turn left on Iris Avenue, then go half a block, and she would be home. It was awfully early in the day to surprise her parents, but she knew they wouldn't mind.

Claire desperately wanted three things: to go to the bathroom, drink a big glass of ice water, and then immediately lie down and sleep. Anywhere would do; the kitchen floor, for instance.

She had just passed the alley behind the Rose and Thorn when she saw something lying in the middle of Peony Street. The neighborhood was shrouded in fog so she had to stop and get out of the car before she could properly see the thing. At first, she thought it was a big duffle bag, like the ones her cousins took with them when they went into military service. When she got closer she realized it was not a thing, it was a person.

"Hey, buddy," she said. "Have a little too much to drink?"

She nudged the man, who was lying curled up on his side, facing away from her. Claire assumed he'd passed out in the middle of the street, a situation that was not that shocking to the daughter of a bar owner.

"You need to move, or you'll get hit by a car," she said, and then walked around him so she could see his face.

It was covered in blood.

Twenty-four hours earlier Claire had been deeply asleep in the tastefully appointed bedroom of a rented flat above a luxury bath goods shop on Church Street in Kensington. When the alarm clock went off her heart began to race, and a feeling of panic rose up in her throat. She tried telling herself she had nothing to worry about; she'd done nothing wrong. She'd given a month's notice, as was stipulated in her contract. She'd collected her last check. The previous night she'd said goodbye to everyone she cared about at the going away party, a party from which her former boss was glaringly absent.

The problem wasn't that she felt menaced or harassed, as was Sloan's tendency when Claire didn't do as she commanded. The problem was Sloan hadn't done anything to her for two days; that scared her more. When she said goodbye to her employer in the entryway of the Milestone apartment, Sloan had ignored her, acted as if she was just another faceless service provider, not someone who had been with her for twenty years. For two decades Claire had waited on Sloan hand and foot, put up with her mean-spirited abuse, and received little thanks for continually rescuing her from every sticky situation. She had expected Tuppy to call her every five minutes with increasingly sweet offers alternating with escalating threats. Instead, there had been only this ominous silence.

Even though Sloan had ceased all communication, she made sure Claire's exit was not completely without drama. The estate agent had claimed the production company extended her lease for another three months.

When they couldn't produce a lease signed by Claire for the additional time, she told them to take it up with the producer, that she would leave the key in their drop box on her way out of town the next morning. The estate agent glared at Claire as she waved cheerily on her way out of the office.

"Bloody Americans," she heard him say to his secretary.

Claire's Boston Terrier, Miss Mackenzie Peabody MacGuffin, rattled the tags on her pink, rhinestone-studded collar as she stretched and yawned.

"Good morning, Mackie Pea," Claire said.

The little dog nuzzled Claire's hand, hopped down to the floor, and went to the door, where she stood expectantly.

"We'll take a nice long walk in the park, pick up gifts for Mom, Dad, and the cousins, and pack our boxes to ship," Claire said. "After that, we'll have some lunch, another quick walk, and then we're out of here."

At just before three o'clock Claire took one last look out her bedroom window at the beautiful view across the street: an ancient stone church surrounded by green leafy trees in a small park. The rain that had steadily drizzled all morning had finally stopped, and sunlight gleamed on the wet cobblestones as black cabs, double-decker buses, and tiny cars wove through the busy street below. This had been her morning and evening view for the past four weeks while Sloan dubbed dialogue in a London studio during the day and led the paparazzi on a merry chase through the most fashionable clubs at night. Claire was usually given the smallest hotel room available to share with another staff member. Renting this flat had been a last-ditch effort by her boss to convince her to sign up for another tour of duty, as in, "see what you'll be missing?"

"This is the most expensive piece of real estate you or I will ever have slept upon," she told the dog. "It's all downhill from here."

The bath goods store manager had agreed to ship Claire's boxes of belongings to the U.S., so Claire carried them down one by one and then paid for shipping.

The cab driver who picked her up in front of the Church Street flat was talkative and nosy, so Claire filled him in on her troubles with the estate agent as he drove her to their office. He waited for her to drop the key and then conveyed her in the direction of Heathrow. Due to a car accident traffic was snarled, and for the full ten minutes it took the cab to convey her one block she considered abandoning it for the underground. She also considered the four-inch heels she was wearing, the overloaded carry-on bag and Miss MacGuffin's travel case, and decided against it.

Her phone played "The Wicked Witch of the West" theme from The Wizard of Oz, which meant her ex-boss was finally calling. She knew Sloan had been invited to an engagement party for the royal couple that was to take place that evening and was probably in a vicious panic. Claire decided it would not help her nerves to hear that ominous tune play over and over all evening, so she turned off her phone.

She took a deep breath and resigned herself to the inevitable Sloan Merryweather temper tantrum. There was no telling what that woman would do next. Claire prayed that Sloan's personal assistant Tuppy had not betrayed her. Otherwise, Sloan might have her thug lawyer waiting at Heathrow.

"La, la, la," she said.

"What's that, love?" the cab driver asked.

"Nothing," Claire said, "just talking to myself."

"You'll want to watch that," he said, smiling at her in the rearview mirror. "There's some will think you're a nutter."

She hadn't realized she'd said it out loud.

Just as she feared, after an agonizingly slow cab ride she reached Heathrow after her flight had departed. Although she felt like collapsing into a sobbing heap in the middle of the concourse, she knew that looking panicked or upset in an airport could mean a one-way ticket to a security hold and a body cavity search. She was able to maintain her composure as she purchased a new ticket for a 7:00 p.m. GMT flight. She kept herself together all the way to the gate of the next available flight. There she realized she'd left her phone in the cab. The tears she'd felt welling up all morning threatened to spill over, so she looked up and blinked hard to force them back.

'Not now,' she sternly reprimanded herself. 'This is not a safe place to fall apart.'

She dug her long nails into her palms until the pain distracted her.

'La, la, la,' she said under her breath. 'Let's just get through this.'

Claire's phone was her lifeline. It not only kept her world organized, but it was also her primary means of communication with her friends, colleagues, and family. Upon waking in the middle of the night on an airplane or in a hotel room, she often had trouble remembering which country she was leaving, going to, or was in, but as long as her phone was nearby, she felt securely tethered to the earth.

She took some deep breaths and willed herself to be calm lest someone suspect she was sad about some terrorist act she might be planning. She reminded herself that all was not lost. She still had her carry-on bag (in which she'd stowed her handbag), Miss MacGuffin's carrier, her passport, and a new ticket.

To pass the time she bought some magazines and tabloids which all featured stories about her former employer. She rolled her eyes at the flattering "exclusives" she knew had been written by Sloan's publicist Ayelet.

These, along with the carefully staged paparazzi photos that accompanied them, were passed off as real interviews by publications willing to flatter Sloan in return for access.

Then there were the tabloid publishers, who had no legitimate access and just threw any wild fabrication on the cover. Sloan was often desperately trying to get pregnant, was already secretly pregnant, or devastated because she wasn't pregnant. They might say she was having a torrid affair with her latest costar, was broken-hearted and bitter, or head-over-heels in love again with an ex, sometimes all in the same week. Tabloid editors were always looking for incriminating evidence they could use to either sell as a shocking expose or use to blackmail Sloan into cooperating with milder versions of the same story. Writers had approached Claire with offers of hundreds of thousands of dollars, but by the use of signed non-disclosure agreements with stiff penalties Sloan had made it impossible for her to take them up on their offers, even if she wanted to.

Two hours later Claire was one of the first to board her flight, as all they'd had left were first class seats. She justified the expense as her reward for all the abuse she'd put up with over the past two decades. After devoting half of her life serving one of the most demanding divas in the movie business, she felt she'd earned a little pampering.

Miss MacGuffin, an excellent traveler, was soon snoring quietly in her carrier, but Claire couldn't sleep. Memories from the past three months kept floating through her mind like a montage on a movie screen. Before she left the British Isles Claire had been determined to see the sites where her favorite movies were filmed. In Scotland that meant visiting the village of Pennan and the beaches of Arisaig, and Morar, where Local Hero was filmed. In Ireland that meant staying a few days in Dawros Bay, in Donegal, where The Secret of Roan Inish was shot; and taking a tour of the Isle of Man in honor of Waking Ned Divine.

She had gone on two Harry Potter tours, one in Oxford and one in Gloucester; and had hired a very enthusiastic film student to take her to many of the London spots featured in Love Actually, Notting Hill, and Four Weddings and a Funeral. The Victoria and Albert Museum fed her Young Victoria craving, and Buckingham Palace represented The King's Speech. After seeing so many of these places immortalized in movies, the British Isles seem to Claire like one big film set. She had felt the same way the first time she went to New York, Paris, and Venice.

Claire would have seemed like the typical American tourist on each of these tours if it weren't for all the crying she did. She may have set a record for Yankees who cry on famous UK landmarks; she didn't know where the standing record was recorded so she couldn't compare her stats. Needless to say, she wasn't the most popular seatmate on the bus or in great demand at dinner stops.

Finally giving notice and then sticking to that decision was something she had dreamed of for so long. The enormity of that decision and the subsequent reality of what her life would be like afterward were only starting to sink in.

As Claire allowed herself to relax, the tears welled up again, so she blinked and sniffed them back. To distract herself she pulled out a small notebook and made a list:

1. Good long visit with Mom & Dad
2. Decide what to do next & where to do it (open salon? Freelance?)
3. Relax somewhere sunny (or go back to LA and look for work?)
4. Order food for Mackie Pea
5. Buy a new phone (move to #1)
6. Sleep for a month

The in-flight movie was a recent cliché-ridden, by-the-numbers romantic comedy featuring leads she knew for a fact to be a heroin addict and a former prostitute; they were also two of the highest paid actors in the film industry.

The supporting actors were actually more compelling, and at least their faces still moved in a natural way. Although a critical failure, the film had recouped its budget and made a substantial profit, so there was a half dozen more similarly themed romantic comedies, or "rom coms" in the works.

After the movie, Claire slept, but fitfully. She kept waking suddenly with a nauseating wrench in her midsection as if her soul had been let out on a long string while she slept and was suddenly reeled back into her body as she was jolted back into consciousness. It felt like waking up on a rollercoaster. Each time she woke she reached for her phone and was grieved anew to remember it was lost.

When they landed in DC, Claire found her connecting flight to Pittsburgh had been delayed due to an approaching thunderstorm. Claire was used to such irritating developments. She had puppy training pads that Mackie Pea used while traveling, so she had no reason to go out in the gale force wind and sheets of rain that lashed the terminal windows.

She reached into her handbag for her phone before she remembered again that she'd left it in a cab in London. She wondered if the cabbie found it before one of his passengers did. She was sure she'd never see it again no matter who found it.

Thunder boomed and lightning shot across the sky as the storm set in, but Claire was used to the hurry up and wait atmosphere of filmmaking, not to mention all the accompanying loud drama. She knew how to block out the noise by focusing on frivolous distractions. She bought some fashion magazines and camped out in the waiting area by her gate.

The storm moved out within an hour but so many flights were backed up Claire realized it would be quicker to drive. She got her ticket refunded from the polite people at the British Airways counter and then stood in line with several dozen other people who suddenly wanted to rent a car. She was exhausted from her journey but was determined to get home.

Once on the road in a rental car, as the terrain changed from hills to mountains, nostalgia overcame her, and she allowed the repressed tears to fall. Even though it had been several years since she'd been home, she didn't need a map or a GPS to find her way back to Rose Hill.

Claire left her car in the middle of the street and ran to the fire station, where she knew someone would be awake. It turned out to be Malcolm Behr, the fire chief, and quite possibly the hairiest man Claire had ever met. Claire could easily imagine him in a kilt with his face painted blue, wielding an ax as he charged across a Scottish battlefield.

"Claire Fitzpatrick," he said. "When did you get back?"

Claire told him what she'd found, and Malcolm called Police Chief Scott Gordon. He picked up an EMT kit and a flashlight and followed Claire back to where the body lay illuminated by her headlights. Malcolm checked the man's pulse and told Claire what she already suspected.

"He's dead," Malcolm said, and then pointed the flashlight at the front bumper of Claire's car.

Claire's father had been chief of police in Rose Hill for thirty years, so she knew where this was headed.

"I didn't hit him," Claire said. "I just drove here from DC after flying there from London, and he's probably been lying here for a while. You can check my plane ticket and make a timetable; I'll help you do it."

"Time enough for all that," he said. "That'll be Scott's problem, not mine."

"Do you know who it is?" she asked.

"He doesn't look familiar to me," Malcolm said. "It's hard to tell with all the blood."

Scott arrived, looking sleepy and rumpled in the foggy glow of the streetlight. Claire, who out of habit always thought in terms of movies and casting, cast Scott in the part of a minor league baseball player and single dad, a romantic anti-hero with a rough exterior that concealed a soft spot for children and dogs. He greeted Claire with a hug and the same quizzical expression Malcolm had given her.

"I didn't know you were coming home," Scott said. "I eat breakfast with your old man every morning, and neither he nor your mother mentioned it."

"It was supposed to be a surprise," she said.

Scott turned on his flashlight, squatted down, and looked at the man. He looked a little green around the gills when he stood back up.

"I don't recognize him," he said and pointed the flashlight at the front bumper of Claire's car.

Claire repeated her alibi, and Scott nodded as he listened.

"I guess I better call Sarah," he said.

"Who's Sarah?" Claire asked.

Malcolm snickered.

"A pain in the ass is what," he said. "She's got it bad for our chief, here."

"Ignore him," Scott said. "She's the violent crimes investigator for the county sheriff's office. She gets all our suspicious deaths. We haven't had many in the past few years."

"It reminds me of how Theo was murdered," Malcolm said. "That was three years ago, January."

"Theo Eldridge?" Claire asked. "Mom told me about that."

"I don't think this one's a bludgeoning," Scott said as he shone the flashlight on the back of the man's head. "It looks to me like he was hit by a car and landed on his head."

"A hit and run," Malcolm said. "It was probably some drunk, under-age college kids."

"The blood's congealed, so it didn't just happen," Scott said. "Plus he's ice cold to the touch, and his clothes are sopping wet."

"That's what I've been saying," Claire said. "I've got a plane ticket and a rental car receipt to back up my alibi."

"I believe you," Scott said. "But Sarah doesn't know you like I do."

"It's gonna be a long night," Malcolm said, "and this weather's not gonna get any better, I'll tell you that. We may have snow by the weekend."

Scott made a call; Claire assumed it was to the county dispatcher. As soon as he terminated the call, he looked at Malcolm.

"Reckon we should take out his wallet and see who he is?"

"Sarah won't like it," Malcolm said.

"Let's live dangerously," Scott said.

Malcolm gave Scott some latex gloves from the EMT kit, and after putting them on Scott took the front hem of the man's raincoat and pulled it back. He could see the man's wallet in his back pocket; he wiggled it back and forth until he worked it loose. He flipped it open and looked at the license.

"He's from your neck of the woods, Claire," he said. "Los Angeles, California. Chance Tupworth."

"Tuppy!" Claire said and then covered her mouth with her hand.

She hurried around the body and crouched down to look at the man's face.

"You know him?" Scott asked her and grabbed her arm just as she reached out to touch the body.

She looked up at Scott, her eyes filled with tears.

"I do," she said. "Oh, my God, Scott, I know him."

Scott led Claire, carrying a restless Mackie Pea, back to the station-house, and called one of his deputies to come and sit with her "just for company" while he dealt with Sarah. This officer turned out to be the grown-up version of a goofy kid Claire had known as "Skippy." The man, now referred to as "Skip," could hardly look Claire in the eye, and blushed as he shook her hand. After Scott left, Skip sat down in a chair at the front desk, put his feet up, and fell sound asleep. Claire reflected that he didn't seem to consider her much of a flight risk, so that must be a good sign.

The station hadn't changed much since her father was chief. It consisted of a small main room with a desk facing the front door and one against the wall; a break room with filing cabinets and a kitchenette, a holding cell, a bathroom, and the chief's office. Now there was a modern phone and computer on each desk, and a large copier/printer/fax machine in the break room, but other than that it was exactly the same.

Claire entered her dad's former office. She let Mackie out of her carrier and spread out a disposable pad on the floor. Mackie daintily did her business, jumped up on the couch, curled up in her carrier, and tucked her nose under her back leg. Claire folded up the pad and threw it in the trash before she sat back down.

The olive green vinyl of the couch was cracked and faded. She could remember sitting on this same sofa, balancing a coloring book on her knees, sharpening crayons in the back of their box, and coloring while she waited for her mother to pick her up after she got off work.

If her mother worked the night shift, Claire would go home from school with one of her cousins and stay overnight with one of their families. If her mother worked in the bar all evening, Claire would go with her, do her homework in the last booth and eventually fall asleep in the back office, curled up in an enormous armchair kept there for that purpose. What seemed in retrospect like an unusual childhood had seemed perfectly normal to her while growing up.

Claire thought about her parents sleeping in their house two blocks away, oblivious to what was going on. She decided to call them, but when she stood up to do so, fatigue overwhelmed her, she lost her balance and fell back onto the couch. It was all she could do to lift her legs up on the seat before her head hit the crackling cushion and she fell asleep.

After Scott woke her, he handed her a cup of coffee as she sat up. He smiled kindly, but his forehead was wrinkled up with worry lines.

"Sarah wants to question you," he said quietly. "I told her you wanted your attorney present."

"I don't have an attorney," she whispered back.

She tasted the coffee; it was lukewarm and bitter. She handed it back, and he set it on the desk behind him.

"I called Sean," Scott said. "He's on his way."

Sean was one of Claire's cousins.

"Isn't he a trust attorney?" Claire asked.

"I'm stalling for time," Scott said. "I'm trying to get someone from the airline to confirm you were on your flight and it's not as easy as you might think."

"I don't have anything to hide..." Claire started to say.

Scott leaned down and put his mouth very close to her ear. A chill ran down Claire's spine, and not in a bad way.

"Trust me," he said. "Do as I tell you."

"Alright," she breathed and looked around for her handbag.

"Sarah has it," Scott said. "Don't worry. I watched her catalog everything that was in it. You'll get it and your carry-on back shortly. Where's the rest of your luggage?"

Claire told him about shipping her belongings ahead of her flight.

"I'll have Skip pick up everything when it arrives," Scott said.

"I just have Mackie's carrier ... Mackie Pea!" Claire said as she noticed the little dog was not inside her carrier

She looked frantically around the room.

"She's okay," Scott reassured her, and then called, "Skip? Can you come in here a sec?"

Skip came to the doorway holding Mackie Pea in the crook of his arm. As soon as she saw Claire, the little dog wriggled until he put her down on the floor, and then she leaped up into Claire's arms and licked her face.

"What kinda dog is that?" Skip asked her. "She looks like a miniature boxer, but I've never seen a black and white boxer."

"She's a Boston Terrier," Claire said. "I call her Mackie Pea."

"That's like the thing you say when you wiggle a baby's toes," Skip said, and then recited, "Mackie Pea, Penny Rue, Worry Ursle, Mary Thornthistle, and Old Tom Bumble."

"It's so nice to be home," Claire said, "where somebody knows that."

"Doesn't everybody know that?" Skip asked her.

"Thank you for taking care of her," Claire said.

"I figured she needed to go out, so I took her across the street to the funeral home where there's some grass."

"And she just went with you?" Claire asked.

"Sure she did," Skip said. "Dogs just love me."

"She's probably starving," Claire said. "Her food is in my carry-on bag."

"I gave her some of my biscuits and gravy," Skip said. "My mom brought it down."

Claire thought of the organic, grain-free dog food she ordered from a specialty store in San Francisco. It cost about the same by weight as filet mignon.

"If you need somebody to look after her while you're here," Skip continued, "my mom said she'd be glad to do it. She loves dogs."

"Thanks," Claire said. "What time is it?"

It seemed like a lot had happened while she slept.

"It's just past eight a.m.," Scott said.

Claire's mother came through the door, took one look at her daughter, and said, "You always did like to make a dramatic entrance."

Claire put Mackie Pea down and stood up to embrace her mother. She couldn't stop her tears. Her mother's arms had always been a safe place in which to fall apart.

At Scott's behest, Delia had brought clothes for Claire to put on so the sheriff's detective could have the clothes she wore when she found Tuppy. Attired in her mother's sweatpants, a Fitzpatrick Bakery sweatshirt, and hideous puffy white tennis shoes, Claire felt like she had been stripped of her identity.

"I look like a high school dropout who works part-time as a cashier at the IGA," Claire said. "Who's going to believe anything I say dressed like this?"

"I'm sorry I didn't take the time to coordinate an outfit," Delia said. "But when the chief of police calls to say your daughter's in jail and needs a change of clothes, formal attire is not a priority."

Claire and her mother sat in Scott's office and talked until Sean arrived. Sean, like Claire, was tall with dark hair and bright blue eyes, inherited from their Irish paternal grandfather's side of the family. He wore an impeccably cut suit and carried an expensive attaché case. Claire knew her clothing and accessory labels, and Sean's were top of the line.

He shook her hand in a formal way and asked everyone else to leave so he could speak with "his client."

"Scott filled me in," Sean said. "Tell me everything that's happened since you last saw this Tuppy guy alive."

29

Sarah Albright introduced herself to Claire with a glare and flared nostrils. She was petite and striking, with short dark hair and big dark eyes. She was dressed like a TV detective in close fitting but business-like dark pants and jacket, a white blouse unbuttoned about two more buttons than was appropriate, and high-heeled pumps. Claire instantly cast her as a ruthless, corrupt cop with no conscience, able to seduce and then kill her victims without hesitation.

"You being related to half the people in this town makes no difference to me, Miss Fitzpatrick," Sarah said. "Being the ex-chief's daughter doesn't work in your favor, either. This town's been run into the ground through lax law enforcement. Anytime I'm called in you can count on the bar being raised."

"You can spend your time insulting my client's family and bragging about yourself, Detective Albright," Sean said, "but you only have fifteen minutes in which to ask questions pertinent to Mr. Tupworth's unfortunate accident. After that, we're leaving."

Claire was impressed by Sean's assertive confidence. Scott stood smirking in the doorway. Sarah gave Sean a vicious side-eye, but then produced a notebook, turned on a tape recorder, and formally questioned Claire. Claire responded to each question with facts if she had them but no speculation, just as Sean had instructed. When Claire told her about discovering she'd left her phone in the cab, Sarah said, "How convenient for you."

After she ran out of questions, Sarah curled her lip in contempt.

"The victim didn't just show up here and get killed without it involving you somehow," she said. "It's just a matter of time before I know why and how."

"Charge her with something, or we're leaving," Sean said. "You have no reason to detain her, and she's not planning to leave town."

"We're keeping her handbag, carry-on, clothes, and rental car," Sarah said. "It's all potential evidence."

Claire looked helplessly at both Sean and Scott.

"She can do that," Sean said. "Sorry, Claire."

"Don't leave town," Sarah said and left the room with Scott behind her.

"Where'd you learn to do that?" Claire asked Sean.

"Television," Sean said.

"What do I do now?" Claire asked.

"Go home, get some sleep, and try not to worry too much. Don't talk to anyone about what's happened and don't let Sarah question you again without me present. I've got a friend in the DA's office in Pittsburgh, and I'll ask him what we should do next. Meanwhile, I'm sure Scott will get this all sorted out."

"I wonder why Tuppy was here," Claire said. "It doesn't make any sense."

"That doesn't matter," Sean said. "All that matters is we can prove you couldn't have killed him."

By noon Claire was in her mother's kitchen eating tomato soup and a grilled cheese sandwich. She couldn't remember the last time she'd eaten white bread, orange-colored processed cheese slices, or soup from a can. It tasted wonderful.

Claire was concerned about her mother. Delia Fitzpatrick was a tall, willowy brunette who had always worn clothes well. She was very particular about her appearance, modest as her wardrobe budget was. Today her gray roots were showing, and the faded cardigan she was wearing was stretched out and baggy over her too-thin frame.

"How are you doing?" Claire asked her.

"I'm fine," Delia said, but without turning around to make eye contact.

"That woman from the sheriff's office is scary," Claire said. "I think if Scott and Sean hadn't been there she might've smacked me around."

"Sarah's aggressive," Delia said, "but Scott can handle her."

When Delia finally sat down, Claire got a good look at the dark circles under her mother's eyes and the deep lines on her face. Mackie Pea jumped up on Delia's lap and gave her a quick little lick on the chin before settling down.

"I always wanted a little dog," Delia said, "but your father was bitten by a dog as a child and never got over it."

"When will Dad be home?" she asked her mother, who was now holding Mackie Pea upside down on her lap, rubbing the little dog's belly while she murmured with pleasure.

"This is your father's schedule," Delia said, "he gets up at 5:00, watches the twenty-four-hour news and weather channels for a half hour, and then he gets his bath and shaves. I take him to the bakery with me at 6:00, and then Scott picks him up there and takes him to breakfast. After that Scott takes him to the service station, where your Uncle Curtis watches him until the bar opens at noon. Then your cousin Patrick looks after him until I pick him up at 5:00, after I get off work at the Inn. We come home, have dinner, and then he watches television until he falls asleep in his recliner."

"I didn't know he needed babysitting like that."

"He falls," her mother said. "Someone has to be with him in case he loses his balance."

"Why doesn't he use a walker?"

"He says they're for old men."

"He's still stubborn; that much hasn't changed."

"Ava says he's like a huge, cranky toddler."

Ava was the widow of Claire's cousin Brian.

"You just said you were working at the Inn. I thought you were working for Ava at the B&B in the afternoons."

"That's a long story for another day after you've had a bath and a good long sleep."

"I'm all for that," Claire said, "but I'd like to wait until I've seen Dad."

Delia was quiet, and Claire said, "What?"

"I want to prepare you for how your father's changed," her mother said, "but I don't know how."

"His memory's bad, you said, but he isn't paralyzed or anything, is he?"

"No," Delia said. "He's had a series of small strokes, not any big one. He'll know who you are, but he may not remember as much as you'd like. He gets confused easily."

"I can handle that," Claire said. "Poor Dad."

Delia was quiet again.

"There's more," Claire said. "Just tell me."

"No," Delia said. "I'll let you see for yourself. Just remember, he's still your father, but he's different. He can't handle problems anymore; he can't tolerate tension of any kind. It agitates him when things change. Try not to worry him about anything."

"Like what happened last night."

"Let's not mention it," Delia said. "He can't help, and it will only upset him."

Claire reflected that her dad had always been the first one she'd gone to for advice when she was in trouble. She couldn't imagine that he wasn't still that strong, protective, invincible man who took the sensible long view in any situation.

"I don't want to worry him," Claire said, "but it would take a miracle to keep a secret that big in this town."

"Your father's very well thought of. People around here know his condition, and they protect him."

"Let's hope that protection extends to his daughter."

Her mother left to pick up her father at the bar. When she brought him back, Claire was surprised at how bedraggled he looked. His shirttail was hanging out, and his undershirt was stained. He did recognize her and seemed glad to see her. She hugged him tightly, and when she kissed his cheek, she noticed his shaving had been more miss than hit.

"What a nice surprise," he said, and Delia steadied him over to his recliner, where he sat down heavily.

He took a handkerchief out of his shirt pocket and wiped his face, which was red and sweating. His jowls sagged, and his eyes were bloodshot.

"Where's Pip?" he asked her.

Claire looked at her mother. Delia shook her head.

"Still in California, I guess," Claire said.

"The heck he is!" her father said. "He was in the Thorn last week. He's grown his hair out long, looked like a hippie. I told him he needed a haircut. He thought that was funny, but I was dead serious. What's the point in being married to a beautician if it's not the free haircuts?"

Claire looked at her mother.

"Claire's had a long trip getting home," Delia said. "Let's let her lie down and get some rest."

"You go on and get a nap," her father said. "When Pip gets here we'll feed him some supper."

Mackie Pea ran into the room and jumped up on her father's lap. Claire was relieved and amazed when her father just laughed.

"Well, who is this little doggie?" he said.

She made introductions, and her father tucked Mackie into the crook of his arm and rubbed the furrow between her eyes. She could hardly believe this was the same man who used to say you couldn't trust any dog and he couldn't see why people kept them.

"You wait 'til old Chesterfield gets a look at you," he told the little dog.

"I can't believe Chester's still alive," Claire said. "Where is he?"

"He's around here somewhere," Delia said. "You might want to be careful with him and Mackie. Chester can be vicious."

"Now, Delia, don't you talk that way about my cat," her father said. "Ole Chester's a good cat."

Claire took Mackie Pea from her father and went down the hall. Her mother followed her back to her old bedroom. Claire could tell her mother had cleared a hasty path to the bed. It looked as if they had been using the room for storage.

"If I'd known you were coming I would've cleaned," Delia said. "I'll work on it tomorrow."

"I can clean my own room," Claire said and kissed her mother on the cheek. "We'll get caught up good and proper at dinner."

"I have to go back to the Inn after I feed your father his lunch," Delia said. "I'll drop your father off at the bar as I go. You need your rest."

"Wake me up when you get home, then," Claire said.

"We'll see," Delia said.

Claire walked down to the bathroom at the end of the hall. The three-bedroom, one-bath house seemed even smaller than she remembered. The bathroom was tiled in the original 1950's jade green. Some of the tiles were cracked now; all of them were dingy. Claire's mother had always been so house-proud, it concerned her how shabby and untidy everything seemed to be.

While she took a long hot bath Claire mentally renovated and redecorated the bathroom. Afterward, she rooted around in the towel cupboard until she found a new toothbrush, and then brushed her teeth.

'I could spend some money updating the house, maybe get some help in to clean it a couple days a week,' she thought. 'Dad could probably use some physical therapy and a nutritionist.'

When she went back to her room, Mackie Pea was not there, and she found the little dog curled up in her father's arms as he reclined and watched the local midday news. She stood in the hallway, reluctant to disturb them.

On the television, the female news anchor had big eighties hair and heavy, dramatic makeup. Dark burgundy blush had been applied like war paint up each cheek, and smoke-colored eyeshadow extended up from her lash line to a slash of white beneath her two narrow, penciled-on eyebrows. Her lips were outlined four shades darker than her frosted lipstick.

The weatherman was the same one she remembered from childhood, only now his hair was snow white. The newsroom set was dated, and the lighting was all wrong, throwing shadows at odd angles and flattering no one. There were awkward pauses between segments, and the anchors couldn't seem to get through one sentence without stumbling over a word.

The commercial that aired on the break was for a local car dealer dressed up in a gorilla suit.

"We don't monkey around with our prices!" he claimed.

Claire sighed. It was like going back in time.

She noticed her father was holding his mouth in an exaggerated frown and was subtly nodding his head. It looked as if he was keeping time to music she couldn't hear. Her mother came up behind her and touched her arm.

"He does that thing with his head when he's agitated. If you touch him or talk to him, he stops. He doesn't realize he's doing it."

"What's wrong with his mouth?" Claire asked.

"That started after the last fall," Delia said.

"Isn't there anything they can do?"

Delia led Claire back into her bedroom, closed the door, and sat on the edge of her bed. Claire got undressed, put on the nightgown her mother had placed on the bed, crawled in and pulled the covers up. She felt 30 years younger in doing so. This was what she and her mother had done every night when she was a child.

"Tell me more about what's going on with him," Claire said.

"He fell a few weeks ago and then couldn't get up. Hannah's little boy Sammy was here with him and went to get help. We haven't left him alone since then."

"When did all this start? You just told me about it at Christmas."

"We first realized something was wrong about a year ago. Your Uncle Curtis and I both noticed he couldn't seem to remember anything, and sometimes struggled to find the right word, but Ian got angry if we mentioned it. One morning last October I found him sitting in the car in the driveway, crying. He couldn't remember how to start the car.

"Doc Machalvie examined him and he failed a short-term memory test, so we went to Morgantown, and they did more tests. An MRI showed he's had multiple little strokes, probably over the past couple years."

"What are they doing for him?"

"He's on blood thinners, blood pressure medicine, and he has a medicinal patch for dementia."

"Dementia?" Claire said, wrinkling up her nose. "That's an awful word."

"It used to be called hardening of the arteries, but now they call it vascular dementia. Every time he has a little stroke, it deprives his brain of oxygen, and more cells die. One of the side effects is a loss of memory function. The patch is supposed to keep it from getting worse."

"Is it working?"

"How can I tell?" Delia said. "His memory keeps getting worse, but maybe without the patch, it would decline even faster."

"What do you do when he has these little strokes?"

"The doctor said there's no point in bringing him to the emergency room when they happen; they can't really do anything to help him. It's just poor circulation, age, genetics."

"But people recover from strokes all the time. They get therapy and reverse the effects."

"This is different," Delia said. "I'm sorry, Claire, but he's not going to get any better."

"How long does he have?"

"Who knows?" Delia said. "It could be years, or it could be tomorrow. We just have to make the best of what time he has left."

"Does he realize what's happening?"

"Oh, yes," Delia said. "He got so down about it Doc put him on an antidepressant."

"What can I do to help?"

"I got great advice from a social worker at the hospital. She said, 'make his world as structured and drama-free as possible and try not to take anything he says personally.' We keep to a schedule, we don't worry him about anything, and we don't argue with him when he insists something's true when it's not."

"There has to be more we can do, better doctors somewhere."

"I know it's your instinct to jump in and fix this," Delia said. "But do you really want what time he has left to be spent going to places he's not familiar with and having people do things that scare him?"

"No," Claire said, "of course not."

"Spend a few days with us and see how it is."

"I can't just sit still and do nothing," Claire said.

"I know," Delia said.

"I can't just accept there's no hope."

"I know," Delia said.

"How can you?"

"Have a talk with Doc Machalvie," Delia said. "He can explain it much better than I can."

"I had planned to stay two weeks, but this thing with Tuppy may mean I'm here awhile."

"We'll love having you as long as you can stay," Delia said. "Were you and Tuppy very close?"

"More like fellow hostages," Claire said. "We had a common enemy."

"It must have been a shock to find him. Why do you think he was here?"

"He knew I was coming here and I missed my plane. He must have planned to travel with me or meet me here for some reason, but I don't know why. If I had my phone, I could check my messages and then I would know."

"Did they find a phone with his body?"

"No, which is weird. That man may have loved his phone even more than I do mine."

"I'm sure Scott will figure it out," Delia said.

"I always thought Scott and Maggie would get together. What happened there?"

"You know how contrary your cousin Maggie is. I think he just got tired of waiting for her to make up her mind."

"Should I pretend to still be with Pip? If Dad's hallucinating conversations with him how do I not upset him?"

"I don't know. Let's worry about that when it comes up again."

"Will you bring Mackie Pea in before you go?"

"If I can pry her out of your father's arms," Delia said. "He's taken a shine to her. He fed her some cheese while you were in the bathroom."

"That dog's gonna have a colon blow-out before the day is through," Claire said.

"I'll take her out before I go," Delia said.

"I love you, Mom," Claire said.

"I love you, Claire Bear," Delia said, and she turned out the light and closed the door.

Claire's last thought before she fell asleep was that the sheets, laundered in the same detergent and fabric softener that her mother had always used, smelled like home.

It was three in the morning before Scott got to talk to someone in authority at the airline. The difference in time zones had been an issue, but not as bad as the cultural barrier. As Scott was thinking the British were just as snotty as he expected them to be, he was sure the man on the other end of the line was thinking Scott was just as obnoxious as he expected an American to be. Scott was getting nowhere until he remembered Ian used to advise him that when he needed cooperation, he should look for common ground.

"What do you think United's chances are against Liverpool?" he asked.

"You follow football?" the man asked, not bothering to hide his surprise.

The UN diplomatic corps would have applauded the improvement in international relations that ensued. By the time Scott terminated the most expensive long distance phone call he'd ever made, he had received a fax of the information needed to corroborate Claire's alibi and a deeper appreciation of an Englishman's devotion to soccer. All those late nights he'd spent watching soccer on satellite television had paid off in an unexpected way.

He scanned and emailed the documents to Sarah's office and locked up the station. Rose Hill was quiet, cold, and drippy, which was not unusual for early spring. There were actually only three seasons: snow, rain, and eight weeks of what passed for summer.

As he crossed Peony Street, he noticed a car with a Maryland license plate parked in front of the Rose and Thorn. He backtracked to the station and retrieved Tuppy's keys from the safe. Sarah had tasked him with finding Tuppy's car, and in his single-minded devotion to clearing Claire, he had neglected to look. Scott's intention was to find the man's phone, see whom he called, and listen to his messages.

The trunk was empty. The man's suitcase and carry-on bag were on the back seat. The driver's side cup holder held an empty coffee cup from an expensive gourmet coffee retailer Scott had heard of but had never visited. There was a cell phone charging cord plugged into the cigarette lighter but no phone. Scott looked under and in between the seats and cleaned out the glove box. He found nothing more exotic than the cellophane from a cigarette pack.

He locked the car, carried the luggage back to the station and put it on the break room table. He put on latex gloves and took out a form on which to catalog the contents. By the time he was through he knew what time the man's plane had been scheduled to take off from Heathrow and land in DC, what time he rented his car and the exorbitant price he paid for the famous coffee. He was also envious of the man's wardrobe and baffled by his toiletry collection.

'What is clarifying lotion?' he asked himself after he read the label on one bottle.

Scott secured the evidence and locked up the station once again. This time he walked down Peony Street, which was no longer blocked off with sawhorses and yellow tape at its junction with Iris Avenue. The lack of broken glass was a puzzle. The force with which Tuppy must have been hit would surely have broken the windshield. Scott imagined a wide circle with the spot where Tuppy had landed as the epicenter. Using a flashlight, he started at the center and spiraled his way out as he went, looking for something, anything that might be a clue as to what had happened. Sarah's team had been thorough; he found nothing.

Scott walked down Iris Avenue and noticed Ian was still up, either watching TV or more likely dozing in his recliner. He wouldn't disturb him; it wouldn't be kind to Delia, and it wouldn't help. He missed talking to Ian about cases, bouncing ideas off him and hearing his opinions. There was no one else who could see things from the chief's perspective or give him advice based on thirty years of experience policing Rose Hill.

Ian knew the past history of every Rose Hillian, along with all their secrets, quirky or dark as they might be. He had been an invaluable resource, a great mentor, a trusted friend. Now he was just a sweet old man Scott took to breakfast every morning, someone who shocked Scott with what he said out loud. Ian Fitzpatrick had been the closest Scott had come to having a father after his own father died, and Scott was determined to never let him know he pitied him or was embarrassed by him.

Scott thought about Claire. He had grown up with her and had witnessed the pain it caused her parents when she left home and then rarely visited. He hoped she would stay even after she was free to leave. Her parents needed her. The thought 'I need her' followed and he shook his head. Where had that come from?

Many years ago, as a lowly deputy in nearby Pendleton, Scott had married a nice girl from that town, but it had not lasted. After Maggie Fitzpatrick's live-in boyfriend Gabe disappeared Scott had become a very supportive friend. Their relationship had blossomed, maybe faster and more intently on his side, but he believed on hers as well. He tried not to pressure her, but he couldn't help himself. He was soon convinced they were meant to be together.

Maggie stayed stubbornly devoted to her missing lover until he returned several years after he disappeared. The truth about the kind of man he really was seemed to break the hold he had over Maggie's heart. After Gabe disappeared again, Scott made the fatal mistake of giving her an ultimatum: commit to being with him or let him go. She let him go.

Maggie Fitzpatrick did not respond well to being bossed around and had a quick temper. She owned a bookstore in town in which she kept a "dry erase board of shame," where the names of people she had banned from her store were listed. Over the years she had to buy bigger boards to accommodate the growing list. Scott was nearly reconciled to the fact that although he was not on the banned list in the bookstore, he was most definitely on the one in her heart.

It had been challenging to break up with her and still live within blocks of each other under the brutal scrutiny of a small town. In an effort to mend his broken heart, Scott had tried to convince himself that he was in love with Maggie's beautiful widowed sister-in-law Ava. He quickly realized, however, that he couldn't substitute his infatuation with one woman for the true love he felt for another. Since then he had been determined to only date women from other towns, and although there had been a few, he just didn't feel that intense passion he felt for Maggie; anything less felt like settling.

He was currently single, and Claire was as well. He couldn't help but wonder. He'd felt something, and he thought she had, too; a strong attraction between them when they touched. It wasn't that irresistible, magnetic force-field he had to contend with in Maggie's presence, but it was something more than just a friendly feeling; it was a spark. Maybe this kind of attraction was a healthier thing than the heartbreaking longing he felt for Maggie. Maybe it would break that spell. He wished something would.

Peony Street by Pamela Grandstaff

Chapter Three - Saturday

Claire woke up to bright sunlight shining through the gap between the white eyelet curtains of her childhood bedroom. For a long moment she was confused, and during that time some protective instinct told her not to be in such a hurry to rush headlong back into consciousness.

She rolled over, intending to go back to sleep, but instead found herself facing a small child standing next to her bed. Its head was covered in tangled blonde curls, its nose was encrusted with dried snot, and its mouth was smeared with what Claire hoped was chocolate. It didn't appear to have any clothes on, at least from the waist up.

"Me Sammy," he said. "Who's you?"

"Hi Sammy," she responded, now understanding that this was her cousin Hannah's son, whom Delia often babysat. "I'm Claire."

He reached out with a grimy little hand and patted her cheek.

"You's pretty," he said.

"Thank you," she said.

As soon as Claire moved he was off like a shot, and she could see from his small, retreating behind that he was indeed naked.

"Mom?" she called out, "Dad?"

There was no response. Looking around she realized that her dog was missing.

"Mackie Pea?" she called out.

Nothing.

She got out of bed and wrapped herself in the flannel robe her mother had left for her. As she left her bedroom, she heard a noise outside the back door, a low growling, and another sound, like a small siren gaining and losing volume. She opened the back door to see Mackie Pea cornered against the house and porch railing by an immense black and white cat. Two big dogs stood out in the yard watching the standoff with what looked like delighted interest. They barked at Claire but came no closer to the porch.

"Shoo, Chester!" she yelled at the cat. "Get out of here!"

The cat turned and hissed at Claire but showed no sign of being intimidated enough to retreat. Claire went back into the kitchen and got a broom out of the pantry. As soon as he saw the broom the cat took off into the bushes; evidently, it had lost that battle before. Mackie Pea was trembling, sitting in a pool of her own urine. The two dogs in the yard came forward now that the cat was gone.

"You were a lot of help," Claire told them.

They wagged their tails and panted happily. Claire scooped up Mackie Pea and took her inside.

"I'm so sorry," Claire said to the whimpering dog, "you poor baby."

She took the little dog to the bathroom and gave her a bath in the sink. Mackie loved a bath, especially the getting rubbed with the towel part afterward. After the bath and rubdown, Claire plugged in her mother's blow dryer to finish drying the little dog's short fur. When she turned off the blow dryer and turned around, she was startled to see Sammy sitting on the toilet, holding onto the front rim with both hands to keep from falling in.

"Me pooping," he said with a grimace.

Mackie Pea tried to wriggle free, but Claire took her to the bedroom and shut her in. When she got back to the bathroom, Sammy was swinging his legs and smiling.

"Me done," he said. "Me need a wipe."

Claire unrolled some toilet paper and wrapped it around her hand, completely prepared to do this small person's bidding, but he frowned, said, "Wipes!" and pointed to the cabinet under the sink. There Claire found a package of wet wipes. Sammy jumped down and bent over so Claire could perform this service. She turned to flush the commode and throw away the wipe and when she turned back around he was gone again.

"Sammy," she called out.

She heard a noise in her parents' room, and when she investigated, she found Sammy in there, pulling on some thermal underwear with dinosaurs printed on them. She watched as he dressed in these, a sweatshirt with a cartoon car on it, and some cowboy boots.

"Don't you have any pants?" she asked him.

He looked at her as if she were stupid.

"Them's pants," he said, pointing at what Claire now surmised were pajama bottoms.

"Of course," Claire said. "Sorry."

As he headed toward the door, Claire quickly closed it and backed up to it, blocking his escape route.

"Where's your mother?" she asked him.

He was frowning at her in as fierce a way as a toddler could. Despite his tiny stature, Claire found she was a little intimidated.

"Move," he said.

"Somebody should be looking after you," Claire said. "Where are your parents?"

"I not telling," he said, and she knew at once that he meant it.

Claire heard someone come through the front door calling out, "Yooohoooo!"

Sammy dove under her parents' bed and Claire opened the door to the hallway. Her cousin Hannah came down the hall and hugged Claire. It surprised her how emotional she felt seeing Hannah. Instead of happiness and joy, she felt a sense of melancholy and loss, which she quickly covered up.

"How dare you sneak into this town, murder someone, and not call me to help you hide the body?" Hannah said.

"There's a little boy under the bed," Claire said. "Is he yours?"

"No," Hannah said. "I don't have any children, especially not any stinky little boys. They're so gross!"

Sammy giggled, and Hannah said, "Let's go have some cookies and milk in the kitchen. Luckily there aren't any stinky little boys around here we'd have to share them with."

"Rowr!" Sammy said.

"What was that?" Hannah asked.

"Sounds like a monster to me," Claire said.

"Oh, no," Hannah said. "Monsters love milk and cookies. I hope he doesn't eat them all up and not share any with us."

"Rowr!" Sammy said. "Me triceratops rex."

"Nice vocabulary," Claire said.

"He knows all of them," Hannah said as they went down the hall. "I can't tell them apart, but he knows all their names. Plus, some of the ones we learned in school have different names now. You wait. He'll show you the book and then give you a quiz. He's a very strict teacher."

"It seemed like he was here all alone," Claire said. "Is that usual?"

"There's one thing you'll quickly learn about Sammy," Hannah said, as she got the milk out of the refrigerator and a package of cookies out of the cupboard. "He's an escape artist. He's supposed to be at my mother's house. She called me a few minutes ago to say, 'I just turned around for a second, and he was gone.'"

Hannah did a spot-on imitation of her mother's high, whiny voice.

"I believe her," Claire said. "He seems to appear and disappear."

"He's fast," Hannah said. "The trick with Sammy is to give him a reason to stay put. He gets bored at her house because she won't play with him."

.

"What about a daycare, where he can play with other kids?"

"He's been kicked out of every daycare in the county. They don't have enough staff to keep track of him, plus the fire department and police are tired of looking for him. Sam thinks we ought to put a GPS ankle bracelet on him, to save time."

"Oh my gosh, Hannah," Claire said. "Don't you worry about what will happen to him?"

Hannah gave Claire the same look Sammy had given her in the bedroom, the one that indicated she must be mentally deficient.

"I'm doing the best I can," she said. "After I got pregnant and Sam got his legs back under him we had an honest talk about what we both needed to be happy. I wanted to buy Lily Crawford's farm so we'd be closer to town, for the baby. Sam wanted to dissolve his business and do contract work instead. He and Coach Riggenbottom started a physical therapy program for returning vets at the community center, but that doesn't pay anything. We want to do what makes us both happy but the mortgage must be paid, we must have health insurance, and Sammy must be fed and clothed, so I must work. I'm still the county's domestic animal control officer, plus I work at the vet's office and waitress at the Thorn. If I'm not sleeping, I'm working."

"Did you sell the family farm?"

"We tried to, but no one wanted to pay what it was worth. We're renting it to Drew Rosen, the veterinarian. Have you met him?"

"No."

"Seriously cute," Hannah said. "I'll set that up for you if you want."

"No, thanks," Claire said. "I've got enough trouble in my life right now."

Hannah's cell phone played "I Feel Good" by James Brown. After she saw who it was, she answered and then listened.

"I'll be right there," she said and ended the call. "There's a doe in the IGA. Can you watch Sammy 'til I get back?"

"Doe as in deer?"

"A female deer, ray, a drop of golden sun," Hannah sang, terribly. "Me, a name I call myself ..."

"Sure," Claire interrupted. "I'll do my best."

"That's all any of us can do," Hannah said, and then she yelled down the hall, "Be good for Claire and I'll bring you something."

"What?" was the reply from under the bed.

"Something for your treasure chest," she called out and then winked at Claire. "Good luck."

Two hours later Claire was sitting at the kitchen table, drinking the last dregs of a pot of coffee while watching Sammy feed Mackie Pea rings of oat cereal. The little dog sat at Sammy's feet, waiting patiently as he pushed each circle to the edge of the table. As soon as it fell the dog would catch it with a loud snap of the jaws that made Sammy laugh. It looked as if the small boy was training the dog but Claire knew better.

"Where's his tail go?" Sammy asked.

"Mackie Pea is a little girl dog," Claire said. "Boston Terriers have their tails docked when they're little."

"Does it hurt?"

"Probably," Claire said.

"When me steps on my dog's tail he say YIPE!" Sammy said. "Why's they's cutting her tail off?"

"People do weird things to dogs," Claire said. "To make them look a certain way."

"They's always trying to cut me's hair," Sammy said, "but me not."

"Good for you," Claire said. "You should grow it down to the ground."

"Down to the ground?" Sammy asked. "Down to me's feets?"

"We'll have to braid it and wrap it around your head to keep you from tripping over it."

"Hairs don't grow down to the ground," Sammy said. "That's silly."

"It will," Claire said. "Unless you cut it before it gets down to your legs you'll trip over it when you walk."

"You have long hairs," he said. "They's pretty."

"Thank you," Claire said, surprised by how much the compliment meant to her, even though it came from a three-year-old.

"You growing your hairs down to the ground?" he asked her.

"No," she said, "just this long."

"Me can cuts my own hair."

"Not on my watch."

"They's never letting me have scissors."

"That's because scissors are sharp. You might cut yourself."

"Me not. Me careful."

"I'm not giving you scissors."

"They's never do," he said with a sigh.

"It's hard to be you, I guess," Claire said.

"Me mad about it," Sammy said. "They's never letting me do nothing."

"Sorry about that."

"That's okay," Sammy said. "Me alright."

"Did you like going to school?" Claire asked him.

"They's have good toys at the white church school. They's have trucks, and bulldozers, and trackhoes, and backhoes, and monster trucks. They's have a big train you can ride on."

"Do you like playing with other kids?"

"Uh huh," Sammy said. "Where's you find this little girl dog?"

"I got her from a lady I worked for."

"What's her's name?"

"Mackie Pea."

"Mappy Pete's likes me," Sammy said and then held up two fingers. "Me gots two dogs. They's names Jax and Wally."

"I've met them," Claire said, not bothering to correct him on Mackie's name or his grammar. "They're out back, asleep on the porch."

Sammy shrugged.

"They's likes me," he said. "You's want to see some treasure?"

"Sure," Claire said.

Hannah opened the back door and entered the kitchen. Sammy slid out of his chair and ran down the hallway into Claire's parents' bedroom. Mackie Pea looked at Claire as if to say, "What was that about?"

"You can see how close we are," Hannah said as she sat down. "He's always so overjoyed to see me. I don't know why I expected him to be more like the dogs."

"He went to get his treasure."

"Cute dog," Hannah said. "Did Sammy give you any trouble?"

"Not a bit," Claire said. "He's going to grow his hairs down to his feets."

"I'd cut it off while he's asleep, but it doesn't seem sporting," Hannah said. "He howls like a banshee if I even try to wash it, and honestly, I'm picking my battles with this one. Left to his own devices, he'd turn feral within a week."

"How did you get the deer out of the grocery store?"

"Popcorn."

"Of course. Where is it now?"

"She's frolicking in the woods beyond the college campus, telling all the other deer about her big adventure in the bright place with all the wonderful food."

"Anyone hurt?"

"Some displays; nothing that can't be washed or restacked. You'll be relieved to know that no tourists were harmed."

"I'm so glad," Claire said. "You know how I worry."

"I've missed you, you big smartass," Hannah said. "Enough of my drama, let's talk about yours."

Hannah got up and rummaged through the cabinets until she found a jar of peanut butter. She brought the jar and a spoon back to the table and sat down.

"I'm sure you've heard all about it by now," Claire said. "I can't believe Ed Harris hasn't shown up to interview me for the Sentinel."

"He's on vacation."

"That's a blessing," Claire said. "I like Ed, but he does have a way of asking only the questions you don't want to answer."

"I don't care who you killed," Hannah said, pointing the spoon at Claire. "It was obviously self-defense, and I will testify to any facts you care to give me."

"He was a coworker, and I have no idea why he came here or who killed him. We weren't what you'd call best pals."

"Not a spurned, jealous lover, then?"

"I guess the scanner grannies have been hard at work this morning."

The scanner grannies were a group of home-bound senior citizens who had figured out how to listen in on cell phone and cordless phone calls using their old-school police scanners.

"The consensus is that your mother is too nice for you to have done it, but there's also a growing conspiracy theory that your years in Hollywood may have corrupted you."

"There's no doubt about that."

"That's your natural hair color, isn't it? It's been so long since I've seen it I almost forgot what it looked like. It's dark like Patrick and Sean's but not quite black. Last time I saw you it was red and cut like a space cadet's."

"It's shocking, I know."

"According to my mother, you're terribly thin."

"She hasn't even seen me," Claire said.

"She doesn't have to," Hannah said. "In my mother's mind, people are either terribly fat or terribly thin. There's no middle ground. I bet when she called your mother this morning the third question she asked was how you looked."

"That's refreshing. In L.A. how you look is always the first question."

Sammy came back down the hall with a battered blue cookie tin with snowmen printed on it. He handed it to Claire. He then leaned against his mother and let her ruffle his hair and kiss the top of his head.

"What you's bring me?" he asked her.

Hannah reached into her jacket pocket and took out a small egg-shaped object that looked like it was made of fur and feathers held together by mud.

Sammy gently took the item and held it close to his face, turning it slowly around and around as he examined it.

"What is it?" Claire asked.

"An owl pellet," Hannah said.

"Gross!" Claire said.

"It not gross!" Sammy said and scowled at Claire.

"Sorry," Claire said.

"You can take it apart and see everything the owl ate," Hannah said. "Sometimes there are mouse bones or chipmunk teeth in them."

"Cooooool," Sammy said in awe.

Claire made a face.

"No say gross!" Sammy said to her.

Hannah leaned down and kissed Sammy on the cheek, a big wet smacking kiss. He smiled but did not break his concentration on the owl pellet.

"Her's my mama," he said, briefly glancing up at Claire. "Her's allowed to kiss me."

"Lucky her," Claire said. "Can I look at your treasures?"

He nodded gravely.

Claire opened the cookie tin and looked inside.

"Takes them all out and puts them on the table," he said. "So we can sees them."

Claire carefully removed each object and put it on the table.

"That frog is dried out that way," Sammy said. "We finded him in the garage."

"He's missing a leg," Claire said.

"It broked," Sammy said with a shrug.

"That's new," Hannah said, pointing to a silver key ring attached to a rectangular key fob that looked as if it had something inside of it, like a Swiss army knife, but it didn't look like a knife.

"I think it has a bottle opener inside it," Claire said. "If you push on one side it should flip out the other."

Hannah and Claire both tried but they couldn't get it open.

"I guess if he can't open it he can't kill anybody with it. Where'd you get this?" Hannah said. "It's not one of Daddy's, is it?"

"Delia gives it to me," Sammy said. "Me never stoled it."

"Mom's always finding little treasures at tag sales and flea markets," Claire said. "She's like a magpie about shiny silver things."

"Like that silver frame on the mantle?" Hannah asked. "It's beautiful."

"Actually, that was a gift from me on their fortieth wedding anniversary."

"That was a great party," Hannah said. "It's a shame you couldn't come."

"I was in Spain," Claire said.

"How does your dad seem to you?"

"Who's you's daddy?" Sammy asked Claire.

"Ian's my dad, and Delia's my mom."

Sammy seemed to reflect upon this new information.

"He's changed a lot," Hannah said.

"He looks so old," Claire said. "Mom says there's nothing that can be done, but I'm going to talk to Doc Machalvie. Surely there's some specialist we can take him to."

"Ian fell down," Sammy said, and then pointed at the living room, "in there."

"Sammy was here when he fell," Hannah said. "He was a brave boy and went up to the service station to get help."

"Me three. Me can counts to twenty," he said, and then proved it.

"That's pretty good for three," Claire said. "So he crossed the S.T.R.E.E.T.?"

"Yep," Hannah said. "He said he thought Grandma Alice would be too scared to help."

"Her's silly," Sammy said. "Me gets up on her's nerbs."

"You have to admit that's a very accurate description of my mother," said Hannah. "When Mom found out I was having a boy she said, 'I've had enough boys; I want a pretty little girl to dress up.' Cause you know I was not having that kind of thing when I was little."

"You were a tomboy," Claire said. "There's nothing wrong with that."

"Grandma Alice is up on me's nerbs," Sammy said. "Her no likes dinosaurs or even trucks."

"His vocabulary is amazing," Claire said.

"What's cabulary?" Sammy asked.

"It means you know lots of words," Hannah said.

"Me gots lotsa words," Sammy told Claire, "but no bad words."

"I have to pay him a dollar for every curse word I say in front of him," Hannah said.

Claire counted the money from the cookie tin.

"At this rate, he'll be able to buy a car by the time he's sixteen."

"Me never says bad words," he said. "Hannah says them all the day."

"Sammy likes his money, and he likes a good trade," Hannah said.

"He calls you Hannah?"

"Sometimes, and sometimes he calls me Mama, but he always calls Sam 'Daddy.'"

"Her's gots 'C's on her necklace," Sammy told his mother. "But her not trade them to me."

"It's Chanel," Claire said. "If I take the logo off how will anyone know how special it is?"

"You could tells them," Sammy said.

"That's not the point," Claire said, and then to change the subject, "you have a mighty fine collection."

"Mighty fine," Sammy said with pride, and then to his mother, "Me hungry."

Claire offered him a spoonful of peanut butter.

"Yuck," he said. "That the dog jar."

Hannah made a face.

"Why didn't you tell me before?" she asked him. "Gross!"

"Ian's gives the dogs peanut butter outta that jar," Sammy said.

Hannah tickled and hugged him until he laughed.

"Her's my mama," he told Claire. "Her's allowed to tickle me."

"He seems very concerned with what you are and are not allowed to do," Claire said.

"We talk about who's allowed to do what," Hannah said. "We're establishing healthy boundaries and learning about stranger danger."

"Stop, drop, and roll," Sammy said in a very serious voice, "when the fire's on you."

"You couldn't have learned any parenting skills from Alice," Claire said, referring to Hannah's mother. "From what I remember she was always in her bedroom lying down with a headache."

"Sam's all over this child-rearing thing. I'm a little more casual in my approach."

"You gots kids?" Sammy asked Claire.

"No," Claire said, "just Mackie Pea."

Sammy looked over at Mackie Pea, curled up on a rug in the corner.

"Mappy Pete's a little girl dog," he told his mother. "They's cut off her's tail."

"Sammy," Hannah said, "Daddy's coming in a little while to take you to the Megamart to get some new shoes."

"Alright!" he shouted and then danced around. "Megamart! Megamart! Me wants a tractor; a big one with big wheels!"

"You have to take a nap first."

His whole body sagged.

"Me no nap," he whined. "Me not sleepy."

"Then no Megamart," Hannah said. "It's the deal."

Mother and son locked gazes, and Claire was not sure who was going to give in.

"Claire said she would rock you and sing songs," Hannah said. "She's allowed to do that."

"You know any good songs?" he asked Claire.

"I know all the ones your Aunt Delia knows," Claire said.

"Her'll be comin' around the mountain?" he asked her.

"And 'I've Been Working on the Railroad,' and 'How Much is that Doggie in the Window,' and 'My Bonnie Lies Over the Ocean,'" Claire said.

"Ian sings old Bonnie lies in the bakery, please keep that old Bonnie away," Sammy said.

"That's not very nice," Claire said.

"Me scared of Aunt Bonnie," Sammy said.

"Me, too," Hannah said.

"Me, too," Claire said.

"Okay," Hannah said. "Here's the deal: Claire will rock you, you lie down for one hour, and then Daddy will take you to Megamart."

"Me gets a new tractor?"

"That's a deal you'll have to make with Daddy. We're working on my deal right now."

Sammy seemed to weigh the acceptability of the deal on the table.

After a short silence, he asked Claire, "I gets to have my passie?"

"Is that okay?" Claire asked Hannah.

"His daddy hasn't let him have a pacifier since his third birthday, but Delia keeps an emergency passie on top of the fridge."

"It's a mergency," Sammy said. "Me needs it."

"Well, since it's an emergency," Hannah said. "I guess it's alright."

To Claire, she said, "I don't care if he sucks on a pacifier until he's in college as long as it makes him feel better. Maybe if every adult had one, there'd be less of a need to self-medicate."

Sammy dragged a chair over to the kitchen cabinet, climbed on top of the counter, and then on top of the microwave. He took a pacifier out of a basket on top of the fridge. Hannah helped him down.

"Got it," he said, holding the pacifier up for Claire to see before popping it in his mouth.

It seemed to have an instantaneous sedative effect. He rubbed his eyes and yawned.

"Do you have to pee?" Hannah asked him.

He shook his head.

"Rock him for five songs, although he will try to get you to do one more about a million times," Hannah said. "Then put him down on the couch and cover him up with the afghan; the soft blue one, not the scratchy red one. Set the kitchen timer for one hour, and he can't get up until it dings, whether he sleeps or not. As soon as he gets up, he has to pee, which he can do by himself, and then he gets some juice."

Sammy removed his pacifier, said, "the yellow sippy cup with the monster truck," and then stuck his it back in his mouth.

"Got it," Claire said.

Claire went into the living room and sank down in the upholstered rocker in which her mother had rocked her and her brother many years before. Sammy climbed up on her lap and snuggled in her arms. He took out his pacifier and pointed it at his mother.

"Bye, Hannah," he said. "Be good."

"Bye, Sammy," Hannah said and waved as she went out.

"Daddy sings everything alright," Sammy said. "You knowed it?"

"I'm sorry," Claire said. "What song is that?"

"Two little birds on the front porch," he sang, "singing sweet songs, melody four and two, singing, this is my messy to you-hoo-hoo."

"That's Bob Marley," Claire said, "I think."

"Sing it," he commanded and put his pacifier back in his mouth.

He snuggled back down with his head on her shoulder, sucked on his pacifier, and reached a tiny hand up around her neck. Claire wished she had thought to make him wash his hands after he held the owl pellet. As she rocked the chair springs twanged just like they had all those years ago.

Luckily Claire knew all the actual words to "Three Little Birds" by Bob Marley, and Sammy was asleep by the end of the second chorus. His body went completely limp, and his hand dropped from her neck. Claire smelled the top of his head. His tangled golden curls smelled like baby shampoo and wood smoke.

Claire reflected that there was no way she could exactly duplicate the many colors of his hair, although she liked to think she could come close. The client would have to be dark blonde, to begin with; a darker shade and she'd have to bleach it and then use toner, which was harder on the hair. Silently she calculated all the colors she would have to mix to get four different shades, from dark caramel to medium golden blonde to light honey to platinum. She would have to use foils and weave the color in a few strands at a time. It would take hours; she would charge a fortune.

Mackie Pea ran into the living room, jumped up on the other side of Claire's lap, turned around two times and curled up. The little dog didn't seem to mind Sammy being there. Claire reflected that Mackie Pea seemed to have a facility for adapting to change; it was a good thing.

Claire considered worrying about being a murder suspect, about how her folks were doing, and about what in the world she was going to do with the rest of her life, but decided instead to just put all that aside and enjoy holding Sammy and Mackie.

"Every little thing is gonna be alright," she sang quietly.

Instead of putting Sammy on the couch she closed her eyes and continued to rock him until she, too, fell asleep.

Scott had been sparring with Sarah for over an hour, but he knew he was right and was determined not to back down. He'd spent the morning interviewing local people, trying to find someone who saw or heard something, anything that would help Claire.

"She says she lost her cell phone," Sarah said. "But how do we know she didn't steal his and hide them both? I say we get a search warrant and turn her parents' house upside down."

"With Claire's permission and her cell phone service provider's assistance I procured her call and text log from the past week," Scott said. "There was no record of phone calls or texts to the victim for twenty-four hours before the time she says she lost her phone, or any calls or texts going out after."

"You expect me to believe that whoever found or stole her phone didn't use it to make calls?"

"Claire's phone has a security feature that requires a pin number to unlock it. Her account cannot be used without that number."

"Can the service provider give us the text content or let us listen to the voicemails?"

"No."

"I bet they could if we were the feds. If we can get that movie star boss of hers involved, we could probably call in the feds."

Scott took a deep breath.

"The victim landed in DC at around eight p.m.," he said. "He rented the car at around eight-thirty. It takes at least four hours, in daylight and good weather, to get to Rose Hill from Ronald Reagan Airport. The earliest he could have arrived was half past midnight. There was thick fog all along the river so Route 1 would've been slow going. I figure it was closer to one or two before he got here."

"Maybe he waited longer to start out. Maybe he was waiting in DC for her to arrive and he followed her."

"Claire landed at eleven p.m.," Scott said. "The quickest she could get here was four hours, again, if the weather was perfect, which it wasn't. She had planned to make a connecting flight to Pittsburgh at midnight and drive down, which would have brought her here by three a.m. at the soonest, but there was a storm, and her connecting flight was delayed.

"She rented a car at Reagan Airport at 11:45 p.m. She came to the fire station at four-ten. The quickest she could have driven here, in perfect weather, mind you, was four hours. That would have put her here at just before four. By the time Malcolm got to the body, it was four-twenty.

"If she killed him at 3:45 a.m., which is the earliest she could have arrived in Rose Hill, and Malcolm saw him at four-twenty, his blood would still have been flowing. Hell, he would have been warm to the touch and possibly still alive. It was 4:30 when I saw him. His skin was cold, his blood was congealed, and the onset of lividity was evident."

"She killed him somewhere else, brought him here, and dumped him."

"Sarah," Scott said. "Patrick saw the victim's car in front of the Thorn when he left at two a.m."

"That's the bartender, right? He's one of those Fitzpatricks you can't walk around here without tripping over. I remember him from the Eldridge murder investigation. I seem to remember he lives in the trailer park down on Peony. Why didn't he see the body? Doesn't he walk home that way?"

"He didn't go home," Scott said.

"Where did he go?"

"To the home of a local woman."

"Did you question her?"

"Not yet, but I will."

"Maybe I should do it."

"You know folks around here won't tell you anything."

"What's Patrick's relationship to the suspect?"

"They're cousins."

"Isn't that convenient?" Sarah said. "He might have conspired with the suspect to commit and cover up the crime. He may have both cell phones."

"What's the motive?" Scott replied. "The victim and Claire both worked for the same person. Claire fulfilled her contract and was coming home for a short vacation before she goes back to L.A. The last she heard from the victim he was still working for their employer and planned to stay in the UK for the foreseeable future. They had no personal relationship beyond work. She says they weren't particularly close, had known each other less than two years, and didn't socialize together on their own time. She doesn't know why he came here, and until we recover one or both phones, we won't know why either."

"I want to see the log again," Sarah said.

Scott gave her the printout.

"So these calls and texts came from four numbers other than the victim's: her former employer, the PR firm, the agent, and a law firm in New York," Sarah said. "It looks like she was still receiving calls and texts up to the point when the report was printed."

"I've left messages with all of them, but so far no one has returned my calls."

"Why would he come here without her knowledge?"

"She doesn't know."

"It's too big a coincidence."

"It's mysterious, that's true. I'm sure if we had either phone we could find out what happened."

"I wish his family would get here. I'm counting on them to get me access to his service provider's call log."

"If they have his username and password," Scott said. "Otherwise we'll have to subpoena the service provider. That could take weeks."

"Claire could have two phones," Sarah said. "She says she has one; maybe she has two."

"Then I'm sure his call log will reflect that."

"I want her to stay put until we get that log."

"Her alibi checked out," Scott said. "She wasn't here when he was killed."

"You're not the medical examiner," Sarah said. "We won't have that report for at least two weeks, maybe four."

"It takes four hours to drive from DC to Rose Hill, and that's in daylight in good weather. Four hours from when she rented her car," Scott began again.

"She knows more than she's telling," Sarah said, "and right now she's my only suspect. I'd really like to get Sloan Merryweather's take on this. I'd like to subpoena her."

"Be careful, Sarah," Scott said. "Powerful people do not like to be bothered, and you can't afford to piss off your boss in an election year."

"Solving a high-profile homicide case could make me and my boss look good in an election year," Sarah said. "If you don't roll the dice you can never beat the house."

"Have you spoken to anyone in Mr. Farthington's family about meeting with us?"

"They're coming down to identify and retrieve the body. I'll tackle them after they get to the morgue."

"With sensitivity, of course."

"Of course."

Sarah left, and Scott walked down to Claire's parents' house. He walked up to the front door just as Sammy was letting himself out.

"Hold it right there, partner," Scott said.

Sammy froze and then looked right and left as if planning his escape route.

"I brought you something," Scott said.

Sammy looked suspicious.

"Shows me it," Sammy said.

"Is Claire supposed to be watching you?" Scott asked. "Does she know you're leaving?"

"Me going to school at the white church," Sammy said.

"I seriously doubt it," Scott said. "Here's my deal: we go inside and see Claire or I take you to your grandma's house and let her give you a bath."

"Me no get bath," Sammy said. "Me not dirty."

"So we go inside, and I show you and Claire what I brought to trade you."

Sammy turned around and opened the door, revealing Claire fast asleep in the upholstered rocking chair. Mackie Pea barked and jumped down from her lap, waking her up.

"Scott," she said, clearly flustered. "Sammy? Were you leaving?"

Sammy wouldn't look her in the eye. Scott smiled.

"Sammy's slick," he said.

"I didn't even feel him get off my lap," Claire said.

"Where's it?" Sammy asked Scott.

Scott reached into his breast pocket and took out a skinny silver pen.

"Me gots lotsa pens," Sammy said, dismissing Scott's potential trade.

"This pen is like the one astronauts use in space," Scott said. "It writes upside down."

"Do it," Sammy said.

Scott took out his notepad, lay down on his back on the floor and motioned for Sammy to join him. Then he held the notepad up in the air above them and demonstrated writing upside down.

"Me's gots a pen do's that," Sammy insisted.

"Show me," Scott said.

While Sammy went down the hall to retrieve his pen, Scott looked up at a bemused Claire.

"You can see how we were all just put here to serve him," he said.

"He's the most powerful person in this town, apparently," Claire said.

"It's charisma," Scott said. "I think he has viable political potential."

Sammy came back down the hall, lay on his back next to Scott, and tried to write with his pen on the pad Scott suspended above them.

"It not work," he said. "It broke."

"No, watch this," Scott said, and turned over on his stomach, put the pad on the floor and gestured for Sammy to try again. Sammy was surprised to find his pen worked. He looked at Scott's pen with new appreciation.

"You's pen's magic?" he asked him.

Scott solemnly nodded.

Sammy took Scott's pen, said, "Okay, me trade," and then got up and ran down the hall with Mackie Pea right behind him.

Scott got up.

"He has a really gross owl pellet he can offer you," Claire said, "or a one-legged mummified frog."

"How will I decide?" Scott said. "How are you?"

"Exhausted, I guess. I didn't mean to fall asleep."

"You've been through a lot."

"Am I still a suspect?"

"Not to any sane person," Scott said.

"But to Sarah."

"She thinks it's just a matter of time before your connection to the Fitzpatrick family murder syndicate is revealed."

"Do Tuppy's parents know?"

"They're on their way."

"This will devastate them," she said.

"Did he have any romantic partners?"

"Only casual hookups or strategic favors. Tuppy's very ambitious ... was very ambitious. His sexual relationships were with whoever was the most insanely good-looking or could help him succeed in some way."

"That sounds incredibly shallow."

"It's show business. If you aren't psychotically devoted to succeeding you may as well stay home."

"You don't seem psychotic."

"Sarah seems to think so."

"Sammy's been gone a long time," Scott said and went down the hall.

Claire heard him curse. She jumped up and ran down the hall to her parents' bedroom, where Scott was looking out an open window.

"You have got to be kidding me," Claire said. "It's at least six feet to the ground."

Scott pointed downward. Claire leaned out and saw that a cast iron gas meter was installed outside her parents' bedroom, just below the window, at the perfect height for a small boy to climb out onto it and then lower himself to the ground.

"I'm starting to think he's a middle-aged cat burglar in a toddler's body," Claire said. "He can't be only three."

"I'll call Hannah," Scott said. "I bet he's headed home."

"What makes you think that?"

"He took his treasure box with him."

"And your pen."

Scott swore again.

"You're gonna have to pay him for every one of those swears, you know," Claire said.

"It won't be the first time," Scott said.

They heard the front door open, and a man called out, "Hey, anybody wanna buy a possum?"

Scott and Claire went down the hallway. Sam Campbell, Hannah's husband and Sammy's father, stood just inside the front door, dangling his son by his legs. He held the toddler, who was clutching his treasure box, out toward Scott and Claire.

"I'm marking him down for a quick sale," he said.

Sammy laughed a deep belly laugh.

"Him's my daddy," Sammy said. "Him's joking you."

Sam put the little boy down on the floor and gestured behind him.

"Is that your dog?" he asked.

Mackie Pea was outside the front door, standing on her back legs, pawing frantically at the glass of the storm door, with Jax and Wally behind her, watching with what looked like amusement. When Claire let her in the little dog danced around Sammy and then jumped up and licked his face.

"You took my dog?" she asked Sammy.

"Mappy Pete likes me," Sammy said. "Her wants to play with us."

Scott looked up from watching Sammy with the dog and caught a look pass between Sam and Claire. It was over in a second, but something about it struck Scott as odd. He wondered what that was about.

"We're headed to Megamart to get this possum some new shoes," Sam said. "Somehow all his shoes are missing except these cowboy boots."

"Me no like shoes," Sammy said. "Me likes boots."

"Nevertheless," Sam said. "We're going to try again."

Sam looked at Claire, and Scott was again struck by a quality he hadn't expected to see in Sam's eyes; it was tenderness.

"How are you?" Sam asked her.

Scott was immediately aware of the electricity dancing between Sam and Claire. It felt like something so intimate that he shouldn't be allowed to witness it.

"I'm fine," Claire said. "Other than the suspicion of murder hanging over my head, parents who seem to be falling apart, and losing your son three times today."

"Come out to the farm tonight," Sam said. "We'll feed you and catch up."

"Okay," she said, and then both of them suddenly seemed to remember Scott was in the room.

"Thank you," she said to Scott, "for everything."

"I better get back to work," Scott said. "I'll let you know when I find out anything new."

"See you later," Sam said.

Scott left with an uneasy feeling and a burgeoning suspicion. Sam and Claire? When would that have happened?

Claire hated how unnerved she felt. She'd met movie star legends, for crissakes; men who made females (and many males) all around the world swoon with desire. She'd developed a cynical lens through which to view them, those charming rogues with smiles that didn't extend to their calculating eyes. Good looks, charm, and charisma, she had come to understand, didn't necessarily signify good character. In contrast, she had no resistance to her attraction to Sam Campbell, who had all of that in abundance.

After he left with Sammy, she went to the bathroom and splashed cold water on her face. She dried her face and looked herself in the eyes in the mirror.

"He's married to one of the people you love most in this world," she said.

"Who are you talking to?" asked Hannah as she came down the hallway.

Claire felt her face flush with shame.

"Myself," she stammered. "It's a bad habit."

"I saw Sam on the way in. He says you're coming out to the farm for dinner."

"Is that okay?"

"Of course it is, silly. I'll come get you after work, and we'll pick up some provisions, make an evening of it. It's warm enough to sit outside for awhile, at least until the sun goes down. We'll fire up the grill, drink some beers, and really get caught up."

After dinner, Hannah took Sammy in to put him to bed. Sam opened another beer for Claire and handed it to her.

"Hannah's been telling me about your work with returning vets," Claire said. "It sounds like a wonderful project."

"It's basically a workout room where we lift weights and do some physical therapy. The real benefit is them having someone to talk to who knows what it's like to be a soldier in a war zone; someone who won't judge them for what they think or feel. I wish I'd had the same when I came back," Sam said. "The truth is it helps me as much as it helps them."

"Hannah seems very happy," Claire said. "You two seem settled."

"I'm lucky to have her," Sam said. "I certainly don't deserve her."

"Do you ever hear from Linda?"

"No," Sam said. "She's working in DC for some lobbyist, last I heard."

"I looked at some old pictures this afternoon. There were several of you and Linda from high school; Homecoming, Prom ... you know the ones."

"I never told her about us," he said.

"No need to," Claire said, her heart beating a little faster. "It was just one of those crazy things teenagers do; too much moonlight, beer, and hormones."

"I never told Hannah, either."

"Oh, me neither," Claire said. "That's ancient history."

"I still think about it," Sam said."Was that why you ran off to California with Pip?"

"No," Claire said. "I thought I was in love with Pip. I thought California was where all my dreams would come true."

"Do you ever wonder what would have happened if you'd stuck around?" he asked.

"I don't," Claire said. "I think everything turned out just like it should have."

"I appreciated your letters," he said. "Not many people bothered."

"That seems like a long time ago," Claire said. "We were different people then."

"Before I married Hannah."

"I hope you've been good to her."

"I'm not easy to live with," he said. "But I would never do anything to betray her trust."

"I'll drink to that," Claire said and held out her bottle to clink with his.

"Does it bother you knowing Pip's with someone else?" he asked.

"I feel sorry for his wife," she said, "but that's all."

"You're not the least bit curious?"

"No," Claire said. "The last time I saw him I was just reminded of what a stupid mistake I made. No one should be allowed to get married that young. If we'd just dated or lived together, it wouldn't be half so embarrassing now. I'm humiliated to think I was dumb enough to marry the guy."

"He's not that bad," Sam said.

"He's very handsome," Claire said. "That was like a drug I had to kick."

"Not the sharpest tool in the shed," Sam said.

"Not by a long shot," Claire said.

"Who are we talking about?" Hannah said as she came back out onto the porch.

"Pip," Claire said.

"What a good-lookin' idiot," Hannah said. "I still can't believe you married that doofus."

Claire gestured as if to say, "What can I say?"

"I'm going to fix her up with Drew," Hannah said.

"I think you should mind your own business," Sam said, and then stood up. "You ladies enjoy the rest of the evening. I'm going to do some work."

After he went inside Hannah said, "You're one of the few women that Sam can stand to be around for very long; you, Maggie, and your mom; that's about it."

"How's Maggie doing?"

"She's gone back to school."

"That's good, right?"

"I guess," Hannah shrugged. "She's too busy to do anything fun anymore, and it's made her a little stuck up."

"Really?"

"Yeah, there's this professor at Eldridge she's got a big crush on. Talks down his nose at everyone and then looks like he's in pain when anyone else talks. A drippy, snobby dweeb, if you ask me. He's renting the apartment over Ava's garage. Maggie's over there every evening, playing scrabble, she says."

"Is that a euphemism?"

"I doubt it. He sets off my gaydar."

"What does Sean say?"

"He hasn't met him yet. You think he'll be able to tell?"

"Without a doubt," Claire said. "No one has better gaydar than a gay man."

"You can ask him tomorrow. We're having a meeting of the Fitzpatrick cousins at the Thorn after church."

"What are we meeting about?"

"Just a get-together; everyone wants to see you."

"That's sweet," Claire said. "So Sean will be there?"

"He will. Sean's going to move back here, you know."

"He told me. I can't imagine why."

"It's not such a bad place," Hannah said. "His family's here. His parents aren't getting any younger, and neither are yours and mine. You ought to consider staying put, helping them out."

"No," Claire shook her head. "After twenty years of indentured servitude I'm free to do anything I want, and that does not include moving back to Rose Hill."

"You don't really want to be free of everybody and everything," Hannah said. "That would be a lonely place to be."

"I'll stay for a good long visit," Claire said, "and I'll come back more often."

"Your mom needs you here," Hannah said. "She probably doesn't want you to know how bad it is."

"I've made a lot of money over the past twenty years. I just sold a beachfront condo for ten times what I paid for it. If Mom needs help I can hire it for her," Claire said. "What she needs to do is quit working so she can look after dad."

"You've changed," Hannah said. "You sound kind of hard-hearted."

"Things look different when you get outside this town," Claire said. "Not everyone lives in their families' back pockets the way our family does."

"There's a benefit to living that way," Hannah said. "If you need help, there are a dozen people you can call, and any one of them will come running."

"Yeah, and they're the same dozen people who can vividly recall every stupid mistake you ever made, and there's nothing more fun for them than to remind you every time they see you."

"Plus there are pictures."

"Not if I find them first."

"We're family," Hannah said. "That means you always have somewhere to go and someone to take you in, no matter what."

"I appreciate that; I do," Claire said. "I'm just not done exploring what life has to offer."

"You're almost forty, cousin; it's time to grow up."

"I have grown up," Claire said. "I just haven't grown old."

"You aren't grown up," Hannah said. "Until you put aside what you want for what's best for someone you love, you don't know the meaning of grown up. I grew up a little when I fell in love with a guy in a wheelchair, and then, even more, when I encouraged him to go to MIT even though I thought he'd probably never come back. When we went through a rough patch a few years ago, I had to adjust my expectations in order to stay married, but I didn't put on my real big girl panties until I had Sammy."

"I've put my wants and desires second to Sloan Merryweather's for the past twenty years. Before that, it was whatever Pip wanted. I never got to do what I wanted."

"I think you must have wanted something about the life you've lived."

"I made a lot of money, that's true. I got to go all over the world, saw some amazing views, and met famous people. But Sloan never for one minute let me forget it was due to my employment; she always made sure I knew my place was in coach while hers was in first class."

"Was she really that bad?"

"You have no idea."

"I can't wait to hear. Spill it."

"I can't tell you. I signed a confidentiality agreement that if broken would cost me everything I worked so hard to earn. It's not worth it."

"Wow. You make her sound like a monster."

Claire smiled at Hanna and clinked her beer bottle against Hannah's.

"No comment."

"Can you dish about anyone else?"

"Oh, sure."

"Oh, goody! Let's start with the hot men."

When Claire got home, her father was asleep in his recliner with Mackie Pea on his lap. Her Uncle Curtis was sitting on the couch watching a golf match on television. Curtis had been so fond of Claire growing up that he had been like a second father to her. For some reason seeing him made Claire's heart hurt.

"Hey, Claire Bear," Curtis said. "Welcome home."

He jumped up off the couch and hugged her, kissed her cheek. He smelled like he always did; a combination of cigarette smoke, gasoline, and the spearmint gum he loved to chew. Her father woke up as she came in and seemed very confused to see her.

"It's awfully late, young lady," he said. "Don't you have school tomorrow?"

Claire exchanged a look with her Uncle Curtis, who gave her a sad smile.

"It's Saturday, buddy," Curtis said. "There's no school tomorrow."

"Where's Mom?" Claire asked.

"She's on nights," her father said.

Claire was pretty sure he was referring to the nursing home where Delia worked twenty-five years earlier.

"She went to a baby shower," Curtis said. "The Deluca gal's."

"Liam's sick," her father said, and Claire felt as if her heart had stopped.

"What?" she said.

"The medicine makes him sick at his stomach so he can't eat. He's losing too much weight. Doc wants to put him in the children's hospital in Pittsburgh."

He looked so bereft. Claire couldn't speak for the tears in her eyes and the lump in her throat. Her Uncle Curtis put on his jacket and squeezed her shoulder. His hazel eyes, just like his daughter Hannah's, were full of sorrow and sympathy.

"I better get on home," he said. "You stop by the station tomorrow, sweetheart. We'll get caught up."

He waved to Ian and left through the front door.

"You might just check on your brother," Ian said. "See if he needs anything before you go to bed."

"I will, Dad," she said and fled to the bathroom.

Claire ran the shower to cover up the sound of her crying. She didn't want to upset her father or have to explain. Her mother was waiting on the other side of the door when she came out. She walked with Claire to her bedroom and shut the door behind them.

"It was so sad," Claire said. "Dad told me Liam was sick and I should check on him."

"He sometimes forgets that Liam died," Delia said. "By tomorrow he won't even remember what was said."

"It's so awful," Claire said.

"He started asking after Liam a few months ago. The first time I told him Liam died a long time ago, and he got so upset Doc had to give him a sedative. Now I just tell him Liam's staying the night at Curtis's, or Fitz's. It's kinder that way, don't you think?"

"Yes," Claire said, wiping her mascara from under her eyes with a tissue. "I'm so sorry you're going through this. It's not fair."

"When has life ever been fair to this family?" Delia asked her. "Or anyone else, for that matter?"

"You deserve to enjoy life," Claire said. "Let me help you. I have money now, lots of money, actually. I can hire people to help you."

"Isn't it just like rich folks to throw money at every problem."

"I'm not just some rich person; I'm your daughter."

"And a very good one," Delia said. "Get some rest, and we'll talk tomorrow."

"I love you, Mom," Claire said.

"I love you, too," Delia said. "Now go to sleep."

"Hey, before I forget," Claire said, "did you give Sammy a silver key ring with a bottle opener on it?"

"No," Delia said. "But if you have a chance to look in that tin of his see if he's got my Kennedy silver dollar. He calls it trading even if he's secretly taken it and hasn't given you anything in return."

Claire lay in bed, tired but not able to sleep. She tossed and turned and stared at the ceiling. Eventually, the alarm clock glowed midnight. Shortly thereafter there was a tap on her window. She parted the curtains and was surprised to see Scott. She knelt on the bed and opened the window.

"What are you doing?" she asked him.

"I can't call or knock on the front door; I didn't want to wake your dad."

"What's going on?"

"I brought your purse and your clothes. You can pick up your carry-on and rental car tomorrow."

"Thank you," Claire said as she hoisted her belongings in through the window. "What's the latest?"

"Tuppy's family came to identify the body today. They don't know his phone password, so we have to subpoena the service provider. It may take weeks."

"If I could get my hands on his phone I could probably figure it out," Claire said. "I'm the one who helped him set it up when he started working for Sloan."

"We may find it, yet," Scott said. "Either way, you can't leave town for awhile."

"That's okay," Claire said. "Mom and Dad need me here. It may take me more than a couple weeks to sort them out."

"I know what that's like."

"Is something wrong with your mom?" Claire asked.

"She caught a cold at Christmas, and it's just held on. Now she gets so short of breath she can't walk very far. Doc Machalvie's been saying for months she should have tests done. I finally talked her into going. Her appointment's on Monday in Morgantown."

"Is it just me, or do you suddenly feel like the roles have reversed?"

"Definitely," Scott said. "I don't know why I'm so surprised, but I never thought about what would happen when my mother got old."

"Your mom and my mom are not old."

"Not yet," Scott said, "but they're definitely slowing down."

Claire shivered, and Scott smiled at her.

"You're going to catch pneumonia," he said, and then glanced appreciatively at her nightgown.

"Stop that," Claire said. "I'm closing the window."

"Sorry," Scott said, but he was smiling.

"Goodnight," Claire said, and then pulled the window sash back down, and closed the curtains.

Claire lay back down and closed her eyes. She went to sleep thinking about Scott, but it was Sam she dreamed about.

Peony Street by Pamela Grandstaff

Chapter Four - Sunday

Her cousin Patrick was already in the Rose and Thorn when Claire arrived.

"Claire Bear!" he called out from behind the bar.

Claire wiped her Jimmy Choo Mary Jane heels on the entryway mat and took off her black Burberry trench coat as Patrick came around the bar, which covered most of the wall to her right. He made his way down the narrow space between the long wall of booths on the left and the small tables in the middle, which had mismatched chairs upended on top of them.

Patrick swept her up in a tight, warm hug and swung her around until she was dizzy.

"Stop, Patrick," she protested. "I'm gonna puke."

He let go and laughed as she tried to regain her balance.

"You look great," he said. "Like a serial killer, but a hot one."

Her Armani white shirt, Calvin Klein black wrap sweater, and Marc Jacobs black pants were on day three and starting to show it. She was looking forward to the return of her carry-on bag.

"Thanks," she said. "You haven't changed a bit."

"I could stand to lose a few pounds," he said, patting his belly. "But then I'd be so damn handsome I'd never get any work done for all the women fighting over me. You see my dilemma."

Patrick did look the same, other than a touch of gray at the temples of his dark hair, some laugh lines, and the extra weight on his muscular six-foot-two frame. His bright blue eyes twinkled mischievously, and his smirky smile was punctuated by a cleft chin that any leading man would envy. As had been the case with every relative she'd encountered so far, Claire felt irrational homesickness just looking at him.

'Why do I still feel homesick when I'm home with the very people I missed when I was away?'

Patrick was playing bluegrass music on the bar sound system, music which also pulled at her heartstrings. Claire couldn't listen to fiddle music without tearing up and went out of her way to avoid it out in the world beyond Rose Hill. It had been next to impossible to avoid it in Scotland, where every other pub played traditional music.

The only thing more difficult than listening to it was singing it; Claire hadn't sung anything for years. She used to be the girl who sang whenever anyone asked her to. In a church or seated on top of the bar in the Rose and Thorn, Claire would gladly sing her heart out. Unfortunately, the naive confidence she had as a teenager in Rose Hill quickly gave way to a self-conscious vulnerability as soon as she left.

"Silver threads and golden needles cannot mend this heart of mine ..."

She hadn't heard that song in at least twenty years but could remember every word. She could remember sitting on top of the bar singing that very song as Scooter Scoley played his fiddle and grinned at her like a possum. He had wanted her to go on the road with his band, The Snufftuckers; instead, she ran away to Hollywood with Pip.

'An impulsive decision that launched my crazy career,' Claire thought. 'I wonder what I would've done differently if I knew then what I know now.'

The bar looked and smelled the same as it had since Claire was a child. It was a pungent combination of cigarette smoke embedded in the yellowed paint, the fragrant oil soap used to clean everything, and what must have been gallons of spilled beer and whiskey soaked into the wood floors. It was acrid, it was sweet, it was sour, and it smelled like home.

The blue vinyl booths and the seats of the swiveling stools attached to the bar were patched with duct tape, and the square tables all tilted slightly at different angles. The huge mirror set into the majestic hand-carved back wall of the bar was smoky around the edges, as befitted a work of art shipped across the Atlantic Ocean over a hundred years before. The only change she noticed was a gargantuan flat screen television affixed to the back wall.

Many evenings Claire sat in the last booth at the back of the bar, completed her homework, drank sodas, and read books while her mother served and cleaned. This bar had been her father's dream, his retirement plan, and a bone of contention in the community when he was promoted to chief of police. As a compromise he sold it to his wife for a dollar, and as far as Claire knew the bar was still in her mother's name. When Patrick came of age, he took over the bartending duties, and later Hannah had come to work as a waitress.

It was in this bar that a nineteen-year-old Claire broke the news to her parents that she was moving to California with Pip. Her mother wept into a white bar towel, and her father slammed his fist on a table top.

"This will all end in tears," he'd warned her.

And it had.

Claire sat down at the bar and accepted the mug of coffee Patrick offered. The rim was chipped, but it was clean and had the logo of his sister Maggie's store, Little Bear Books, on the side: a drawing of a bear cub wearing big glasses, sitting with a large book propped open on his little bear legs.

"Too cute," Tuppy would have said, "nauseatingly so."

Thinking of Tuppy, Claire felt a loss where two days ago, with him alive, she would have felt next to no regard at all. Claire hadn't kidded herself that they were ever real friends; Tuppy had formed a strategic alliance with Claire despite his being an unrepentant, pretentious snob. He'd made many cracks about what a redneck Claire was, what a bump on the log she came from, and had slyly asked if her family tree forked or was everyone "related?" But he had also looked out for her when it was important and hadn't thrown her under a bus in order to look good to their boss, which he could so easily have done many times.

"Think you'll do much time for killin' that guy?" Patrick asked her.

"I'm still walking around," Claire said. "They must not think I'm too dangerous."

"Tiny Crimefighter just wants you to think you're off the hook," Patrick said. "When Theo got murdered, I was one of her prime suspects, and she stalked me like a buck in deer season. Of course, she also wanted to jump my bones."

"Tiny Crimefighter?" Claire asked. "Do you mean Sarah?"

"Hannah named her that," Patrick said. "Sarah's the sharp claw of the law."

"She's very intense, isn't she?" Claire said. "Did you sleep with her?'

"Naw," Patrick said. "The crazy ones are great in bed but more likely to shoot you if they catch you running around."

"Where is everyone?"

"Church," he said. "Unlike you lazy Methodists, we Catholics go visit the Lord's house every Sunday."

"You're here."

"I go to the early Mass. Father Stephen skips the homily, and we're out in thirty minutes. Everyone else goes to the later one, the long one."

Although Claire's father was raised Catholic her mother had refused to convert, something that had made a sworn enemy out of her mother-in-law Rose. Claire's Grandma Rose used to say to Claire, "You may look like one of mine, but you've got that French blood in you; that's what killed your brother." Grandma Rose was not a cuddly kind of grandparent. She loved her three sons and her Catholic grandsons, but everyone else was viewed as a potential underminer or usurper of her role as matriarch.

Claire held out her mug for a refill and Patrick obliged.

"What's this meeting about?" Claire said. "Hannah was kind of vague about it."

"The old folks are starting to wear out. We need to sort out what will happen to the businesses."

"Isn't that up to them to decide?"

"And let my mom stick me with the bakery? No, thank you. It's better if we come to an agreement among ourselves and tell them how it's gonna be."

"Why involve me, though? I don't live here. I don't have a stake in the outcome."

"This bar should rightfully pass to you."

"You're the one who's kept the business going. You deserve to have it. I certainly don't want it."

The front door opened and an unfamiliar person came in. He was dressed like one of the many mountain biker/hiker/campers that swarmed the area in the late spring and summer: rain poncho, olive-colored fatigue pants, hiking boots, and a sunburned nose. Claire was reminded that tourists always underestimated how cold it was here in late spring, and couldn't believe that you could freeze at night but still get sunburned during the day.

"You open?" he said.

"No, sorry," Patrick said, "not on Sundays."

The man looked confused but left.

Patrick took the "Private Party" sign from under the counter and went up to the front to put it on the outside of the door. Meanwhile, Claire looked around.

'Do I want this?' she asked herself.

She imagined working behind the bar, serving the locals, students, and tourists at the tables and booths, late into the night, every day but Sunday.

"I don't want it," she told Patrick when he came back.

Patrick shrugged.

"Suits me," he said. "But your folks need you here."

"Don't worry. I'll get them sorted out before I go. Mom says they're doing fine."

"Well, she would, wouldn't she? Delia's the first in line to offer help and last in line to ask for it."

"If she needs someone to clean the house, or someone to help with Dad, I can pay for that. It doesn't have to be me."

"So you'd pay some stranger to help your own family before you would?"

"That's not such a horrible idea, Patrick. I'm not a bad daughter because I don't want to move back to Rose Hill and babysit my senior parents. I can pay for an assisted living facility or a nursing home when they need it, but I don't think they're going to need that for a while."

"That's so cold," Patrick said. "Family used to mean something to you."

"I'm completely normal," Claire said. "It's just the rural, backward, clannish way everyone lives around here that seems normal to you."

"We take care of our own."

"Exactly. You don't want some outsiders coming in here, trying to change things, trying to bring the town into this century, let alone the second half of the last century."

"I guess you like those new condos down on Lotus Avenue."

"Mom said they replaced a row of condemned houses full of black mold and asbestos. Change happens. It's not all bad."

"Soon none of us will be able to afford the property taxes we'll have to pay in order to live here."

"You're exaggerating."

"I'm not. You think anyone who grew up in Glencora still lives up there? Not unless they sold some huge piece of property to a developer or started a tourist business."

"Lots of tourist money comes into this place," Claire said.

"But they used to go back up the mountain after closing time," Patrick said. "Now they're buying second homes here and renting them out. The woman who bought the diner doesn't even make hamburgers. I ordered a turkey sandwich, and it came covered in this green slime that looked like frog snot. For crissakes, there's a friggin' tea room next door."

"A tea room?"

"Knox Rodefeffer's second wife opened it. Her son goes to Eldridge, and she's from Boston, where according to her they do everything right. My mom got into a huge, screaming fight with her. We could hear it in here over the music."

Claire pictured her fierce Aunt Bonnie having a go at the unlucky tearoom owner and pitied the poor woman.

"I'm sorry to hear about next door," Claire said. "I know you wanted to buy it and expand the bar."

"She outbid me. I had the mortgage lined up and a down payment saved, and she offered Gwyneth twice what it was worth. She offered to buy the bar, too, said it was an eyesore. Rich witch, with that smug smile on her face, looking down her nose at me. We'll be lucky to hold on to this place. You can't smoke in here anymore, you know, and there's an actual law against smoking on the street out front. If our taxes keep going up, it's just a matter of time before we have to sell it to some trust-funders who think they're gonna get rich roasting gourmet coffee or micro-brewing beer."

"That's awful," Claire said. "I'm sorry about what's happening in Rose Hill. I don't want any of the family businesses to close."

"That's why I wanted to expand the business, to try to save the place," Patrick said. "We need some new fixtures, a commercial kitchen, and a dance floor with a stage for a band. I'd like to have a trivia night and a karaoke night. We have to market this business to the college kids and tourists, not just Jimbo, Pudge, and the rest of the locals."

"I'd pay a lot to see Pudge Postlethwaite sing karaoke."

"He's actually a very solid baritone. I bet you didn't know that."

"You should have the bar, Patrick," Claire said. "It means more to you than anyone."

"It doesn't matter who runs it if it goes under. None of us wants the bakery, and I can't run the gas station and the bar. You remember Hatch?"

"Hannah's boyfriend in high school; of course I do."

"Curtis is of a mind to sell the gas station to him."

"What about Curtis's four boys? What about Hannah?"

"I can't see Hannah sitting in there all day chewing the fat with those old geezers, can you? None of Curtis's boys are moving back here to Rose Hill. They're like you; they can't stand the place."

"I never said I couldn't stand the place."

"You've been back, what, five times in the past twenty years?"

"My work took me all over the world, Patrick. I had contracts to honor and obligations to fulfill."

"You could cut hair in Rose Hill," Patrick said. "Denise's looking for a buyer for The Bee Hive."

Claire could barely suppress a shudder at the thought.

"Doing hair and makeup for films is completely different," Claire said. "It pays better, for one thing."

"You've got above your raising, Claire Fitzpatrick. You think you're too good for us."

Patrick said what he did with a humorous gleam in his eye and a grin, but she thought he was only half-kidding.

"It's true," she said. "I've gone posh."

Hannah and Maggie came in. Maggie was tall and blue-eyed like Claire but with more of an Amazonian bombshell figure. Her flaming red curly hair corkscrewed out like fireworks going off in all directions around her head and shoulders, and her pale skin was covered in fine freckles.

As they walked up the aisle, Claire estimated it would take an entire day for Maggie's hair to air-dry after it was washed, and if straightened it would fall clear down past her hips. There were a few silver and white strands now among the red and pronounced frown lines between Maggie's golden brows. Claire immediately thought of all the different shades she'd have to mix to cover the gray and match Maggie's glorious mane. She also reflected that if Maggie were in show business, she'd need some nerve paralyzers and wrinkle fillers. Nothing extreme, just some preventative maintenance work now so that any changes made through plastic surgery later wouldn't seem so dramatic.

'If she lost weight she'd be striking enough to be a lead actress,' Claire thought. 'But she'd break the nose of any producer or director who suggested she take a turn on the casting couch. Plus, with that temper, no one would want to work with her twice.'

"Mary Margaret," she said as she hugged her cousin. "It's so good to see you."

Maggie's hugs were always quick as if she endured them rather than enjoyed them, so Claire knew it for the compliment it was. Maggie smiled at Claire with real pleasure at seeing her, but then quickly recovered. She was Bonnie's daughter and a granddaughter of the formidable Rose, after all. That much genetic starch doesn't wash out.

"It took you long enough to come home," Maggie said. "I forgot what you looked like. The last time I saw you your hair was short, spiky, and platinum blonde."

"Have you lost weight?" Claire asked her. "You look great."

"She's so busy she doesn't have time to eat," Hannah said.

"You stay busy, and I notice you never miss a meal," Maggie said to Hannah, who was known to have a voracious appetite and the metabolism of a hummingbird. To Claire, she said, "I swim every morning at the college and walk the rail trail every evening. Between school, the bookstore and the bakery it's the only time I have to myself."

"She's got a new boyfriend," Hannah said.

"He's not my boyfriend," Maggie said, but her face and neck flushed a deep red.

"He's a teacher at Eldridge," Hannah said. "They got him from some fancy school in England. He talked Maggie into going back to school and got her a scholarship."

"I'm considered an adult returning student," Maggie said, rolling her eyes at Hannah. "Professor Richmond wrote the letter of recommendation that helped me get a grant to pay for school."

"That's great, Maggie," Claire said, as they all sat down in Claire's booth. "What's your major?"

"English Lit," Maggie said, "with a minor in American Lit."

"There are lots of jobs, apparently, in the Lit field," Patrick said. "Our Maggie will be able to wrangle Lit on either side of the Atlantic."

"Shut up," Maggie said to her brother. "I'm getting an education, not building my resume."

"Her boyfriend teaches a class on Shakespeare," Hannah told Claire. "I can't understand a word he says, but Maggie thinks he's dreamy."

"Hark!" Patrick said. "Wouldst thou care for a wee drop of ale?"

"Verily I would," Hannah said. "But alas, I am a Capulet and cannot imbibe from the frosty mug of a Montague."

Maggie scowled at Hannah.

"Aren't you hungry," Maggie asked Hannah. "Why don't you go order us a pizza?"

"I might miss something."

"You might miss my foot up your behind," Maggie said.

"I've missed you two," Claire said.

That lonely, aching, homesick feeling overwhelmed her again, and to her embarrassment, she felt tears fill her eyes. She quickly blinked them away.

As Hannah went out Patrick and Maggie's brother Sean came in. He was a thinner, more polished version of Patrick, but with the same piercing blue eyes, dark hair, and cleft chin.

'Sean's a leading man,' Claire thought. 'Put him in a tux, and all the women and gay men would swoon.' She looked at Patrick in comparison and decided he was more the western or action adventure type. 'Classic bad boy,' she concluded.

She embraced Sean, and he said, "I stopped by Scott's on my way here, and he says you can pick up your carry-on bag and rental car anytime this afternoon."

"Good," Claire said. "I loved these clothes when I bought them, but I'm getting a little tired of wearing them."

"You look great," Sean said. "Too classy for this dive."

"What's that supposed to mean?" Patrick said.

He threw a wet bar towel at Sean, who ducked.

"How's everything back home in Pittsburgh?" Claire asked Sean.

"This will soon be his home," Patrick said. "Sean's moving back to Rose Hill."

"He told me," Claire said, and couldn't hide her horror.

91

"Don't make that face," Sean said. "Mom and Dad are getting on, and I've had my big city experience. I sold my house, and I'm going to fix up the second apartment over Maggie's bookstore."

Claire caught a quick look pass between Patrick, Sean, and Maggie. Hannah came back in with two huge pizza boxes, set them on the table, and hugged Sean.

"Hey, good-looking," Hannah said to Sean. "When's the big day?"

"My last day at the bank is May 30th."

They all sat down, and Patrick brought over a pitcher of beer and some glasses.

"What will you do for work?" Claire asked Sean.

"I'm going to polish up my lawyering skills and open a family law practice," he said. "The community college in Pendleton has a paralegal program, and they've offered me a part-time teaching position. I'll still do estate planning, of course, but there's not a big demand for that here. Rose Hill is a great place to invest right now, so I'm looking at buying one of the empty buildings downtown. They all need to be renovated, and that will take some time. I'm hoping to have the apartment finished by the end of the summer and an office open by October."

Claire again saw the quick warning looks pass between the siblings.

"What's going on?" she asked. "Is there some big secret?"

"Pip's going to do all the work," Hannah said. "He's back."

"Hannah!" Maggie snapped, and Hannah yelped as she was kicked under the table.

"We were going to tell you," Maggie told Claire.

"After this meeting," Patrick said.

"Sorry," Sean said. "I thought you knew."

Claire felt her consciousness recede back into her head as she resisted this information. Her cousins seemed to be waiting for her reaction, so she quickly attempted to gather her wits.

"Did he bring his wife and kids?" she asked, in what she had intended to be a neutral tone that actually came out a little shrill.

"Left them, apparently," Hannah said. "He came back alone."

Claire pushed Sean out of their side of the booth.

"Where are you going?" Patrick said. "We have business to discuss."

"Don't be such a big baby," Maggie said. "We were going to tell you."

"Here's the thing," Claire said, addressing everyone at the table. "I'm not moving back to Rose Hill. I don't want any of the family businesses, and I'll sign any papers Sean draws up to confirm that. I'm only staying as long as the police make me, and then as soon as I get my parents sorted out I'm out of here. I love you guys, and I love our crazy family, but this is not where I belong. I don't know where I belong, but I know it's not Rose Hill. It's my turn to be happy, it's my turn to have a life of my own, and if I come back here I'll just disappear; absorbed by this family, by these businesses, by this town. I'm sorry, but I just can't do it. I won't do it."

Claire turned and walked purposefully toward the door as her cousins broke into applause. Claire's face burned as she grabbed her coat and flung open the door, determined not to look back.

"As God as my witness," Maggie called after her, "I'll never be hungry again!"

"Brava!" Sean shouted. "Bellisima! Encore!"

"I think she really means it," Hannah said, to which Patrick replied, "She's not going anywhere."

As soon as Claire's feet hit the sidewalk in front of the Rose and Thorn, she turned right, having made an impulsive decision not to go back to her parents' house. The door to the bar slammed shut behind her, blocking out her cousins' laughter. Down the street, she saw her Aunt Alice turn the corner by the old diner, headed in her direction. She was walking with some old busybody whom Claire recognized but couldn't name. Claire ducked into the nearest door, which advertised in golden gilt letters, "Dashwood Antiques, Gifts, Tea Room."

Sleigh bells attached to the door jangled as she went in. As Claire attempted to take in the pink and white floral chintz explosion that greeted her inside, her nose was assailed by the sickeningly sweet scent of candles poured into glass jars, the clean floral scent of expensive soaps, and the wonderful, exotic aroma of many fragrant teas. Claire had learned a lot about tea in the UK, fancied herself sort of a self-taught tea snob, and thought she knew good tea when she smelled it. There was some good tea in this shop.

"Good afternoon," someone said from the back of the shop, but the sense of Claire not being welcome was clearly communicated by the woman's tone. "With what may I assist you?"

Claire turned toward the sound of the voice, and her enormous handbag got hung up on a spinner rack of greeting cards trimmed in handmade lace. She grabbed the rack before it fell over onto a display of porcelain Beatrix Potter figurines.

"You're quite the proverbial bull, aren't you," the voice said, and Claire recognized the mocking smugness of which her cousin Patrick had warned.

The woman who approached her was slight in form, with half-readers dangling on a frayed silk cord around her neck, and pink lipstick haphazardly smeared on thin lips ringed with disapproval lines. Upon her head, a grosgrain headband held back a poorly cut bob of mousy brown hair that was aggressively graying, but not in an attractive, dramatic way.

She was dressed in the kind of clothing Claire had come to recognize as "old money," which is to say, slightly shabby but with impeccable labels on the inside, rather than the outside, where they would be considered a vulgar display.

Claire was taken aback by the marks visible on one side of the woman's face, marks she had been unable to completely conceal with makeup. Claire didn't miss much when looking at a person's face; this woman had been slapped recently, and hard.

Claire immediately cast her as the betrayed society wife of a womanizing executive type; brittle, bitter, and recently replaced by a mistress less than half her age. Maybe they'd had a slap fight. Claire had seen one of those up close, and they were not pretty.

"I'm so sorry," Claire said in what she hoped was an imperial manner. "I wonder if you have any Darjeeling Yellow Tea? I'm particularly fond of the tea from the Goomtee Estate in India. It has such a sweet, honey fragrance. Are you familiar with that blend?"

The woman momentarily stared at Claire before stating, "You're not from here."

"No," Claire said. "I live in South Kensington."

"London?"

The woman's facial display of disbelief was insulting.

"I'm only here for a short visit."

"Do you have a child at the college?"

The look she bestowed upon Claire clearly indicated that such an occurrence could not possibly be true, so revolting was Claire's stumbling entrance and flashy appearance. Her eyes raked Claire from her high heels up to her bright red lipstick, and she curled her lip in derision.

"No, no children," Claire said. "About that tea?"

"I have Darjeeling, yes, and it's Indian, but I don't know from what estate. I'm not usually interrogated about provenance."

She said this with marked disapproval as if in addition to her vulgar appearance Claire was further guilty of being unreasonably interested in whence came the tea.

"I'd love to try it," Claire said.

Claire dropped her handbag on a fragile white chair with spindly legs and a tiny seat she was sure would collapse if she had the temerity to sit upon it. She knew her expensive handbag wouldn't impress this woman, so she shrugged off her coat and draped it over the handbag in a way that the label inside the coat could clearly be seen.

"My mother had a Burberry trench," the woman said. "She bought it on her year abroad, after Wellesley but before she married Daddy."

"It performs its function, that's all I care about," Claire said, and thought she remembered that line from one of Sloan's scripts. "If it's good enough for the Queen..."

"Quite a nice family before the commoners married into it," the woman said, and turned away, leaving Claire open-mouthed and appalled at such blatant bad manners.

Claire picked up her coat with the intention of leaving immediately, but saw her Aunt Alice and the busybody out in front of the shop looking in the window at the ruffled silk peonies stuck in an antique silver pitcher, starched linen handkerchiefs transformed into a fleet of origami swans, and a handmade wooden cradle full of collectible china dolls and Steiff teddy bears.

Claire moved to the table farthest away from the entrance, at the back of the shop, hidden behind a mountain of quilted fabric handbags and matching accessories, all in a ghastly bandana print of acid green and antacid pink. On the wall by the table were framed illustrations of Scandinavian children, some in sunny nurseries, and some lolling about with puppies in a garden under the watchful eye of a knitting nanny.

"What's worse than twee?" she imagined Tuppy asking. "What's twee to the twentieth degree?"

She was amazed to find she missed him. She also found it impossible to believe that the witty, energetic, ambitious young man she had known for such a short time could really be dead. Any minute she expected him to dash in, take a wide-eyed look around, and say, "Well. It's all just too darling, isn't it?"

She sighed. A phone rang, and she heard the shop owner answer. She imagined the woman's first name would be a family name, maybe even one of those last names for a first name: Blair, Spencer, Cavender, or Kennedy, and there would be a nickname associated with it like Bitsy or Kiki. Katherine Hepburn would have played her in tennis whites.

The woman raised her voice in anger, and the implication of drama, like the smell of freshly baked bread, immediately attracted Claire's attention. It produced a delicious combination of curiosity mixed with the promise of schadenfreude.

"Don't come here," the woman warned. "Are you insane? I'm working ... I have customers ... my husband could stop by any minute. My son ... I won't let you. It's over ... there's nothing to talk about. I'm sorry you feel that way, but I really have no choice."

The kettle wailed, and the woman went to the back room where Claire could not hear the rest of the call. When she came back to serve Claire her face was flushed, and her hands trembled. Her attention was not on what she was doing, and she had to go back for a spoon and then a serviette. Claire could feel the tension building and decided to sip slowly, to wait and see if anything else happened. The caller was obviously a spurned lover, possibly a younger man, a married man, or a woman.

Within five minutes her patience was rewarded. The sleigh bells tied to the front door rattled violently, and the woman gasped, then rushed to the front of the store. She tried to keep her voice down, but Claire could hear everything.

"I told you not to come," she hissed. "It's too dangerous."

A deep voice, a man's voice, said something Claire could not decipher, but all the hair rose up on her arms and neck.

'Why would I have that reaction?' Claire wondered.

"You'll ruin everything," the woman hissed. "I won't allow it."

Again she heard the man's deep voice, too low for Claire to discern the words, but something about it made her deeply uneasy, almost panicked. Claire thought this was probably her intuition warning her that something awful was about to happen.

She quietly gathered up her handbag and raincoat, put a twenty on the table, skirted around the backside of the hideous handbag display, and tiptoed up the side of the store, hoping to slip out unnoticed. She decided not to look at the man in case he might kill her if he thought she could pick him out in a line-up. She was almost to the door, just beyond the shabby chic pillow slips covered in tiny yellow rosebuds and the display of "Team Darcy" and "Team Heathcliff" t-shirts, when the woman noticed her.

"You didn't pay," the woman spat.

"I left it on the table," Claire said.

Her hand was on the polished brass doorknob when the man said, "Claire?"

A rippling goose-bump-covered shudder rolled up one side of Claire and down the other. Her stomach contracted, Darjeeling tea threatened to leave the way it came in, and her fight or flight response got stuck on 'stunned and paralyzed.' More than anything else in the world Claire did not want to turn around. When she did, she watched the color drain out of the face of the woman standing next to Phillip Hobart Deacon, also known as "Pip," also known as her ex-husband.

"Hi Pip," she said and fled.

Claire rushed out of the tea room and ran right into a man built like a fire hydrant. He caught her by the arms as she bounced off of him and almost fell.

"I'm so sorry ..." she began, but then he said, "Claire? Claire Fitzpatrick?"

Claire recognized him but couldn't come up with a name.

"It's Dominic," he said. "Dom Deluca. We've only known each other since kindergarten."

"Of course I know you, Dom. It's just I suddenly don't feel well, and I need to get off the street as quickly as possible ..."

"Sure, sure, sure, come with me to the shop," he said, as he grabbed her arm and pulled her down the sidewalk. "You remember Denise Gambini? We got married after she graduated beauty school; we've got three kids and one on the way. She'll be thrilled to see you. I haven't seen you since your Grandpa Tim's funeral."

"Actually, I didn't come home for that," Claire said, as they arrived at The Bee Hive Beauty Salon. The logo painted on the window was a woman's head with a towering hive-shaped hairdo around which bees were buzzing. It had to be seen to be believed.

"I coulda swore I saw you at that funeral," Dom said. "It was the same week your cousin Brian escaped from prison and died in a car accident. His poor mother; we felt so bad for her. Are you sure you weren't there?"

"I was in Prague," Claire said.

"Yeah, in the movies or something, your mom is always saying."

Dom flung open the door and shouted, "Hey Denise! Look who I ran into! We really did run into each other, too; she almost knocked me over!"

As they entered the hair salon, Claire inhaled the familiar chemicals of her chosen profession: the eye-watering sting of ammonia and peroxide mixed with hair color, the sharp tang of the permanent wave setting solution, and a multitude of beauty products spiked with scents from floral to fruity to spicy, with various combinations in between.

A heavily pregnant Denise was artfully teasing and combing a woman's hair, valiantly trying to cover her sparsely populated pink scalp, which was quite a feat given how little she had to work with. Claire could see Denise was in the zone: tease, comb, spray, tease, comb, spray, tease, comb, spray.

Denise squealed when she saw Claire and waddled over to give her a side arm hug.

"We went to beauty school together!" Denise announced to the room.

There were two women sitting under hood dryers; they raised the hoods up and leaned forward so they could hear. Claire recognized them but couldn't come up with their names. The woman in the hydraulic chair who had been getting her hair teased seemed to be asleep or possibly dead (it had been known to happen).

"Oh, my God, tell me everything," Denise said. "I know you've been working for that movie star, that red-headed one whose husband left her for that teenager, the one with the chest out to here. She won that award for playing a prostitute, and her dress fell apart on stage. Oh, my God, I can't believe I can't think of her name. It's Sonya, or Samantha, or something ..."

"Sloan Merryweather," Claire said.

"Oh, my God, yes! That's the one. She's so gorgeous. You do not know how many people come in here and ask for the haircut she had in that movie about the Internet thing where she fell in love with the guy who was her dog walker but was secretly rich."

"Tweetheart," Claire said.

"That's the one! Oh my God, what's she like? Is she nice?"

Claire hated these questions because there was really only one way to answer.

"She's a legend," Claire said. "Very talented and always professional."

"It's just awful what that husband did to her, so humiliating. I felt so bad for her. That he had the nerve to bring that skank to the award show."

"Well, Sloan did win the Oscar," Claire said. "So something good came out of it."

"It was because they couldn't have children or something, wasn't that it? She couldn't give him the son he wanted so badly. I guess he and that teenager have like five kids now, but all girls. God showed him."

"Sounds like us," Dom said. "We got three girls and another one on the way."

"It looks like any minute," Claire said. "Shouldn't you be in bed?"

"We didn't do the test," Denise said. "Last time we did the test the doctor said it was going to be a boy, and boom! We got Giana. Big surprise. And us with everything blue in the nursery. So we don't know what it is, but we got our fingers crossed and a yellow and green in the nursery."

"This might be my son," Dom said with tears in his eyes, pressing his hand to Denise's belly.

Claire was surprised to feel tears fill her own eyes as Denise took her hand and pressed it against her burgeoning bump. The skin was tight as a drum, and Claire felt something roll out against her hand, something like an elbow, or a knee, but so tiny.

"Isn't it a miracle?" Denise said. "It's why God made us."

Claire thought but didn't say that was certainly one point of view, but not necessarily her own. She loosened her hand from Denise's grip, wiped her eyes, and said, "That little guy is strong. Shouldn't you be sitting down with your feet up?"

"My due date was two weeks ago," Denise said. "I don't want him gettin' too comfy in here. I'm off tomorrow, and I'm gonna clean my whole house. I got Giana moving in the right direction by vacuuming the stairs."

"We had to replace the carpet," Dom said while beaming at his wife. "We got hardwoods now. They're much easier to keep clean."

Claire thought it must be nice to be adored like Denise so obviously was, even when she looked like she was smuggling a basketball under her smock.

Claire heard Tuppy's voice in her head saying, 'She's the goose that lay the golden Delucas.'

Claire had always enjoyed Tuppy's snide comments when they weren't directed at her, but she hoped he wasn't setting up shop in her brain. It would be just like Tuppy to haunt her out of spite or boredom with the hereafter.

The woman in the hydraulic chair snored so loudly she woke herself up. Denise gave her one last spray, whirled off her nylon cape and brushed her neck and shoulders with a big fat powder brush. Claire walked over to a display rack to see what products Denise was pushing. The women under the dryers lost interest, sat back, and pulled their hoods back down. Claire was reading the list of ingredients on a bottle of something that claimed to stimulate hair growth when she heard Denise swear.

"Oh, my God, Dominic," Denise said. "My water just broke."

"He's coming!" Dom said and began to cry again. "Oh, honey."

"About time," Denise said. "Don't just stand there bawling, you big dope, go get the car. Call Mama and tell her to have Stephie bring the overnight bag. Hurry, but don't drive crazy." To her customer, she only said, "Don't forget your change, sweetie."

Claire looked down, and immediately realized she hadn't expected the watery mess at Denise's feet to have a smell. She felt a little nauseated.

"I'll get the car!" Dom yelled and ran out of the shop.

Denise calmly gave her customer her change, and the woman toddled out, oblivious to what was happening.

"You should sit down," one of the women under the dryers said.

"You should cross your legs," the other one said.

Denise was putting on her coat.

"What can I do?" Claire asked her.

"Finish those two and lock up," she said and tossed Claire the keys to the shop.

Tires squealed as Dom pulled the car all the way up on the curb.

"Wish me luck that God willing, this is Dom Junior's birthday," Denise said, "because I'm not doing this again."

"Good luck," Claire said and watched as Dom carefully shepherded his wife into the car, and gently, slowly backed out into the street and drove away.

"I'll comb myself out," the first woman said as she tied a plastic rain hat over her curler-studded head and slipped on her coat. "No offense, but I don't let just anybody touch my hair."

"I do have a license," Claire said, but the woman gave Claire a weak smile and left the shop.

"How about you?" Claire asked the second.

"I'd love for you to do mine," the woman said as she moved over to the hydraulic chair. "I want to know what all those people in Hollywood are really like."

Claire jacked up the chair. It had been over twenty years since she graduated from beauty school, and at least that long since she'd done a roller set comb out that wasn't for period costume, but it was like riding a bicycle.

"Heavy tease and spray?" she asked the woman.

"Better lay it on pretty thick; it's got to last through Tuesday," the woman said. "I've got the Interdenominational Women's Society meeting on Tuesday night at the Owl Branch Missionary Baptist Church. We're doing a cookbook to sell as a fundraiser for Pine County Hospice. I'm going to have a fight on my hands getting my broccoli casserole in there instead of Sister Mary Margrethe's."

As the woman filled Claire in on the fierce political battles being waged over the charitable cookbook project, Claire loosened the rollers and pulled them away from the woman's thick, unnaturally black hair, which sprang right back into crisp, roller-shaped curls. Claire pictured Myrna Loy in The Thin Man and Joan Crawford in Mildred Pierce. No, not quite right. She wished the woman had a big white streak in front or something that would make it more interesting. She pictured the Bride of Frankenstein and smiled to herself. She'd done that one before, on herself for a Halloween party.

"Did you ever see Rosalind Russell in Auntie Mame?" she asked the woman.

"That's one of my favorite movies," the woman said. "Do you like old movies?"

"Love 'em," Claire said, and set out with fresh enthusiasm to recreate the hairstyle Mame Dennis was wearing when Beauregard Jackson Pickett Burnside fell in love with her while shopping for the orphans' roller skates at Macy's.

As Claire was finishing up with what she thought was Denise's last client of the day, her Aunt Alice and the busybody came in. They were surprised and delighted to see Claire, who enthusiastically faked the same reaction. As she took Auntie Mame's money, she glanced at the appointment book and saw two more customers were scheduled after these two. The first was Scott, and the other name was smeared and illegible.

"This is wonderful," the busybody said. "You can tell us what all the movie stars are really like."

"You're so thin," Aunt Alice said. "The last time I saw you your hair was blonde and curly, and you were carrying an extra twenty pounds. You're not anorexic, are you? I hope you're not hooked on any of those drugs because that would kill your mother. She has enough to worry about with that crazy father of yours. How did you get your teeth so white? They don't look real. "

Claire wondered how she would get through the next hour.

After Alice and the busybody left, Claire finally dealt with the gross puddle Denise had left on the floor behind the front counter. Her eyes watered and she fought her gag reflex with rubber gloves on her hands and a whole roll of paper towels. She threw everything that had gotten wet in the trash and bleached the floor.

She called her mother to tell her where she was and what she was doing.

"That's awfully nice of you," Delia said. "I'll have to make them a meatloaf tonight and run it over there in the morning."

She still had some time to kill before Scott's appointment. She worried that if she sat still she might think too much and this was definitely not a safe place to fall apart. She swept the floor, wiped the counters, washed out the sinks, washed and dried a load of dirty towels and then folded them. She organized the supply shelves and made a list of things Denise was out of. It was quiet, she was surrounded by familiar objects and smells, and hardly anyone knew where she was. It felt completely natural to be there.

'Could I do this every day?' she asked herself.

She envisioned the energy it would require and the competition she would have if she started her own business in L.A. If Sloan followed through on her threat to blackball Claire in the industry, there was no point in even trying. There were so many younger and hotter-looking kids coming up, and all of them were probably more talented and skilled than Claire. Her ace up the sleeve had been her connection to Sloan. Without that she might as well buy The Bee Hive, pull on some support hose, and get her teasing arm back in shape.

'I'd be right back where I started,' she thought.

It seemed to Claire as if the opportunity for her potential life, the one that would eventually include settling down in one place with a really nice husband and at least one cute kid, had passed by without her realizing it. She was almost forty. It was too late to start over in her chosen career and about a minute before too late to have a child. How was it that three years ago when she'd signed her last contract with Sloan, it had seemed like she had so much time left to start the next chapter, the really meaningful chapter? Now it looked as if her best years had been squandered.

Reluctantly she let herself think about the man she'd left in Scotland. Drama professor Carlyle McKinney wasn't handsome, but with a crooked smile and laughing brown eyes, his face had character. He was barely as tall as Claire, and she blushed to think how readily she gave up high heels for him.

Although a master of accents, Carlyle's trained speaking voice was pure Masterpiece Theater. Claire had been thrilled every time a little Scots burr sneaked in during his unguarded moments. Speaking of which, the unguarded moments had been brilliant as well, an intoxicating mixture of passion, tenderness, and laughter.

The producers on Sloan's last movie had hired Carlyle to be Sloan's dialect coach, and as a consequence, he and Claire spent many long days shivering under the same umbrella. He made her laugh, which for Claire, now immune to the physical beauty of the gorgeous actors she met every day, was a potent aphrodisiac. Of course, as soon as Sloan caught wind of what was going on, she found a way to ruin it, and Claire had given her final notice.

'I miss him,' she thought, and then immediately scolded herself for her weakness.

"La, la, la," she said, but these feelings, once dug up and brushed off, would not be buried again so easily.

'You've got to quit being such a romantic,' Claire told herself. 'There is no perfect man.'

"Hello," Scott called as he came in. "Hey, Claire. I didn't expect to see you here."

She filled him in on Denise, and he said he didn't mind if she cut his hair.

"I hope it's not a conflict of interest or anything," she said. "I don't want you to get in trouble with Sarah."

"If you knew how little I care about what that woman thinks of me," he said. "Plus you can't be chief of police in this town and not trip over a conflict of interest at every turn. Your dad forgot to tell me that before he retired."

"Do you think they'll clear me for take-off soon?"

"Maybe by the end of the week," Scott said.

Scott reclined in the chair at the shampoo bowl, and Claire washed his hair.

"It's getting a little thin on top," he said with some embarrassment.

"That just means you have an elevated testosterone level," Claire said. "Just proves you're a manly man."

"I want that printed on a tee shirt," Scott said, "which I will then wear every single day for the rest of my life."

"High levels of testosterone cause something called DHT to gum up the hair follicles," Claire said. "The hairs get thinner and thinner, and eventually quit growing altogether. High levels of testosterone can also cause prostate cancer, so you'll need to watch out for that."

"This conversation just took a weird turn," Scott said.

"Hairstylists are like shrinks; nothing's too personal. Plus, now that we've spent a night together in jail we should be able to talk about anything," Claire said. "There are some supplements I can recommend that are supposed to block the enzyme that converts testosterone into DHT. It takes a few months, but I've seen good results with the people who've tried it."

"It's not like that heart medicine people put on their scalps."

"No, but some people swear by that, too."

"I don't want any of those hair plug thingies."

"They're much less obvious these days," Claire said. "The trick is to cut your hair really short and plant several crops over a long period of time; that way the change isn't so dramatic. It's very expensive, though; at least a hundred grand to do it right."

"I could just shave it all off like Sam does, but I'm not sure I have the right shaped head."

"You don't need to do anything drastic," Claire said. "There's one actor I know who had part of his scalp removed, the bald part, I mean, and then they sewed the edges back together. He has to part his hair on the side to cover up the scar."

"That seems like a big risk to take just for vanity's sake."

"When your entire career is based on how you look those risks seem more reasonable."

"I guess I'm lucky, then," Scott said. "I can do this job bald and fat."

"Just tell people your bald spot is a solar panel for a sex machine."

"Another great tee shirt."

After they were finished with the shampoo and scalp massage, Scott moved over to the hydraulic chair. Claire trimmed his hair, shaved his neck, and against his protestations, worked on his eyebrows.

"It's called manscaping," she said. "Chicks don't dig the unibrow."

"It wasn't that bad."

"No," she conceded. "But look how good you look now."

She turned him toward the mirror, but instead of looking at himself, he was looking at Claire's reflected image. His newly groomed brows were separately furrowed.

"What?" she asked his reflection.

He turned the chair and faced her.

"There's something in my inside jacket pocket that I want to show you, but you can't tell anyone I did."

"Okay ..." Claire said.

She went to where his jacket hung by the door and reached inside the interior pocket.

"You have got to be kidding me," she said when she removed the plastic baggie which held a phone.

"I think it's Tuppy's," Scott said. "Someone turned it in earlier today. Evidently, when he got hit, his phone flew several yards and landed in the bed of a pickup truck parked on the street. The owner moved it before Sarah's team performed their search; she doesn't know I have it."

"What is it you want me to do with it?"

"I'm hoping you have a charger that will work with it so we can power it up and check his messages."

"But I don't know his password."

"You said you might be able to figure it out."

"You could get in so much trouble," Claire said. "Why are you doing this?"

"Because you're Ian's daughter; because you're an old friend; because I never for one minute thought you could murder anyone, but Sarah thinks you did, and she's determined to prove it."

"Ambitious?"

"She'll stoop to anything she thinks will raise her profile."

"You think if his messages clear me she might erase them and say there weren't any."

"I know Sarah better than just about anyone, and I can tell you that is exactly what she'll do."

"Jiminy Christmas," Claire said.

Claire rummaged in her bag until she found her phone charger. Being very careful to keep the plastic between her fingers and the phone's surface, she plugged it in and set it on the counter to charge. They looked at each other.

"Got any cards?" Scott asked.

Chapter Five - Sunday/Monday

Claire dealt the cards, but halfway through the first hand, Scott put his down on the counter.

"What's the deal with you and Sam Campbell?"

Claire could feel herself blush and cursed her thin, pale Irish skin.

"I've got to learn to cover it up better," she said. "I don't want Hannah to find out."

"Find out what, exactly?"

"You can't tell anyone; not Maggie, not Patrick, not Ed, nobody."

"I solemnly swear," Scott said.

"It happened when we were in high school, the summer Brad Eldridge drowned," she said. "One night Sam and I ended up out at the lake alone. We'd been drinking beer, and one thing led to another."

"Really?" Scott said, smiling broadly. "You and Sam?"

"This is so embarrassing," Claire said. "I'd had a crush on Sam for ages and Linda was away at cheerleading camp. He was my first."

"But what happened? Why didn't you two get together? I saw the way he looked at you yesterday."

"Brad drowned the next day," Claire said. "Everyone was freaked out about that. The next time I was alone with Sam, he said he was sorry, that he felt like he took advantage of me. He said we should forget it ever happened. He broke my heart if you want to know the truth. I wanted to die, but I couldn't tell anyone about it."

"I'm so sorry," Scott said. "He never told any of us."

"Afterward, I decided I was already ruined, so to speak, so I might as well have fun. Pip was the lifeguard at the pool that summer. What a loser, when you think about it now. He had graduated two years before but was still hanging out with high school students, and lifeguarding was his actual profession. Back then we were all crazy about him. I decided to seduce him, and it wasn't difficult."

"I don't know anyone who would have turned you down."

"I wasn't thinking about the future. I didn't think there might be consequences."

"What consequences?"

"We got caught."

"Your dad?" Scott said.

"Oh, yeah," she said. "He said if Pip didn't marry me he'd arrest him. And you know my dad; he meant every word he said."

"Pip's lucky Ian didn't shoot him instead."

She could remember the shame and embarrassment she'd felt on that night as if it had happened yesterday; her father's disgust and disappointment; her mother's grief and subsequent emotional withdrawal from her. That was the reason she'd quit high school, got her GED and went to beauty school. That's why as soon as she had her cosmetology license she left Rose Hill and ran off to California with Pip; she couldn't stand the way her parents looked at her, how little they thought of her. She was diminished in their eyes, and to her teenage brain, it seemed that no redemption would ever be possible.

Her eyes filled with tears; she stood up, not sure where she was going but determined to run somewhere. Scott stood up as well and took her in his arms.

"You've carried that burden long enough, Claire," he said as he hugged her. "You were so young. You made a perfectly human mistake, and you paid for it. You've got to forgive yourself, now. You've got to let it go. You sweet, sweet girl."

Claire clung to Scott and wept. It felt like a safe place to fall apart.

The timer she had set went off, and she broke their embrace to turn it off. She wiped the mascara from underneath her eyes, blew her nose in a tissue, and tried to laugh.

"Being a cop's a lot like being a shrink, too, isn't it, Scott?"

"We're friends from way back, and we'll be friends 'til way yonder," Scott said. "It will always be our secret."

"I might as well tell you the rest of it," Claire said. "Since you're the only one I'm going to tell."

Scott sat back down, and Claire wiped her eyes again.

"Sam and I kept in touch. Even after I married Pip and went to California and he went into the service. We wrote to each other. He told me the things he couldn't tell Linda, about how scared he was to go to Kuwait, and that his fellow soldiers felt more like his family than his real family did. He knew marrying Linda was a mistake and had only got engaged to her because both their mothers pressured them to marry.

"In turn, I told him about what I really got up to in L.A., the kind of people I was working for, and how scared I was to admit it had been a huge mistake to marry Pip and move clear across the country. I had this dream that we would eventually go back to Rose Hill and be together. It was only a fantasy, I knew, to get me through a difficult time, but there was a tiny part of me that thought it might actually happen.

"When Sam got hurt they sent him to a hospital in Germany for several weeks before he came back to the states. I borrowed money from my boss and flew to DC to see him at Walter Reed. He was so medicated he couldn't communicate. The doctor thought I was Linda, who had never once come to see him, so he took me into his office and sat me down. He said Sam would probably never walk again, and that men who had been through what he had often had severe emotional difficulties the rest of their lives. He asked me if I was willing to go through that with him and

I said I was. I meant it. I was. I decided I was going to leave Pip, move back to Rose Hill and help Sam recover.

"The day I had to leave I visited Sam one more time. He was not so out of it that morning but was in a lot of pain. He was so glad to see me. He just held onto me and cried. I told him what I planned to do and he told me not to do it, that he didn't want me to give up my life to take care of him. At that point everything looked so bleak to him; he believed he would never walk again, and that there was no point in living if he couldn't. He was so depressed I thought he might kill himself if he had the opportunity. I stayed until his pain got so bad they had to medicate him again. It was awful. I told the doctor what I was afraid he would do and he said they knew that, that they were closely watching him.

"Pip thought I was coming home for a visit, so I had to drive over here before I went back to California. I went to see Sam's mom, and she acted like he was already dead. I saw Linda, and she was mostly worried about what people would think of her if she was married to a cripple, plus she was upset thinking they would always be poor. It made me sick. I visited my parents for a couple days and then flew back to California, determined to break up with Pip and move back to Rose Hill.

"On the plane back to California I made a plan. I set myself a deadline of six months, which was how long the doctor thought Sam would be at Walter Reed. I had to earn enough to pay back the money I'd borrowed to fly to DC, plus enough money to move back to Rose Hill. Denise's mom still owned The Bee Hive, and I knew she would give me a job.

"When I got to California Pip had a surprise for me. He'd forged my name on a mortgage to purchase a condo in Malibu. I found out later he was sleeping with my boss, who put him up to it. Her slimy boyfriend owned a mortgage company that churned out those crazy loans that are illegal now. If it had just hurt me, I would have defaulted on the loan, but it turned out he'd forged my parents' names as cosigners, so I couldn't just walk away.

"On top of that Pip had been fired in the middle of a renovation job and we were being sued. I had to work two jobs just to make the mortgage payment. Pip lost his lawsuit, and I had to borrow more money from my boss to pay the lawyer and the settlement. Six months turned into a year, and I was still in so far over my head that I couldn't leave L.A.

"I kept tabs on Sam through Maggie and Hannah, so I knew when he came home what bad shape he was in. They told me how good you, Ed, and Patrick were to him, and how you wouldn't let him give up. I knew you helped him get rehabilitated and then convinced him to go to MIT. His mother wouldn't let me talk to him when I called, and I didn't dare write to him at her address. It was one of the darkest periods in my life. I knew where I wanted to be, but I couldn't get there.

"Eighteen months after Sam came home I finally caught Pip cheating on me with my boss. I kicked him out and quit my job. I thought I might be able to sell the condo at a loss, and I was willing to face the consequences of not repaying my terrible boss. As soon as I made the decision I wanted to tell Sam I was coming home. I called the Thorn on a night I knew he would be there with you guys, and Hannah answered the phone. She told me she had made Sam laugh for the first time since he came back and that she was in love with him. I heard the happiness in her voice, and I knew that if she could make Sam laugh, then she was doing what I had wanted to do for him.

"You know how much I love Maggie and Hannah. When we were in grade school, and Liam died, my parents were so devastated they couldn't be there for me. Aunt Bonnie is such a pill and Aunt Alice is so ditzy; there was no adult I could turn to. Those two little girls took care of me and got me through it. I could never hurt them; I won't let them be hurt."

Scott looked at her with great compassion and concern.

"For what it's worth, I think Hannah and Sam have been as happy as anybody could be, considering the circumstances," Scott said. "Sam went through some dark times, but Hannah stuck by him, and he's doing great now. I think you did the right thing."

"Doing the right thing sometimes hurts so badly, doesn't it?" Claire said.

"It's the worst," Scott said. "Sometimes I think having a conscience is a curse."

"It felt good to get all that out. Thanks for listening."

"Anytime," Scott said. "We do-gooders have to stick together."

"Let's try Tuppy's phone."

Claire got some latex hair color application gloves out of the supply closet and put them on. Scott hung over her shoulder and watched while she tried several passwords.

"His password is always his latest crush plus the year. What was that stage manager's name? Nigel? No. Trevor? No. It was Irish."

"Sean, Patrick, Brian, Ian, Curtis, Timothy..." Scott said.

"It wasn't one of our family names. It's right on the tip of my tongue. Tuppy made a crude nickname out of it."

"I'm not comfortable suggesting anything," Scott said.

"That's okay," Claire said. "I've remembered. It's Declan2011."

"I don't need to know the nickname. I can imagine."

It worked.

There were voicemails waiting, but his full voice mailbox required another password she couldn't figure out. She was able to pull up Tuppy's last text messages. It looked like he erased his text history as soon as he got to DC. There were four outgoing and two incoming texts cached after that. Three of the outgoing were to Claire, the two incoming were from Sloan, and the first outgoing one was to someone named Morty. They read:

To Morty at 1:00 p.m. GMT: "I will be in NYC early enough on Monday to have lunch before the meeting. Looking forward to working with you, Chance."

To Claire at 4:45 p.m. GMT: "Wr u? M on yr pln. Nd to tlk."

Incoming from Sloan at 8:05 p.m. EST: "Yr as gd as ded."

To Claire at 8:07 p.m. EST: "In dc. Wl mt u n rh. Btw I qt! Mr ltr."

Incoming from Sloan at 2:11 a.m. EST: "No whr u r cmn 4 u."

To Claire at 2:12 a.m. EST: "Yr swt dad has bk. Kp safe. Btw njoy yr 3dm. Yr wlcm."

"Do you understand all that?" Scott asked her.

"He got a ticket for the same flight as me, but I didn't know it. He said we need to talk. He went ahead and took the flight to DC, and then wanted to meet me in Rose Hill.

"He said he quit his job and I should enjoy my freedom. I don't know why he said 'you're welcome' and I don't know what book he's talking about. Maybe Morty is a potential employer in NYC. He didn't abbreviate anything in that text, and he used Chance instead of Tuppy so it must be important. Sloan's texted him twice, once to say he is as good as dead, and the last to say she knows where he is and she's coming for him."

Claire felt a chill as she said the last message out loud. She met Scott's gaze and grimaced. Scott wrote down all the phone numbers and carefully transcribed all the texts on a sheet of paper, along with Claire's interpretations and all the times translated into Eastern Standard Time.

"His last text was at two-twelve p.m. Eastern Standard Time."

Claire looked at his phone log and saw that his last call was made to her.

"I need my phone," Claire said. "He may have left me a voicemail telling me what was going on."

"It sounds like your employer meant to do him harm."

"Sloan's got an oversized sense of entitlement and loves to create drama. She'd say worse to a bartender who brought her drink five seconds later than she expected it."

Scott studied Tuppy's texts again.

"I'm surprised how few texts he has from her. I would think she'd harass him pretty much nonstop as soon as she knew he'd gone."

"Sloan's a screamer, not a texter. Part of Tuppy's job was to do the texting if she needed any done. She probably made Teeny do it."

"Teeny?"

"He's Sloan's stylist; part of the team."

"But why didn't she text or call him again after the one where she says she knows where he is and is coming for him?"

"I don't know," Claire said. "There are no texts or calls after that from her management team, either."

"They wouldn't need to," Scott said, "if they knew he was dead."

"Someone could have followed him from the airport. But why wait until he got here to kill him?"

"Maybe they wanted to see where he was going."

"None of this makes any sense," Claire said. "He was just an employee who quit in a huff. Why kill him at all?"

"I wish I knew what happened after he left your parents' house. Look at the timeline. He may have been hit right after his last call and text to you."

"It would be so like him to walk into traffic while texting someone," Claire said, "or while reading a text."

"There's not a lot of traffic on Peony Street in the middle of the night."

"Then it had to be a drunken hit and run. It was so foggy it could be they just didn't see him crossing the street. No one in Rose Hill knows him, and nobody knew he was here unless they followed him, or had him under some kind of surveillance."

"Or had your phone."

"I left it in a cab in London. It's probably been sold three times by now."

"And if by some miracle the cab driver returned it to your last known address, who would have it?"

"The estate agent; but I didn't make the best impression on them."

"Give me their address."

Claire took her address book out of her handbag, looked up the estate agent's contact information, and wrote it down for him.

"Did you give them a forwarding address?" he asked.

"Yes."

"Wouldn't they then put your phone in the mail to you? Or at the very least, contact you?"

"That gives way too many people the benefit of the doubt."

"Hollywood has made you cynical."

"Life has made me cynical," Claire said. "Why aren't you?"

"I'm tempted daily," he said, "but there are still a lot of good people left in Rose Hill."

"But someone in Rose Hill ran over Tuppy and didn't call 911."

"It was either someone who had a lot to lose by taking responsibility for the accident or someone who intended to kill him."

"Do you really think it could have been murder?"

"I haven't had that many murders to investigate, but in every one there was a motive, and it was either money or revenge. Your employer seemed to have a great deal of animosity toward your friend."

"Nasty threats are not unusual for Sloan, so those don't necessarily mean anything. I've heard her threaten to do outrageous things to lots of people, but that's just her way. It sounds to me like she's just mad that he quit and took off with no notice."

"What about the book?"

"He was always saying he ought to write a book," Claire said. "Maybe he was meeting with a publisher in New York. Maybe that's who Morty is."

"So he may have secretly written a book, and left a copy with your Dad for you to read."

"Not just to read, but to keep safe."

"Because there weren't many copies?"

"Or because of what the book was about," Claire said.

"Blackmail is a strong motive."

"Except we have ironclad confidentiality agreements with Sloan. Tuppy couldn't tell anyone anything about her. No book advance could cover the penalty he'd have to pay. Plus ..." she started to say but stopped.

"What?" Scott asked.

"Sloan's attorney is not someone you want to mess around with," Claire said. "He's pretty scary."

Scott took the phone from Claire, turned it over, and looked at the back of it.

"Are you familiar with what one of these is supposed to look like inside?"

"Sure," Claire said. "I'm the one who always installed the batteries and memory cards. Sloan can't be bothered to do anything like that."

Scott handed the phone back to Claire.

"Let's look inside," he said.

Claire pried off the back cover.

"Pop the battery out," Scott instructed her.

"That's strange," she said as soon as it was out.

"What's that?"

"There's an extra piece in here that my phone doesn't have," she said, "and it certainly wasn't in here when I set up this phone for Tuppy."

"Don't touch it," Scott said, looking at the small flat square piece that looked like a tiny circuitry board. "I think it may be a bug or a tracking device. If it's a bug, we just gave the whole game away."

"Oh, no," Claire whispered. "All that stuff I told you about Sam and me!"

"The phone was dead and charging while you told me all that," Scott said. "I'm pretty sure the phone would need to be charged up in order for it to work, but I'll have to ask Sam."

The door to the salon opened with a bang on a gust of cold air. Scott and Claire both jumped. Scott quickly gathered the pieces of the phone and tucked them in his pocket.

"Hello?" a woman called out in an irritated tone. "Is anyone even here?"

Claire groaned and went to greet the owner of the tea room from which she had fled earlier in the day.

"Where's Denise?" the woman demanded. "What are you doing here?"

Claire explained what was going on but did not offer to take the appointment.

"I couldn't read the name on her appointment book, and there was no phone number," Claire said, "so I couldn't call you to cancel."

"It's Huckle," the woman said. "Meredith Stanhope Huckle."

"Her late father was a famous senator," Scott said.

"As was my late husband," Meredith said.

"She's married to Knox Rodefeffer," Scott said, "the bank president."

"He's running for the U.S. Senate," Meredith said.

"I know Knox," Claire said. "I also know his ex-wife Anne Marie; very well, as a matter of fact."

Meredith ignored this.

"My son Peyton is at Eldridge," Meredith said, "in Humanities."

"Ah," said Claire. "I know something else about you."

"What's that?" Meredith asked.

"You've been having an affair with my ex-husband."

"That's a slanderous lie," Meredith huffed.

"Not if it's true," Claire said.

Meredith Stanhope Huckle turned on her heel and stalked out of The Bee Hive Hair Salon with as much dignity as she could muster.

"Pip?" Scott asked. "Really?"

"I overheard them and then saw them."

"Well, well, well," Scott said. "Just what Knox needs, another scandal."

"Another scandal?"

"I think he tried to kill Anne Marie before they were divorced. She was running around with college students and getting into all sorts of trouble, embarrassing Knox. She was in a car wreck, and even though Knox had an alibi, I always suspected he had something to do with it. It was freezing cold outside, but she wasn't wearing a coat and had no ID or handbag. She was in a coma for several days. When she woke up, Knox put her in a rehab where she had a nervous breakdown. When she got back here she acted really crazy, and Caroline Eldridge took her out to California, to some ashram or commune. She decided she was a psychic or something. They got divorced soon after."

"I know the rest of this story," Claire said. "I ran into Anne Marie's sister out in Los Angeles a couple years ago, and she took me to see Anne Marie, who did a psychic reading for me. I thought it was really accurate. I took my boss to see her and although she wasn't happy with what Anne Marie said it turned out to be true. She spread the word about Anne Marie's talent, and now lots of people go to her. She has a huge following. My boss has her on speed dial."

"Well, I'll be," Scott said. "This is just like a movie."

"The problem is it's my life," Claire said, "and I'd much prefer a romantic comedy to a murder mystery."

Claire cleaned up, locked up, and Scott walked with her down to the station to pick up her carry-on bag and rental car. He then rode home with her.

"I'll call the realty company and see if someone returned your phone," he said as he got out of the car.

"You're such an optimist," she said. "Hasn't life beaten that out of you yet?"

"It's my biggest weakness," he said. "But I'm also a thief. I didn't pay for my haircut."

"That one's on me," Claire said, "Lucky for you we aren't in L.A. where it would cost several hundred dollars."

"It's all about context, isn't it?"

"Kind of like how in Rose Hill being Ian Fitzpatrick's daughter is more valuable than being a movie star's hairdresser. It's probably saving me from doing hard time."

Scott touched her arm and said, "I don't want you to worry. I think everything's going to be alright."

Claire said goodbye to Scott, went inside, and was surprised when Mackie Pea didn't run to greet her as she opened the front door. Then she saw her father was sound asleep in his recliner, with Mackie Pea cuddled up on one side of his protruding belly with the evil black and white Chester on the other. The TV was on with the volume turned up high. Claire turned it down and searched the house for her mother, but she wasn't home.

Claire went to the kitchen and seriously considered eating some of the cinnamon rolls that were on the counter. She knew they were from her Aunt Bonnie's bakery and would be full of buttery, sugary calories. She hid them in the microwave so she wouldn't have to look at them. As she sat down to eat a lettuce and tomato wrap instead, her mother came in the back door. Claire was struck by how haggard she looked.

'Hannah was right,' she thought. 'Our parents have begun to look old.'

"Hi sweetheart," her mother said, and kissed the top of her head.

Claire jumped up.

"What can I fix you?" she asked.

Delia took off her coat and sat down at the kitchen table.

"Some tea would be lovely," she said.

While Claire made tea Delia told her about her day.

"I went to church, where the Robinson's new baby Georgia was christened. She's named after her grandmother, who you went to school with. She's as bald as a cue ball and screamed the whole time. Afterward, there was a reception in the fellowship hall; I helped serve and then stayed to clean up. Then I went to the Inn and covered the front desk so the desk clerk could go to the store. I can't wait for you to see what Gwyneth has done to the Inn; it's completely restored. After that, I went to Hannah's and chased after Sammy while Sam and Hannah cleaned out the barn. Everyone seems to be spring cleaning this weekend."

"The farm looks great," Claire said. "They've really made it their own."

"The bulbs Lily planted years ago at the farm are all peeking out of the ground. She always had such lovely flowers," Delia continued. "I went to Bonnie and Fitz's, where we turned all her mattresses and took the curtains down and laundered them. I starched and ironed them while she mended Fitz's socks. For someone who walks as little as that man does you'd be surprised how he goes through socks. Then I stopped at Alice's to pick up your father, and they gave us dinner: it was that chicken casserole with the water chestnuts that Ian hates so much. I brought your father home and got him settled in his chair. I just ran some aspirin over to Alice; another one of her headaches. I knew your father would be fine for a few minutes."

"You must be exhausted," Claire said. "Why do all these people have you working for them but none of them are over here helping you?"

"They help," Delia said. "This tea hits the spot."

Claire told her mother all about her day, concluding with, "why didn't you tell me Pip was back?"

"I thought you'd high-tail it out of here if I did," Delia said.

"I'm legally obligated to remain within the city limits until Sarah says I can go."

"I'm sorry if you feel stuck."

"It's nothing against you or Dad," Claire said. "I love seeing you, but Rose Hill just feels so small. It's like wearing a turtleneck with a too-tight neck."

"You think Pip's involved with Meredith?"

"Oh, yeah," Claire said. "There's no doubt in my mind. That man is a serial seducer; he can't help himself."

"Meredith's not exactly a femme fatale."

"It doesn't matter to him. He will bed anything."

"Your father never liked him," Delia said.

"Neither did you," Claire pointed out.

"It wasn't so much that I disliked Pip; I never knew him that well. It was more that I didn't like who you were when you were with him."

"Ouch," Claire said.

"I love you, sweetie," Delia said, taking Claire's hands in hers across the table. "But it was like you became someone else when you were with him. Everything he liked you liked, everything he wanted, you wanted. It was always all about him and what he thought, and you changed yourself to suit him. When I think about all that blonde hair..."

"I never was a good blonde," Claire said. "Plus a permanent wave on top of double processing is never a good idea."

"What I'm trying to say is Pip's not a bad man, he's just not the man for you. You were still figuring out who you were, and instead, you let him decide for you."

"I really thought I loved him," Claire said.

"You were both so young," Delia said. "Chemistry is a powerful force when you're a teenager. Plus you think you know it all at that age and no one can tell you any different, especially not your mother."

"I'm sorry I disappointed you."

"It's your life to live, sweetie, I just hated to see you make a bad choice. I knew you would eventually be hurt."

"He's evil."

"Oh, I wouldn't say that," Delia said. "Pip's not too bright, but he's very skilled at manipulating women to get what he wants. He's lazy and likely to quit as soon as something gets difficult. Plus he's too good looking for his own good. That's made it easier for him to get his way."

"That's him in a nutshell," Claire said. "You missed your calling, Mom. You should have been a psychologist."

"I'd never be able to resist telling people what I think they should do," Delia said.

Claire got the cinnamon rolls out of the microwave and put them on the table. Delia declined, saying her stomach felt a little queasy, so Claire started picking at one side of them. They were even better than she remembered, tender and buttery with way more pecans and cinnamon than anyone else used. Before she realized what she was doing she had eaten two.

"I'm so hungry," Claire said. "I can't seem to stop eating."

"You've just been missing our good home cooking," Delia said.

The phone rang, and it was Dom Deluca tearfully and joyfully reporting the birth of Dominic Junior. He said that Denise's sister Stephie had broken her ankle rushing down the stairs of her house to go to the hospital, and she would not be able to cover Denise's appointments for the next six weeks.

"I'm going to be here a week at the most," Claire protested.

"Even a week would be wonderful," he told her. "It's closed tomorrow so you wouldn't have to be there until Tuesday. Four days. It would be such a blessing."

Claire said she'd do it, "But only this week,"

She groaned as she hung up.

"You're sweet to help them out," Delia said. "I'm too tired to cook for them tonight."

"Denise's mother will be cooking enough to feed an army," Claire said. "Don't worry about it. Tonight we need to find that book."

Delia and Claire looked all over the house but did not find Tuppy's manuscript.

"Your father may not remember what he did with it," Delia said.

"We can start fresh in the morning," Claire said. "We both need some rest."

"I'm at the bakery at six tomorrow morning," Delia said. "Then I have the front desk at the Inn from noon to five and the bar in the evening."

"You need to start telling people 'no,'" Claire said.

"You try that first," Delia said, "and then let me know how it works out for you."

At two o'clock in the morning, Mackie Pea began to growl low in her throat, and Claire awoke to a tapping on her window. Even though she was half asleep, she knew who it was before she pulled back the curtains. She unlocked and opened the window just a crack. Cold air poured in.

"Go away, Pip," she said.

"I need to talk to you," Pip said in a pleading voice Claire knew so well.

"Go talk to Meredith," she said.

"That's not what it looked like," he said.

"I don't care if it is," Claire said. "You're no longer my problem."

"I need your help," he said. "I'm in big trouble."

"Big surprise," Claire said. "I'm still not interested."

She began to lower the window sash.

"I know who killed your friend," he said.

"Wait there," Claire said.

Claire quickly got dressed and then climbed out the window, much to Mackie Pea's displeasure. She started to bark in protest, so Claire reached back in, picked her up, and tucked her down inside her raincoat.

Outside she could see her breath and noticed the dew on the grass had turned to a light frost.

"It's friggin' cold out here," Claire said. "It's April, for crissakes."

"Welcome home," Pip said.

He held out his arms for a hug, and Claire shook her head.

"Ground rule number one," she said, "no touching."

Pip hadn't changed much in the ten years since she'd seen him. He was dressed like a stoner who just discovered reggae music, complete with a Baja hoodie, leather necklace, and pierced ear. His hair was still a surfer dude tangle of sun-bleached golden curls, and the hazel eyes flecked with gold were still fringed with thick long lashes. Not surprisingly there was more sun damage to his skin and wrinkles around his eyes, but just like all handsome men, Pip was aging well.

Claire didn't feel the pangs of attraction or regret she once had. After all, he'd put her through, seeing Pip just reminded her that the shallow nature of teenage attraction was a poor predictor of long-term suitability. He looked like trouble wrapped in ignorant bliss; he smelled like pot smoke.

Claire took a deep breath of clean, crisp air, looked up and was amazed at the number of stars visible in the dark sky. She had forgotten how beautiful night could be away from all the ambient light of the cities she'd lived in.

"C'mon," Pip said.

Without discussing it first, they walked down to the old depot, which was where they used to secretly meet over twenty years before. Back then it had been a boarded up relic, and now it was the "Mountain Laurel Depot Bar and Grill." They sat on the steps to the platform, facing the river.

"What happened to Tuppy?" Claire asked him, moving as far away from him as she could on the broad stairway, cradling Mackie against her chest.

"What kind of name is Tuppy?" he asked her.

"His last name was Tupworth," she said. "It was a nickname."

"Was he your boyfriend?"

"We worked together," Claire said. "He was Sloan's personal assistant."

"How is Sloan these days?"

"Ruthless and evil, same as ever. Now cut to the chase. Who killed Tuppy?"

"It was an accident. He was just in the wrong place at the wrong time."

"Did you see it happen?"

"No, but I got there right after it happened."

"Why didn't you tell the police?"

"It's complicated."

"Which just means you're involved somehow and afraid you'll get in trouble."

"I saw you with Scott, earlier. He hit on you?"

"You know, Pip, not everyone lives their day-to-day life as if it's a porn movie. Sometimes men just talk to me, and there's no sexual subtext."

"Not straight guys," he said.

"You have five seconds to start confessing what you know. Five, four, three ..."

"You always were a ball buster."

"Two ... one ..." and she got up to leave.

"I'm in trouble, Claire," he said. "I've got this situation with these two ladies I've been dealing with, and they're both being complete bitches about something that is totally not my fault. On top of that, there's Knox, who I'm pretty sure has a hit out on me."

"So you've been screwing around with Meredith and who else?"

"Knox's secretary, Courtenay."

"How is this related to Tuppy's death?"

"I'm getting to that. Let me finish. You're always in such a hurry to twist my words and think the worst."

"And zero," she said and stood up.

"C'mon, Claire," he said. "You never let me finish."

"Hurry up," she said. "I'm freezing."

"Knox bought this condo for Courtenay after he married Meredith, to keep her happy on account of he had been screwing around with her but then didn't marry her. Meredith's from some powerful political family and Knox is running for something; congressman, governor, I forget what."

"Senator."

"Okay, yeah, whatever," Pip said. "He has this second post office box where he gets all the mail he doesn't want anyone to see, right? Well, somehow Meredith found out about it and talked the lady at the post office into giving the mail to her. Knox's credit card bills were in there and some other stuff. Anyway, Meredith figured out about the condo and all the crap he gave Courtenay. She called him out on it. She was super pissed and said she was gonna divorce him, take him to the cleaners. He talked her out of it; said Courtenay was blackmailing him, which is bullshit.

"Meredith likes the idea of going back to DC as a politician's wife, and after she thought about it a while, she decided he could keep on seeing Courtenay until after he's elected, and then they'll figure something out."

"Like kill her," Claire said, "and throw her body down in the Hell Hole where no one would ever find it."

"That's a good idea," he said, "but no, nothing like that; more like pay her off."

"So how did you get involved?"

"I was doing some odd jobs for Knox at their house, and Meredith asked me to work on some stuff at her store. One thing led to another ..."

"I get the picture, fast forward."

"So Meredith comes up with this plan where I bone Courtenay and get her to fall in love with me, and then she'll quit bothering Knox."

"I immediately see the flaw in this plan."

"What?"

"Courtenay likes money and power, and you have neither."

"Meredith was going to bankroll me, see, so I could buy Courtenay all that crap she likes."

"I know seducing Courtenay was a cake walk for you, so let's skip past that part, assume she's now crazy about you and ready to break up with Knox."

"Yeah, she is crazy about me but she doesn't want to break up with Knox, and he doesn't really want her to."

"But what about Meredith?"

"After he's elected Knox is going to pretend to end it with Courtenay, but really he's going to move her to Virginia so they can keep seeing each other. Meredith won't know about it."

"What about you?"

"Courtenay wants me to go, too, but Knox can't know about it."

"Does that bother you at all? I mean, sharing her with Knox?"

"Not really."

"Of course not. Proceed."

"I can't see any reason not to go along with it. As long as we keep Meredith and Knox from finding out what's going on, we'll be rolling in it."

"What does this have to do with Tuppy?"

"I'm getting to that. The other night I was at Courtenay's when Knox was supposed to be in DC. He came back early, and I had to climb out the second-floor window to get away before he saw me. I was buck naked."

"So you're outside in the cold with no clothes on."

"I was hiding in the bushes trying to decide the best route back to Mom's house when Meredith's car turned in the driveway, and her headlights almost caught me."

"She was following Knox."

"Yep. She was loaded, too. She pounded on Courtenay's door and liked to scream down the neighborhood. When she stopped long enough to take a breath I heard the window above me open and there comes Knox."

"Did he see you?"

"He almost landed on me."

"Was he dressed?"

"Yeah."

"I would've loved to have seen the look on his face when he found you hiding underneath his girlfriend's window with no clothes on."

"He was super pissed off, but he decided we would be better off working together. He boosted me back up into Courtenay's window so Meredith would catch me in the bedroom instead of him."

"Then what happened?"

"I got my clothes on, and Courtenay and I went down to the front door."

"Meredith was surprised."

"Uh huh; she thought Knox was gonna be there. She was so pissed."

"Then what happened?"

"She left. I got the hell out of there. I took off across Marigold and cut through Davis's backyard. Phyllis was having a party, but the keg was empty, so I didn't stay. I got to Peony Street right after it happened."

"Who hit him?"

"I don't know. Meredith and Knox were both outside of their cars, looking at the guy in the road. Then Meredith screamed, and Knox slapped her hard across the face. She went down and was just crying like crazy. Knox hauled her up, put her in his car, and took off. I got the hell out of there."

"Why didn't you check to see if he was still alive?"

Pip shrugged.

"Why didn't you call 911?"

Pip shrugged.

"Did Knox come back and get Meredith's car?"

Pip shrugged.

"If Meredith left Courtenay's first she must have hit Tuppy," Claire said, "or she was waiting around the corner to see if Knox's rental car left Courtenay's condo and followed him. In that case, Knox could have hit him."

Pip shrugged.

"Did you tell Meredith you saw them at the scene of the accident?"

"No. Today was the first time I saw her since that night."

"When I was in the store."

"Yeah. You surprised the crap out of me. I didn't know you were back."

"It was supposed to be a surprise for my parents. You know the county cops think I killed that guy."

"Why would they think that?"

"I found the body and I'm the only one who knew him."

"Damn, that's harsh."

"So you have to tell Scott what happened."

"No way."

"Pip, you have to tell him what happened or they're going to blame me."

"Yeah, well, that might be sorta complicated."

"Why's that?"

"I kind of stole Meredith's car."

"You what?"

"After Knox left with her, I got in her car, and the keys were still in it."

"Where is the car now?"

He shrugged.

Claire remembered the lying shrug very well. It meant he didn't want to tell her the truth because he knew she'd be mad.

"What time did all this happen?"

Pip shrugged.

"Phillip Hobart Deacon, I am this close to calling Scott. What time was it?"

"I know it was after 2:00. I went to get a drink at the Thorn afterward, but it was closed."

"So at the scene of a crime, instead of assisting the victim, or calling the police, you stole what may very well have been the vehicle in which manslaughter was committed. You stashed the car, probably in your mother's garage, and then walked down to the Thorn for a drink."

He shrugged again.

"Pip," she said.

"It was cold," he said. "She left the keys in it."

"Jeezus, Pip."

"I told you I was in trouble."

"Yeah, and now I'm in double trouble. Now they'll think we conspired to commit the crime together. They'll get us for manslaughter, hit and run, and grand theft."

"What should I do? You gotta help me."

His bottom lip turned down, and his eyes squeezed almost closed as he started to cry.

"Turn off the waterworks," Claire said. "That doesn't work on me anymore."

"That's really mean, Claire," he sniffed. "You used to love me."

"I need to think about this," she said. "Does anyone else know what you did?"

He shrugged.

"Who did you tell?"

"I told Courtenay."

"Great."

"She's crazy about me. She won't say anything."

"You're such an idiot," Claire said.

"Well, you're a bitch."

"I'm going home," Claire said. "I'd tell you to stay away from both women, but I know that's impossible."

"Give me a reason not to," he said, in what she knew he thought was an irresistibly seductive manner.

"Get knotted," she said and got up to leave.

"What's that supposed to mean?"

"I don't know, exactly," Claire said. "But it perfectly describes what I wish you would do with that heat-seeking missile you cannot keep in your pants. Tie a knot in it or something."

"You never had any complaints," he said.

"I didn't know what I was missing until I had better," she responded.

Mackie Pea whimpered, and Claire cradled her inside her coat as she ran all the way home.

Back inside her parents' house she changed into her nightgown, got back in bed, and turned off the light on her bedside table. Mackie curled up next to her and laid her little face on the pillow.

"Your life with me has been one big crazy adventure so far, hasn't it?" she said to the little dog. "Don't worry, though. I'll figure it all out."

Mackie Pea licked Claire's chin and then snuggled down to sleep. Claire turned over, stared at the ceiling, and worried.

The next morning when Scott left his house at 5:00 a.m. he saw someone walking down Sunflower Street towards him. Although the morning fog was thick, he recognized this person's unusual gate.

"I was coming to see you," Sam said.

"Come in and have some coffee," Scott said. "I need to show you something."

Sam's prosthetic lower limbs were undetectable to someone not looking for them. Walking close next to him, on a quiet night like this, Scott could hear the subtle hiss and click of the gas-cushioned pistons adjusting to the pressure of each step. They were a miracle of engineering developed by Sam's MIT roommate, who was inspired by Sam to make designing prosthetics his life's work.

As they entered the house, Sam said, "Where's your big cat? I haven't seen him prowling around town lately."

"Maggie has Duke," Scott said. "I guess you could say I lost custody."

Scott made some coffee, and they sat down at his kitchen table. Scott took a small plastic bag out of his jacket pocket and handed it to Sam.

"What's this look like to you?" Scott asked.

"It's a tracking device," Sam said.

"Not a bug?"

"No," Sam said, "just a GPS transmitter. I've installed them myself."

"Are they illegal?"

"They're perfectly legal," Sam said. "You can, however, use one to engage in illegal activities."

"It was in the victim's phone."

"May I see it?"

Scott gave Sam some disposable plastic gloves from a stash he kept in his work bag. He then took the phone out and handed it to Sam, who used a couple tools on his Swiss Army knife to expertly remove the back and take the phone apart. When he was through, he put it all back together.

"There's nothing else in there that doesn't belong," Sam said.

"That's good," Scott said. "After our experience with the FBI a few years ago I have mixed feelings about being tracked and bugged. On the one hand I resent it; on the other hand, it saved my life."

"Is Claire in any real danger?"

"She's nearly in the clear. It would help if we could find the cell phone she lost in the UK before she flew home."

"Where did she leave it?"

"In a cab."

"Has she checked to see if anyone returned it to her last address?"

"She thinks that's unlikely, but even if someone did, she thinks the rental company may throw it away out of spite."

"Do you have the name and address of the rental company?"

Scott got out his notebook, found the page with the address, and slid it across the table to Sam. Sam took out his cell phone and called someone.

"Rodney, hey, this is Sam Campbell; how are you?"

Scott got a refill while he listened to one side of the phone call. After some pleasantries and some gossip about a mutual acquaintance, Sam asked his friend to go to the rental agency and get the phone if they had it. After Sam hung up, Scott offered him a refill, which he accepted.

"It amazes me that you can pick up the phone and make a request like that," Scott said.

"Rodney and I were in the same unit. He works at the embassy, which is on the other side of Hyde Park from South Kensington. It's just past 10:00 a.m. in London, so he's going over there now."

"Have you done any network security work for the embassy?"

"I couldn't say if I did," Sam said and smiled one of his enigmatic smiles.

"Don't you worry about scanner grannies?" Scott asked him.

"Well, first of all, this is a satellite phone, not a cell phone; and it's encrypted."

"Of course," Scott said.

"Police scanners manufactured before the mid-nineties can still tune into analog home phones and some cell phones, even though it's illegal. Nowadays most home phones are digital, and you can't legally buy a scanner with cell phone frequency capability. Plus the newer cell phones use a more secure system."

"Meaning if our victim made a cell phone call on a phone the scanner grannies with newer scanners probably didn't hear it, but the ones with older equipment might have."

"It would be worth checking," Sam said and made another call.

"Hi honey," he said, "I'm with Scott, and we're talking about Claire's predicament. Would you check in with some of your grannies and see if they heard any unusual calls around two a.m. the night that guy got killed? Thanks, babe."

Sam put his phone back on the table and took a drink of his coffee.

"There's something I've meant to ask you," Scott said. "I've been reading about all the trouble in the middle-east, and how the governments there managed to turn off the Internet. It seems like that would be an impossible task in this country, even if someone wanted to do it."

"It wouldn't be hard at all," Sam said. "It could be done within a few hours, actually."

"But with all the different service providers there are, how could they get everyone to cooperate?"

"They wouldn't have to," Sam said. "Our Internet system is attached to the rest of the world through submarine communications cables. Cut the cables, and we're cut off."

"What about satellite connections?"

"We could easily interfere with the signal," Sam said, "or destroy the satellite."

"I never feel better after I talk to you," Scott said.

Sam laughed, and his phone buzzed at the same time.

It was Hannah; Sam handed the phone to Scott.

"Hey, Lone Ranger," she said. "I was wondering when you would get around to calling in your old pal Tonto."

"I apologize for not thinking of it sooner. You know how it offends my law-abiding sensibilities to collect evidence through illegal activity."

"Not me. I'm the Masked Mutt Catcher. I do some of my best crime-fighting that way. Garnet Bloomenthal is your key granny in this case. She was up and on the scanner all night Friday, and she took notes. Claire's boyfriend made one call at around two a.m. to a woman he called 'Miss

Clairol.' He said he left a book with her daddy and no offense, but he was getting the bleep out of Rose Hill. He may even have called our beloved hamlet creepy."

"Will she talk to me?" Scott asked.

"No way," Hannah said. "She knows she's breaking the law. She may be ninety-three, but she's no dummy."

"At least we know he was alive at 2:00 and not with Claire."

"I'll keep poking around," Hannah said.

"Thanks," Scott said and handed the phone back to Sam.

As Sam put it back on the table, it buzzed again, and Sam answered.

"That's great," Sam said and motioned to Scott for something to write with.

He wrote down some information and thanked his friend before he terminated the call. He turned the paper around and slid it to Scott.

"The estate agent had the phone, was holding it for ransom against some unpaid bill they claim Claire owes them. Rodney was able to convince the agent that cooperating with the American Embassy was a smarter course of action. The phone will be on the next flight to DC. A courier will pick it up there and drive it straight to you. You should have it by five o'clock."

"That's outstanding," Scott said. "I've seen you do this kind of thing before, but it always impresses the hell out of me. Rodney must owe you some huge favor."

"It's not about favors," Sam said as he stood up. "It's something you can only understand if you've been where we were and went through what we did. Those of us who made it out alive have a bond that no one can sever. There are only a handful of men and women left from my unit, but each one of us knows all we have to do is call, and whatever we need one of us will move heaven and earth to get."

"Claire will really appreciate it," Scott said.

Sam shook his head.

"This was all you," he said. "You can't tell anyone I did this."

"I can't do that," Scott said. "I can't take credit for something you did."

"Think of it as my gift," Sam said. "Claire needs someone to look out for her in the long term, and I wouldn't mind if it was you. If making you look like the white knight helps that along, I'm honored to assist."

Scott was speechless. Sam shook his hand and left the house. Scott watched his friend walk up Sunflower Street until he disappeared into the fog.

Chapter Six - Monday

Claire woke up to her father outside her bedroom door, calling her name. It was still dark out. Claire scrambled out of bed, scaring Mackie Pea, who yipped. Claire put on her robe and slid her feet into slippers.

"What is it, Dad?"

"Your mother's sick," Ian said. "She needs you."

Claire hurried past her father into the hallway.

"She's in the bathroom," Ian said, and then went back to the living room.

Claire found her mother sitting on the edge of the bathtub, a cold cloth on her forehead. The room smelled like she had been ill. Her mother's face was pale, and her skin was clammy to the touch.

"Mom," Claire said, as she knelt next to her. "What's wrong?"

"I think your Aunt Alice may have food poisoned me," Delia said.

"Dad seems alright."

"He didn't eat it. He hates her cooking, so she bakes frozen fish sticks for him."

"What can I do for you?"

"When I stand up I get dizzy. I need you to help me get back to bed."

Claire grasped her mother around the waist, and Delia put an arm around her daughter's shoulders. Her mother swayed, and Claire steadied her. They slowly made their way to the bedroom, and Claire helped her get in bed.

"I'm calling Doc Machalvie," Claire said.

"It's probably just salmonella," Delia said. "I think most everything that was in is now out, so I just need to sleep it off."

"I'm calling him," Claire said, "just to be sure."

"It will rattle your dad too much," Delia said.

"Too bad," Claire said.

Claire went to the kitchen and looked up Doc's number in the slim Pendleton County phone book. He answered on the first ring and was in their house within 15 minutes. Claire's dad was agitated, so Claire sat in the living room and talked to him until Doc came back.

"Is Liam sick?" her father asked her for the tenth time.

"No, Dad," Claire said. "Mom's sick, but she's going to be alright."

After a few minutes, Doc came back down the hall and sat down on the couch next to Claire. He gave her a quick hug.

"Nice to see you, young lady," he said.

"What's wrong with Liam?" Ian asked him.

"He's fine," Doc said without missing a beat. "It's your wife I came to see."

"What's wrong with Delia?"

"I think she's caught a virus that's going around," Doc said. "She's let herself get run down, and her immune system is weak. She needs to rest, drink lots of fluids, maybe some broth when she feels up to it. Good thing Claire's home to look after her."

"Claire will take care of her," Ian said.

Claire could tell he was still agitated because he was holding his mouth in that exaggerated frown and was swinging his head.

"Could I trouble you for a cup of coffee?" Doc asked Claire and nodded toward the kitchen.

"Of course," Claire said, and jumped up to accommodate the request.

"Get Doc some coffee, Claire Bear," Ian said. "It's the least we can do."

Doc followed Claire into the kitchen and sat down at the table. Claire filled and started the coffee maker and then offered him some of Bonnie's cinnamon rolls, which he seemed delighted to accept.

"Doris won't let me have anything this good in the house," Doc said. "I think a little treat once in awhile is actually good for a body."

Claire quickly calculated that Doc must be at least seventy years old, but he looked and acted like someone much younger. He had delivered Claire and her brother. He was with Liam when he died, and had grieved along with them.

"You doing okay?" he asked her as she poured the coffee.

"I'm fine," she said, "but my parents seem to be falling apart."

"I'm glad you came home. Your mother has worn herself out working and worrying about your father. I bet she didn't tell you she took out a mortgage on this house to pay for his medical expenses. I think Knox probably took advantage of your folks, interest-wise."

"That slimy weasel."

"Knox Rodefeffer is the stinkiest polecat in a family of skunks, that's for sure," Doc said. "I've known him since he was a boy; he was a spoiled brat then, and his sense of entitlement has only grown, along with his stomach."

"I'll jerk a knot in his tail, don't you worry about that," Claire said. "I won't leave until I've got everything whipped back into shape here."

"I'm going to be brutally honest with you, Claire. With your father, it's going to be a progression of small strokes and general debility, although a more severe stroke could happen at any time. As bad as it sounds, the most we can hope for is that his body fails before his mind is completely gone. If not, eventually it will be too much for your mother to deal with and he'll have to go into a facility. Delia's going to need you for more than a couple weeks."

Claire opened her mouth to say she could hire help, but the pointed look Doc was giving her stopped her.

"I have money," she said instead. "I can pay off the mortgage."

"Good," Doc said. "That will help relieve her mind. She's got to slow down, but I don't think she will unless you stay and help."

"I really don't want to move back here," Claire said. "I've got plans..."

Doc shrugged.

"Have you ever heard the saying that if you want to make God laugh tell him your plans?" he said.

"It seems like the whole town is conspiring to keep me here."

"None of us wants to grow up, but eventually we have to, or someone will suffer the consequences. I know you don't want your family to have to suffer for you not taking responsibility."

"It's just so depressing," Claire said. "I know I'm whining; sorry."

"I've got pills for that," Doc said, and Claire laughed.

"I'm not joking," he said. "If it gets to be too much and you can't cope, come see me. There's nothing wrong with asking for help."

Claire thanked Doc and saw him out. Her father was already back to sleep, and Claire covered him with a blanket. She took a big glass of water down the hall to her mother, who was also sleeping. She set the glass on the bedside table and looked down at Delia. She looked so much older, so frail, and so vulnerable. Claire knew Doc was right; she had to stay.

At five o'clock in the morning, Claire woke up her dad so she could start living her mother's day. With him bathed and shaved, and her mother bathed, hydrated, fed some dry toast and sent back to bed, Claire looked for clothes suitable to work in the bakery.

After considering and rejecting everything she'd brought in her carry-on bag, she went through her closet; it was like an archive of unfortunate fashion choices from the past 30 years. In amongst the hip-hugging bell bottoms and skinny-legged Capri pants she found some faded straight leg jeans, a Fitzpatrick Bakery sweatshirt, and some work boots she'd purchased back in the 90's when grunge was in fashion.

After she dressed, Claire pulled her long dark hair up into a knot on top of her head so she wouldn't have to wear the dreaded hairnet. She put on one of her father's insulated Carhartt canvas jackets, put Mackie in her Louis Vuitton carrier and then caught sight of herself in the mirror over the mantle. She looked like a redneck kidnapping some rich person's dog.

Claire's father was standing by the door, waiting for her. She set Mackie's carrier down so she could comb his messy hair and wipe shaving cream off his earlobe. She helped him get his coat zipped up, took him by the hand, led him out of the house, and locked the door behind them. They then walked arm in arm down the street, slowly, as if he was a child who had not quite mastered balance. Mackie Pea was jostled in her carrier, but she didn't make a sound.

"You need a walker," Claire said.

"Walkers are for old people," Ian said.

"I'm getting you one this week," Claire said. "I'm also cutting your hair and trimming those eyebrows. You look like Boxcar Willy."

"You didn't use to be so bossy."

"You didn't use to be such a mess," she said, and then immediately regretted her words. "I'm sorry, Dad."

"I'm glad you came home," he said, patting her hand. "Your mother needs your help."

They arrived at the bakery at just past six o'clock and found Scott there drinking coffee and eating donuts.

"This is how stereotypes are created," Claire said.

Scott looked her up and down.

"That's an interesting look for you," he said. "Where's Delia?"

While Claire was explaining about her mother being ill, her father began to tug on Scott's jacket.

"We're late," Ian said. "We need to go. I don't want anybody to get our table."

"Alright, let's go," Scott said. "Although I think Phyllis will hold our table for us."

He winked at Claire, wiped his mouth, downed the last of his coffee, and took Ian by the arm.

He called out "thank you" to Bonnie and Ian shushed him.

"Don't you call that she-devil out here," Ian said. "I've had enough of her lip to last me a lifetime."

"Dad," Claire started to admonish him, but Scott shook his head at her.

"C'mon, partner," Scott said. "Let's go get some breakfast."

"I'm working Mom's schedule," Claire said. "If you need me I'll be wherever she would usually be."

"I'm taking my mom to Morgantown for tests later this morning," Scott said. "I probably won't be back before five."

"I hope it goes well," Claire said.

"Thanks," Scott said and helped her impatient father out the door.

Claire took a deep breath and looked down at Mackie Pea. Bonnie was not going to like this one bit. Quietly she looked up a number in Bonnie's phone book and then used the bakery phone to call Skip, who said he would be glad to come down and get Mackie Pea. He arrived just as Bonnie came out of the kitchen with a tray of cinnamon rolls. The warm air of the bakery was redolent with the scent of cinnamon, sugar, and butter.

'I'm gonna gain five pounds today,' Claire thought to herself.

"There's the sailor home from sea," Bonnie said when she saw Claire.

She came around from behind the counter and stood with her hands on her hips.

"Your mother called me this morning and said you were working for her today, but I didn't believe it. What's that dog doing in my bakery?"

"Skip's mother is going to look after her," Claire said.

She hurriedly thanked Skip and handed him the carrier. Mackie Pea looked curious but not worried as they went out the door. Skip looked odd wearing his police uniform and carrying the fancy pet carrier, but then Claire didn't know anyone in Rose Hill who wouldn't; it didn't fit in here.

Bonnie Fitzpatrick was not a big person, and Claire was always surprised to be reminded of that. In her imagination, Aunt Bonnie was huge and terrifying. She was actually much shorter than Claire, round in figure, with beautiful white curly hair and sharp blue eyes.

Having been married to an alcoholic for almost fifty years (and having feuded with her mother-in-law for half of those years), Bonnie had an iron will that had been forged into steel. There were many stories told about her famous temper, and the tongue lashings she had been known to deliver were legendary; consequently, everyone tip-toed around her.

"Let me look at you," she said, and Claire felt incredibly self-conscious like she was twelve. "You're too thin, but we'll fix that. C'mon back to the kitchen. I can tell by those fancy fingernails you'll be worse than useless, but poor help is better than none at all. Put on an apron and wash your hands."

For the next six hours, Claire worked harder than she ever had in her life. Everything was heavy: the enormous trays of baked goods, the deep stainless steel bowl of the huge electric mixer; even the wooden rolling pin she used to roll out the croissant dough was a heavy wooden dowel the size of a baseball bat.

Throughout the morning Claire consumed at least one of every donut, croissant, scone, and cinnamon roll that wasn't deemed perfect enough to sell. Her Aunt Bonnie kept putting bits and pieces on a plate for her and Claire ate until she felt like she might burst. Each bite was so rich and delicious it made Claire's eyes roll back into her head in ecstasy.

The kitchen was stifling hot, stuffy, and the pace was brutal. By the end of her shift Claire's back ached, her feet were sore, her head hurt, her stomach stuck out, her skin was clammy with perspiration, and she wanted nothing more than to take a bath and crawl into bed.

Her Aunt Bonnie, on the other hand, never broke a sweat. During a short lull, she sat on a stool behind the cash register and sipped some strong, black coffee while Claire guzzled ice water and nibbled on a broken scone.

"Patrick said you had a fight with the tea shop owner," Claire said.

"Yankee cheapskate," Bonnie said. "She asked me to bake some tea cakes for her shop but then wanted to pay me half the agreed upon price."

"She's a piece of work, alright," Claire said. "I can't imagine why she's lowered herself to work in retail."

"The rumor is she needs the money," Bonnie said. "Evidently she lost a lot of money in the stock market crash, and you know how stingy Knox is."

"Yet she acts like it's beneath her to take money from customers."

"She's one of those Yank bahookies that trace their ancestry back to the Mayflower like that's something to brag about," Bonnie said. "Being related to them that were kicked out of one country only to make mischief in another is naught to be proud of."

Aunt Alice came in for her shift and said, "I went over to see your mother, Claire, and she's very ill; she really shouldn't be alone. I'm afraid of what might happen."

Claire grabbed her coat and ran all the way home, only to find her mother dressed, sitting at the kitchen table having a cup of tea and reading a newspaper.

"You know how Alice exaggerates," Delia said. "She loves to stir up trouble."

Claire took a shower, dried her hair, and then looked through her carry-on for something suitable to wear to work at the Eldridge Inn reception desk. The fashionable designer clothes that were perfectly suitable for LA, New York and London seemed too showy for Rose Hill. All of a sudden they looked to Claire like costumes from a chick flick shot in Manhattan. It would be about a fashion magazine editor who's engaged to a Wall Street barracuda but ends up falling for the irritatingly charming, scruffy musician/artist/writer whom she is accidentally handcuffed to/trapped with/rescued by after a ludicrous series of unlikely mishaps. They were not clothes for a real person with a real life in a small town with no dry-cleaner.

Out of the time-traveling closet of dated fashions, she pulled a pair of black wool pants and a charcoal gray twin set she could wear with her mother's pearls. Her swollen feet refused the heels she tried to push them into, so she wore black ballerina flats. She applied and then wiped off her favorite bright red lipstick. As soon as it was on, she realized it just didn't work here. It looked garish, not glamorous.

When she was finished getting ready she looked in the mirror. She looked like someone's spinster aunt, she decided. Not the hip, fun kind, but the sensible, dependable kind; the kind of person who could be counted on to do the right thing. This was the person she seemed to be turning into whether she liked it or not.

"The only thing missing is a black velvet headband," her mother said when she saw her.

"The better to cover my new lobotomy scar," Claire said.

"You're getting your sense of humor back," Delia said. "That's a good sign."

"I'm hoping it will make me more popular in prison," Claire said. "If I make the tough ones laugh they might not shiv me."

"Scott and Sean both say you have nothing to worry about," Delia said.

Claire thought but did not say that Scott and Sean didn't know what Pip had done the night of the accident. If that bit of information came to light, she'd probably be charged with conspiracy to commit murder.

"Curtis is taking your father over to the bar at noon and Patrick will order him some lunch," Delia said. "Just pick him up there on your way home after five."

Claire looked askance at her mother, to see if she was secretly enjoying seeing Claire struggle through her daily schedule, but Delia hugged her and kissed her cheek.

"Thank you for staying," she said. "I don't know what I'd do without you."

Claire's feet were so sore she drove her rental car to the Inn rather than walk the five blocks.

The Eldridge Inn sat on Morning Glory Circle at the end of Morning Glory Avenue. It was the northernmost street in Rose Hill, where the more well-to-do people lived. The Inn was a larger version of the Eldridge's Edwardian home at the end of the cul-de-sac and was situated between that residence and Rose Hill City Park.

The grounds also adjoined those of Eldridge College, an obscenely expensive private school where rich people sent their offspring after more prestigious schools kicked them out. The effect of so much manicured splendor was intimidating to most Rose Hillians, and before she'd seen the rest of the world, Claire had been intimidated by it too.

Claire came in through the side entrance and found Inn owner Gwyneth Eldridge at the front desk, berating a woman dressed in a maid's uniform.

"I don't care if she's sick, we need her here," Gwyneth said. "I'm certainly not going to wash bed linens all day. Either she comes in, or you will have to work her shift."

Gwyneth Eldridge was around ten years older than Claire. She was the eldest of the Eldridge siblings descended from the college founder. The younger brother Brad had drowned under mysterious circumstances when they were all teenagers. After the older brother, Theo was murdered a few years ago, Gwyneth and her flaky sister Caroline had inherited the Inn along with many other properties and assorted trust funds.

Gwyneth had an anorexic look Claire had come to accept as the television and film industry standard, and her clothes were classically tailored and expensive looking. Her blonde bob was expertly streaked and beautifully cut. A simple looking haircut is not always the easiest, and Claire had seen many butchered bobs, much like Meredith's at the tea room.

'The trick is you have to account for the ears,' Claire thought. 'You have to leave the hair that falls over the ears a little longer so it will hang perfectly even when it's dry.'

The edges of Gwyneth's bob were razor straight, dead even, and perpendicular to the line of her shoulders. The length was exactly where it should be on her neck; any shorter and it would widen the line of the jaw; any longer and it would look too youthful. This was an admirable haircut, professionally maintained. Claire was impressed.

Claire could tell that Gwyneth's face had been surgically enhanced by a skilled surgeon. She'd had a facelift and some eye work done, but it was subtle. The only give-away to her real age was her hands. It was almost impossible to combat aging in the hands. Sloan had tried everything, only to end up with something much worse than what she started with. You rarely saw her hands in editorial spreads, and if they were visible, they were digitally manipulated to appear flawless or replaced by someone else's via digital trickery.

When Gwyneth turned and saw Claire she smiled a chilly smile, no doubt assuming Claire was a guest.

"How may we help you?" she asked.

Claire recognized the affected British accent that seemed to afflict particularly keen anglophiles of a certain financial standing. Her previous employer was susceptible to the same inclination. Claire doubted they ever fooled anyone.

"I'm Delia's daughter Claire," she said. "I'm here to cover her shift."

Gwyneth's smile contracted into pursed-lip disapproval.

"Do you have any qualifications?" Gwyneth asked while giving her a merciless up-and-down appraisal.

"I was the personal assistant to a celebrity for many years," she said. "You may have heard of her: Sloan Merryweather."

Gwyneth's face lit up, and she preened a little.

"I have often been told that I look just like her," Gwyneth said.

Without hesitation, Claire said what she always said to the delusional people who claimed this distinction.

"I think you're much prettier."

Gwyneth was delighted with this answer. She was even more delighted when Claire demonstrated her expertise with Gwyneth's phone and personal computer.

"You're hired," Gwyneth said after Claire was through organizing her day.

"Just until my mother feels better," Claire said.

"I'd actually prefer you," Gwyneth said. "Nothing against your mother but I do think a younger person smartly dressed makes a better first impression."

'Just like in show business,' Claire thought, but she held her tongue and smiled.

The Inn didn't have many guests, and Claire spent most of the afternoon drinking coffee, eating the shortbread that had been put out for guests, surfing the Internet, and occasionally answering the phone. It was a nice, quiet break after spending the morning toiling in a hot kitchen. She slipped off her shoes, sank her toes into the thick wool carpet under the desk, and struggled not to fall asleep.

Gwyneth had done an excellent job restoring the inn. It looked as though no expense had been spared on the renovation and redecoration. The most impressive thing to Claire was that every piece of furniture was the real thing; there was not a reproduction antique in sight. There was a gas fire in the fireplace, soft classical music played over a discreetly installed sound system, and the air was perfumed by many expertly styled floral arrangements. Claire had stayed in many four and five star accommodations, and in her opinion, the Eldridge Inn could definitely compete on that level.

At four o'clock an extraordinary thing happened: Sloan Merryweather came through the front entrance. Claire was struck by a sense of time having slipped sideways, of parallel universes colliding, and half expected a loud crack of metaphysical thunder.

"Hello, darling," Sloan said. "Miss me?"

Sloan was in full on movie star mode. She made a grand entrance, and the force of her personality radiated out and bounced off the ceiling and walls. The room seemed suddenly brighter. Claire reflected that Sloan instinctively knew how to find the best light in any room, and would do whatever it took to be the only one standing in it.

She wore a Calvin Klein traveling outfit of black pants, a slender black tunic sweater, and a matching cashmere wrap. Her Louboutin platform pumps were six inches high, but she was still shorter than Claire in her flats. A heavy gold necklace in a modern design rested against her bony chest, and a thick gold cuff bracelet hung on her delicate wrist. A large dark emerald ring overwhelmed her slender hand but exactly matched her eyes. Claire couldn't see what earrings she was wearing, but she guessed they would be the heavy gold ones that matched the necklace and cuff.

Sloan's famous mane of thick auburn hair was the only jarring note in her otherwise flawless appearance. Claire knew Sloan's hair issues better than anyone on the planet, and things were not looking good. It looked as if it hadn't been washed in a while, for one thing.

Behind her, the pro linebacker turned fashion stylist nicknamed Teeny struggled with a mountain of bags, and the small, harried-looking Juanita carried her employer's bottle of spring water, carry-on tote, and an umbrella. That used to be Tuppy's job.

"What are you doing here?" Claire asked as she stood up.

"I heard about Tuppy, darling, so of course I came as soon as I could. I'm devastated, naturally, for his family's loss, and if there is anything I can do to help with arrangements, I would be only too glad. I can't believe they could think you had anything to do with his death. I'm fully prepared to make a statement to that effect to whatever law enforcement agency is keeping you here, plus any media outlets."

"There are no media here, Sloan," Claire said. "What's going on with your hair?"

"It's your fault," Sloan hissed. "You know I can't do it myself."

"Are you looking for a room?" Claire asked, and made a point of looking at the almost empty reservations page.

"I can't believe this is where you've ended up," Sloan said. "I keep expecting to see barefoot pregnant women dressed in overalls holding corncob pipes. No wonder you got the hell out of here as soon as you could. Don't worry about the police, darling, Stanley's coming, and he'll clear up everything."

"I have an attorney," Claire said. "Do you want a suite, or do you want to rent the entire second-floor south wing?"

"Yes, dear, but the kind of attorney you could get here, well, let's be serious. Stanley's the best. This unpleasantness will all be resolved in no time, and then you can come home with us, where you belong."

"No, thanks," Claire said. "I don't work for you anymore, and I don't want to accept any favors that might obligate me. I like things just the way they are."

Sloan leaned over the desk, way too close to Claire's face for her comfort, put her mouth next to Claire's ear, and made a profanity-laced threat in a very low voice no one else could have heard. The gist of the message was that if Claire knew what was best for her, she would stop being so obstinate and cooperate, and if she refused Sloan's help, there would be dire consequences. Within this message, anywhere Sloan could insert a profane word as an adjective or a noun, she did.

Along with the verbal venom, Claire also received a huge dose of Sloan's signature scent, created especially for her by a famous Parisian perfumer. It was called "Petit Renard," which meant "little fox" in French. Tuppy had called it "Urine de Renard," and on that point, Claire had to agree.

"Do you understand?" Sloan said as she straightened back up, and despite her resolve, Claire felt her knees wobble.

"Luckily the whole south wing on the second floor is available, and the suite at the end is very nice," Claire said. "It certainly doesn't meet the demands made on your contract rider, but you can have an empty room on each side of you, just as you prefer. Teeny, Juanita, and Stanley can have the next three and that leaves three rooms. Will anyone else be arriving?"

"Angus and Ayelet will come if I need them to; I haven't decided yet."

"Will anyone else be joining you?"

"Carlyle's in Scotland," Sloan said, eyeing Claire with sly contempt. "I guess he just wasn't interested in seeing you again."

"Will you need room service?" Claire asked as she felt her face flush in humiliation. "There's a diner, a pizza place, and a burger joint; those are your choices."

"I knew there could not be a decent restaurant this far out in the wilderness; will they let Juanita cook for me in the kitchen?"

"I think the owner would be only too delighted," Claire said. "It seems many people think she looks just like you."

"One of those, huh?" Sloan said. "Where is she?"

Claire called Gwyneth, who lived in the former college president's residence at the end of the cul-de-sac. Once she heard who had arrived, she made amazing time and came in breathless and star struck.

"Such a pleasure to meet you," Gwyneth said. "I'm just another slobbering fan, I'm afraid."

"It's like looking in a mirror, isn't it, Claire?" Sloan said. "I'm just lucky you didn't decide to become an actress."

Gwyneth almost levitated with pleasure. Sloan's request about the kitchen was met with total approval, but then Gwyneth upped the ante.

"I just happen to have a four-star chef employed in my home," Gwyneth said. "I would be honored if you would allow me to provide you with all your meals while you're here. Everything's organic, of course. Are you vegan?"

"Heavens, no," Sloan said. "I like my steaks bloody and my Scotch neat."

(Claire knew this was a lie; Sloan only ate steamed green vegetables and chicken, fish, or eggs that were poached in her French spring water with no butter or oil. She ate 500 calories a day, tops, and didn't drink hard liquor because of its aging side effects. The steak and Scotch retort was dialogue from a play in which she was meant to portray a femme fatale back in the forties.)

Gwyneth clutched her pearls but didn't miss a beat.

"I'm sure we can accommodate any preferences you might have. Just give Claire a list, and I'll have Renaldo do the rest."

Gwyneth insisted on personally seeing Sloan to her room, but before she followed her up the stairs, Sloan turned to Claire.

"I hardly recognized you, you've gained so much weight," she said. "I'll see you later."

Teeny and Juanita smiled nervously at Claire and followed their employer. Claire was so relieved to see the desk clerk for the next shift coming through the door from the kitchen she almost hugged the woman. Claire grabbed her coat and handbag and ran out to the car. As she pulled out of the service drive onto Morning Glory Avenue, she saw a long dark sedan with New York plates pull up to the entrance of the Inn, and knew Stanley had arrived. It had been a narrow escape.

Scott waited until his mother was settled in her bed, kissed her forehead, and turned out the light.

"I don't want you to worry," she said. "If you call your sister I'm sure she'll come. I don't want this to disrupt your work."

"We'll talk about it later," Scott said. "Get some rest."

Scott locked the front door behind him and stood outside, enjoying the fresh air; his mother's house was so overheated he couldn't stand to stay in it very long. It had been a long day spent pushing his mother's wheelchair from waiting room to waiting room in different parts of a labyrinth-like hospital, allowing her to be taken away for tests, and then waiting an interminable amount of time to talk to a doctor about what the results meant. His mother was exhausted; he was also worn out but went down to the station to check in.

His deputy Frank was there and handed Scott the courier delivery package that held Claire's phone.

"Everything's been real quiet," Frank said. "I like this time of year."

"Has Sarah been by?" Scott asked.

"Around noon," Frank said. "I didn't tell her anything, and I didn't open the safe for her. I told her I didn't have the combination."

"Good man," Scott said. "You go on home; I'll stay awhile."

Scott opened the courier's package and smiled at the rhinestone-studded pink leather case holding Claire's phone. He slipped it out of its case, pried off the back, took the battery out, and was relieved to find no tracking devices. After he reassembled it, he took Claire's charger out of his desk drawer, plugged one end into the wall behind his desk, and the other into Claire's phone. Then he used his own phone to make a call he didn't want to make to the sister he knew would not want to hear what he had to say.

Claire walked into the Rose and Thorn and was immediately hailed by the regulars sitting on swiveling stools attached to the bar like mushrooms on a log. She couldn't remember all of their names but the faces, though older, were familiar. Her father was sitting in what she thought of as her booth, watching a basketball game on the flat screen television on the back wall.

"Hey, Dad," she said. "Are you ready to go home?"

"Look at the big television Patrick put up there," Ian said. "It's a modern miracle, that is."

Pip came out of the bathroom and sat down across from her father, where she could see he had a beer waiting.

"What are you doing here?" Claire said.

"Is that any way to talk to your husband?" her father said. "And him having come all the way from California to see you."

"It's alright," Pip told Ian with a wink. "I'm used to her ways. She's all bark."

Pip tried to grab Claire around the waist, but she was too quick for him. It was all Claire could do not to pour his beer over his head. Instead, she sat down next to her father and regarded her ex-husband.

"Pip's staying at his mother's house, Dad," she said, pointedly. "So he can help her work on some things."

"If you're missing me," Pip said, "I can certainly spend every other night at your place."

"You're welcome to stay," Ian said. "We've plenty of room."

"My mom's sick," Claire said. "I'd like to keep things quiet for her."

"I can be quiet," Pip said and waggled his eyebrows.

Claire kicked him, and he yelped.

"What's the matter?" Ian said.

"Pip's back is bothering him," Claire said. "He gets these pains."

"The only pain I'm having is in the neck," Pip said. "I'd like to speak to you privately, sweetheart."

"Hello, young lovers," Patrick said and put a pitcher of beer on the table.

Claire stuck her tongue out at him, and he laughed as he went back to the bar.

"You two go on," Ian said. "I want to see the end of this game."

Claire got up and walked to the back room with Pip right behind. Once they were inside, she shut the door and said, "Well?"

"Meredith still won't talk to me," he said. "Courtenay wants me to tell the police Meredith ran over your friend and then asked me to hide the car. She thinks if I turn Meredith in they won't charge me, and then Meredith will be out of the way, permanently."

"First of all, you're an idiot," Claire said. "Courtenay probably wants both of you out of the way. With Meredith in rich people resort camp for manslaughter and you in federal prison as an accessory after the fact, Courtenay will have a clear shot at having Knox all to herself."

"She wouldn't do that to me," Pip said. "You don't know her like I do."

"If you mean intimately, then, no," Claire said. "But if you mean I don't know her type that's where you're wrong. Courtenay's the Russian starlet and Knox is the brilliant director. Meredith is Sloan, the famous actress, the wife with the money and the connections, but a total drag to be married to; and you, my dear ex-husband, are the personal trainer who fools around with both women but gets dumped in the end. Don't you remember Lars?"

"You're just jealous."

"Oh, honey, bless your heart, I'm not jealous; I'm just smarter than you," Claire said. "And trust me; I'm not that exceptional in the brains department."

"If you're so smart then what should I do?"

"You need to talk to Sean," Claire said. "Do you have a working car that hasn't been stolen or used in the commission of a crime?"

"My mom's car."

"I'm going to give you Sean's number. Call him and make an appointment to go up to Pittsburgh and talk to him. Maybe he can figure a way out of this mess."

"You go with me."

"No, Pip," Claire said. "Just this once do something difficult without some woman holding your hand. You're forty-two years old, for crissakes. Grow up!"

"Courtenay's expecting me to come over tonight. Knox is in DC."

"Is there any point in me telling you that isn't a good idea?"

He shrugged.

"Sloan's in town," Claire said and was gratified to see real fear in his eyes.

"Does she know I'm here?"

"Not yet," Claire said.

"Well, whatever you do, don't tell her," Pip said.

"Are you sending your wife any money to take care of your children?" Claire asked.

"Her parents are taking care of them," Pip said. "They hate me."

"Big surprise," Claire said.

"It's not my fault," Pip said. "Crap just always happens to me, and everybody always blames me."

"It's never your fault, is it?" Claire said. "I can't imagine why you continue to have such rotten bad luck. It couldn't possibly be the poor choices you make, could it?"

"Courtenay says she's going to help me start my own business. She says there are lots of rich people in DC who will pay big bucks for the stuff I do."

"As a prostitute or as a carpenter?"

"I hate you, Claire," Pip said and banged out the side door.

Claire went back to the front room and collected her father, then led him by the hand, out the door and all the way home.

"I don't like Pip," Ian said as Claire helped him take off his coat in the front entryway. "I know he's your husband, but I think he's an idiot."

"There's nothing wrong with your mind," Claire said. "He is an idiot."

"Why don't you divorce him and marry some nice boy like Scott."

"I think Maggie may have a lock on that deal," Claire said.

"Your cousin Maggie blew her chance," Ian said. "I think you could snag him."

"You think so?"

"She's as mean as that mother of hers. I told him he should thank his lucky stars; he made a narrow escape."

"What did Scott say to that?"

"He said there's a lid for every pot, and he's Maggie's."

Claire got him settled in his chair, brought him a glass of juice, and exchanged the medication patch on his back for a fresh one.

"That patch is really helping my shoulder," he said. "My bursitis is much better since we started using it."

Claire washed her hands as she reflected on the worth of a patch that was supposed to save her father's memory in light of the fact that he couldn't remember what it was for. Her mother said the patch cost over two-hundred dollars a month; their insurance only covered it for nine months out of the year, and only after the deductible was met.

Claire wondered how people survived; people who worked hard for decades and had so little to show for it at the end of their lives. What did people do who didn't have children to care for them? What would she do?

Claire checked on her mother, who was lying in bed reading a book. She considered telling her everything that had happened that day, but her mother looked so rested, and relaxed Claire didn't have the heart to burden her.

"How was your day?" Delia asked.

"It was fine," Claire said. "How are you feeling? What can I do for you?"

After Scott had fully charged Claire's phone, he tucked it in his interior jacket pocket and locked up the station. Loud bluegrass music from the Rose and Thorn was pouring out of the open front door and echoing against the mountain on the other side of the river. Sometimes when there was a lot of moisture in the air, the river sounded like it was running right through the middle of town. Two new dams installed after a devastating flood three years before made sure it never could.

Scott knocked on Ian and Delia's front door, and Claire answered. She invited him in, and he saw Ian was napping in his chair. They went to the kitchen, where Scott sat down while Claire poured him some coffee.

"How's your mom?" she asked.

Against his will, Scott felt his eyes well up. Claire put her arm around his shoulders, hugged him, sat down next to him, and clasped his hand on the table. He wiped his eyes and cleared his throat.

"It's cancer," he said. "They think it started in her uterus and now it's everywhere. The cough and shortness of breath are from where it's spread to her lungs. The oncologist wants to do radiation and chemo, but the internist wasn't very encouraging about that. He said if it were his mother he would call Hospice and try to make what time she has left as good as possible."

"Oh, Scott," Claire said, tearing up in sympathy. "Your poor mother."

"She's always been a bit of a hypochondriac," Scott said. "I never took her seriously. Maybe if I had intervened earlier..."

"Don't do that," Claire said. "Your mom is a grownup and responsible for her own health. How could you know when it was just for attention and when it was real? She could have called Doc Machalvie any time any day, and he would have come right over to see her. Please don't get stuck blaming yourself. You can't rescue everyone."

Scott leaned into Claire, and she embraced him.

"Thank you," he said. "I'm so glad you came back. I really need a friend right now, and somehow I don't think Patrick or Ed could handle this quite as well."

"What about Maggie?"

Scott shook his head.

"We aren't even friends anymore," he said. "The worst part is I'm the one who set fire to that bridge."

"Well, it looks like I'll be here awhile, so I'll be glad to help you however you need me to."

"You're staying?"

"Just for the summer," Claire said.

"That long?" Scott said.

"I don't know how long, exactly, but enough time to get everything organized here."

"I see."

"I don't have to decide today. We'll see how it goes."

"Don't worry," he said, smiling. "I'm not asking for a long-term commitment."

"I know how I sound; I just can't help it."

"You just got here," Scott said. "It may take some time for you to figure out what you really want to do."

"What I want to do tomorrow is drive to Pendleton and buy a new phone. Do you think Sarah will think I'm making a break for it?"

"I have a nice surprise for you," he said and took her phone out of his jacket pocket.

"No way!" she said, and held her beloved phone up to her lips and kissed it. "How did you find it?"

"I know people," Scott said and blushed.

Claire hugged him again and kissed him.

"I said you should get divorced first," Ian said from the doorway. "Don't go puttin' the cart before the horse, little girl."

Scott was confused, but Claire laughed.

"Don't worry, Dad," she told her father. "I'll do everything in the right order."

Claire found a notebook and she and Scott transcribed her calls and texts, starting the day she flew home, putting everything in order.

4:45 p.m. GMT: Tuppy called Claire: "Clairol, you in danger, girl. Seriously, this morning Frau Schlechtwetter instructed me to nuke your world. I have a marvelous plan that will deliver us both from evil, but it's too dangerous to leave in a voicemail. I thought we would fly to DC together and have a good chinwag on the way over, but you were a sneaky little devil and did something else. Call me as soon as you get this."

5:15 p.m. GMT: Sloan called Claire: "Claire, Tuppy says you're on your way back to us, and I'm so glad. I promise to make it worth your while. You won't regret it. I've missed you. See you soon."

8:14 p.m. EST; Sloan called Claire: "I don't know what you two think you're doing but it's a big mistake. You of all people should know what bad luck it is to cross me. Stanley will be in touch; you won't enjoy it, but he will."

8:15 p.m. EST; Tuppy texts Claire: "In dc. Wl mt u n rh. Btw I qt! Mr ltr."

"Same as before; it says he's in DC and will meet me in Rose Hill," Claire said. "He also says he quit and will tell me more later."

8:16 p.m. EST; Tuppy called Claire: "I'm in DC; where are you, my little minx? I left the Queen of Hearts with no notice, and she's all, "off with his head!" I'm going to drive to that godforsaken burg from which you hail to meet you at your parents' house. Please, please call me. I have got to talk to you."

2:05 a.m. EST; Tuppy texts Claire: "Wr r u? Im n yr crpy tn. Call me!"

"Where are you?" Claire translated. "I'm in your creepy town."

2:11 a.m. EST; Tuppy calls Claire: "Miss Clairol, this town is tiny and creepy; you do not belong here. Come with me to New York where I am soon to be a rich and famous author. You can be my personal assistant, and I promise not to be half as mean as Brunhilda. Seriously, your hometown is like a fifties horror movie; I cannot wait to get out of here. Your dad was sweet but seemed a little confused. I gave him something to give to you. Read it, and the truth will set you free. I hope you're alright, Claire. I'm getting a little worried. Please call me."

2:12 a.m. EST; Tuppy texts Claire: "Yr swt dad has bk. Kp safe. Btw njoy yr 3dm. Yr wlcm."

"Your sweet dad has the book," Claire said. "Keep it safe. By the way, enjoy your freedom. You're welcome."

Tuppy's communications stopped there. All the calls and texts after that were from Sloan or someone on her P.R. triage team, by turns threatening and cajoling.

"I notice they didn't stop communicating with you after he died," Scott said.

"Is that good or bad?" Claire asked.

"It's interesting," Scott said. "About this book ..."

"I haven't been able to find it," she said.

"Did you ask your dad?"

"I'm afraid it will upset him."

"Let's ask him now," Scott said. "Just be real casual about it like you don't really care."

They went to the living room where Ian was watching the news.

"Hey, Dad," Claire said. "Did somebody stop by here the other night and leave something for me?"

Ian looked at Claire, wide-eyed.

"I thought I dreamed that."

"No, that was a friend of mine," Claire said. "Tuppy."

"That's the one. Good-lookin' fella," Ian said. "Talked funny."

"That's him," Claire said. "Did he give you something?"

"It was the darndest thing," Ian said. "He tried to tell me it was a book."

"What was it?"

"It was a key ring," Ian said. "Now, what did I do with that?"

"A key ring?" Scott said.

"Are you sure?" Claire said, and immediately Ian got agitated, and his head started to nod.

"Well, I think so," Ian said. "My memory's not what it used to be."

"That's okay," Scott said. "It's not important. Claire can get another key ring."

Ian's nodding slowed down, and his attention drifted back to the television.

"It's probably around here somewhere," he said, losing interest in the subject.

Claire drug Scott by the arm back into the kitchen.

"I know what it is and where it is," she said. "It's a flash drive on a key ring that Sammy's got in his treasure box. He showed it to Hannah and me and said Delia gave it to him."

"I'll call Sam," Scott said.

"It's late," Claire said. "Let's just wait until morning. It's probably safer in Sammy's tin box in Sam and Hanna's house than in the station safe."

"Right next to my pen," Scott said.

"I've got to work at The Bee Hive tomorrow," Claire said. "I'll ask Hannah to bring him down in the morning, and I'll trade something for it. I'll see if I can't tempt him with a toy, or money, or something. As soon as I have it, I'll plug it into Denise's computer, and we can read it together."

There was a knock on the door, and Ian said, "It's like Grand Central Station in here. Claire, will you get that?"

It was Skip bringing back Mackie Pea.

"I forgot all about her," Claire confessed to Scott. "How awful is that?"

The little dog was excited to see Claire but rushed straight past her to Ian.

"There's my little girl," Ian said and cuddled her as she licked his chin.

"Thank you so much, Skip," Claire said. "Thank your mother for me, too."

"She says Mackie can come every day if you want. They had a big time. Mom's going to knit her a little sweater."

"I'm so grateful," Claire said. "Tell your mom to come down to The Bee Hive this week, and I'll give her a free haircut."

"Thanks!" Skip said. "She'll love that."

Skip left, and Scott followed him out.

"Try to get some sleep," he told her. "I'll come see you in the morning at work."

"You, too," she said. "I'm so sorry about your mom."

Scott smiled and waved goodbye.

When someone tapped on her window in the middle of the night, Claire groaned.

"What do you want, Pip?" she said as she lifted up the sash.

"I'm in big trouble," Pip said.

His eyes were wide and his skin pale.

"What did you do now?"

"I kind of owe Sloan a lot of money," he said.

"And?"

"And I kind of owe a lot of back child support."

"And?"

"And I kind of have some tax issues."

"And?"

"I know you sold the Malibu condo; by rights half of that dough is mine."

"I figured you didn't read the divorce papers before you signed them; if you had, you'd know that's not true."

"You gotta help me, Claire," he said. "Sloan's gonna kill me if I don't pay her back."

"I'm done bailing you out," Claire said. "I've got my own family to worry about."

"What should I do?"

"Borrow the money from Courtenay, since she loves you so much."

"Courtenay says Knox and Meredith are going to frame me for the hit and run."

"See? You should have gone to Scott right away."

"I'm going to tow Meredith's car down to the Hell Hole and push it in there."

"That's about the stupidest thing I ever heard, plus it's impossible. That's a state park; you won't get within ten miles of that cave before the park rangers stop you."

"Then I'll leave town, maybe go to Mexico for awhile."

"Buena suerte," Claire said. "No dejas que la puerta te pega en el culo, saliendo de aqui."

"Please, Claire," he said, and his lip turned down, and his chin trembled, right on cue.

Claire was reminded that Sloan had once set up Pip with an audition for a small part in a film. He was handsome enough and willing to have sex with anyone, so he probably would've gotten the part except he blew off the audition to get high with someone he met on the bus on the way to the studio. Pip had acting skills, no doubt, but they were so intertwined with his naturally manipulative behavior that she didn't think he even realized it was an act.

"No way," she said. "You made this bed, and you can lie in it."

"There's a warrant out for me in California," he said. "Sloan will probably call the police as soon as she knows I'm here."

"Her attorney's in town, too," Claire said. "She's got a new one, and he's even meaner than the last one."

"I'm toast, then," Pip said. "Please, Claire."

Claire considered her options.

"Meet me up at the Thorn at midnight," she said. "I'll take care of everything."

"Thanks, babe," he said and gifted her with a thousand kilowatt smile. "I knew you wouldn't let me down."

Claire pulled the window sash back down and got out of bed. First, she had to make a call, and then she had to get dressed.

Knox Rodefeffer lived on the other side of Morning Glory Circle, across from the Eldridge Inn. He was still up and seemed very surprised to see Claire under his front portico so late in the evening. He was dressed in khakis and a white shirt, but his tie was undone, and his collar loosened. He had on worn leather slippers and was holding a tumbler of what smelled like whiskey. Claire could hear a twenty-four-hour news station on the television in the background.

"What can I do for you, Claire?" he asked, and then looked behind him as if to see who might be lurking in the hallway.

"I came to talk to you about my parents' mortgage," she said.

"You'll need to talk to our loan officer about that," Knox said, "down at the bank tomorrow."

"I also wanted to know if it was you or Meredith who ran over my friend Tuppy," Claire said. "I'm on the way to see Scott, and I want to be sure I have the facts straight."

Claire watched all the florid color drain out of Knox's heavy jowls and all three of his chins.

"I don't know what you're talking about," he said.

"Maybe you should call the county sheriff's department, and we can let them help us sort it out."

"What do you want?" he said, and came outside, closing the door behind him.

"I'm here to warn you," Claire said. "If you, Meredith, or Courtenay try to pin this on Pip I will make you very sorry."

"I don't know what you mean, and pretty soon I won't care," Knox said. "I'm done with this conversation."

He turned and opened the storm door.

"I had a long talk with your ex-wife this evening," Claire said.

Knox stopped and turned back around, letting the storm door hiss shut.

"Go on," he said.

"Anne Marie says Meredith is dangerous," she said.

"My ex-wife is mentally ill," Knox said. "Was this one of her so-called visions?"

"She told me you married Meredith in order to ally yourself with her late father and late husband's political friends. She said there's something you don't know about Meredith that's going to derail your campaign at the last minute."

"What?" he said, now looking very interested.

"Anne Marie said Meredith has taken a life twice before and may do so again," Claire said. "If she killed my friend he's the second; that would mean there was another death before that. It also means you could be the next to go."

"That's preposterous," Knox said, but he stayed on the porch.

"If you know she killed my friend, you better turn her in before she goes off the deep end and turns on you," Claire said. "Or worse, waits until the most crucial part of your campaign to wig out on live TV."

"Did Anne Marie say she'd flip out at a press conference?"

"She said whatever the trouble is it will come to light in a very public way."

"I heard Anne Marie was telling fortunes for a living, and by all accounts, she's making a ton of money doing it, but I thought it was a scam."

"She's been tested at Duke University," Claire said. "She achieved 98% accuracy."

"If she's so accurate why didn't she tell you how Meredith supposedly killed these people or who they were?"

"Anne Marie says her visions are like being in a dream while she's awake," Claire said. "She said she saw Meredith with blood on her hands, and a red numeral two was visible above her to the left, and the number three was fading in and out on the right. She's done so many readings now she can translate the symbols she sees much more easily. She said blood on the hands means taking a life, and the numerals were written in blood. The left side refers to the past and the right side to the future."

Claire was good at reading people. She knew Knox was inclined to believe every single word she was saying, maybe had observed things in Meredith's behavior that backed up these new suspicions. He may also have been thinking about an attempted murder he himself got away with.

"I'm sorry my ex-wife wasted your time, Miss Fitzpatrick," Knox said. "I hope she has enough sense left not to broadcast her slanderous delusions. Neither my wife nor I had anything to do with your friend's death. I was in DC that night and Meredith went to bed early with a headache. Her car was stolen that evening so perhaps whoever took it hit your friend. In any event, I'm sorry for your loss. If you come down to the bank tomorrow, I'll see to it that your parents' mortgage is refinanced at a much lower rate, and I'm sure you'll be happy with the terms."

"And Pip?"

"Tell that loser if he knows what's best for him he'll leave town and never come back," Knox said. "As long as he leaves my wife and secretary alone nothing will happen to him."

Knox went inside and closed the door. Claire hurried down the steps and ran back to her rental car, which was parked around the corner. She drove down Morning Glory Avenue to the very end, past the library, where a narrow gravel road known as Possum Holler began. About a quarter of a mile out this road, just past the entrance to the Rose Hill Cemetery, was a shabby farmhouse with an old sofa on the front porch. Claire parked in the rutted driveway, got out of the car and walked around to the back of the house, choosing her steps carefully to avoid tripping over the multiple rusted metal objects and broken plastic items that littered the muddy path.

Claire looked through the dirty window of the back door and saw Pip's mother sitting in the kitchen. A cigarette dangled from her lips as she took colorfully-decorated cards from a deck and placed them in an intricate pattern on the table. Claire tapped on the glass, and the older woman looked up, scowled, and waved her in. The screen door hinges screeched as Claire opened it, and she knew from past experience that in order to open the interior door it had to be raised up an inch by pulling up on the doorknob as she pushed.

The smell inside the house was a musty combination of mildew, fried food, and cigarette smoke. The sink was piled high with dirty dishes and a small television on the counter was broadcasting a shopping channel. The house was heated by an old gas box stove that sat in the corner of the room. A blanket was draped over the wide opening that led to the front room in order to keep the heat in the one room in which Pip's mother spent most of her time. Claire knew this because she had lived in this house for a year after she married Pip.

"Well, if it isn't the empress, daughter of the mighty one," Mrs. Deacon said.

"How are you, Freda?" Claire asked as she sat down across from her.

"I'm worried about my son," Freda said. "I've tried every spread I know, and everyone ends with this dad-blasted card ..."

She held up a card that featured a weeping woman with a display of swords hanging points-down behind her.

"What is that?" Claire asked.

"It's the Nine of Swords, baby girl, and it's reversed, which is as bad as things can get."

"Pip's in trouble, alright," Claire said. "He needs to stop running away from his problems and start taking responsibility for his actions."

"There's more going on than just Pip having some bad luck," Freda said. "There's real evil involved, someone powerful and wicked."

"Is the car still in the shed?" Claire asked.

Freda eyed Claire through the smoke from her cigarette, looking as if she was trying to decide whether or not to lie.

"Pip told me it was here," Claire said.

"It's gone," Freda said. "It was here when I left for work and gone when I came home. Someone cut the padlock on the shed and towed it away. They rutted up my driveway something awful."

Claire thought but didn't say that it would be hard to prove that anything done to Freda's property could actually make it any worse.

"Was the front end banged up?"

"I couldn't tell ya," Freda said. "I never laid eyes on it, myself."

"Of course," Claire said. "Well, I better get going ..."

"I'll do your cards," Freda said, and then lit her next cigarette with her previous one.

"That's okay," Claire said. "I need to get home."

"Shuffle and then cut the cards three times," Freda said as she held out the cards. 'We'll just do a quick and dirty simple one."

Claire did as she was told, and then handed them back. Freda fanned the cards and asked Claire to pick out three. As Claire picked them out, Freda placed them on the table.

"This here's your past," Freda said as she pointed to the first card Claire drew, which depicted a goat-headed fella who reminded Claire of several men she'd met in L.A. "This is the devil. He represents ambition, greed, and a lust for material things."

"Sounds about right."

"This is your present," she said, pointing to the card in the middle of the spread. It featured a man in a dark, hooded cloak, holding a scythe, which Claire figured couldn't represent good news. "This is death, but it doesn't mean you're gonna die. It means the end of the old way of life and the beginning of the new; an abrupt and complete change."

"That's true enough," Claire said.

"This here's your future," Freda said, pointing at the last card, featuring a sundial surrounded by cherubs in a bright blue sky. "And it's about the luckiest card there is. It's the Wheel of Fortune. You're going to have unexpected and great good fortune. I'm not a bit surprised; you always did land on your feet."

"Only after Pip dropped me from a great height," Claire said and got up to leave.

"Pip's a catbird, I know that," Freda said. "But he's my only son, and I love him. We gotta look out for him, 'cause Lord knows he can't look out for himself."

"I know," Claire said. "I'm trying to help him."

"If he needs money it'll have to come from you," Freda said. "I'm flat broke."

"Are you working?" Claire asked.

"I'm cleaning at the college; same as always."

Freda went back to shuffling cards, her cigarette clamped in one side of her mouth, the eye on that side shut to avoid the smoke.

As Claire opened the back door something on the filthy floor caught her attention; she reached down and picked it up. It was part of a bank deposit envelope; it looked as if someone had torn off the top end, took the cash out, and then dropped it. It was from Knox's bank.

"You got a bank account downtown?" she asked Freda.

"I don't trust them banks," Freda said. "Matt Delvecchio cashes my checks at the IGA."

Claire held up the deposit envelope.

"Knox Rodefeffer must have paid you well for housing his wife's car," Claire said, "and for lying about what happened to it when you're asked."

Freda lay down the cards, took her cigarette out of her mouth, and pointed it at Claire.

"You always were too smart for my son," she said, with a crafty smile. "Pip takes after his father in the looks and brains department. Me, I'm not much to look at, but I can take care of myself."

When Claire got to the bar, Patrick had a message from Pip.

"He said to meet him at the depot," Patrick said. "He said it wasn't safe to stay in here."

"Well, for once he's right," Claire said. "It's probably the most sensible thing he's done this week."

"What's he done now?"

"What hasn't he done?" Claire said. "If he's talking he's lying, if there's a woman within five feet he's trying to get in her pants, if there's a fool nearby with any money he's trying to get hold of it, and if there's the least bit of hard work required he's suddenly nowhere to be found."

"I gave him a hundred bucks," Patrick said. "He said you'd pay me back."

"Somehow," Claire said, as she took out her wallet, "I never get a drink, but I always end up paying his tab."

When Claire arrived at the depot, Pip wasn't there. She sat on the steps to wait and shortly thereafter she heard a car pull in and a car door close. Sloan's attorney Stanley came around the corner.

"Hello, Claire," he said.

"He's not here," Claire said. "I was supposed to meet him, but he's skipped town."

"I'll track him down eventually," Stanley said. "It's you I want to talk to."

"I'm not coming back to work for Sloan."

"Suits me," Stanley said. "You've been nothing but a pain in my ass since the day I met you."

"Then why do you need to talk to me?"

"This unfortunate accident with Tuppy," Stanley said. "Was Sloan implicated in any way during your questioning?"

"No, of course not."

"We received a call from the county sheriff's office; they want to question her."

"Probably because of the mean texts and voicemails she left Tuppy right before he was killed."

"Do you know the content of these communications?"

"She said she knew where he was and was coming for him. She said his ass was as good as dead."

"Unfortunate phrasing to use, in retrospect," Stanley said, "but said in the heat of passion, with no real intent to act upon those feelings."

"Sounds like you've got her defense ready."

"Has anyone questioned you about Sloan's relationship with Mr. Tupworth?"

"All I said was that we both worked for her. I honored my confidentiality agreement."

"Your confidentiality agreement won't be upheld by a court of law in a homicide investigation," Stanley said. "If you refuse to answer any questions based on your agreement with Sloan you'll be found in contempt of court."

"So I either go to jail or lose all my money."

"Just one more reason to return to the fold and allow me to handle your defense."

"I don't need a defense," Claire said. "I didn't kill Tuppy."

"The combination of circumstantial evidence, an ambitious detective, and a judge running for re-election has often resulted in the incarceration of innocent people."

"So you've met Sarah."

"I had the pleasure."

"Well, no thanks, Stanley," Claire said. "I will honor my confidentiality agreement even if it means I go to jail. At least my parents will still have my money."

"An honorable stance," Stanley said, "but I wonder if you'll be able to maintain it when faced with actual imprisonment. Your fellow inmates probably won't think your smartass comments are that cute, either."

"I don't think it will come to that," Claire said. "You're a smart guy. Who do you think killed Tuppy?"

"Based on your movements over the past two days I'd say your ex-husband or the bank president."

"Well, you can watch me walk home now," Claire said, "and tomorrow you can watch me go to work at The Bee Hive."

"I'd like you to sign a new confidentiality agreement."

"Why? Wasn't the last one I signed in force for perpetuity?"

"It's just a precaution," Stanley said and withdrew papers from his inside breast pocket. "You know how cautious we legal-types are."

"No," Claire said. "You're not the boss of me anymore, Stanley. I don't have to do anything you ask me."

Claire got up and attempted to walk past the attorney, but he grabbed her arm. Claire pulled away and rubbed her arm.

"Keep your hands off me," Claire said. "You don't know how pissed off we hairdresser-types can be when we're bullied, or how apt we are to file assault charges."

"Don't threaten me," Stanley said. "I'm cordial now. You haven't seen one-sixteenth of what I'm capable of doing."

Headlights illuminated them, and the city police car pulled into the parking lot next to Stanley's sedan.

Skip got out and said, "Claire, you alright?"

"I could use a ride home," she said.

Once in the car, she breathed a sigh of relief.

"Who was that guy?" Skip asked.

"The devil," Claire said. "A product of unbridled ambition, greed, and the lust for material things."

Chapter Seven - Tuesday

Scott's mother was gasping for air as he fumbled with the cylinder of oxygen and attempted to rig up the cannula, the slender plastic tubing that would deliver oxygen to his mother's lungs via her nose. He then remembered the breathing treatment apparatus called a nebulizer that they'd brought home from the hospital. He helped her use it and was relieved to see her wide-eyed look of panic relax into grateful, deep breaths as it took effect. He turned the oxygen up to the level recommended by the doctor and draped the cannula around her head with trembling hands.

"Call your sister," she said between ragged breaths.

"I did," he said. "She's coming today."

Doctor Machalvie arrived and let himself in. Scott waited in the kitchen while Doc attended to his mother.

"These crisis events will get very bad very fast," Doc said when he returned from his mother's room. "I gave her an injection of Terbutaline to help her breathe and a sedative to help her relax. You'll notice I elevated her arms on some pillows and turned the heat down. You can wipe her face with a cool, damp cloth, and put a fan in her room; these things may help her breathe easier. When she gets panicked have her breathe through pursed lips. She's stabilized now, but this is going to be a recurring experience. You need to either get her into a nursing facility or call Hospice."

"She wants to stay home," Scott said, "but I can't call Hospice ... I just can't."

"Then you'll need to hire a nurse and get all the necessary medical equipment set up here. Will her insurance cover that?"

"I don't know," Scott said. "I don't even know where her policy is."

"I'm going to give you the name and number of a social worker I know at Pine County Hospice," Doc said. "Talking to her doesn't mean you're signing your mother up; you're just getting all the information you need to make an informed decision. You need to know what your options are."

"I don't want them to come in here and shoot her full of morphine," Scott said. "She wouldn't want that."

"First of all, no one can do anything without my permission," Doc said. "Even if you sign her up today, I'm still her primary physician, and everything they do has to be run by me. Second of all, I've worked with PCH for over twelve years, and I've never seen even one instance of them over-medicating a patient. There are strict guidelines that have to be followed, and they are subject to the same accreditation requirements as the hospitals. Thirdly, your mother will decide how much or how little pain medication she needs. She may want less medication and tolerate more discomfort in order to be coherent longer. It will be up to her, with my guidance. So don't make that the reason you don't call for help. That's a common fear about Hospice, but it's not a fact."

"I'll talk to my sister about it," Scott said.

"Your mother is the one dying," Doc said. "It's her decision to make."

It was the first time someone had said it so bluntly, and to Scott's embarrassment, he started crying and couldn't stop. Doc sat with him while he did.

"I'm only a phone call away," Doc said before he left.

Scott thanked him, put the phone number on the fridge and anchored it with a magnet. He'd never really paid attention to the magnets on his mother's refrigerator before. In a weird coincidence, he realized the one he'd used was an advertisement for Pine County Hospice.

After a thorough search of his mother's less than ideal filing system, Scott found her will and her insurance policy. He set the will aside and attempted to decipher the insurance company's explanation of what they would and would not cover. He considered himself to be of average intelligence, but the policy seemed to contradict itself in several instances, and the complicated stipulations seemed like a grown-up math story problem: "If A is true, but B is not met, then C will apply, but only if D is also true." Within minutes he felt the beginning symptoms of a migraine and took some ibuprofen. He called Pine County Hospice and left a message for the social worker. She called him back within the hour and made an appointment to visit later in the day.

There was a knock on the door, and Scott answered it to find Sister Mary Margrethe, sibling to Father Stephen, the priest at Sacred Heart Catholic Church. She was carrying a covered dish. Scott took it from her and invited her into the kitchen.

"Mom's just had an episode, and Doc gave her a sedative," Scott said. "We need to let her sleep."

"I wouldn't dream of disturbing her," Sister Mary Margrethe said. "That's one of my broccoli casseroles; you can refrigerate it now and heat it up for dinner."

"That's very kind," Scott said and put the dish in the fridge.

"I came as soon as I heard," she said as she sat down at the kitchen table. "You must let me arrange for people to sit with your mother so she won't be alone."

"Thank you," Scott said. "You know Rose Hill's police force is just me, Frank and Skip. There's an investigation going on, and I really need to be working, but I can't leave her alone."

"Let us help you," Sister said. "That's what your church family is for."

"The social worker from Hospice is coming over later to help me figure out her insurance," he said. "Doc says we need to put her in a facility or sign her up for Hospice."

"That's a very hard decision to make," Sister said. "I've seen firsthand how much help Hospice can be to families in this situation; you'll be glad you asked for their assistance."

"It's up to Mom, really," Scott said. "Penny's on her way; she can stay for awhile and help."

"Meanwhile, why don't you let me stay here this morning, and I'll set up a rota of ladies to take turns sitting with her."

"Thank you so much," Scott said. "I don't know what I'd do without your help."

"You always were a conscientious child," Sister said, "albeit a very fidgety altar boy."

Claire's mother insisted she was well enough to go back to work at the bakery, but Maggie covered her shift instead. Skip came to the house to pick up Ian and take him to breakfast and told Claire that he would deliver him to Curtis's service station afterward. He also offered to take Mackie Pea to his mother's house. Claire knew Mackie Pea would enjoy spending the day at Skip's mother's house, where she would probably eat tons of junk food and get fitted for her new sweater. Claire hadn't wanted to impose yet again, but Skip assured her that his mother loved Mackie, and it gave his mother something to do with her time.

"She'd take her to raise if you'd let her," Skip said. "She's gonna cry her eyes out when y'all go back to California."

With all her dependents taken care of, Claire left for The Bee Hive. As she passed Meredith's tea room, she noticed all the lights were on, but when she tried the door, she found it locked. A sign taped to the interior side of the window promised someone would be back in fifteen minutes.

Further down the block Claire unlocked The Bee Hive and turned on the lights. Her first appointment was at ten, which gave her an hour to prepare. According to the barely legible appointment book, there were sixteen clients scheduled with only a one-hour break in the afternoon. It felt to Claire as if she was facing a 5K marathon and was completely out of shape. All her muscles were sore from working in the bakery the day before, so she did some light stretches to warm up.

For her new temporary job, Claire had assembled an outfit that was more of a tribute to function than form. She wore a large Fitzpatrick Bakery apron over a short sleeved t-shirt and jeans, the better to protect her skin and clothes from the endless stream of water and chemicals she would be applying to the heads of various Rose Hillians during the day. On her feet, she wore her mother's cushiest tennis shoes: big, puffy, white monstrosities with thick rubber soles and a padded interior that felt like soft feather beds for her swollen feet. She wound her hair up in a twist on the back of her head and secured it with a large hairclip she found in a drawer.

"Morning, Sunshine!" Hannah called as she entered the salon with Sammy in tow.

"Thanks for coming," Claire said. "Hi, Sammy."

"No problem," Hannah said with a wink. "I promised him you weren't going to try to cut his hair."

Sammy looked suspiciously doubtful that no shenanigans were planned in regard to his hair.

"Sammy, I want to make a trade," Claire said.

Sammy clutched his treasure box with a look of alarm.

"How would you like this?" Claire asked, and opened her handbag to remove a dinosaur toy that had been Liam's.

"Delia lets me play with that all the times," Sammy said. "Me gots lots of dinosaurs at me's home."

"Then how about this?" Claire said and drew out the sparkly necklace with the Chanel emblem that she would likely never wear again.

"They's for girls," he said with disgust.

"How'd you get to be such a chauvinist piglet?" Hannah asked him.

"Okay," Claire said. "How about cold hard cash?"

"You gots dollars?" the small boy said.

"I gots lots of dollars," Claire said and withdrew her billfold. "I have American dollars and euros."

"What you's want me's to trade?" Sammy said.

"The key ring Delia gave you."

"Me never stoled it," Sammy said, clutching his tin tight to his chest.

"I know you didn't," Claire said. "I'll give you all my dollars and all my coins for that key ring."

He seemed to consider this.

"Whaddaya say, kiddo?" Hannah said. "Sounds like a good deal to me."

"Me want that," he said and pointed to Claire's handbag.

"Pocketbooks are for grownup girls," Claire said, and then to Hannah, "Please forgive me for perpetuating a sexist preconception."

"No, not that," he said, still pointing at the handbag, "That!"

"You're going to have to be more specific," Claire said.

Sammy reached over and tugged on the essential accessory that distinguished Claire's Blue Jean Blue Hermes Birkin handbag from the knock-offs sold on every other street corner in New York. It was a long, slender leather leash also called a "cadena." At one end was a leather clochette that concealed two small keys; at the other end was a small padlock you could use to lock the handbag. This tether wrapped around one handle and dangled down the front of the bag.

"He just wants the dooflotchy," Hannah said as if to say, "what a relief; it's no big deal."

"You don't understand," Claire said. "I can't do that. It would ruin the value."

"It's just a purse," Hannah said. "I can get you another one."

"It cost fifteen thousand dollars," Claire said.

"It did not," Hannah said. "Really? For a blue leather purse with a dooflotchy hanging off the handle?"

Up until this moment, Claire had never been anything but proud to carry the exclusive handbag, given to her by Sloan as an incentive not to quit after a particularly bad trip to France. Now she looked at the bag and saw what Hannah saw: a baby blue leather purse trimmed with some fancy platinum hardware and a dooflotchy hanging off the handle.

"Here," Claire said, as she removed the clochette, leash, and lock, and handed them over to Sammy.

His eyes lit up. He put his tin down on the floor so Claire could wrap the leash around his waist and secure it so it wouldn't fall off.

"This is the most expensive belt any three-year-old has ever worn," Claire said.

"This me's police belt," Sammy said. "This me's jail lock for bad guys."

"Really?" Hannah said as she examined the handbag. "Fifteen grand for this? I paid less than that for my truck."

The door opened, and Claire's first customer came in. Claire stood up to greet her as Sammy grabbed his tin and dashed out the door before it closed.

"That little stinker," Hannah said and jumped up to follow him. "Don't worry, Claire, I'll catch him."

Claire picked up her naked-looking Birkin Bag and stowed it in the supply room. The spell had been broken; it was now just an outrageously overpriced souvenir from her former life.

On her break, Claire went over to the bank to pay off her parents' mortgage. The loan officer turned out to be someone named Amy that Claire went to school with. She looked up Claire's parents' mortgage agreement and shook her head.

"I want you to know I didn't write this," Amy said. "I would never put someone's residence in a variable interest mortgage with a six-year balloon payment. If it was a development property, maybe, but never on someone's home."

"I want to pay it off," Claire said. "I can write a check or arrange a wire transfer from my bank in Los Angeles."

"You know your parents only paid twenty-five thousand for that house in 1974?" Amy said. "It's probably worth six or eight times that now."

"I didn't realize real estate values had gone up so much here," Claire said.

"It's like beachfront property," Amy said. "There's only so much ski resort property up at Glencora, so rich folks are buying up anything they can get their hands on within twenty miles. Most of the land in this county and the next is state park property or federally protected. They're building a new ski resort up at Glencora, and a new highway is supposed to connect it to Interstate 81 in Virginia within three years. Property values in this area are only going to continue to rise."

Claire filled out the necessary paperwork for a wire transfer, signed several documents, and Amy notarized the paperwork.

"I'll run these over to your mother to sign later on," Amy said. "I've been meaning to stop by and see her anyway to thank her for helping my mother while she was recovering from surgery last month."

Claire thanked her and shook her hand after she rose to leave.

"By the way," Claire asked. "Who did write this mortgage?"

Her friend lowered her voice to a whisper.

"Knox's secretary," she said. "Her name's Courtenay, but we all call her Knoxlay behind her back."

Claire felt her face get hot as she considered this new information.

"Where's Knox's office?" she asked.

"It's on the second floor," Amy said, "but you can't go up there without someone using a special key in the elevator."

"Do you have that key?"

Amy grinned and produced it out of her desk drawer.

There was no one in Knox's outer office, and his office door was closed and locked. Claire could hear voices inside, so she pounded on the door.

"Police!" she shouted. "Open up!"

The voices were instantly silent, and then there was the distinct sound of a heavy door swinging shut, a door that needed to have its hinges oiled. A flustered and red-faced Courtenay fumbled with the lock on the office door before she opened it to the outer office.

"Hi Slutney," Claire said. "Bang any of my ex-husbands lately?"

"You!" she said. "What do you want?"

Knox came around from behind his desk, his white face quickly flooding with color.

"What do you think you're doing?" he asked her.

Claire pushed Courtenay aside and didn't stop until she was right up in Knox's face.

"That mortgage your girlfriend wrote for my parents was criminal," she said. "I'm going to file a complaint about it with the Federal Reserve; then I'm going to put an ad in the Sentinel and find out if anyone else in this town has been swindled by your bank. I bet there'll be plenty. We may band together and file a class action suit."

"I said I would fix that," Knox sputtered.

"Oh, it's fixed alright," Claire said. "I just paid it off."

"You what?" he laughed. "I didn't think beauticians made that kind of money. Been selling more than haircuts, Claire?"

Claire reared back and walloped Knox in the jaw, and he fell backward against the desk. She had never hit someone before. She didn't realize how much it could hurt a hand to do so. It felt broken.

"Yeow!" Claire cried and clutched her aching fist while Knox cursed at her.

"Knox!" Courtenay cried. "Your face!"

"Call security!" Knox yelled to Courtenay.

"Better yet, call the police," Claire said.

"Don't call anyone!" Knox shouted to Courtenay. "What is it you want, Claire?"

"I want to know what happened to my friend Tuppy," she said.

Knox was still rubbing his jaw.

"Don't just stand there, you idiot; go get me some ice," he said to Courtenay, who ran out of the office.

"He was already dead in the road when Meredith found him," Knox said. "I thought we'd better stay out of it, considering we're just seven months out from the election. Meredith was so upset by what happened she's experienced a lapse in her sobriety. She left earlier today to admit herself to a private rehabilitation facility, just as a precaution."

"If she didn't hit him, why did you pay Pip's mother to keep quiet about the car?"

"Meredith was so hysterical I had to drive her home. When I returned to retrieve her car, it was gone. I discovered your do-less ex-husband had stolen the car when he tried to blackmail me for its return. His mother was much more reasonable to deal with."

"What did you do with the car?"

"I sold it to a dealer who will break it down into parts and sell it to multiple body shops. Since I reported it stolen it would be very inconvenient for it to be found. There would be questions."

"Why destroy the car if she didn't kill him?"

"When it comes to damage control," Knox said, "I prefer a scorched earth approach."

"What did you do to Pip?"

"I suggested that he might want to leave the country for awhile."

"You didn't kill him."

"I'm ambitious, Claire," Knox said, "but I'm not a monster."

"I'd like to speak with Meredith."

"That's not possible," Knox said. "No one can speak with her."

Something about the way he said this sent a chill down Claire's spine.

"When did she leave?" Claire asked.

"Early this morning," Knox said. "I had someone drive her."

"And she went, just like that, gentle as a lamb."

"She didn't have a choice," Knox said, and the look in his eyes was mercenary. "I've told you everything, Claire. He was dead when she found him. You can call the police and turn me in for leaving the scene of an accident, but in return, it will be very easy for me to implicate you in Pip's car theft and blackmail."

"If neither you nor Meredith killed Tuppy then I don't care what any of you people did or didn't do," Claire said. "As far as I'm concerned our business is concluded."

"Let's bottom-line it," Knox said. "I can give you five figures in cash, but if you want more, we'll have a paper trail to contend with."

"I don't want your money," Claire said. "I want to know who killed Tuppy."

"Then let me share this," Knox said. "There was a dark sedan with New York plates driving around Rose Hill the night your friend died."

"That doesn't help me much."

"I saw the same car parked at the Eldridge Inn this morning," Knox said. "The driver looked like a thug, and the passenger looked like the type that employs thugs."

"Three piece suit?" Claire asked. "Rolex, slicked back hair, and a goatee?"

"That's the one."

Claire met Courtenay coming up the back stairwell as she went down.

"He has a press conference this week," Courtenay said. "How is he going to explain that bruise on his face?"

"He told me what happened," Claire said. "I'm not going to tell the police."

"How much did he pay you?" Courtenay said.

"Nothing," Claire said. "As long as he doesn't try to pin it on Pip or me I'm not going to make trouble for him."

"He had the tar beat out of Pip," Courtenay said. "I bet he didn't tell you that."

"No," Claire said. "What a jerk."

"I told him if he killed Pip I was leaving him, and I meant it. Pip's going to call me every night, and if he misses one call, I'm outta here."

"I didn't realize you cared that much for Pip."

"I love him," Courtenay said. "And the only way to keep him safe is for me to stay with Knox until after the election is over. Then I'm leaving Knox and going to be with Pip. We're going to get married."

"Pip's lucky to have you," Claire said, although she doubted either party was going to feel very lucky after the sexual attraction wore off and Courtenay discovered Pip was already married with a bunch of kids and some very serious money problems.

"He's lucky Knox didn't kill him the night we all got caught," Courtenay said.

Someone opened the door to the stairwell on the floor below.

"You mean when he caught him outside your condo?" Claire said quietly.

"No, stupid," Courtenay said. "When Knox ran over your friend thinking he was Pip."

"Did you see him do that?" Claire asked.

"No," Courtenay said. "Meredith told me."

Courtenay ran up the stairs past Claire, leaving her stunned and speechless.

Claire got back to the salon just in time for her next customer. Despite a swollen hand that hurt like hell she was able to perform the required services but was preoccupied with what Knox and Courtenay had told her. Knox claimed he and Meredith found the body, but Meredith alleged Knox hit Tuppy thinking it was Pip. This didn't make sense. According to Pip, on the night of the accident Meredith left Courtenay's condo first and then Knox left. If that was true, they both must have assumed Pip was still with Courtenay. It made more sense if Meredith was the first to arrive at Tuppy's accident and Knox followed unless Pip lied.

'How can I believe anything any one of them told me?' Claire thought.

A tall, thin, older woman came in, and Claire did a double-take when she saw how this woman was dressed. At first, she thought the woman might be homeless, based on how many tattered tote bags she was carrying and the multiple layers of worn, faded clothing she was wearing. Anticipating a request for a handout Claire opened the cash drawer, thinking she would give her a five dollar bill and send her on the way as kindly as possible.

"Can I help you?" Claire said, glancing outside, expecting to see a shopping cart piled with all the woman's worldly goods.

"Rodefeffer," the woman said, glaring at Claire in an imperious manner through her dirty cat-eye glasses. "Mamie Rodefeffer. I have an appointment."

Now Claire recognized the woman as the oldest living heir to the Rodefeffer Glass fortune, probably the richest woman in town, and Knox's aunt. It had been so many years since Claire had seen Mamie, and she had seemed old then. Claire estimated she must be close to ninety now.

She leaned forward to examine Claire through her thick lenses, which magnified her eyes to an unnaturally large size, and said, "You're not Stephanie."

Claire explained the situation and Mamie said, "I guess I'll have to make do with you. Try not to muck it up."

"I'll do my best," Claire said.

"Your teeth are so white," Mamie said, getting even closer to Claire's face. "Are they your own?"

"Please take a seat in the shampoo chair," Claire said as she backed away. "I'll be right with you."

"I washed it this morning so you can't charge me for a shampoo," Mamie said. "Just wet it with the spray bottle and cut it. I'll set it myself at home."

Mamie was known for her miserly ways; Claire knew her tip would be a quarter at most. Mamie put all her tote bags down and peeled off several layers of cloth coats and cardigans.

Claire wanted to get Mamie to talk about Meredith, but she needed to get there in an indirect way.

"I saw Ann Marie recently," Claire said. "She told me to tell you hello when I saw you."

"That gal doesn't have the brains God gave a goose," Mamie said. "Drank like a fish, liked to sniff the drugs up her nose, plus she chased after anything in long trousers. Knox kept sending her somewhere to dry out, but she would start right back where she left off. She almost died in a car accident, you know; flying down Pine Mountain Road in a snowstorm with no clothes on, probably late for an orgy. She was in a coma and was never right in the head afterward. Knox was well shut of her."

"And then he fell in love with Meredith."

"Hah!" Mamie said. "Fell in love with her family's political connections is more like it."

"Meredith certainly has a nice tea room," Claire ventured.

"She can't wait for me to die," Mamie said. "She'd like to get her hands on my glass collection but she won't. I'm not leaving a single thing to those spoiled brats. I don't cotton to Knox's politics, and Richard can't keep his Johnson in his pants. No, I'm leaving it all to someone who will knock their socks off. I wish I could be there to see their faces when the will is read."

"Does Knox know what's in your will?"

"I told him there was no point in trying to do me in like he did Ann Marie because he wasn't getting a penny. He tried to have me declared incompetent, but the judge laughed him right out of the courtroom. 'I've never met anyone saner in my life,' the judge said. That put the bucket of lard in his place, I'm telling you."

"You don't really think Knox would hurt you," Claire said.

"I wouldn't put it past him," Mamie said. "And I wouldn't turn my back on that new wife of his, either."

"What makes you say that?"

"First her father dies, then her husband dies, and each time she inherited a fortune. So how come she's trying to borrow money from me behind Knox's back? Said all her money was tied up in trust funds. Poppycock! She's going to poison the soup one of these nights, and then Knox will find out just how her husband and father shed their mortal coils. I made sure she knows not one penny will come to her if something happens to me. I'd rather leave everything to the lowest common guttersnipe; in fact, I did."

Mamie cackled like a witch and Claire couldn't help but enjoy her dark sense of humor.

"Does the guttersnipe know?" Claire asked.

"Heavens, no," Mamie said. "I wouldn't trust that floozy as far as I could throw her."

Claire wondered who the lucky heir was. Mamie tipped her a quarter, just as she anticipated.

"Looks like you didn't completely ruin it," she said as she left. "I might even be back in a month."

While Claire's next customer was under the dryer, Hannah came in the shop.

"Sammy's hiding under my mother's house and I can't reach him," Hannah said. "Sam's going to hang around there and wait him out. He'll come out as soon as he's hungry."

"I'm sorry for dragging your whole family into this," Claire said. "After we get that book I swear I won't bother you again."

"Are you kidding? I love this kind of stuff," Hannah said. "It beats catch-and-release possum duty any day."

"It's nice to have a partner in crime," Claire said. "I'd got so used to only having myself to rely on I forgot what it was like to have a trusted friend."

"I'm psyched," Hannah said. "I've always wanted to be part of a vicious gang, but the ones around here are so religious."

"Are you sure you want in on this?" Claire said. "We may be entering dangerous territory."

"Listen," Hannah said. "I once tased the crap out of someone who tried to kill Scott; I'm not afraid of Knox Rodefeffer."

"Mom sent me the newspaper clipping," Claire said. "I was very proud."

"I thought the least they could do was name something after me, like a drinking fountain or something," Hannah said, "or declare that day a holiday, but no. My bravery was not recognized by the mayor or his evil minions."

"It was heroic," Claire said. "You are clearly a fearless force to be reckoned with."

"So spill it," Hannah said.

Claire told Hannah about her adventure at the bank.

"How's your hand?" Hannah asked when she was through.

"It's not broken, but it hurts like hell," Claire said. "I keep running cold water over it to take the swelling down."

"Okay, bruiser," Hannah said. "So either Meredith killed Tuppy or Knox killed him and is going to blame Meredith."

"Meredith may have told Courtenay Knox did it hoping to drive a wedge between them," Claire said.

"I wonder where Meredith is," Hannah said.

"Will you see if you can find out?" Claire said.

"Haven't you heard?" Hannah said. "I'm the Masked Mutt Catcher! I'm sworn to uphold the law whenever it's most convenient."

"The door to the tea room was locked this morning, but the lights were on, and there was a sign up saying she'd be right back. Why would she do that if she knew she was leaving for a long while?"

"She must not have known she was leaving," Hannah said, and then changed her voice to a deep, dramatic timbre, "and death lasts a very long while."

"I'm going to call Anne Marie," Claire said. "Maybe she can pick up on what's going on."

"I'll go up to their house," Hannah said. "I think there may be a possum up there that needs to be captured."

"Be careful," Claire said.

Hannah whipped one of Denise's haircutting capes around her shoulders and stood with her hands on her hips.

"Never fear!" she said. "The Masked Mutt Catcher is here!"

Claire had to wait another hour before she had five minutes to call Anne Marie.

"I'm sorry, Claire," Anne Marie said. "I've caught a horrible cold, and my instrument's gone all wonky. I couldn't do a reading right now if my life depended on it."

"You know Knox better than anyone," Claire said. "If he wanted to do away with Meredith, or quickly hide her somewhere, what would he do?"

"He used to lock me in his office safe," Anne Marie said. "There was this one time I was drunk off my ass, and the parents of this really lovely young tennis player were looking for me ..."

Claire recalled the sound of a creaking hinge she heard just before Courtenay opened the office door.

"Where is the safe hidden?" Claire asked. "I was in there this morning, and I didn't see it."

"There's a bookcase in front of it that's on hinges. You have to push a button under his desk to unlock it, and then it swings outward. I don't have the combination, though."

"Weren't you afraid you'd suffocate in there?" Claire asked.

"Oh, no," Anne Marie said. "It's climate controlled to keep the Cuban cigars fresh. I would just sleep off whatever it was I was on, and eventually, he'd let me out."

Hannah came back to report that none of the staff at Knox's house had seen Meredith since she left for work that morning. She certainly hadn't packed anything or notified anyone she was leaving. Claire told Hannah what Anne Marie had said.

"She's in that safe," Claire said. "I'd bet on it."

"Yeah," Hannah said. "But is she dead or alive?"

Scott was sitting at the kitchen table in the Campbell's farmhouse, negotiating with Sammy while Sam watched with barely concealed amusement.

"You took my pen without giving me anything in trade," Scott said. "I want the keyring Delia gave you."

Sammy was clutching his tin box to his chest, and his cowboy boot-clad feet were dangling from his booster seat. He shook his head vigorously and frowned at Scott.

"I'll trade you something else, then," Scott said. "What do you want?"

"Me no give it," Sammy said. "Delia gives it to me and me never stoled it."

"I know you didn't steal it," Scott said. "I want to trade you for it."

"You gots dollars?"

"I can't give him money for what may be evidence," Scott said to Sam. "Help me out, here."

"I'll give you ten dollars for it," Sam said.

"Shows it to me," Sammy said.

Sam took a ten dollar bill out of his money clip and laid it on the table. Sammy leaned over to look at it.

"That's one, zero," he said. "Me can count twenty."

And he did.

"Well done," Scott said.

"Do we have a trade?" Sam asked.

Sammy grabbed the ten and was scrambling out of the chair when his father caught him by the back of his thermal underwear pants.

"Wait just a minute, son," Sam said.

"Me gotta poop," Sammy said as he swung back and forth through the air, still clutching his tin box.

"Then I'll hold the box for you," Sam said.

"No," Sammy said. "Me gotta poop bad, Daddy."

Sam carried his son into the half bath in the hallway off the kitchen, shut and locked the door. Scott could hear intense negotiations being made between father and son, and eventually, Sam came out holding the tin box.

"He doesn't have it," Sam said.

"What?"

"He traded it to somebody, and he doesn't know that person's name. Somebody he met at Curtis's gas station."

"That could be anyone."

"Sorry," Sam said. "I'll talk to Curtis and see if he remembers."

"You know how important that flash drive is," Scott said. "Claire's friend may have been killed over it."

"Do you think Claire's in any imminent danger?"

"No," Scott said. "Sarah would've liked to have dragged her into it, but now that a movie star's involved she's changed her focus. That movie star's lawyer looks like someone I wouldn't want to tangle with, but you know Sarah."

"Let me know if Claire's in any trouble," Sam said. "Otherwise I'm staying out of it."

"I can take care of Claire," Scott said.

"So I've noticed," Sam said.

Scott left the farm and drove down to City Hall to see the mayor. He wasn't in but his secretary Kay was. Since Kay basically ran the town, she knew more than the mayor did, anyway. Scott told Kay what was going on with his mother.

"I need to know if I can take Family Medical Leave to look after my mother."

"I'm so sorry," Kaye said. "We don't have it. You have to employ 50 or more people in order to be eligible, and we don't employ anywhere near that number."

"Can I use my vacation or sick leave to take care of her?"

"If it were up to me you could," Kay said. "Unfortunately the city's leave policy states that if you're off more than a week, the city has to have someone qualified take charge of the police force. I don't think Frank or Skip have the qualifications the council would require so they'd have to hire someone to do it temporarily. You know the bureaucratic red tape around here. They'd have to call a special session to discuss it and then form a committee to address the situation. It would take them some time to write a job description, post it, and interview candidates; probably eight weeks to get someone hired. And how would the city pay for that?"

"So I'm stuck," Scott said.

"I'm so sorry," Kay said. "Is there anything I can do to help?"

"Quadruple my salary so I can afford around-the-clock care," Scott said. "Her health insurance won't even pay for a decent nursing home. I can barely afford to pay home health care aides to stay eight hours every day, and you know my job is 24-hours a day. My sister's coming over to help, but she has a job and a family she needs to take care of. Sister Mary Margrethe is going to arrange for some sitters, but Mom has to have nursing care. I can't put that responsibility on volunteers."

"I'll call some of my friends and see if we can't find some retired nurses," Kay said. "With your permission, I'd like to share information about your mother's condition with the congregation at my church and see what we can come up with."

"Sure," Scott said. "Go ahead; I would appreciate any help I can get."

"I'll see Sister Mary Margrethe at the Interdenominational Women's Society meeting tonight. Between the two of us, we can muster the town's Catholics and Protestants on your behalf."

"Thank you so much," Scott said. "I don't know how I'll ever repay your kindness."

"It's prepaid every day," Kay said. "Every day when you show up for work and do the right thing on behalf of this town."

"You should run for mayor," Scott said. "I'd campaign for you."

"I've been considering it," Kay said. "I'll let you know."

Hannah had agreed to meet Claire at The Bee Hive after her last customer. Claire was cleaning the salon when she arrived.

"Evidently my precious angel traded the key ring to someone at Dad's station," Hannah said. "Dad doesn't remember seeing it happen but he's going to ask around."

"Well, crap," Claire said. "I need that book."

"What's the plan, Stan?" Hannah asked as she sat down in the hydraulic chair and spun it around a few times. "How are we going to defeat the evil Knox and free the fair Meredith?"

"I've been thinking about this," Claire said. "I think Knox can't move Meredith until after the bank closes at six, which is in fifteen minutes. He has to wait until the staff is gone, which is probably a half hour after that, but has to do it before the cleaning crew arrives. That's a narrow window of opportunity."

"Cleaning starts at seven," Hannah said. "Gail Goodwin works seven to eleven at the bank; everyone knows that. The night security guard lets her in and out."

"Knox will probably have Courtenay distract the security guard," Claire said.

"With her astounding intellect, no doubt."

"Knox will have to take Meredith out the back door to his car in the alley," Claire said and outlined her plan.

"I think it's genius unless that safe turns out to be empty," Hannah said when she finished. "Cause then we'll get arrested and go to jail. I'd hate not to be able to vote against Knox in the upcoming election."

"The only way we're going to find out what happened to Tuppy is if we get Meredith to spill the beans," Claire said. "She's more likely to testify against Knox now that he's shown her what a cad he is by locking her in a safe. If neither of them killed Tuppy, then the worst that happens is some public embarrassment for Knox because they didn't report the accident."

"If they didn't kill him, then who did?" Hannah asked.

Claire didn't want to answer, as she was pretty sure her confidentiality agreement prohibited her from doing so.

Hannah and Claire walked into the bank five minutes before closing time. Claire's old friend Amy was cleaning up her desk. Claire noted that Amy had an uninterrupted view from the front entrance to the elevator.

"Did you see Meredith in here today?" Claire asked her.

"She came in this morning, just after I got here," Amy said. "I had to use my key to let her go up to the second floor.

I didn't see her leave, though. She might have gone out the back way or left while I was at lunch, but it's not like her to stay that long. She hates Courtenay."

"I think Knox has Meredith locked in his office safe," Claire said. "Hannah and I are going to rescue her."

"Are you sure about that?" Amy asked. "I'd hate to rile up Knox for no reason."

"We think she's in there," Hannah said. "I mean, we sure hope she's in there."

"I'm trying to stay out of the limelight, policy-wise," Claire said. "So I'm hoping you'll help us find out if she's in there, and if she is, let her out."

Amy motioned to the security guard to come over, and to Claire's alarmed expression she said, "Don't worry; Roy's my husband."

"Roy, honey," she said when he got to her desk. "Knox has gone and locked up Meredith in his office safe, and these two ladies want to convince him to let her out."

"Not again," Roy said and shook his head. "That man will never learn."

"Could you turn off the security camera pointed at the elevator for a minute?" she asked him. "We don't want anyone to get in any trouble."

Roy smiled and winked at Claire.

"No problem," he said.

Claire thanked her old friend, who just shrugged and said, "It's not the first time this has happened. When Knox was married to Anne Marie he used to lock her up in there once a month, it seemed like."

As soon as her husband gave her the high sign, Amy produced the key from her desk and walked them to the elevator.

"I'm going to give you fifteen minutes, and then Roy'll turn the camera back on," she said. "If you get in trouble you need to leave by the back stairs; the cameras in there are not even hooked up, per Knox's orders. I hope y'all know what you're doing. I've seen some of the people Knox meets with, and let me tell you, he's not someone you want mad at you."

Hannah looked at Claire with wide eyes, but Claire was resolved. Her friend turned the key and pressed "2."

"Good luck," Amy said.

Courtenay was at her desk and rolled her eyes when Claire and Hannah came in her office.

"What now?" she said. "Knox isn't here."

"We know Meredith is in the safe," Claire said and was rewarded with the astonishment and guilt that overtook Courtenay's expression.

"I don't know what you're talking about," Courtenay said, but she choked on her words.

"The police are on their way," Claire said. "If you let Meredith out before they get here you won't be arrested as his accessory."

"I didn't have anything to do with it," Courtenay said. "All I did was lock the door to the office."

"That's, um, exactly what an accessory does," Hannah said. "Assists the criminal in the commission of a crime."

Courtenay quickly stood up and was looking toward the door to the stairs as if she was about to make her escape.

"Help us rescue Meredith," Claire said. "You'll be a hero, then."

"Meredith hates me," Courtenay said, "and Knox will kill me."

"Knox couldn't have hit Tuppy, thinking it was Pip," Claire said. "Knox was the one who boosted Pip back up to your bedroom window. He knew Pip was still in there with you when he left."

Courtenay tilted her head to the side just like Mackie Pea did when she didn't understand something Claire said.

"Meredith just wanted to make you hate Knox," Claire said. "She wanted you to leave Knox for Pip. She knew you were in love with Pip because she planned it. She paid him to seduce you."

"You're just jealous," Courtenay said. "Pip would never do that. He loves me."

"The police are on their way," Claire said. "You don't have time to escape, but you do have time to save yourself and Meredith. Then you'll be free to be with Pip."

Courtenay seemed paralyzed with indecision.

"Wait a minute," Courtenay said. "I need to think."

"I can smell the dust burning," Hannah said, and Claire elbowed her.

"Give me the combination," Claire said, "and I'll open the safe and tell the police you helped."

Courtenay unlocked her desk drawer, took a card out of her Rolodex, and handed it to Claire. It had a series of numbers on it but nothing else. Courtenay relocked the drawer and started gathering up her things.

"How do we know this is the correct combination?" Hannah said.

"I'm outta here," Courtenay said. "You're on your own."

"Don't let her leave," Claire said as she raced into Knox's office.

"Get out of my way!" she heard Courtenay say.

"Oh, no you don't," Hannah said, and Claire could hear sounds of a tussle.

Claire pulled the desk chair away from Knox's desk and looked underneath. There were three buttons: one red, one blue and one black.

"Great," Claire said. "Which one is which?"

She hesitated a moment before she chose the blue one, surmising red must be for security. She pressed blue and watched the bookcases. Nothing happened, but she could hear the door to Knox's office lock. She pressed it again and the door unlocked. She then pressed the black button, and an ear-splitting alarm went off.

"Crap!" she yelled and pressed the red button.

The bookcase behind Knox's desk clicked and swung outward about two inches. She pulled hard on it, not realizing how well-calibrated the balance was, so it swung back against the wall with a thump and many of the books fell out. It also made the same creaking noise she had heard earlier from outside the office. Behind the bookcase was a small vestibule and a huge walk-in safe with a digital keypad. The alarm was blaring, but she could still hear Hannah and Courtenay yelling at each other. Her hands were shaking as she held up the Rolodex card in the dim light and punched in the code. Nothing happened.

"Holy crap," Claire said as she pictured herself trying to explain to Tiny Crimefighter why she had punched the bank president and attempted to break into his safe.

Just then the mechanism clicked, and the handle turned. As Claire gripped the handle and pulled it, she heard something behind her. She looked around and ducked just in time to avoid being hit with the golf club Knox Rodefeffer was wielding. His face was blood red and veins were bulging in his forehead. He swore and swung again, just missing her as she jumped backward. The door to the vault swung open so hard it knocked Claire off her feet. Meredith came out swinging what looked like a collectible coin case, and she clocked Knox upside the head with it. As he went down Meredith started screaming like a crazy woman and continued hitting him over and over with the coin box.

"Meredith!" Claire screamed, and Meredith turned on her with crazed eyes and bared teeth.

"You!" she screamed and raised the coin box as Claire watched in horror.

"Don't kill me!" Claire yelled over the loud alarm. "I'm the one who rescued you!"

Meredith paused and looked Claire in the eyes; at that moment she seemed to come to her senses. She dropped the box and slumped to the floor. Claire glanced at

Knox, who seemed to be down for the count but was still breathing. She could hear Courtenay screaming in the outer office, but Hannah was strangely silent. Claire knelt down next to Meredith, who was crying so hard she was gasping.

"Did you hit my friend Tuppy?" Claire asked her.

Meredith looked up.

"What?" she asked. "Who?"

"My friend Tuppy was in the street that night you left Courtenay's," Claire said. "Was he already dead or did you hit him?"

Meredith shook her head, crying pitifully.

"Is that what he told you?" she wailed. "It's a lie. That poor man; I told Knox we should call the police ..."

"Did Knox do it?" Claire asked her. "I need to know, Meredith. Tuppy was my friend."

"There was no pulse," she said. "He was already dead when I found him. Knox came afterward. Knox wouldn't let me call the police. He said it would cause a scandal. We should have called! Now look at us ..."

She dissolved into tears again, and Claire felt like she had just heard the truth.

Claire stood up, stepped around Meredith, over Knox, and ran to the outer office, where Hannah was sitting on top of Courtenay, who was lying face down while Hannah held her arms behind her back.

"Get off!" Courtenay shrieked, but Hannah just grinned at Claire.

"She's feisty," Hannah said. "Plus she bites."

"C'mon," yelled Claire, and ran for the back stairs.

Hannah jumped up and followed. In the stairwell the alarm wasn't nearly as loud, so as Claire and Hannah hit the landing after the first flight they could hear Courtenay panting and running close behind, her high heels tapping on the metal stairs. Just before the door to the stairwell on the second floor closed behind her, they heard the ding of the elevator arriving on the second floor.

"Go, go, go!" Courtenay said. "That will be the police!"

"Won't the alarm go off if we open the back door?" Claire said when they reached the main floor.

"The alarm is already going off, you big dummy!" Courtenay said. "It's the same one!"

They reached the back door, flung it open, clambered down the back steps, and then ran down the alley to the back door of Little Bear Books, to which Hannah had a key. Courtenay tried to follow them through the door.

"Why should we help you?" Hannah said, barring her way.

"I'm your witness, and you're mine," Courtenay said. "If anyone asks me we've been in here since I got off work at six."

"I owe you an apology," Claire said. "You're smarter than you look."

Once inside the bookstore, Hannah pulled Claire along to the café and pushed her into a chair. Courtenay flung herself down in a chair at the same table and yelled, "Service! Service here, please!"

"That's enough of that," Maggie said, from behind the café counter. "What are you three up to?"

"Establishing an alibi," Hannah said.

Maggie shrugged.

"You better be prepared to spend some money, then," Maggie said. "Alibis don't come cheap in here."

Peony Street by Pamela Grandstaff

Chapter Eight - Wednesday

The next morning Claire was sweeping up the hair from her third customer when Hannah came in The Bee Hive.

"Sweet, sassy molasses!" Hannah said. "I've got gossip so juicy I feel like I'm gonna pop."

"Come in, come in," Claire said. "I've been dying to know what happened after we left the bank but I'm scared to ask anyone."

"Our dear friend Meredith is now residing in a very exclusive mental health facility in Maryland," she said. "And that's just part of my story, morning glory."

"Why don't you let me cut your hair while you tell me about it?"

"And cheat on my nail scissors? I wouldn't think of it."

"If you want me to listen you have to let me cut your hair," Claire said.

Hannah took off her baseball cap and let Claire wash her hair.

Hannah was a small, thin person with mouse brown hair. She had a prominent nose, and her small hazel eyes were a little too close together. Claire reflected that plastic surgery would only destroy the features that made Hannah so distinctly herself. A character actress wouldn't profit from looking like every ingénue off the bus from the Midwest. Hannah was better cast as the wise-cracking sidekick, the comic relief who often stole the movie from the lead actors.

"Spill it," Claire said. "Tell me everything."

"The bank alarm is connected to our humble police station, in which Tiny Crimefighter just happened to be using the litter box when it went off. Lucky for us she had to resort to Sir Skipsalot for backup; he saw everything, and he couldn't keep his mouth shut to save his life."

"My dad says he doesn't have a lick of sense," Claire said.

"Picture it with me now," Hannah said. "The crime-fighting kitten rushed into the bank with her back arched, and her tail frizzed, expecting to thwart a bank robbery, only to find Meredith sitting in Knox's office having a nervous breakdown and Knox out cold on the floor."

"She knew she'd better handle the situation with kid gloves," Claire said. "Knox has a lot of power around here."

"Exactly," Hannah said. "While they waited for the ambulance Sarah called her boss, who told her to take Meredith to the hospital for a psych evaluation while Knox had his fat head examined."

"If you had seen how she was going to town on him," Claire said. "You'd be surprised he's still alive."

"Skip says he has a concussion and looks like he's been beaten all to hell, but he's going to be okay. When Knox came out of it, he refused to press charges, saying that Meredith had a complete mental breakdown and couldn't be responsible for her actions."

"That's actually kind of true."

"So the hospital says, yes, she's definitely got monkeys missing from her barrel, so Miss Meredith is being transported to the Trembling Hands Home for Wealthy Psychopaths over in Maryland."

"And there was no mention of the three witnesses who were allegedly sipping cappuccinos at Little Bear Books when all this went down?"

"Why would he rat us out? We could only make things more uncomfortable for him with Detective Fuss-in-Boots."

"That's one I hadn't heard."

"I just made it up, and I love it. I'm keeping it in the rotation."

"So that's that," Claire said. "We're so lucky; when I think about what would have happened if Meredith had not been in that safe ..."

"I haven't even told you the juiciest part, yet," Hannah said. "Evidently Meredith told Skip and Sarah that she not only killed her father and her first husband but that she also intended to kill Knox."

"Mamie was right!" Claire said. "Those must be the two murders Anne Marie saw in her vision."

"She overdosed them with their medication and got away with it."

"But why would she tell it now?"

"I guess being locked up in Knox's safe all day freaked her out so much she went bat-poop bonkers and lost her ability to lie. On the way to the hospital, she told Sarah and Skippy about finding your friend's body and Knox not letting her call the police. She also told them that she married Knox because she lost all her family money in a Ponzi scheme and couldn't get her hands on her son's trust money. When Knox found out she was broke, he canceled her credit cards and cut off her funds. Tony Delvecchio told Frank Meredith recently took out a multi-million dollar life insurance policy on Knox."

"She told Sarah all that?"

Hannah made the cuckoo sign with her finger circling the air next to her head.

"I'm telling you Skip said this stuff was pouring out of her as fast as she could tell it," Hannah said. "Sarah kept repeating her Miranda Rights, but Meredith wouldn't stop talking. Of course, Knox's lawyer is claiming she wasn't competent enough to be questioned. They're going to say it was all inadmissible because she's just been crowned Miss Crackaloop Crazypants."

As Hannah brought her up-to-date Claire shaped her unevenly cut mop of fine hair. It was a challenge to take such a randomly butchered coif and turn it into art, but Claire did her best. What she really wanted to do was highlight it to look like Sammy's, but she knew Hannah would just pull it back in a ponytail and slap her hat back over it as soon as she was done.

"What about Courtenay?" Claire asked.

"Our fair Courtenay is now free to join King Pipster in the kingdom of Pipsalot."

"Pip's a one-trick pony; all he has to do is bat those long eyelashes, cry like a baby and feel sorry for himself," Claire said, "and the women line up to save him."

"If he cried in the self-pity Olympics," Hannah said, "he'd win gold."

"I'm hoping his mother doesn't come looking for me today," Claire said. "She's liable to pitch a fit as soon as she finds out where he is."

"What are we going to do now?" Hannah said. "How will we find out who killed your friend?"

"I was all for believing Knox or Meredith killed Tuppy until yesterday. Now I think Tuppy must have had something on Sloan, something really bad or she wouldn't have brought her thugs here."

"You think Sloan had someone kill him?"

"Everybody who was there that night lied about something, but each person also told me something true; I just have to sort it all out."

Maggie came through the door.

"I worked your mother's shift at my mother's bakery and lived to tell about it," she said.

"Thank you," Claire said.

"I'm headed up to the Inn after lunch to cover Delia's shift," Hannah said. "You want me to sneak up to the second floor and spy on Sloan?"

"Better not," Claire said. "These are not friendly people, and Stanley is probably armed."

"Your hair looks better," Maggie said to Hannah.

"We always look better after Claire's been home a week," Hannah said.

Hannah left without putting on her ball cap, and Claire was touched.

Maggie sat down in the hydraulic chair and spun around a few times, just like Hannah had.

"Your dad's at the service station," Maggie said. "Uncle Curtis will take him over to the bar at lunchtime."

"I don't know what I'd do without you guys," Claire said.

"We're your family," Maggie said. "This is what we do. When one cog in the Fitzpatrick fun machine breaks down, another cog fills in."

"Your mom doesn't seem to be slowing down or falling apart," Claire said.

"If you don't have a heart it can't be attacked," Maggie said. "Plus she's too mean for germs to live on her very long."

"I only worked there Monday morning, and I'm still sore."

"Is that how you hurt your hand?"

"Yeah, let's say that."

"So I guess you won't be volunteering to take over the bakery when Mom retires," Maggie said.

"No way," Claire said. "Are you?"

"No, thank you. When that old lady finally lays down her rolling pin the business will be sold or closed."

"How's your dad?"

"Come see him this evening. He's been asking about you."

"When's a good time?"

"Call first," Maggie said. "That way if he's too drunk or passed out you won't waste your time."

"Still done with doctors?"

"Oh, yes," Maggie said. "He hasn't changed his mind about that. His back is still so screwed up he can barely walk.

After Grandpa Tim and Brian died, he gave up hiding the booze. Now he and my mother live under the same roof but never speak a word to each other. It makes family dinners so much fun."

"If he can't get around how does he get the alcohol?"

"Doc gives him the pills and Patrick gives him the booze. When he finally has too much of both and keels over, they'll have to share the blame."

"Everything's so depressing today," Claire said. "Let's flat iron your hair."

"I was hoping you'd offer," Maggie said. "It hasn't been done since the last time you were home."

When Maggie lay back in the shampoo chair, her unruly red hair filled and exceeded the capacity of the bowl. Claire wet it with the sprayer, and it instantly deflated. Claire washed it, deep-conditioned it, rinsed it, and then treated it with an anti-frizzing serum before leading Maggie back to the hydraulic chair. Clair pumped the chair up as high as it would go and started detangling the matted mess from the bottom, using a wide tooth comb.

"Where's your little dog?" Maggie said. "I heard it's really cute."

"Skippy's mom has it," Claire said. "She's like my daycare now. She's knitting Mackie a little sweater that I'm terribly afraid she will be forced to wear home today."

"Ouch, Claire," Maggie said. "You're pulling too hard."

"You'd think that when God gives you hair like this you'd get a tougher scalp to go with it," Claire said. "Once I get it detangled I'm going to trim it just a little before I blow dry it. You're going to be here at least an hour, so start at the beginning and don't leave anything out. The last time I saw you, Scott was still chasing you around, and Gabe hadn't come back."

Maggie got her caught up on the events of the past few years while Claire detangled her hair and then pinned it up in sections so she could blow dry the underneath first, using a large flat paddle brush. She had the flat iron heating up on the counter.

"So after Grandpa Tim died and Brian got killed Gabe disappeared again," Maggie said half an hour later. "That was three years ago."

"You think Gabe had something to do with Brian's death?"

"No," Maggie said. "The feds let Gabe out of prison early so he could testify against the drug dealer we think killed Brian. One of the drug dealer's thugs kidnapped Gabe and Scott and tried to drown them in the river. Gabe escaped, and Scott got rescued, but I'm not entirely sure which one of them killed the thug. Gabe disappeared right after that, and no one has seen him since."

"I always thought Gabe was such a nice guy," Claire said. "I can't believe he did all those things."

"He had us all fooled."

"I hate it when someone doesn't live up to my expectations," Claire said. "But it seems to happen all the time, so maybe it's my fault for having unrealistic expectations in the first place."

"I lived with him for three years, and I had no idea Gabe was a drug-dealing ex-con," Maggie said. "Even after I knew he was a liar and a criminal, I still believed he loved me; for a little while, at least."

"The heart is not the best judge of character," Claire said and looked Maggie in the eye in the mirror.

"No," Maggie said, meeting her gaze. "It's not."

"So what about Scott?"

Maggie shrugged.

"C'mon," Claire said. "It's me you're talking to. We don't have any secrets."

"I hear you've been spending a lot of time with Scott," Maggie said. "Any secrets you'd care to share?"

"He's been a lifesaver and a great friend," Claire said, "but that's all."

"He's always there when you need him," Maggie said. "He's the best man I know."

"So why aren't you with him?" Claire said. "He'd take you back today if you'd let him."

"Sometimes," Maggie said, "you can put someone through too much. Sometimes the kindest thing you can do for someone you love is to let them go."

"You're wrong about that," Claire said. "He doesn't want to be let go."

"I've burned that bridge," Maggie said. "Trust me on that."

"And Scott thinks he's to blame," Claire said. "Clearly y'all need to talk."

"I've moved on," Maggie said.

"To the professor that Hannah keeps talking about?"

"He's just a friend," Maggie said. "Just like you and Scott."

Claire didn't meet Maggie's gaze in the mirror.

"Look how long your hair is when it's straight," Claire said. "It looks about a third as thick, too."

"It's just too much hair, isn't it? Be honest with me."

"I think we should take off some more length but not do anything drastic."

"Let's cut it," Maggie said. "Let's cut it all off."

"I'll buy it from you," Sloan said from the doorway.

Maggie and Claire were startled, not having heard the door open.

"How much do you want for it?" Sloan asked Maggie.

Sloan hadn't made a movie star entrance, and in her casual clothes, she looked just like the well-heeled tourists who swarmed Pine Mountain. Maggie didn't seem to recognize her, and Claire could tell from her cousin's bored expression that she wasn't impressed.

"Tourists," her look seemed to say, "are so tiresome."

"It's not for sale," Maggie said, and Claire felt a frisson of apprehension at how Sloan might react to Maggie's blunt refusal. No one talked to Sloan Merryweather like that and got away with it.

Before she could react, Sam and Hannah came in, holding hands with Sammy between them. As soon as Hannah saw Sloan, her eyes widened, and she dropped Sammy's hand.

"Sloan Merryweather!" she said. "Can I have your autograph?"

Sloan smiled.

"Of course you can; how sweet of you to ask."

"Who?" Maggie said.

Sloan gave Maggie a seriously cutting side eye that no one but Claire seemed to notice.

"Sloan Merryweather," Hannah said to Maggie. "She was in Tweethearts and that remake of All About Eve called Bumpy Night. You know, Sloan Merryweather."

Maggie rolled her eyes at Claire. Sloan took a sticky note off the front counter and used a pen attached to a chain there to write something. She then handed the note to Hannah. She then wrote on another note and handed it to Maggie.

"I'm not really an autograph collector," Maggie said.

"That's what I'm prepared to pay for your hair," Sloan said. "It's for a cancer charity I represent. They make wigs for kids who lose their hair from chemo treatments."

"She's not interested," Claire said.

"You'd pay me that much?" Maggie said. "That's more than my store nets in a year."

"What business is that?" asked Sloan. "I'm thinking of investing in this area."

"It's the bookstore down the street," Maggie said.

"It's not for sale," Claire hastened to add.

"Everything's for sale," Sloan said quietly while looking at Claire.

Claire introduced Sammy to Sloan. Sammy stuck his tongue out at her, but Sloan's eyes were on Sam. She was looking him up and down in an appraising manner.

"These are my friends Sam and Hannah Campbell," Claire said, "and here comes Scott."

Scott walked in and pretended to try to catch Sammy, who scurried around behind his father.

"Sam Campbell," Sloan said. "Isn't this the guy you went skinny dipping with in high school?"

Claire felt all the air go out of her lungs and couldn't remember how to inhale. Of all the personal details about her life that Claire had been unwise enough to share with Sloan, who could not have cared less, this was the one tidbit she chose to remember.

"What?!" Hannah said, and Claire could clearly see how vulnerable she was to what Sloane was about to dish out. It would be like kicking a puppy, cruelty of which Mackie Pea knew Sloane was perfectly capable.

Before Claire could think of how to respond, Scott did.

"No, that was me," he said.

"What?!" Maggie said, but the look she gave Claire was more pissed off pit bull than a kicked puppy.

"Didn't I ever tell you about that?" Scott said to Maggie. "Patrick and Sam went to a keg party at Fitz's hunting cabin and ditched Claire and me out at the lake. We drank all the beer in Theo's boathouse."

"Claire?" Maggie said.

"Claire?" Hannah said.

Claire was picturing her name being added to the top of the dry erase board of shame in Maggie's bookstore. She'd be banned for life.

"Remember how cold the water was?" Scott asked Claire.

"Sure," Claire said, while intentionally avoiding everyone's eyes.

"Unfortunately it was too dark to see anything," Scott said. "Claire told me if I touched her she would kill me."

"Holy Hottentots!" Hannah said. "How did you keep that a secret?"

"Where was Ed?" Maggie asked Scott. "You two were always joined at the hip."

"That was the summer Brad drowned," Scott said, and Claire was impressed with how smoothly he embellished his lie. "Ed wasn't allowed out at the lake after that."

Maggie stood up and pulled on her jacket.

"How much do I owe you?" she asked Claire in an icy tone.

"On the house," Claire said.

"Oh dear," Sloane said. "Did I say something I shouldn't have?"

"It was no big deal," Claire said. "Just a late night swim with a friend."

"I was kind of disappointed," Scott said, "at the time."

Maggie left in a huff with Scott on her heels, and Sloane looked smugly satisfied.

"You just love creating the drama, don't you?" Claire said to her. "You just have to stir things up and try to make a fool out of me."

Sloane shrugged and tried to look innocent.

"I don't know what you're talking about," she said.

"You're not that great of an actress," Claire said.

"I think the Academy of Arts and Sciences might disagree with you on that point," Sloane said. "And as far as making a fool of you, that's Carlyle's forte, not mine."

"Hey," Hannah said. "That's my cousin you're talking to. Watch your mouth."

Sloan turned on Hannah before Claire could intervene.

"Looks like Claire took all the pretty DNA and left you with the rest."

"Stop it," Claire said. "I won't let you do this to my family."

"Don't stop her! This is better than a movie," Hannah said. "I wish I had some popcorn."

"C'mon," Sam said, hoisting the squirmy Sammy a little higher in his arms. "Let's get Junior home and put him down for a nap."

"I'm not ready to go," Hannah said. "I wanna see what she looks like when she's really mad, not just pretending to be mad. Her face is so jacked up I can't tell what she's actually feeling. Isn't that important for an actress, Sloan, to be able to demonstrate emotions?"

"C'mon, hon," Sam said to Hannah and made the briefest eye contact with Claire. There was relief in his eyes.

"So nice to meet you, Sam," Sloane said, "And your wife, Anna, of course."

"I know you know my name's Hannah," Hannah said. "But I don't even mind the insult, coming from you. You're just as pretty as you were in that movie where you played the prostitute. I was sorry to hear your husband was carrying on with the actress who played your daughter. I guess all the money and fame in the world are no guarantee you'll be happy."

Sloane's face turned beet red, and Sam tugged Hannah's arm to get her to follow him out.

"What do I always tell you about torturing the tourists?" Sam said to his wife. "It doesn't keep them from coming back; it just irritates them."

"I'd like to know what in the world your handsome husband sees in you," Sloane said to Hannah. "You're not even ugly in an interesting way. You're just plain forgettable."

"Alright, that's enough," Sam said, but Hannah just laughed in Sloane's face.

"You're just gonna keep getting older, lady," Hannah said. "Don't you ever forget that."

Sammy stuck his tongue out at Sloane over his father's shoulder. Hannah was still holding the post-it note with Sloan's signature on it, and she waved it goodbye to them as they went out.

"What horribly ordinary people," Sloan said. "I don't know how you can stand being associated with such boring nobodies."

"What are you doing here?"

"What are you wearing, Claire?" Sloan said. "You look like a teamster."

"What do you want?"

"Stanley didn't want me to come," Sloan said. "But I wanted to see you, to warn you in person."

"About what?"

"What might happen if you accuse me of arranging Tuppy's accident."

"Did you?"

"Of course not."

"Then why worry?"

"It's not the kind of press I need right now," Sloan said. "The focus needs to be on my engagement to Carlyle, the film being released in October, and then the Oscar campaign."

"By all means," Claire said. "Let's remember what's really important."

"Don't be ugly, Claire," Sloan said. "It's not your style, and you can't win. I've got more money and better lawyers."

"And no conscience."

"If I did send someone to rough up Tuppy and he died as a result, why would I then come here and put myself right in the middle of the investigation? That would be pretty stupid, wouldn't it?"

"I've asked myself that," Claire said. "And you know what? I think you'd do it just for kicks; because you get off on the risk and the drama; because you really believe you can get away with anything. And why not? You always have."

"Don't be ridiculous," Sloan said. "You have an overactive imagination. Lucky for me I have a signed confidentiality agreement with your name on it. I could confess anything to you, and there's nothing you could do about it."

"Go away, Sloan," Claire said. "There's no way in hell I'm coming back to work for you."

Sloan just pretended she didn't hear Claire as she checked herself out in the wall of mirrors behind the styling stations, turning this way and that.

"Ayelet wants me to adopt an orphan to be delivered between Thanksgiving and Christmas. Either that or pretend to be pregnant and hire someone else to actually carry the brat."

"But you don't like children."

"I won't have to spend much time with it," Sloan said. "What do you think of 'Always' as a name? That's what Ayelet suggests."

"Why not Artichoke or Asparagus?" Claire said. "If you're going to be silly about it."

"That would be asinine," Sloan said. "Everyone knows when it comes to baby names you choose fruits, not vegetables."

"You couldn't even take care of that dog," Claire said. "You'll have to hire three nannies to raise one child. There's a lot that can go wrong, you know. It's easier to get rid of a dog than a child."

"What's that supposed to mean?"

"I wasn't referring to anything."

"You can't talk about that."

"Don't worry, Sloan," Claire said. "I will abide by my confidentiality agreement."

"Stanley wants the book Tuppy was writing," Sloan said. "We know Tuppy gave it to you."

"I don't have it," Claire said. "He said he left it here for me, but I can't find it."

"I wouldn't want anything to happen to you," Sloan said. "Stanley is very impatient to have this taken care of."

"If I had it I would gladly hand it over to you or your flying monkey."

"Your life with me wasn't so bad," Sloan said. "We had some good times."

"Your idea of a good time usually led to my idea of a bad time," Claire said.

"When we lived in Brentwood you had your own guest house and a pool."

"Paid for by a porn producer with an expensive drug habit; the dealers and porn stars were always fighting outside my bedroom window at three a.m."

"There's no drama like hopped-up hooker drama, that's true."

"Consider what went on in that pool," Claire said. "I never swam in it."

"I helped you get that condo in Malibu."

"You forged my name on a mortgage so your boyfriend would get the commission. Then I caught you having sex with my husband in our bedroom."

"Dear old Pip, the delicious dimwit. He owes me quite a bit of money, you know. Whatever happened to him?"

"I don't know, and I don't care."

Sloan wandered around the salon, picking up things, pretending to examine them, and then setting them back down. It was a piece of business she'd learned while acting in a Broadway play. It had upstaged and enraged the lead actor, but she got away with it because she was sleeping with the producer.

"What about the two months we spent in Paris?" Sloan asked.

"You tormented the director until he had a nervous breakdown," Claire said.

"Jean-Marc," Sloan said. "A rank amateur, thinking he could tell me how to play Collette."

"It was horrible to watch the way you tortured him."

"But the city, you have to admit, was fabulous."

"You stayed at the George V; I shared one bathroom of a moldy rental with nine alcoholic crew members who didn't value personal hygiene."

"What about the time we spent in Vancouver shooting Tweetheart?"

"You used the makeup and hair trailer to have an affair with your married costar while I stood outside and kept everyone out."

"Mmm, Clifford," she said. "He has such wonderful hands."

"And a jealous wife; there are still fundraisers you aren't invited to because of that affair."

"She gets all the muscle disease kids, and I'm stuck with the bald ones; they're not nearly as cute in commercials."

"It could be worse; they could find a cure, and then you'd have no sick kids to pimp for P.R."

"I'm overlooking your sarcasm, but I can still recognize it."

"I can say anything I like; I don't work for you anymore," Claire said. "I tried to leave on good terms, but obviously that's impossible."

"I know you enjoyed Scotland."

"Until you stole my boyfriend."

"You made out all right," Sloan said. "There isn't another personal assistant or hair stylist in the business that has made more money than you."

"I'm thankful for all the money," Claire said. "But silly me, I thought when I quit working for you I could start a new life without you in it."

"Here?"

"Yes, here," Claire said. "My family is here, and they need me."

"You're too spoiled. You'll miss our life."

"I want a simpler life."

"There is no simple life," Sloan said. "That's just a gimmick they use to sell lifestyle magazines and overpriced shacks in the Hamptons. Take a month off, get this delusion out of your system, and then come back to work for me."

"Your world is the fake one," Claire said. "I have roots here; I belong here."

"No, you don't. You're like me now," Sloan said. "Don't you know you can never go back? People like us don't belong anywhere but on the road or on the stage. We weren't meant to settle down; if we stop dancing, we'll die."

"I helped you learn that dialogue," Claire said. "I seem to remember one theater critic said you chewed the scenery like a cow in clover."

"Every show was sold out for the entire run on Broadway," Sloan said, "and that critic is fat and bald."

"Other people can perform the same service I do," Claire said. "Just hire someone, already. I'll train them if you want."

"I need you, Claire. Look at me; I'm a wreck. I have two editorial shoots and three covers coming up. I may have to do re-shoots on Mary next month."

"I'll do it for you here if you want, but I'm not going anywhere with you."

"I can't do it here. It's not safe."

"It will be fine," Claire said. "Come back after six, and I'll close the curtains, lock the door, and we'll take care of business."

"I'll pay you."

"It's on the house," Claire said.

"What's the catch?"

"You have to let me go afterward," Claire said.

Sloan considered Claire for several seconds.

"I'll be back," she said.

Claire felt like she'd been holding her breath the whole time Sloan was in the salon. She watched her walk to the curb and get into the back seat of Stanley's long, dark car. The driver was someone Claire hadn't seen before. He was big with that menacing look Stanley seemed to favor. Claire wondered if he had killed Tuppy.

Scott had followed Maggie out of The Bee Hive and ran to catch up.

"Maggie," he said. "Talk to me."

Maggie stopped in her tracks, turned around, and walked back toward him with such menace that he started to back up, with his hands outstretched.

"Now, wait a minute," he said. "You and I were not boyfriend and girlfriend in high school."

"No," Maggie said. "It's not that you swam naked with my cousin Claire back when we were teenagers. It's not that I've heard all week about how cozy the two of you have become since she came back. It's that I'm still finding out things that you've kept a secret from me. I don't know why I'm still surprised and disappointed, but I am."

"I'm sorry," Scott said. "For the millionth time and for everything I ever did wrong; I apologize."

"It doesn't matter," Maggie said and turned to go.

"Except it does, doesn't it?" Scott said to her retreating back. "It still matters because you still care. You're jealous because deep down, you know I should be with you."

Maggie just kept walking away, and Scott was immediately aware of all the people on the street who had stopped whatever they were doing to watch their fight. A couple of college students walked by, and one of the young men shook his head as he said, "Bitches," as if in sympathy.

"Watch your language," Scott said to the boy, but his heart wasn't in it.

Scott wasn't looking forward to his next assignment. He walked up Pine Mountain Road, also known as County Route 2, to the Rose Hill Bed and Breakfast.

The B&B was a large, ornate Victorian with white gingerbread trim and a round turret that rose past three floors at one corner. Inside the vestibule, Scott could smell something delicious baking in the kitchen. No one was sitting at the front desk, which was an elegant table in the front parlor, so he walked back past the stairs through a narrow corridor to the kitchen. He took a deep breath and steeled himself before he saw Ava.

Ava Fitzpatrick had won the genetic lottery when it came to beauty and grace. In a small town full of ordinary people she stood out like a movie star, even though she played down her looks with plain clothes and little makeup. Her dark hair and dark eyes were set off by a knee-weakening bright smile, and her figure reminded Scott of a dancer's. She seemed fragile, but in fact, Ava was one of the most resilient people he had ever met.

Ava's late husband Brian was Maggie's oldest brother. He abandoned Ava when their children were small, disappearing around the same time as Maggie's boyfriend Gabe. It turned out that they went on a drug run together, and when their car crashed Brian escaped, but Gabe ended up in prison. Brian returned, years later, after he heard that Ava had received a generous bequest from Theo Eldridge.

Brian created havoc in Ava's life by bringing her into contact with a ruthless drug lord. He got arrested, escaped, and then died all in the space of a couple months. He also left behind a child from a bigamous marriage to a woman he murdered for her money.

Scott had offered his support and a shoulder to lean on during this time in Ava's life, and a crush from which he had suffered since his teenage years had blossomed into an infatuation. Encouraged by Ava to think his feelings might be returned, he had allowed himself to be drawn into her life after Brian died and Maggie rejected him.

Ava was glad enough to let Scott be of service to her and the children and to do all he could to protect her reputation, which had been damaged by her husband's many crimes. He quickly realized, however, that Ava's affection, although warm and seemingly sincere, was more a method of self-preservation than a genuine interest in any kind of relationship. Ava had built a fortress around her family, and Scott learned that while any man might be allowed to serve the queen, he should never kid himself that he belonged in the palace alongside her.

Ava was sitting at the kitchen island, sipping coffee and reading the newspaper. The bakery smell was most intense in here, and Scott could see a cooling rack full of muffins on the kitchen counter. When Ava looked up, there was a moment's wariness in her eyes before she warmly welcomed him.

"It's so good to see you," she said and invited him to sit with her and have a muffin and a cup of coffee.

Scott was strong, but he wasn't made of steel. He accepted both but sat on the opposite side of the island from her.

"How are the kids?" he asked her.

"Charlotte's enjoying the consolidated school, which surprised me," she said. "She was always such a bookworm, but when she turned fifteen, suddenly it was all about boys and makeup."

"She's a beautiful girl," Scott said, but didn't add, "just like her mother."

Charlotte was the spitting image of Ava when she was a teenager, with the same dark hair and eyes. Scott thought she probably had boys following her around much like Ava had, fighting over who got to carry her books.

"She's glued to her phone," Ava said. "I told her as long as her grades stay up she can keep it; but the minute they drop, it's gone."

"How's Timmy?"

"He'll be nine this month," she said. "You know Hatch, who works at the service station? He's raising his sister's son Joshua; Joshie and Timmy have become inseparable. You never see one without the other."

Scott knew the town gossip was that Joshua had been fathered by Ava's late husband as well; he and Timmy looked like red-headed, freckled twins.

"Little Fitz is almost four," Ava said. "He goes to daycare at Sacred Heart. He's my little sweetheart; just loves to be cuddled."

Little Fitz was the baby Ava's husband had abandoned when he came back after all those years. Ava had adopted him and treated him just like one of her own. He also had red hair and freckles.

"How are you doing?" Scott asked, even though he really didn't want to be taken into her confidence anymore. It wasn't safe there; he didn't trust himself not to become intoxicated and lose his way.

"I'm fine," she said, and to his relief, he could tell she wasn't going to be any more forthcoming.

"Did Patrick tell you I would be coming to talk to you?" he asked.

"He did," she said. "He came here right after the Thorn closed and he stayed until five in the morning."

"Alright, then," he said. "That's all I needed to know."

Patrick had fallen into the same trap Scott had, but much longer ago, right after his brother Brian left Ava. They broke up after Theo was killed because Patrick was a suspect and Ava didn't want their relationship to be seen as a possible motive. Scott hadn't realized they were seeing each other again until Patrick admitted it when questioned about the night Tuppy was killed. Patrick's mother had doted on her oldest son Brian, so their love affair had to be kept hidden.

Scott pushed back his chair.

"Stay and finish your coffee," Ava said.

The back door opened and a man came in, smiling at Ava. He was older than Scott, who guessed him to be in his early fifties, with floppy hair, a pronounced, beak-like nose, and close-set eyes. He was dressed in a rumpled suit and tie and carried a battered briefcase.

"Hallo, Ava," he said, with a pronounced English accent.

Ava introduced him as Professor Richmond, and as each man heard the other's name, they both took a moment to size each other up. Professor Richmond did so with an amused air and one raised eyebrow. Scott could feel a little steam build between his ears and reminded himself to be professional.

"We have someone in common," Professor Richmond said. "The formidable Mary Margaret Fitzpatrick."

"Is that right?" Scott said and rose to leave.

"Stay and have tea with us, do," Professor Richmond said, making Scott realize that he had interrupted Ava preparing tea for this man. "I've heard so much about you, all terribly flattering, of course, and I would be delighted to make your acquaintance."

"We'll have to do that some time," Scott said, and thanked Ava for her time before he left.

Gail Godwin was coming in the front door as he went out, and she followed him outside to try to get the gossip on Knox and Meredith.

"You probably know more than I do," Scott said.

"I heard she cracked up and Knox stuck her in a loony bin," Gail said. "I never liked her, but she didn't seem crazy to me."

"I think she must have been under a great strain," Scott said.

"Being married to Knox Rodefeffer would drive any woman crazy," Gail said. "I clean the bank, you know. I've seen what goes on there late at night ..."

"Anything the police should know?" he said.

"Oh, no, nothing like that," she backtracked, reminded that this wasn't just little Scotty Gordon she was talking to, this was the chief of police. "Just nonsense with that secretary of his; they aren't fooling anyone."

"You hear anything about that accident on Friday night?" Scott asked.

"I heard a couple things," Gail said. "Nothing I'd swear on the Bible about."

"Tell me anyway," Scott said. "I won't hold you to it."

"Well," Gail said. "I heard Phyllis Davis had a wild party at her place that night and there were some underage college kids there. I guess everybody got stinking drunk and there may have been drugs involved; you know Phyllis. Seems two of the boys got into a fight over something and decided to settle the argument by drag racing up Peony Street."

"This was Friday night?" Scott asked. "Why didn't anyone call me?'

"It was after midnight," she said. "Ed Harrison lives on one side of her, but he was out of town, and on the other side are Ian and Delia, but Delia didn't remember hearing it. I don't dare bother Ian with anything like that nowadays, poor man."

"Delia said she didn't hear anything?"

"Delia Fitzpatrick once slept through a thunderstorm that tore off our carport and dropped it in their front yard," Gail said. "So I wasn't surprised."

"You live right behind Phyllis on Marigold, and you didn't hear it?"

"I clean the bank until 11:00, and then I do the IGA," Gail said. "I don't get home until 3:00 am, and it was quiet then."

Scott reflected that Tuppy was lying in the middle of Peony Street at 3:00 am. If Gail had walked that way home, she would have seen him, but that was way out of her way.

"You have any names for me?" he said. "Of the college kids?"

"No," she said as she shook her head. "And you know Phyllis probably didn't even bother to ask."

"You said you'd heard a couple things," Scott said. "What else?"

"That movie star staying up at the Inn showed up on Monday," she said, "but that man who's staying with her was driving around town a few days before. No one else in town has a car like that with a New York license plate."

"On Friday night?"

"I have it on good authority that he was."

"Did you see him?"

"I said a good authority," Gail said, "but not one stupid enough to get involved."

"Thanks, Mrs. Godwin," Scott said. "I better not make you late for work."

"Ava's not a stickler about that," Gail said. "Besides, she'll be having her tea with the professor about now, and I don't like to interrupt."

"What do you think of him?" Scott asked her.

"He's a stuck-up snob, and I can't understand him half the time," Gail said, "but nothing for you to worry about when it comes to Maggie."

Scott didn't even bother to pretend not to understand; it was a small town.

"Really?" he said. "Why's that?"

"Let's just say he prefers grad students," she said, "of the male variety."

Scott considered that the best news he'd heard all day.

Claire had a very deaf older woman in her chair and was trying to coax her wiry gray hair into some semblance of a Doris Day-style from her Rock Hudson period. When the door opened, she thought it was her next appointment, but it was Stanley. He nodded to Claire and took a seat in the waiting area. Claire leaned back so she could see his driver standing outside the door, blocking the entrance.

"She's completely deaf," Claire said. "Go ahead and say whatever it is you came to say."

Stanley stood up and walked over to sit in the second hydraulic chair. He smiled at the older woman, who clicked her dentures but didn't respond.

"We're going to need that book," Stanley said.

"I told Sloan earlier," Claire said, "I don't have it. I know Tuppy said he left it for me, but I can't find it. Believe me, Stanley, there's nothing I want more than to be done with Sloan and all her crazy drama. I wasn't in on some plot with Tuppy; this was all him."

"I'm going to need you to sign a new confidentiality agreement."

"Why?"

He shrugged.

"Just a precaution."

"I'll show it to my attorney, and if he thinks I should sign it, I will."

Stanley sighed as he stood up.

"Don't make this harder than it has to be," he said.

His quiet tone scared her more than if he had shouted.

"I don't want any trouble," Claire said. "I don't trust any of you, and for a good reason. I've seen your work."

"I'll have the agreement hand-delivered to your attorney this evening. I want it signed and returned to me by noon tomorrow."

He walked toward the front door.

"Don't you want his name and address?"

Stanley shook his head.

"Already got it," he said.

He left the salon, and Claire felt her stomach unclench.

"Was that your boyfriend?" the woman asked.

Claire shook her head.

"Snappy dresser," the woman said.

At five o'clock Claire picked up Mackie Pea from Skip's mother's house and feigned delight over the pink coat she had made for the little dog. It had purple crocheted trim all around the hem, and purple crocheted buttons down her tummy. Her little front legs were stuck through its sleeves, and it had a little pink hood with a purple tassel.

"I just love her," the older woman said. "It gets so cold here at night, and I hate to think of her shivering."

Claire thanked her and made her promise to come in for a free haircut. She then took Mackie Pea for a walk to the Rose and Thorn to collect her father. Mackie seemed to be proud of her new sweater and strutted down the sidewalk with her head held high. Claire didn't have the heart to take it off.

"All this time I thought you were so high class," she told the dog, "when actually you're just a good ole girl at heart."

Ian was sitting in the back booth with Sam and Scott. He scooped up Mackie Pea, set her on the table in front of him and began feeding her peanuts.

"Look at your fancy new coat," Ian said to Mackie. "Aren't you the prettiest girl I've ever seen?"

"Well?" Claire said to Scott and Sam. "Where's the key ring?"

"Sammy traded it to someone at the service station but doesn't remember the name," Scott said.

Claire felt what was left of her courage drain away.

"Has something happened?" Scott asked her.

"What's going on?" her father asked.

"Nothing, Dad," Claire said. "Are you ready to go home? I have another appointment at six, so I need to get back."

"I can take him home," Sam said. "You and Scott go on."

"I can take my own damn self home," Ian said. "I don't need a babysitter."

"I'm just hoping Delia will give me some dinner, Ian," Sam said. "You know Hannah's idea of dinner time is whenever she gets around to it."

"I'm sure she would," Ian said. "Our Delia's a mighty fine cook."

Claire mouthed "thank you" to Sam, who nodded in return.

She reached for her dog, but her father batted her hands away.

"You leave my little sweetheart alone," he said. "She's staying with me."

Sam winked at Claire and gestured with his head for her to go on.

Scott followed her outside.

"I guess you heard about Meredith and Knox," he said. "What a mess."

Claire hoped Scott could not see her face flush with shame. It was so complicated to be friends with a policeman, especially when you and your cousins couldn't seem to stay out of trouble.

"I don't think they killed Tuppy," Claire said. "A confidentiality agreement I signed during my former employment prohibits me from speculating on who might have, so infer from that what you will."

"I heard that gossip, too," Scott said. "Unfortunately Stanley got Senator Bayard to come down on Sarah through her boss. She's been made to understand that going after Sloan is no longer an option."

"Even if she's guilty?"

"There were threatening phone calls and texts," Scott said. "But she was thousands of miles away when it happened."

"But Stanley was here."

"Yes, but just like with Knox, there's no proof, and Sarah's not allowed to look for any."

"Sarah must be foaming at the mouth. Do you think she'll come after me again?"

"No," Scott said. "Knox is the next best thing to a movie star around here. She thinks derailing his political plans will do in a pinch."

"Senator Bayard isn't interested in protecting him?"

"They're all distancing themselves in preparation for the scandal."

"What happened with the cars?"

"That's a dead end," Scott said. "The pieces of Meredith's car are probably in a hundred resale shops by now, and Knox's car is at the dealership in Morgantown, getting some work done."

"How convenient."

"So we're left with Meredith's word for what happened," Scott said, "and she's not exactly a reliable witness. Plus there's every chance that nothing she said on the way to the hospital can be used against her. Thanks to Knox, Pip's wanted for leaving the scene of a crime, not to mention unpaid child support and tax evasion. Sarah's not sure who will get to him first, the feds or the police."

"He may be safer in jail," Claire said. "He also owes a lot of money to my previous employer."

"There's a warrant out for Pip's arrest," Scott said. "Any idea where he went?"

"None," Claire said, and then wondered why she continued to protect her ex-husband when he so thoroughly deserved every consequence coming to him.

"Did Sarah talk to Tuppy's family?"

"It didn't come to anything," Scott said. "I'm sorry."

"I'm relieved not to be the prime suspect," Claire said, "but I don't want anyone to get away with murdering Tuppy. I don't think she who must not be named would come here unless she was very worried. I don't think her attorney wanted her to come. He usually cleans up her messes alone."

"Maybe it's just the book Sloan's after. There must be some pretty damning information in there."

"We may never know," Claire said.

"You want me to hang out with you until it's time to go home?" Scott asked her.

"No," Claire said. "You probably need to be at your mom's."

"My sister's there," he said. "She's still in denial about what's going on; she doesn't want us to call Hospice."

"Surely she doesn't want your mom to go through all that chemo and radiation," Claire said.

"She does," Scott said. "She wants Mom to fight this. She doesn't want us to give up."

"What are you going to do?"

"I called in my version of Stanley," Scott said. "Father Stephen's coming over after dinner."

Claire smiled.

"That's good to see," Scott said. "Try not to worry too much."

"Keep me updated," Claire said.

"I will."

As soon as Claire got back to the salon the phone rang.

"Hi," Hannah said when she answered, but she was whispering.

"What's going on?" Claire said.

"Um, I may have put on a maid's uniform, and I may have sneaked into Sloan's room, and I may be hiding in her closet."

"Hannah!" Claire said. "I told you not to do that."

"Can you help me?" Hannah said. "She's getting ready to come to The Bee Hive to let you do her hair, but I'm not sure if the mean guy is going with her or not."

"I'll be right there," Claire said.

When Claire arrived at the Inn, she came in through the back entrance and sneaked through the kitchen. When she peeked into the front parlor, she was just in time to see Sloan and the driver departing. Stanley was not with her. She asked the front desk clerk where Stanley was, and the woman pointed upstairs.

"He said he didn't want to be disturbed," the woman said, "and I wouldn't if I were you; he's scary."

"He knows me," Claire said. "He won't mind."

Claire ran up the stairs two at a time while she tried to think up a plan, but when she reached the top, she was as clueless as when she started. She knew which room every member of the entourage was in, which was a plus; unfortunately, she'd have to pass Stanley's to get to Sloan's. She knocked lightly on Juanita's door, and was relieved when Juanita answered with a whispered, "Oh, my God, Claire, come in here!"

Claire was used to the sight of the ex-pro football player nicknamed "Teeny" sitting on Juanita's bed painting his toenails. He jumped up and gave her a bear hug.

"She just left," he said. "Wasn't she going to see you?"

"She was," Claire said. "She left something in her room, and she called and asked a maid to look for it, but the maid can't find it, so she sent me to help the maid look. I don't want Stanley to know I'm here, so I need your help."

Neither of them questioned her lie; Claire felt a little bit bad about that. They may have been comrades in arms while they worked for Sloan, but Claire knew either one of them would rat her out in a skinny minute to save their own hides.

Juanita led Claire out into the hallway, tip-toeing even though the floor was covered in plush carpet. She put her finger to her lips and gestured for Claire to follow her down the hall. Teeny stayed back in the hallway to watch for Stanley; he was supposed to make a ruckus if Stanley came out of his room.

As they passed Stanley's room, Claire could hear him through the door, talking on the phone. She was relieved they were staying in the new, thick-carpeted section of the hotel and not in the original part where the hundred-year-old wood floors creaked. Claire opened the door to Sloan's room, quickly went inside, and closed the door behind her.

Claire opened the closet door. Hannah was huddled in a knot down in the corner of the closet with her hands covering her eyes, and her head tucked forward as if she was trying to make herself as small as she could, if not invisible.

"Don't kill me, I'm the mother of a small child," Hannah said.

"Hannah," Claire hissed, "come on."

Hannah uncovered her eyes and crawled out of the closet. She had on a crisp white maid's uniform with her grubby hiking boots and brown socks.

"I thought I was a goner," she said.

"We're not out of the woods, yet," Claire said. "I told them I was sent to help a maid look for something of Sloan's, so if anybody asks, that's what we're doing."

Claire slipped her cover off her phone and stuck it in her pocket. When she opened the door to the hallway, Stanley was standing just outside.

"What are you doing?" he asked.

Claire's heart was pounding as she told the story she had manufactured and hoped Hannah looked convincing behind her. While she was explaining her presence, Hannah walked past them carrying an armload of dirty towels, and for some reason waving a toilet brush in the air.

"Ah couldn't find it nowhere, ma'am," Hannah said in her version of a country hick accent. "Ah tried my bayest."

Hannah kept going down the empty hallway, past the closed doors of Teeny and Juanita's rooms.

'So much for their help,' Claire thought.

Claire was holding her breath, trying to look casually innocent, which in this case meant looking irritated at having to do Sloan's bidding but not overly emotional about it because it happened all the time.

"Well," Stanley said impatiently. "Did you find it?"

Claire held up her phone, which was just like Sloan's except for the pink rhinestone-studded case, the one she had pulled off and stuck in her pocket just moments before.

Stanley rolled his eyes.

"You know how she is," Claire said.

Stanley shook his head and stood aside to let Claire pass. She knew all he'd have to do is call Sloan's number, and if this phone didn't ring, he'd know it was a ruse. Claire's heart was pounding as she walked quickly down the long hallway.

"Claire," Stanley said, just as she reached the top of the stairs.

She was sure he saw her jump at the sound of her name, but when she turned, he said, "I'll see you at noon tomorrow."

Claire waved and then ran down the steps. Hannah was in the downstairs staff bathroom changing back into her clothes.

"You are a danger to yourself and others," Claire told her when she came out.

They left through the kitchen and then stood on the back porch while Claire put the cover back on her phone.

"She didn't kill your friend," Hannah said. "But she thinks Stanley might have done it."

"Tell me everything she said."

"Stanley came in and told her he had given you the papers to sign, and he didn't think you were going to give them any trouble. Sloan said she wanted you to come back to work for her and if he didn't get you to do that then she was going to fire him. Stanley said he knew too much for her to fire him; if she knew what was good for her, she'd shut that talk right up. Sloan goes, 'Did you kill him?' and Stanley goes, 'No, I didn't, we were just lucky.' Then he left, and she got a phone call. She was really mean to whoever it was she talked to; she said 'you might as well enjoy it because there's no turning back,' whatever that means."

"That was probably Carlyle."

"It was," Hannah said. "I heard her use that name."

"Anything else?"

"Her feet are really small," Hannah said. "I had some time to look at her shoes while I was in the closet. They're like hooker heels for tots."

"You were insane to take that risk," Claire said. "But it's good to know Sloan didn't have him killed."

"You think Stanley was telling the truth?"

Claire shook her head and said, "I don't know."

"I'll tell you one thing," Hannah said. "I'm going to need a gallon of de-skunkerizer to get the smell of her perfume off me. It's awful!"

"I better go back to The Bee Hive," Claire said.

"If I were you I'd snatch her bald-headed," Hannah said.

"Claire laughed.

"I just may do that."

245

Peony Street by Pamela Grandstaff

Chapter Nine - Wednesday/Thursday

Claire ran back to the salon, where Stanley's long sedan was parked out front. As Claire unlocked the salon door, Sloan exited the car.

"If you leave that car parked out here someone will come in and check on me," Claire said.

Sloan spoke to the driver, and the car glided off down the street.

Claire had closed all the curtains earlier, so all she had to do was lock the front door behind Sloan.

"Okay," she said to Sloan. "Let's get this over with."

Sloan shrugged off her jacket, loosened the collar of her blouse, and sat down in the hydraulic chair. Claire jacked up the chair and considered her former employer in the mirror.

"This is the last time," Claire said, and then with painstaking dexterity, she went about the tedious task of separating Sloan's famous hair from her head.

"Where's your spare?" she asked her.

Sloan gestured at her enormous handbag.

"I'll do that one, too," Claire said. "But they will only look good for about two weeks of wear, and only if you're careful. That means that within a month you have to find someone else to do this for you. It wouldn't hurt to get a few new pieces ordered."

"You'll have changed your mind by then," Sloan said.

Claire was used to the appearance of Sloan's bald head, but she wrapped a towel around it so Sloan wouldn't get cold.

"I won't," Claire said. "My parents need me here."

"I can hire someone," Sloan said. "Hell, I'll hire staff and buy them the biggest house in town. We'll call it The Sloan Merryweather Home for Claire's Hick Parents."

"When I first got here that was my inclination, too," Claire said. "I forgot what it was like to have people in your life you can trust, who want to help you even if there's nothing in it for them. The people in my family help each other and their neighbors because it's the right thing to do, and not because they get great PR from it or expect some big reward. I have a really great family. I'm just glad they're letting me back in."

"In a month you'll be begging for your job back."

"No," Claire said. "I'm staying."

Sloan's hair pieces were made from human hair; some of the finest craftsmanship Claire had ever seen. When properly seated and styled, it was impossible to detect they were fake. Unfortunately, Sloan had neither the skill nor inclination to learn to do anything so pedestrian for herself.

"Tell me about the redhead," Sloan said. "She has gorgeous hair."

"Maggie's hair is actually very curly, to an almost unmanageable degree. It would make a beautiful hairpiece, but it would be a huge headache to maintain. Plus it's too red for you. It would be a distracting change from your signature color."

"I'm ready for a big change," Sloan said. "Imagine me walking the red carpet with a wild titian mane and a baby bump; in an emerald-colored pre-Raphaelite dress, Carlyle on my arm..."

Claire flinched, and Sloan honed in on it immediately.

"I would give him up if I could have you back."

"I don't want him anymore."

"Liar," Sloan said. "That's why you could never win playing poker. You can't hide your feelings."

"At least I have them."

"If I'm not being paid to show emotion I can't see why I should bother," Sloan said. "Real emotions are dangerous. On the other hand, controlled emotions make excellent tools."

"Or weapons," Claire said. "Are you being kind to him, at least?"

"What do you care?"

"He's a nice man, Sloan," Claire said. "Unfortunately for him, nice men are like snack foods to you."

"It wasn't hard to convince him," Sloan said. "I'm sorry if that hurts."

"No, you're not," Claire said. "You're especially pleased that it hurts."

"That's true," Sloan said. "To answer the question you didn't ask, yes, he regrets what he did."

"He said that?"

"He didn't have to," Sloan said. "It's there in his eyes: disgust and contempt."

"And it doesn't bother you that he looks at you that way?"

"It's not me he's looking at that way; it's when he looks at himself in the mirror. He's always perfectly divine to me."

Claire gently washed each hairpiece, affixed them to wig blocks, and dried them to just barely damp with a diffuser on the end of the hairdryer, set to low; best to keep the heat damage to a minimum. Sloan stood up and leaned toward the mirror, where she very closely examined every pore on her face, starting at what would have been her hairline had she any hair.

"I'm thinking of having some maintenance work done," Sloan said. "What do you think?"

"It won't settle in time for the campaign," Claire said.

"You're right," Sloan said. "Who will tell me these things if not you?"

Claire sectioned the damp hair and secured it with large clips. She used large soup-can-sized rollers and a special setting lotion that was water soluble so it wouldn't leave any residue. Once the wigs were set, she propped up each of them on a milk crate under a hood dryer set to low and set the timers.

"Did you go to the engagement party?" Claire asked her.

"I did," Sloan said. "I met Mario Testino; he's shooting me for Vanity Fair."

"Did you reschedule British Vogue?"

"It's this weekend," Sloan said. "We're going up to Blenheim Palace."

"That should be beautiful. The flowers will be blooming."

"You could come."

Claire didn't answer. She remembered one cold, rainy afternoon she and Carlyle spent in Woodstock, near Oxford, wandering through what Carlyle referred to as "a monument to Baroque excess." They were newly in love; at that stage where it was imperative to always be touching. When parted for even a brief period of time her longing for him had been an ache in her chest. Sloan hadn't known about it, yet; no one did. It was still their delicious secret.

"You were sweet together," Sloan said.

Claire reflected that Sloan always had an uncanny way of reading her mind.

"I admit I was jealous," Sloan said. "I saw how he looked at you. No one has ever looked at me that way. With lust, yes; or pride of ownership, always; but not love. I hated you for making me think about that every time I saw you together."

"That's amazingly honest."

"Why not be honest?" Sloan said with a shrug. "You can't tell anybody."

"So you took him out of spite?"

"That was just a bonus," Sloan said. "He perfectly fits the role I need him to play. He gives me credibility in British theater circles, which I'm determined to have, and he looks great in a kilt. The mean queens who run everything will adore him. He's got rough edges, genuine talent, and an accent."

"I warned him," Claire said. "I've seen you do it before; to business partners, costars, producers, directors, nobodies who you couldn't care less about, and people who thought they were your closest friends."

"Don't be too hard on him," Sloan said. "He's only a man, after all; and an actor. He knew what the opportunity could mean, what it does mean. He's already getting offers."

"I'm glad he didn't come."

"I didn't tell him where I was going," Sloan said. "He thinks I'm at a spa in Arizona."

"Does he know Tuppy's dead?"

"I doubt it," Sloan said. "He was in Scotland when I left."

"He liked Tuppy; they used to get drunk together and play pub quizzes. No one could beat them when they teamed up."

Sloan didn't say anything. In her examination routine, she was down to her neck, holding her head this way and that, using a hand mirror to inspect all angles.

"You need to ease up on the Botox," Claire said. "You look great in photographs, but it will ruin your re-shoots."

"It's impossible to win," Sloan said. "If I let myself age naturally I'll have no work; if I fight against it, I'll work longer but lose everyone's respect. It's a fine line."

"Nice pun," Claire said. "The most important thing is to be able to emote on screen in close up. If you turn yourself into a waxworks, no one will be able to see your actual talent."

"My next project doesn't start until after awards season," Sloan said. "I can shoot my forehead silly between now and then, just not around the mouth. Winners need to smile."

"Don't go overboard with the fillers," Claire said. "If you don't go pumping your lips full of anything, and don't get those awful cheek implants, you can get away with everything else for a long time."

"You should be a plastic surgery stylist," Sloan said. "It could be your new career."

Claire sat in the second hydraulic chair and put her feet up on the counter.

"Those shoes," Sloan said. "Really, Claire?"

"My feet hurt," Claire said. "Leave me alone."

Claire hadn't realized how tired she was until she sat down. It felt so familiar to hang out with Sloan, talking about her and obsessing over what she should do or wear. Despite herself, Claire could feel herself being drawn back into her old role.

"When is your Actor's Studio interview airing?"

"In September," Sloan said, "to coincide with the Vanity Fair, Vogue, and People covers."

"You're winning the trifecta there," Claire said.

"Ayelet is worth every penny," Sloan said. "The woman never sleeps."

"Are you going to do that sci-fi thing with the haunted spaceship?"

"No," Sloan said. "I'm doing the rom-com with Clifford."

"Aren't you two getting a little old for romantic comedy?"

"Our last movie together did a half billion worldwide," Sloan said. "That's some serious chick flick coinage."

"What are you getting out of it?"

"Ten million plus one percent of the gross," Sloan said. "It's my best deal, yet."

"I'm surprised his wife is letting him off the leash for that."

"Ticket buyers love to see us together. We're negotiating a relationship."

"What about Carlyle?"

"Carlyle's contract ends after awards season. Clifford doesn't have anything in contention this year. He's shooting a World War II thing in Austria right now and then that Harvey remake in North Carolina right after, so he's not available until next March; which is perfect timing."

"Won't stealing America's Sweetheart's husband create negative press?"

"It all depends on how well it's orchestrated," Sloan said. "Ayelet used to work for Clifford's agent. They're putting together a media strategy for it. Plus, his wife can use the sympathy to boost her own profile. She's already got a younger lover on the side, and he'll be credited with healing her broken heart. We'll get a lot of tabloid coverage out of it, and that will boost ticket sales, so everyone wins in the end."

"What will happen to Carlyle?"

"After award season we'll break up, due to the Oscar curse, of course. Then I'll cry on Clifford's shoulder, and we'll fall madly in love, despite how wrong it is."

"He's so high maintenance, though, and such a drama king. You fought over every scene."

"That was passion, darling, and it translated into onscreen chemistry. As long as I don't forbid him from wearing women's lingerie in private, we'll get along famously in public."

"Is he gay?"

"No, sweetie, he just likes to feel pretty."

"That's dialogue."

"It's also the truth."

Sloan finished her above-the-neck inspection and Claire had every reason to believe she might strip and continue downward. Claire got to her feet just as the timer dinged, removed both wigs from under the dryers, refastened them to the stands clamped to the countertop, and left them to cool. Sloan picked up a tabloid paper and some celebrity gossip magazines and sat back down in the hydraulic chair to read.

"I guess you heard that russkiy shlyuha bore Sid another girl," she said.

"That makes five, doesn't it?"

"She's banging her trainer. This last one may not be Sid's."

"Does he know?"

"He probably doesn't care. He's got something going on with his new assistant."

"Where's Portia?"

It was Sloan's turn to flinch, but Claire pretended not to notice.

"Boarding school somewhere," Sloan said, feigning disinterest.

"She should be graduating soon," Claire said. "She was five when she lived with us, and that was at least twelve years ago."

"Yes, and if it weren't for you she'd be dead; isn't that what you're thinking?"

"I try not to think about it," Claire said.

"She said she could swim."

"She was afraid to displease you," Claire said.

"She needed too much attention," Sloan said. "She yapped all the time. It drove me nuts."

"She was just a little kid," Claire said. "That's how they are. That's why you shouldn't adopt one."

The phone rang, and Claire answered, explained why Denise wasn't there and made an appointment for the customer.

"Are you thinking of buying this place?" Sloan asked her after she hung up.

"I'm just helping out an old friend," Claire said.

Claire removed the rollers, combed out and styled the hairpieces, and gave them a light fixative spray. She then loosely tied a hair net around each one to support the weight of the hair so it wouldn't flatten the style before Sloan wore it.

"I could teach you how to do most of this," Claire said. "You've seen me do it enough."

"No," Sloan said. "I haven't done my own hair since I met you."

"We've come a long way from the Palomino Club."

"I loved that job; it was so simple. Take off your clothes, shake your ass, and collect your money."

"That's how you met Sergio."

"Good ole Sergio; he was my first submissive. I didn't know what in the hell I was doing."

"I never could understand why men would pay you to be mean to them."

"Powerful men like to be worshipped in public and abused in private," Sloan said. "Once a beautiful woman understands that she can rule the world."

"Did you like that job better than the porn?"

"I learned a lot about lighting from doing porn."

"And you met Vincent."

"I still put flowers on his grave every summer. He was the best producer I've ever worked with."

"He really believed in you."

"He took Tammy Jo Hogsett and turned her into Sloan Merryweather," she said. "I owe all I have now to him."

Claire put the hairnet-covered hairpieces on Styrofoam forms, lowered them carefully into two shopping bags and loosely covered them with tissue paper. Sloan pulled the towel from her head and dropped it on the floor. She put on her ski jacket, flipped up the hood, slung her handbag over her shoulder, and took the shopping bags from Claire.

"We're leaving tomorrow," Sloan said, "as soon as you sign the agreement."

"I should have that to you by noon," Claire said.

She was feeling nostalgic and soft-hearted toward Sloan, whom she couldn't help but excuse for being no more or less than exactly what she always had been. They had been together for twenty years. Sloan had shown her the world and made her rich; that should count for something.

"Good luck, Sloan," Claire said. "I hope everything works out for you."

"Oh, I forgot to tell you," Sloan said, as she paused at the door. "I banged your brother last night."

"My brother died over twenty-five years ago," Claire said.

"The bartender," Sloan said. "Something Fitzpatrick: Peter? Paul? Perry?"

"Patrick," Claire said. "Did he tell you he was my brother?"

"He didn't have to," Sloan said. "He looks just like you."

Claire shook her head.

"Goodbye, Sloan," she said.

"Call me when you're ready to come back," Sloan said, and as if by magic, the dark sedan appeared out of the darkness, pulled up to the curb, and swallowed Sloan whole.

Claire cleaned the shop and locked up. She walked down to the corner, where what used to be Davis's Diner was now the Pine Mountain Cafe. It was eight o'clock, and the restaurant was filled with students and tourists. Claire read the menu posted on the window and was reminded of the bistros in Aspen or Big Sky. What Patrick had referred to as "frog snot" on his sandwich had actually been pesto.

She crossed the street diagonally where Pine Mountain Road met Rose Hill Avenue, and walked past the bank, up to Maggie's bookstore, Little Bear Books. Through the window she could see more students and tourists sitting in the café, drinking out of either very big or very little coffee cups. She walked on down the street to where Rose Hill Avenue ended at the gates of Eldridge College. She waved to the night watchman, who was an old friend of her father's.

Claire crossed the street and walked back toward town; past the Bijou Theater, currently hosting a short films festival, and then Delvecchio's IGA, which now had a big red movie rental kiosk outside and a sign on the door that read, "Lift passes and trail maps sold here."

She walked past the post office, then the Rodefeffer Realty office, and turned down Pine Mountain Road toward the river. Instead of turning right on Iris Avenue she went all the way down to where the road ended in the water, between the old train depot and the glassworks. The Mountain Laurel Depot Bar and Grill seemed to be packed with people as well. A sign on the gate of the old Rodefeffer Glassworks announced it was soon to become "Wilberforce Cycles," a bicycle factory specializing in racing and mountain bikes.

The train tracks by the river had been converted into a rail trail. Claire stood in the middle of the path and took deep breaths of cold air. Claire enjoyed the sound of the water rushing by, and how clean the cold air felt and smelled as it rolled across her face. She thought of all the oceans, lakes, rivers, and streams she had stood next to over the past twenty years. Only this particular water looked, felt, and smelled like home.

Claire backtracked and walked past the new condos on Lotus Avenue. She was trying to decide which end unit was Courtenay's when she realized Stanley's car was parked outside the one on the farthest end. Claire's heart was racing as she got nearer, determined to see the license plate in order to be sure. The door to the last condo opened, and Claire ducked down behind the car parked next to Stanley's. She heard a man's deep voice say, "We'll be in touch." Claire duck-walked to the front end of the car she was hiding behind and raised her head up high enough to peek through the windows. She saw Stanley's driver get in Stanley's car.

She only heard one car door close, so Claire surmised either Stanley had stayed in his car, or the driver was alone. The car backed out, and Claire stayed hidden in the shadows until it was gone. Then she quickly walked home.

When she opened her parents' front door, she was shocked to find Stanley sitting in the living room with her father. She looked back out the front door, but his car wasn't there.

"Hello, Claire," Stanley said.

"What are you doing here?" Claire said, and then to her father, "are you alright?"

"He's looking for that keyring your friend gave me," Ian said. "I told him we can't find it. My memory's not what it used to be."

"It's okay, Dad," Claire said. "It's no big deal."

"It's actually quite a big deal to me," Stanley said. "Sloan told me she didn't leave her phone at the Inn. I'd like to know what you were doing in her room."

Claire's father was nodding his head, and his exaggerated frown was back. He was also rocking a little, back and forth; this was new behavior.

"I want you to leave," Claire said to Stanley. "Right now."

Stanley rose and smiled at Claire, but not with his eyes.

"Your father and I were having a nice chat," he said.

"My parents are off limits to you and Sloan," Claire said. "I'll get a restraining order if I have to. I'll call the press."

"It was a pleasure to meet you," Stanley said to Ian, who looked bewildered.

Claire opened the front door. Stanley walked through it and then paused.

"Don't ever threaten me again," he said in a low voice, still smiling. "You should know better than to underestimate what I can do."

"Don't you threaten me anymore," Claire said. "Don't you underestimate me or anyone else in this town. We don't care how much money Sloan has or how mean you are. We'll do whatever we need to in order to take care of our own."

"Cute dog," Stanley said to Claire. "It's actually Sloan's dog, I believe, isn't it? I don't think you ever had the paperwork changed to reflect the new ownership."

Claire closed the door in his face and locked it.

"What's wrong, Claire?" Ian asked her. "Who was that man?"

Her father was clearly agitated, still rocking slightly and nodding his head.

"That was not a nice man," Claire said. "If he comes here again, don't let him in. Call Scott instead. Where's Mom?"

"She's asleep. He wanted to speak to her, but I said she wasn't feeling well. He thought she might know where the key ring was."

Claire went down the hall and looked in on her mother, who was snoring. She realized she was trembling all over. She didn't know what to do but felt she had to do something. She couldn't call Scott; he was busy with his mother and besides, as kind and honorable as he was, he was no match for Stanley. She realized there was only one person on her side who was; she went to the back porch to make the call so her father wouldn't hear.

Scott, his sister Penny, a social worker from Pine County Hospice, and Father Stephen all sat on either side of his mother's bed. Scott's mother was crying into a tissue, and his sister's eyes were swollen and red.

"I spoke to Doctor Machalvie," Father Stephen said to their mother. "He's been conferring with the specialists in Morgantown, and he agrees that chemo and radiation would only prolong your life for a very short time, and the side effects would probably make you miserable. He's ready to make the referral to Hospice."

"Can't we just pray for a miracle?" Penny said. "If our faith is strong enough we can heal her, can't we?"

"I believe miracles happen," the priest said. "I believe that prayer can heal. I also see good, faithful people die all the time. A time comes for us all."

"If we bring in Hospice it means we've given up," Penny said. "I won't do that."

"You want your mother to be as comfortable as possible, don't you?" the social worker said. "A nurse will come to the house to check on her and help manage her symptoms; we can set up any medical equipment she needs here at home; aides can come to help take care of her personal needs. She'll be free to focus on resting and spending time with her family and friends. We'll help you take good care of her. People who go into Hospice care early enough tend to live longer, better quality lives."

"You can prepare for the worst and still hope for the best," Father Stephen said.

"Can she have chemo and radiation if she's in the program?" Penny asked the Hospice social worker.

"Only if it's for palliative care, which means treatments that are given to alleviate painful symptoms," the social worker said. "Right now the Medicare guidelines stipulate that she can't seek curative treatment while in the program. That may change in the future, but that's the law right now."

"What do you want to do, Mom?" Scott asked her.

"I'll do whatever you both want me to do," she said. "You decide."

"I'm going to leave this information with you," the social worker said, and laid some brochures on the bedside table. "If you have any questions please don't hesitate to call us."

Scott walked outside with her and said, "I hope we can convince Penny it's the best thing."

"It's not unusual for family members to disagree," she said. "It's good if everyone can be on board, but that's not always the case. You need to be designated her medical power of attorney; then if she becomes incapacitated, you can make the decision for her."

"I hope it won't come to that."

"Be sure to take care of yourself," she said. "Get some sleep."

When Scott got back to the bedroom, Penny said, "I'm afraid they'll just come in here and shoot her up with morphine and then she'll die."

"Mom will decide how much pain she can tolerate and how much medication she wants," Scott said. "Plus Doc will be in on every decision. He wouldn't recommend Hospice if it wasn't the best thing."

"I can't do it," Penny said. "I'm not giving up."

"Don't fight," their mother said. "Please don't fight."

"Why don't you all sleep on it," Father Stephen said. "Pray about it and ask for guidance."

"Pray with us now," Scott's mother said. "Let's all hold hands and pray."

Scott didn't understand why he felt so resistant to holding hands with his family and letting Father Stephen pray over them. He'd been raised in the church, and while he wasn't what anyone would call a strict Catholic, he did believe in God.

As he listened to Father Stephen quote from Corinthians and then ask for mercy and forgiveness for his mother, his resistance turned to resentment. What had his mother ever done that she needed to ask for forgiveness?

Why should anyone have to beg to be let into heaven? There wasn't a person Scott could think of who was perfect enough to please the kind of God they were praying to. Why bother?

Afterward, as he walked out of the house with Father Stephen, Scott felt his irritation boil over.

"It doesn't seem fair," Scott said. "My mother's a good person, a good Christian; why did this happen to her? There are plenty of evil people who live long, unproductive lives."

"We can have faith that for those who have done well, everlasting enjoyment shall be given; while to lovers of evil shall be given eternal punishment."

Scott had heard this rhetoric his whole life, but he wasn't sure he believed it anymore. It seemed more like something with which you would threaten a child in order to make him behave than something a reasonable adult person would believe.

"Let me ask you something, Father," Scott said. "How does anyone get into heaven if we're all so damaged and wicked down here? Why does God care what happens to such sinful people?"

"We live so that God may experience the world through us," Father Stephen said. "We are like his wayward children, his stray lambs. He cares what happens to us. He loves us."

"So why does He let us go to hell if He loves us so much?"

"Call it universal tough love," Father Stephen said with a smile. "Everyone has a choice how they end up; there are many forks along the road, many opportunities for redemption."

Scott wasn't convinced by this argument. He could agree that there were consequences to every action, but he could more easily believe hell was suffering from experiencing those consequences here on earth rather than an actual place he would be sent in which to burn after he died. He knew it was pointless to argue with Father Stephen about it; the man's life's calling was based on faith. It would be more productive to ask him for help with his sister, who was a fervent believer.

"Why can't my sister think of what's best for our mother, not for herself?"

"It's normal to feel all kinds of strong feelings when someone is dying," Father Stephen said, "Anger, denial, guilt; try to be patient with your sister as she comes to terms with losing her mother."

"It's not like I want this to happen," Scott said. "I just can't see sense in making her suffer because we aren't ready to let go."

"Penny will come to that realization, too. Give her time."

"We may not have time," Scott said.

After Father Stephen walked away, Scott decided he wasn't ready for round two in the hothouse with Penny. He walked down to Claire's parents' house and arrived just as Sam was leaving. Sam seemed to be in a hurry to get going, so they only exchanged brief greetings. Claire invited him in, and he made some small talk with Ian before joining her in the kitchen.

"I've just realized I spend most of my time talking to people in a series of kitchens," Scott said as he sat down.

"Thank you for what you did today at The Bee Hive," Claire said. "I couldn't bear it if something Sam and I did a long time ago hurt Hannah now."

"It wasn't totally selfless; I enjoyed Maggie's reaction."

"She's probably not going to speak to me for awhile."

"She'll get over it," Scott said. "What was Sam doing here just now?"

"Just checking on me," Claire said, but she wasn't looking Scott in the eye. "How's your mom?"

Scott told her about the uncomfortable family meeting.

"Father Stephen says Penny will come around, but I'm not so sure," Scott said.

"How long is she staying?"

"She said just until she got Mom squared away."

"I remember saying that what seems like a hundred years ago, last weekend," Claire said. "Can she stay longer if you need her to?"

"She can get family medical leave at work, which I don't have, and I don't think they'd be strapped for cash if she had to be off a long time. Her husband Kyle has a good job."

"They have kids?"

"Twins: Kyle Jr. and Kylene; they're fifteen."

"I don't know Penny very well; she was so much younger than us."

"She's got a very strong faith," Scott said.

"You do, too, don't you?"

"I want to believe, but the older I get, the more it all sounds like a fairy tale. 'Be good down here, and the old man in the sky will reward you up there.' It sounds like a pretty flimsy premise on which to base your whole life."

"I can't imagine you turning to a life of crime," Claire said.

"I know, right?" he said. "Even if it turned out it was all hokum I'd probably still do what I think is the right thing. Not because of some reward I'm hoping to get after I die, but just because I want to be that kind of person."

"You're the best person I know," Claire said and laid her hand on his arm. "I'm lucky to know you."

Scott took her hand and held it in his.

"What are you and Sam up to?"

Claire withdrew her hand, got up, and moved some things around on the kitchen counter.

"C'mon, Claire," Scott said. "I'm not stupid; don't shut me out."

Claire turned around and leaned back against the counter.

"I'm not going to tell you," she said. "Not because I'm ashamed of anything or I don't trust you. I'm not telling you because what I'm going to do next isn't exactly legal, and if you don't know about it you can't get in trouble for it."

"Claire," Scott said. "It would be dangerous to play around with these people. You know that better than anyone."

"Sean's coming in the morning, and we're going to meet with Stanley at noon. I'm going to sign a new confidentiality agreement, and then Sloan and her entourage are going to leave Rose Hill."

"That sounds legal enough."

"It is," Claire said. "Now stop asking questions."

"I trust Sean," Scott said. "Does he know what you're going to do?"

"I didn't want to talk about it on the phone," Claire said. "He'll know everything after he gets here in the morning."

"Do you want me to keep an eye on The Bee Hive, or hang out with your Dad all day?"

"No, it will all be fine," Claire said. "You take good care of your mom. I'll call you as soon as they leave."

"I don't like this," Scott said as he stood up. "I wish you trusted me more."

"You're a sweetie pie," Claire said, and then she hugged him.

The instant attraction he felt surprised him, and he kissed her before he could decide if it was the best idea. To his further surprise, she kissed him back.

"I don't want anything to happen to you," he said when they stopped.

"Don't worry so much," she said. "I may not be as smart as Stanley, but I'm definitely smarter than Pip."

"I can't find anything wrong with it," Sean said the next morning, looking over the agreement Stanley had delivered to his home the night before. "It basically says you can't talk about Sloan or anything that happened while you were in her employment, forever and ever, amen."

Sean and Sam were sitting in the hydraulic chairs at The Bee Hive while Claire paced the floor. Mackie Pea was watching her from her carrier, which was perched on the back counter.

"I drew up the agreement making you the legal owner of the dog," Sean said. "But what would compel her to sign it?"

"This would," Sam said and held up the key ring with the flash drive attached.

"I thought that was lost," Sean said.

"Sammy had it," Sam said. "I just thought it would be safer in my hands than in anyone else's."

"I'm guessing Scott doesn't know you have it."

Sam gave Sean a pointed look.

"Okey dokey," Sean said. "I guess we'll call that privileged information."

"Sarah can't pursue Sloan now, anyway," Claire said. "So I might as well use it to get custody of Mackie Pea."

"Do you even know what's on the flash drive?" Sean asked. "There was some mention of a book."

"Tuppy wrote a book about Sloan," Claire said. "I don't know why he bothered; the penalty for breaking his confidentiality agreement couldn't possibly cover any advance a publisher could pay."

"Did either of you read it?" Sean asked.

"I skimmed through it," Claire said. "Tuppy's only known her for eighteen months. His stuff is inflammatory but nowhere near as damaging as revelations about her past would be."

Sean looked at Sam, who was wearing one of his inscrutable poker faces, like a puzzle box that seemed impossible to open.

"Okay, then," Sean said. "We offer the key ring in return for the transfer of ownership of the dog."

"Here's the thing," Claire said. "Stanley's going to think I had the book all along, and that I've made copies of it. He's going to be really mad thinking I've tried to one-up him. He may just refuse our offer and then burn down the whole town."

"You're exaggerating," Sean said.

"I assure you I'm not," Claire said. "You remember that scene in the Godfather where the producer wakes up to find his prize thoroughbred's severed head in his bed? That's Stanley's favorite part; he laughs his ass off. That movie is a workplace comedy to him."

"What if he refuses to sign?" Sean asked.

"We have a backup plan," Sam said.

"Please, I beg you," Sean said, "no guns."

"No guns," Sam said. "Just many, many witnesses, too many to kill; trust me."

"I trust you," Claire said.

Stanley's car glided up to the curb across the street from The Bee Hive, and Sam stood up. He held the door open for Stanley to come in as he went out, and walked away without looking back.

"Sloan's staying in the car," Stanley said. "I guess you said your goodbyes yesterday evening."

Stanley shook hands with Sean and seemed very pleased with himself.

"All signed?" Stanley said to Claire. "Ready to start your new life?"

Sean gave Stanley the signed confidentiality agreement, which Stanley quickly looked over, folded, and put it in his inside jacket pocket.

"There's one more thing," Sean said and held up the key ring.

Stanley's face turned blood red. If he had been a character in a cartoon, steam would have come out of his ears.

"I know you won't believe this, Stanley," Claire said, "but I didn't find it until after you left our house last night."

"If you ask for one penny I'll have you arrested for extortion so fast your empty little head will spin," Stanley said, and then pointed at Sean, "and you will be disbarred."

"I don't want any money," Claire said. "I want custody of the dog."

"Out of the question," Stanley said. "How do I know you haven't made a dozen copies? A publisher may pay millions into an offshore account for the chance to publish it, but I would know it was you who did it. There wouldn't be a cave deep enough in which you could hide from me."

"The kind of people you're used to dealing with might do that," Claire said, "but I don't need any more money, and I certainly don't want to get it that way. I just want to be as far away from Sloan Merryweather as possible. All I need is for her to sign the paperwork making Mackie Pea my dog, and you'll never have to deal with me again."

"No," Stanley said. "You'll come back for more. I don't do business with blackmailers; I bury them."

Stanley's back was to the front door and the windows of The Bee Hive, so he couldn't see the people quietly lining up outside between the building and his car. Almost every person in Claire's extended family was there, plus neighbors, students, and tourists, all people who'd been told that Sloan Merryweather was in The Bee Hive and would be signing autographs. The Pendleton Press had sent a photographer and a features editor. A local television station news crew was setting up to record the event.

As the crowd swelled, Stanley's driver blew the horn and Stanley's phone buzzed. He finally turned around.

"What the hell?" he said.

"I told you not to underestimate me or this town," Claire said. "All those people believe that Sloan Merryweather came to town just to give me the dog, as a gift in return for all my years of service. All I need is for her to do so, in front of everyone, and you can have the book."

"I won't allow it," Stanley said.

"Too late," Claire said and pointed toward Stanley's car.

Like a flame lit to please a million moths, Sloan Merryweather emerged from Stanley's car in full on movie star mode. She had on skintight black pants, knee-high black high-heeled boots, a black turtleneck, and a short black trench coat. Her auburn hair flowed in big soft waves from a side part, and huge dark sunglasses completed the glamorous ensemble.

The crowd parted as she walked slowly across the street to the door of The Bee Hive, greeting people and touching hands along the way. When she reached the salon door, she turned, pulled off her sunglasses, and posed for the cameras. Claire watched her run through her repertoire of stances and hand gestures, intuitively adjusting for the angle of the sunlight reflecting off her gorgeous hair.

"Hi, how are you?!" she said to every person, one by one, as she pointed and waved. "It's so good to see you!"

Sam emerged out of the crowd, opened the front door of The Bee Hive, and gestured for Claire to come outside. Sloan turned and saw Claire.

"You did this for me?" she asked.

"All for you," Claire said, and then opened the carrier and took out Mackie Pea, resplendent in her pink and purple coat.

She could see Stanley was about to implode.

"Sloan," he said.

"Not now, Stanley," Sloan said. "I'm talking to all these wonderful people."

Claire started past Stanley, and he grabbed her arm. Suddenly Sam was between them. Stanley made a funny "oof" sort of noise and had a weird look on his face. He let go of Claire, and she went out front to have her picture taken with Sloan.

"Let's get one of you holding Mackie Pea," Claire said to her. "You know how people love dogs and babies."

Sloan reluctantly took Mackie, who was growling low in her throat. She then handed the small dog right back to Claire, all with her open-mouthed movie star smile. She pointed, waved, winked, and blew kisses as the brisk spring wind blew back her newly styled hair as if it had been directed to do so.

The newspaper photographer's camera clicked, and the TV station's video camera whirred while several dozen cell phone users photographed and digitally recorded her with the intention of immediately uploading the footage to the Internet; it would be impossible for her team to stop it from happening.

"Y'all are just so lovely," Sloan enthused. "There's a real special place in my heart for this town; Y'all have made me feel so welcome."

"Great accent," Claire said under her breath, "if we were in Texas."

"Shut up, I'm working," Sloan said under hers.

"So the dog is a gift to Claire?" the reporter asked, and shoved the microphone into Sloan's face.

"Oh, yes," Sloan said. "Claire just loved the little dickens so much I just had to give it to her."

"She's such a generous person," Claire said, "and cares so much about children and animals."

Sloan put her arm around Claire so they could get some more shots. As always, Sloan intuitively knew just how long to stay before leaving them wanting more.

"Y'all are so sweet," Sloan said. "I hate to leave, but I have to fly to London this afternoon for a little ole Vogue cover shoot."

Sloan let go of Claire to sign some more autographs, and to have her picture taken with some small children. Claire watched Sloan do this trick where she held a child in one arm while she grasped their sticky little mitts with her free hand so they couldn't actually touch her. Each child was held for less than three seconds; long enough for a photo to be taken but just under the amount of time it took urine to soak through a diaper into whatever Sloan might be wearing.

Claire turned around in time to see Sam escorting Stanley to his car. Stanley seemed to have shrunk in stature and had a look on his face Claire had never seen there before; it was fear. As soon as Sam let go of his arm and walked away Stanley turned and beckoned impatiently for Sloan to follow.

"What a lovely send-off," Sloan said to Claire. "Thank you so much."

"It was my pleasure," Claire said. "I was happy to do it."

"Call me when you change your mind," Sloan said.

Claire just shook her head and waved as Sloan took her movie star exit. Everyone waved and cheered as the car pulled away from the curb, and Sloan blew kisses from the open window. Claire snuggled the wriggly little dog in her arms, satisfied that no one could take her away.

Sam made his way to Claire and stood with her next to the entrance to The Bee Hive, away from the dispersing crowd. He smiled with his whole face and Claire's heart melted.

"That went well," he said.

"How did you get them to show up all at once like that?"

"First we announced she'd be at the Thorn; once they were all assembled there after we saw Stanley go in the salon, we changed the venue to The Bee Hive."

"That was amazing."

"Here," he said. "It's a going away present from Stanley."

He pressed something into her free hand. It was the confidentiality agreement she had just signed and turned over to Stanley.

"What on earth did you do to him?" she asked.

"We had a short, meaningful conversation," Sam said. "He won't bother you again."

"Tell me something," Claire said. "Did you actually read Tuppy's book?"

"You mean this?" he said and held up the key ring. "I'm going to hold onto it if you don't mind; just for security purposes."

"You're amazing," she said. "I don't know what I'd do without you."

As soon as she said it she regretted it; it was too much. Sam's face closed up like a door slamming shut.

"All I meant was thanks, Sam," she said.

He nodded and walked away, but with a brief backward look that made her heart skip a beat.

Scott worked his way through the crowd toward her.

"What's going on?" he asked.

"Sloan's leaving," Claire said, "and she likes to make a big exit."

"You're free to leave, too," Scott said. "Sarah doesn't have enough evidence to hold anybody. Courtenay tipped the feds off about Pip's whereabouts; he's been arrested in Mexico and will be extradited to California later this week."

"Courtenay, who loved him so much she was going to give up Knox," Claire said, shaking her head.

"She found out he was married," Scott said. "Someone told her all about his financial problems."

Claire thought about Stanley's driver leaving Courtenay's apartment.

"I didn't know they were involved," Scott said. "How did you know?"

"Hannah told me," Claire said, and hoped that would be as far as that line of questioning went.

"Your cousin is an excellent detective but a terrible gossip," Scott said. "But I have to admit that comes in handy pretty often."

"So whoever killed Tuppy got away with it," Claire said.

"Maybe," Scott said. "There are still some loose ends to follow up on."

Claire looked thoughtful.

"I recognize that look, Claire," Scott said. "I've seen it on Hannah and Maggie. Don't get involved."

"Okay," she said with a shrug.

"Claire, I mean it."

"Alright," Claire said. "I'll let it go."

After the crowd dispersed, Claire went back in The Bee Hive and put Mackie Pea down on the floor. She sat on one of the hydraulic chairs and turned on her phone. Her latest voicemail was from Carlyle. The sound of his voice caused an actual pain in her chest. As she listened, all the feelings she'd been repressing came pouring out in a rush so powerful it made her dizzy with longing.

"Claire, I've been trying to get hold of you, but I don't know where you are. I just heard about Tuppy; a bit of a shocker to say the least and I know you're gutted. Listen, there's something you should know, something he told me after your going away party. He swore me to secrecy, but that cannot matter now, can it? When Sloan changed solicitors a year ago the cow didn't half cheese off the bastards she sacked. For revenge, they bunged her files down to a previous address and the man who lives there now called Tuppy to come get the lot.

"Before he delivered them to Stanley's office our Tuppy went through the files and ferreted out your confidentiality agreements; all of yours and his own, as well. He shredded them. So you're no longer beholden to that shelter belter, hen, haven't been since the cow hired Stanley. Do with this information what you will just don't let the madbit bully you.

"I've got my own solicitor now, looking over my contract, trying to find a way out. I know you probably don't give a shite, but I'm sorry, hen. So sorry. If there's any way I can make it up to you, please just tell me. You're missed, love. You're sorely, terribly missed, is all I'm saying. Please forgive me."

Even more than his heartfelt words was how Scottish he sounded; it was proof, to her mind, of how sincere he was; he was most himself when he dropped his polished English accent. Oh, how she missed him.

The front door opened and Claire quickly dried her eyes.

"I guess I missed all the excitement," the woman said. "I heard there was a movie star downtown, but she's gone. You know anything about that?"

"No," Claire said. "I don't know anything about that movie star."

After Claire closed up the shop that evening, she and Mackie Pea went down to the Rose and Thorn to pick up her father, and then walked him down to Machalvie's pharmacy to purchase a walker. At first, he stubbornly refused to even go in the shop, but then he agreed to at least look at what they had. As soon as he saw the brightly colored aluminum walkers with their handbrakes, baskets, and a place to sit, all on four multi-directional wheels, his only hesitation was deciding which color he wanted. Claire lifted Mackie Pea and put her in the basket.

"What do you say, my little darlin'?" Ian said to the little dog. "Should papaw take his sweetheart for a ride?"

"Papaw?" Claire said under her breath, laughing to herself at the idea of Ian referring to Mackie as his grandchild, but nonetheless, feeling touched.

Claire paid for the walker and then had to run to catch up with them. There her father went, tooling down the sidewalk holding onto his bright purple rolling walker with Mackie Pea in the basket. The hood of her pink and purple coat was pulled up over her head, and the purple tassel was sticking straight up in the air.

When they arrived back at her parents' house, they found her mother had cooked a pot-roast dinner, and it smelled heavenly.

"You must be feeling better," Claire said.

"Amy from the bank brought the mortgage payoff papers for me to sign," her mother said, while she hugged her. "Now that you've bought our house for us I thought it was the least I could do."

They all sat down to eat, and Claire found she was ravenous; in all the excitement of the day, she had skipped lunch.

"Where's Liam?" her father asked. "Does he have soccer practice this evening?"

Claire set down her fork, her appetite gone.

Delia didn't even pause before answering, "He's staying at Fitz and Bonnie's house tonight."

Her father just nodded and kept eating. Claire's eyes filled with tears, but when she looked at her mother, Delia just smiled sadly and said, "Eat your dinner, Claire."

After dinner, Delia loaded the dishwasher while Claire wrapped up the leftovers. Ian lay in his recliner with Mackie Pea on his lap; he was talking sweetly to her about what a good girl she was.

"I've decided to stay for good," Claire said, "if you and Dad don't mind."

Delia laid a hand on Claire's arm and said, "Are you sure that's the right thing for you? I hate to see you get tied down here if you'd rather be somewhere else."

"You know, a week ago I felt completely different," Claire said. "But then I kept having this homesick feeling every time I saw someone in our family. I think it must have been regret because I was planning to leave again, and deep down I really didn't want to go. As soon as I decided to stay that homesick feeling went away. After staying here with you and Dad, and seeing what you're going through, I realized I want to be the one you can count on to help. I want to be part of the family again and go through this next bit with you. There's really, truly nowhere else I'd rather be."

Delia wiped her eyes and hugged her daughter.

"I'm so glad," she said. "Thank you."

Maggie called and invited Claire over for a movie night sleepover, something they used to do when they were teenagers.

"I thought Maggie was mad at me," Claire said. "I don't want to pass up a chance to mend fences if she's willing to offer."

"Go on," her mother said. "We're fine, and I can always call you if I need you."

Claire went in the living room to collect Mackie Pea, but her father wasn't having it.

"You leave this sweet girl here with me," he said. "I don't want her gallivanting around the neighborhood in this weather; she might catch a cold."

Scott reviewed the advance directive form the social worker from Hospice had helped him and his mother fill out. The social worker completed the "do not resuscitate" order as well but told them they would have to wait for Doc Machalvie to sign it in order for it to be official. Sister Mary Margrethe provided a witness signature to the advance directive, and Kay from the mayor's office notarized it.

"This is so everyone knows what your wishes are," the social worker told Scott's mother. "If you reach a point in your illness where a breathing or feeding tube would be used to keep you alive, neither of those measures will be taken. If your heart stops, nothing will be done to re-start it."

His mother's handwriting was spidery and weak as she signed, but she was able to say, "I understand," when the social worker asked if she did.

Scott walked out to the porch with the social worker and thanked her again.

"As soon as the doctor signs the 'do not resuscitate' order post it next to her bed," she said. "That way if emergency personnel are called they will know not to apply CPR."

"I'll let you know as soon as she makes her decision," Scott said. "It really needs to be what she wants, not what Penny and I want."

"I wouldn't put it off too long," the social worker said. "We could really be helpful right now."

Scott's sister Penny was pouting in the kitchen when he returned. The other women were preparing to leave.

"Anything you need," Kay said as she went out, "anything at all; you just call."

"Thank you," Scott said.

"Miss Penny," Sister Mary Margrethe said. "Have we forgotten our manners?"

"Thank you," Penny murmured, but it was grudgingly said.

"I'll be back in the morning," Sister said. "I put a list on the fridge of the ladies who will be taking turns here for the next few days along with their telephone numbers. I chose only the most sensible people, and as you know, there aren't that many to choose from. If you need anything in the night, please call me. It's been many years since I was a nurse, but I can still be helpful."

Scott walked outside with Sister Mary Margrethe, and she lowered her voice as she said, "I had a word with Penny, but she refuses to accept how serious this is. I've seen this happen many times before; adult children can get stuck in denial and refuse to let go of the parent. I'm glad you got your mother's wishes down on paper so she can't interfere."

"I just wish Penny would calm down," Scott said. "Mom needs peace and quiet so she can conserve what energy she has left."

"I'll work on her again tomorrow," Sister said. "Sometimes I have to use my Sunday school voice to get my point across; it's a big stick, but I'm not afraid to use it."

She patted Scott's arm and then left the porch.

Scott went back inside to face his irate sister.

"You've just given up," she said in a loud voice. "She takes a little turn for the worse, and you've got her planning her funeral."

"Please keep your voice down," Scott said quietly. "Our mother is very sick. You need to accept that and spend some quality time with her before she goes. Keeping us all worked up with your drama is only making it harder for her to rest."

"She was fine last week when I talked to her," Penny said. "We were planning a shopping trip to the outlet malls."

"The cancer has spread throughout her body and is growing at a very fast rate," Scott said. "Her lungs are filling with fluid, and her heart is failing. The oncologist said she would go downhill fast after she reached this point. She's very susceptible to pneumonia or other infections, and if she gets one, it will probably kill her. She doesn't want feeding tubes or a ventilator, and she doesn't want to be in any pain. She's ready to let go, Penny. You have to let her go."

"I can't," Penny cried. "I'm not ready!"

"This isn't about you," Scott said. "This is about Mom and what's best for her."

Penny left the kitchen and went down the hall to the bathroom, loudly weeping. Scott went back to his mother's bedroom and stood by her bed. She seemed to be sleeping, but he could still hear the rattle in her chest that didn't bode well. She opened her eyes and smiled when she saw him, and he sat down on the edge of her bed and held her hand. She could hardly talk above a whisper, so he leaned down when she tried to speak.

"You're a good son," she said. "I love you."

Scott could barely speak for the lump in his throat, but he said, "Are you sure about what we plan to do? Do you want Doc to sign the 'do not resuscitate' order?"

She nodded and squeezed his hand.

"Take care of Penny," she said.

"I will," he said.

"She's a bit of a pill, isn't she?" she said and smiled.

Scott laughed, and his mother tried to, but started coughing and got choked. He helped her turn on her side, careful not to dislodge the oxygen cannula. Her cough was deep and sounded as if it hurt. Scott helped her administer a breathing treatment, and it seemed to help.

"Did you sign me up for Hospice?" she said, as soon as she was able to speak again.

Scott shook his head and took a deep breath.

"Call them," she said, and then relaxed back onto her pillow as if it had taken all the strength she had left to say those two words.

Scott called Doc and told him what his mother wanted. Doc said he would make the referral and then come over and sign the DNR form. The home health aide Scott had engaged earlier in the day arrived, and Scott told her they were calling in Hospice.

"You'll be glad you did," she said. "I used to work for Pine County Hospice, and they're the best. They'll take good care of her."

"Why don't you still work there?" Scott asked.

"It's wonderful what they do," she said. "The work was very meaningful to me at the time, and I'll probably go back to it someday, but honestly, I just needed a change. It's hard to get close to my patients only to lose them, over and over. This morning I helped a new mother with her baby, and then I visited a lady who just had hernia surgery. It's nice to work with patients who get better."

The aide went back to check on his mother. When she came back, she smiled at him with such kind compassion that he knew what she was about to say would be difficult to hear.

"I've been around a lot of dying people, and although everyone's different, I'd say she doesn't have much time left," she said. "I'm sorry."

Scott felt an overwhelming urge to do something: run a mile, build a house, swim the river; something. Instead, he went home to take a shower.

He let himself in his back door and walked past the utility room, where two empty bowls sat on the floor. Anger filled his chest and turned into a rage that he knew was all out of proportion to his irritation over the loss of a cat; nevertheless, he let it take over his will and flood his mind with the sense of having been cruelly used. Duke was his cat. He needed that cat. How dare Maggie take that away from him, along with everything else he loved?

Chapter Ten - Thursday/Friday

"Alright," Maggie said, as she paused the movie. "What in the hell is wrong with you?"

"What?" Claire said, wiping her eyes with her shirt tail. "Can't a girl be happy for Helena Bonham Carter? I mean, look at that glorious head of hair. That woman was born to wear period clothing."

"That's not the reason. We've done this a million times. We watch A Room with a View and then Enchanted April, but we don't cry until Hugh Grant comes back for Emma Thompson in Sense and Sensibility; not until she makes that asthma attack noise in the front sitting room."

"I do too cry during Enchanted April; during the part when it turns out Michael Kitchen can't see well because of his war injury, and he loves Polly Walker because of who she is inside, not because she's a beautiful, rich slut from a well-connected family."

"You're sad and pathetic."

"I know," Claire said. "I can't help it."

"So what's this really about?"

"Maggie, I love you, but you're not the most sympathetic person to talk to about feelings."

"I can be sympathetic," Maggie said. "Try me."

"Well ..." Claire started.

The phone rang in the kitchen.

"Hold that thought," Maggie said.

Claire followed her to the kitchen and refilled her wine glass.

"What?" was how Maggie answered the phone.

"He's in the front room, sleeping," Maggie said, by which Claire guessed she meant the cat Duke, who was the only male creature in the apartment that wasn't a fictitious literary character played by a handsome British actor on a well-worn DVD. "He ate his dinner, and now he's sleeping. I think he just wants a quiet night in."

Maggie paused to listen to her caller and then responded, "Drew says we should give him his space and let him decide where he wants to live."

Claire didn't even try to hide her eavesdropping.

"I did not hijack your cat, Scott," Maggie said. "The truth is I'm home more than you, and he just feels safer here. I'm sorry if that upsets you, but this isn't about you. This is about what's best for Duke."

Maggie rolled her eyes at Claire and then sighed in exasperation.

"Alright," she said. "Come over tomorrow after dinner and use your key. I'll be home about ten."

She hung up the phone and shook her head as she refilled her wineglass and joined Claire at the kitchen table.

"Scott?" Claire said.

"Uh huh," Maggie said. "Duke is Scott's cat, but he prefers living with me."

"I thought you hated cats."

"I don't hate cats; I'm allergic to them," Maggie said. "I get allergy shots now. You know how Rose Hill used to be overrun with feral cats?"

"Hannah told me there was a relocation project and that's why there are so many chipmunks and squirrels all over the place now."

"They brought in these federally funded Liberty Corp volunteers to help. They used humane traps to catch all the cats, euthanized the ones that were too sick or injured, and then spayed, neutered and relocated the rest. People were supposed to put special collars on their pets so if they got caught in the traps they could be returned to their owners. Duke's a wild thing that cannot be tamed, of course, so he kept taking off his collar. After he went missing for a week, we realized he'd been relocated. It took some time to find him but we did and brought him home. Since then he doesn't want to go out."

"Understandable."

"Scott's just using it as an excuse to bug the crap out of me."

"Hannah said she and the new vet ran this program. I haven't met him yet."

"He's the guy who's renting Hannah's farm. Drew bought the practice after Doc Owen died. Duke was originally Doc Owen's cat, and Drew thought he was the office's feline blood donor until he tried to take his blood. Needless to say, he and Duke did not hit it off, so Scott took him in."

"And what's happening tomorrow evening?"

"Scott's coming over to see Duke."

"It sounds like you're having child custody issues."

"It's ridiculous how crazy Scott is about that cat," Maggie said. "He was downright hostile on the phone just now."

"You know his mom's really sick."

"Isn't she always?" Maggie said, rolling her eyes.

"No, I mean really sick," Claire said. "Like dying sick."

Claire filled her in on the situation, and Maggie looked thoughtful.

"I wonder why he didn't tell me."

"Maybe because he thinks you don't care."

"I care," Maggie said. "Scott and I are still friends."

"Dad says Scott's still in love with you."

"I doubt that," Maggie said. "He took up with Ava right after Grandpa Tim and Brian died. Right after Grandpa Tim's funeral, he gave me an ultimatum: then or never."

"He told me that thing with Ava was all a big misunderstanding."

"I understood perfectly," Maggie said. "No teardrop falls from Ava Fitzpatrick's eye without it being caught by some stupid man."

"So why did you turn him down?"

"I don't want to talk about it," Maggie said. "Bores me to tears. Besides, you were just about to spill your guts about some dude that ripped your heart out. Is this the Scottish guy?"

"Mm-hmm," Claire said. "Carlyle McKinney: drama professor, dialect coach, and rabidly ambitious actor."

"Classic narcissist."

"Maybe not," Claire said. "He's simply a male of the species, and therefore weak in certain regards."

"You always were too nice," Maggie said. "What happened?"

"He was working on Sloan's most recent film as her dialect coach, and we spent a lot of late nights giggling into our pints in a local hostelry. Oh, Maggie, the man is so funny."

"Which is like honey to a Claire Bear."

"And he has this amazing talent with accents."

"I get that, I really do," Maggie said, "Look at all my DVDs. I spend more time with the virtual Colin Firth than I do with my real friends."

"He has this cultured, proper British speaking voice but sometimes the Scots burr sneaks in."

"Mmm, Rob Roy."

"I see your Rob Roy, and I raise you Her Majesty, Mrs. Brown."

"Oh, yes, you win; so what happened?"

"Sloan happened," Claire said. "As soon as she caught wind of what was going on between us she made him an offer he couldn't refuse."

"An acting job?"

"Sort of," Claire said. "He's going to pretend to be her fiancé until after the Academy Awards next winter."

"What?"

"I know it sounds crazy, but in that world, the movie business, it's standard practice," Claire said. "It's part of the packaging of Sloan as a product. She sells herself as a romantic heroine off-screen to help sell her performance as Mary Queen of Scots on-screen. If she wants an Oscar, she needs a compelling personal drama to keep herself in the public eye between the film release and awards season.

"Ayelet will tip off photographers so they can get carefully set-up candid shots of her and Carlyle for the tabloids. They'll build on that buzz through talk shows, fashion magazine covers, press junkets, and a half-dozen award ceremonies. All this leads up to February when Sloan will tearfully thank her management team as she accepts her Best Actress Academy Award. More movie tickets will be sold, more DVDs will be rented, her price will go up, and she'll go back to getting the first refusal on all the best scripts."

"So he sold his soul to the devil," Maggie asked. "Is it just for money and fame or does he really want to be Mr. Merryweather?"

"He teaches at the Royal Scottish Academy of Music and Drama, but at heart, Carlyle is an actor. He's really very good, but even brilliant actors need a lucky break. With Sloan, he has access to her management team, good scripts, and opportunities he wouldn't have on his own. In return, she'll get British theater credibility, American and European press, and if all goes well, the aforementioned award outcome."

"You should have known better than to fall in love with someone who teaches drama," Maggie said. "That's like the warning label on a bottle of crazy pills."

"I have a weakness for the creative, smart, funny guys," Claire said. "I can't help it."

"So he betrayed you."

"Not very gracefully, either," Claire said. "Sloan arranged for me to catch them sealing the deal, so to speak."

"Good riddance, then," Maggie said. "To hell with him and the bitch you worked for."

"The problem is I can see his side of it," Claire said. "You don't know how many times over the past twenty years I planned to walk away from Sloan. I knew that job was sucking the life out of me, but I always went back. The truth is I loved the money and the travel, and I admit it, I loved the drama. I can't blame Carlyle for wanting to experience that too. This is his big break. He might have turned her down and then resented me for it."

"You're giving him way too much credit," Maggie said. "He was a fool to let you get away."

"I still have this secret fantasy he'll realize what a farce it all is and run away to be with me."

"Screw that," Maggie said. "If a man loves you he will move heaven and earth to be with you. Anything less is unacceptable."

"Mary Margaret Fitzpatrick," Claire said. "You're a closet romantic."

"I'm delusional, is what I am," Maggie said. "After our talk the other day I changed the sign over the romance section to 'Unrealistic Expectations,' but Jeanette made me change it back."

"Scott would move heaven and earth for you."

"The day he gave me an ultimatum the words, 'no, sorry' were barely out of my mouth when he ran right over to the B&B and cried on Ava's shoulder."

"Everyone makes mistakes."

"Except Scott's big mistake made me waste several years of my life."

"What are you talking about?"

"He knew why Gabe left me the first time; he was there that night. He gave him an ultimatum, too; leave town or be arrested."

"And then he kept it a secret from you; now I remember."

"For seven years I wondered and waited for Gabe to come back to me. I didn't know if he was dead or alive. When the postmistress died Hannah and I uncovered a huge stash of stolen mail hidden in her house, but Scott caught us before we could look through it. There was a letter from Gabe to me in there written the week after he left. Scott found it but was not going to tell me about it. It fell out of his jacket pocket."

"Maybe he was going to give it to you."

"He had seven years to tell me what happened and he didn't."

"I can kind of see his side of it," Claire said.

"Of course you can," Maggie said. "You're the queen of fair play."

"Don't you Catholics believe in forgiveness?"

"We also believe in eternal damnation," Maggie said. "That's more my style."

"It's such a terrible waste of time," Claire said. "Here's this man who loves you so much he hasn't been able to make it work with anyone else. Why postpone happiness? Why defer your joy? You're not getting any younger."

"You sound like my mother."

"Do you love him?" Claire asked.

Maggie hesitated.

"I don't not love him."

"Well, there you go."

"Listen," Maggie said. "Every time I see him with one of those chicks he dates I feel this pain in my chest that makes me want to hurt somebody. I don't think that's pretty enough to be called love."

"Sounds pretty passionate to me," Claire said. "Sounds like an epic romance."

"It's hard to explain," Maggie said. "It feels like if I give in to it, I'll lose something really important."

"Independence? Autonomy?"

"Yeah, but also, I'll have to be nice to him every day. I mean, even if I don't feel like it. I'll have to be affectionate in public, and other people will see it. I can't bear the thought of people seeing me be squishy with him. It feels like admitting weakness."

"In other words, you're afraid if you marry Scott you'll have to be a better person than you are capable of being."

"That's it," Maggie said. "That's it, exactly. You're good."

"You need therapy," Claire said, "and lots of it; maybe even a tag team of therapists so when you wear one out another one can jump in."

"I know," Maggie said. "I do love Scott, but right now I just don't feel compelled to do anything about it."

"You're just stuck in a tar pit of pride."

"That, too," Maggie said. "When Knox's crazy wife Anne Marie came back from rehab she went into some kind of trance and told me my sin was pride."

"She's a rich and famous psychic now."

"That's all hokum," Maggie said. "There are things you can tell anyone, and they'd be true."

"Such as?"

"You're about to go through a big change in your life; a transition; some people will enter your life, and some will fall away. You're making big decisions."

"That's all true," Clair said.

"But don't you see? That's true of everyone. Everyone is always going through big life changes. Psychics just make general pronouncements and watch how you respond. 'The name starts with a J; the color blue is significant.' Con artists do the same thing."

"So nothing Anne Marie told you was specific to you? There was nothing she said that no one else could know?"

"Well," Maggie said, but then she hesitated. "I thought so at the time, but no, it was all just her warped imagination and my susceptibility."

"I thought she was really good."

"What did she tell you?"

"She said I would travel across a large body of water and then fall in love with an educated man," Claire said. "She said I would have two lives in one, but the second one would bring me the most happiness."

"Maybe your second life is here in Rose Hill."

"We'll see."

"Do you want to finish the movie?"

"No, I'm tired. Do you?"

"It's not like we don't know how it ends. I'm tired, too. Let's go to bed."

Claire lay next to Maggie under their grandmother's quilt, staring at the ceiling. Moonlight filled the room, and Duke the cat was curled up between them, purring loudly. Claire felt like she was eight years old, at a sleepover at Grandma Rose's house with Hannah and Maggie. The upstairs of that house had not been heated, and the three of them used to snuggle together for warmth under a mountain of quilts, like baby rabbits in a burrow.

"I'm wide awake now," Maggie said. "What are you thinking about?"

"How we didn't know we were poor when we were growing up," Claire said. "I was looking through your photo albums earlier, and things look so much shabbier in retrospect."

"We never went without anything we really needed," Maggie said. "We always had a roof over our heads and a meal on the table."

"I remember being so jealous of all the toys and clothes Caroline Eldridge had, and how ashamed I felt when her sister Gwyneth made fun of us. I didn't know anything about class prejudice; I just thought she was mean."

"Gwyneth was always such a snotty, stuck-up snob," Maggie said.

"She still is," Claire said.

"Caroline's mother was always very gracious to us," Maggie said.

"Where is Caroline now?"

"Traveling around the world, I guess, from ashram to monastery; saving the world one trust fund payment at a time."

"Being born into wealth must make it easier to spend," Claire said. "Now that I have money I'm scared to death I'll lose it all. I want to hoard it. I'm going to end up like Mamie Rodefeffer, wearing twenty cardigans and carrying ten tote bags. What are in those tote bags, do you think?"

"Romance books," Maggie said. "She's one of my best customers."

"Romance? Really?"

"The more torrid, the better," Maggie said. "She likes the bodice rippers."

"I wish I'd known that," Claire said. "I would've given her more of a B movie hairstyle."

"Are you going to buy The Bee Hive?"

"I don't know," Claire said. "I've kind of enjoyed it this week, but I'm not sure I want to do that every day for the rest of my life."

"It doesn't have to be the forever thing, just the next thing," Maggie said. "How are your parents?"

"My dad's a mess," Claire said, "and my mom is worn out taking care of everyone. I want to make their lives better, easier somehow."

"Good thing you're rich, then," Maggie said. "You can fix everything."

"I don't know if that's possible," Claire said. "My mother thinks I should just accept things the way they are."

"That's very Zen," Maggie said. "I sometimes think Buddhist philosophy is basically that shit happens and you're stupid for thinking it should be different."

"I think there's more to it than that."

"Sure there is; I just like my version better."

"How does that compare to Catholicism?"

"The Catholic philosophy is that not only does shit happen, but it's all your fault because you're such an awful sinner."

"The Protestant faith I grew up with is the surfer dude of religions," Claire said. "We're all 'hey man, just be cool, and like, don't hurt anybody; but if you do, just say 'my bad, bro,' and it's all good.'"

"I love to reduce thousands of years of theology into short, pithy sentences."

"And to think some people like to crochet," Claire said.

"I'm glad you're home," Maggie said. "I didn't realize how much I missed you until you came back."

"I won't tell anyone," Claire said. "I wouldn't want to expose your weakness."

"I'd deny it," Maggie said with a yawn, "even if you did."

"I'm glad to be home," Claire said. "And no one is more surprised about that than me."

"I'm still mad at you for not telling me you went skinny-dipping with Scott."

"That was a long time ago," Claire said. "Nothing happened."

"I know," Maggie said. "I can't help it, this jealousy thing. I don't want him, but I don't want anyone else to have him; even though I know that's not fair."

"Oh, for mercy's sake! If you love Scott you need to do something about it," Claire said. "He doesn't deserve to be treated like this, and you're only hurting yourself."

"Your accent came right back," Maggie said. "It's been less than a week, and you're back to talking like you never left."

"Shut up and listen to me," Claire said. "Two very wise people recently told me that I wouldn't really be grown up until I put aside my selfish wants to do what's best for someone I love."

"Your point being?"

"Maybe it's time for you and me both to grow up."

"I've changed my mind about missing you," Maggie said.

"Too late," Claire said. "No take-backs."

Scott's mother was struggling to breathe; the rattle in her chest sent panic rushing through his nervous system so that he felt like he might jump out of his skin. He could hear Penny on the phone in the kitchen exhorting the 911 operator to send an ambulance right away. He had done everything he knew to do and still his mother couldn't breathe. He held his mother's hand and tried the pursed-lip breathing, encouraging her to do the same.

Doc Machalvie arrived and immediately gave his mother another breathing treatment, injected her with something, and then adjusted her oxygen to a higher level. He looked so gravely concerned that it made Scott's heart thud hard in his chest.

Doc nodded toward the kitchen and Scott said to his mother, "I'll be right back." The panic in her eyes had changed to sadness, and there were tears on her face. He left, shutting the door to his mother's room behind him.

"Do you really want to drag her to the hospital?" Scott asked his sister, as soon as he entered the kitchen. "The trip alone might kill her; and if she does live she'll probably catch something in the hospital that will kill her there."

"We have to do something!" Penny cried.

"Stop it. Just stop and look at what's happening," Scott said. "You're not helping her; you're making it worse."

"She needs to be in intensive care," Penny insisted. "They can build up her strength so she can take the chemo treatments."

"You're the only one who believes that," Scott said. "She's dying, Penny."

Penny burst into tears and fled to her old bedroom.

Scott went out on the front porch and looked up at the dark clouds passing beneath the full moon. The wind was sharp and wet, and it chilled him to the bone, but he didn't want to go back in the house for his jacket. What he wanted to do was run screaming down the hill and jump in the river; anything to get away from what was going on inside.

He thought he might pray, but what would he ask for? A merciful death? A miraculous recovery? What did he really want for his mother, for Penny, for himself? He took out his phone and chose a name out of his list of contacts. It was all he really wanted; his call was his prayer.

A little while later he saw someone coming down the street, running down the street, her long hair flying out behind her like a flag. When she reached the steps to the porch, she leaped up two at a time until finally she reached him, embraced him, and hugged him so hard it took his breath away

"Thank you," he said through his tears. "I need you."

"I'm sorry it took me so long," Maggie said. "I'm here now."

It was so early on Friday morning that stars were still twinkling in the dark sky. Claire had to hurry to catch up with Ian, who was pushing his walker down Pine Mountain Road with Mackie Pea in the basket.

"Wait up!" Claire called after him.

Her feet were so sore she was having trouble walking, even in her mother's gigantic pillow sneakers.

"We're late!" he called over his shoulder.

"It's not even the crack of dawn," Claire protested as she caught up to him. "It's practically still yesterday."

"I've never heard that one before," he said, even though he was the one who taught it to Claire.

There were several cars and trucks parked outside the Laurel Mountain Depot Bar and Grill; Claire was surprised to see it so busy. Her father led her up the wheelchair ramp and in through the side door, where several people greeted him by name. A dark-haired waitress whom Claire judged was showing way too much cleavage for this time of day called out, "I saved your table for ya, Chief."

Ian led his daughter to a table in the corner by the window, which would have a great view of the river had it been light enough outside to see it. He parked the walker, lifted Mackie Pea out of her basket and tucked her in the crook of his arm before he sat down. Claire looked around and realized that besides the waitress she was the only woman in the room.

Many of the men were locals; she recognized them but couldn't place names to faces. Most were dressed in the blue-collar uniform of a ball cap, tan cotton canvas jackets, overalls and work boots. There were a few students who looked like they'd been up all night. There were several men in suits who looked out of place but seemed to feel right at home.

The waitress brought them two coffees and winked at Claire.

"I thought you stood me up," she said to Ian in a deep smoker's voice.

Claire immediately cast her as a hooker with a heart of gold. She looked to be in her late forties or early fifties; her eyes were hard, her makeup had been heavily applied, and the smoker's wrinkles surrounding her lips made her look even older. Her hair color was a few shades too dark, and the big, teased style had been more suited to music video vixens in the eighties.

"This is my daughter," Ian said. "She's home for a visit."

"I know Claire," the woman said, but it took Claire several awkward moments to superimpose this woman's face over that of one of the wildest teenagers who had ever attended Rose Hill High School. Claire was appalled to realize Phyllis was younger than she was by at least two years.

"How are you, Phyllis?" Claire asked.

"Oh, I'm alright," Phyllis said. "I can't complain, and even if I did no one would care. How about I give y'all some sausage gravy and biscuits?"

"What'll you give me?" a man at a nearby table asked her.

"The only thing I can give you, old man, is a heart attack," Phyllis said and rolled her eyes at Claire while the other men laughed.

Phyllis went back to the kitchen, and Claire sipped her coffee.

"This is good," she said.

"We were late," Ian said. "I leave the bakery at six and Scott gets me here by 6:05. It's 6:38 now."

His head started bobbing, and his mouth turned down into the exaggerated frown.

"I think it will be okay," Claire said quietly.

"I have a schedule," her father said loudly. "My mind isn't what it used to be. I need to keep track of things."

"Okay, Dad," Claire said. "It's okay now. Phyllis is going to bring your breakfast, and we're in no hurry, we can take our time."

"I get to Curtis's station by 8:00," he said, almost shouting. "We have to leave here by 7:50."

"We will," Claire said, acutely aware of the attention he was drawing to their table. She was embarrassed and then mad at herself for caring so much what other people thought. She thought if she heard even a hint of a snicker from anyone in the room she could easily do grievous bodily harm to the snickerer. But instead, everyone seemed to be accommodating, some even sending her kind, sympathetic smiles. Claire remembered what her mother had said about the townspeople protecting her father. They were probably used to his outbursts. With this thought, she was flooded with a feeling of gratitude toward everyone in the room.

'As the Mood Swings,' she heard Tuppy say in her head.

'It is kind of a soap opera,' she thought. 'I've got to get hold of myself and calm down.'

Phyllis was having a heated discussion with the college students, who looked like they were giving her a hard time. Claire couldn't hear what they were saying, but it looked like she knew them better than just as customers.

Someone came in through the front door, and several people greeted him.

Her father called out, "Ed! Where ya been, buddy?"

Claire immediately recognized Ed Harrison, Scott's best friend who owned The Rose Hill Sentinel. His family owned the house next door to hers, so he was a familiar person from her childhood and teen years. In high school, he had been so shy he blushed bright red if Claire even so much as looked at him. If she tried to talk to him, he stammered and fled as soon as he could. He made his way over to their table, and Claire got up to accept a hug. He sat down across from Ian and seemed to instantly gauge his agitation level.

"I'm sorry I'm late," Ed told Ian. "We got back so late last night we both overslept; we almost didn't get to the office in time to meet the Pendleton paper delivery."

"We were late," Ian said. "Claire couldn't get out of bed this morning; she's been staying out all hours of the night."

"It's true," Claire said, rolling her eyes. "I've let everyone down. I'm so sorry."

Ed winked at her and said, "You'll just have to try harder in the future."

"Why didn't Scott bring me?" Ian asked, for the fifth time that morning.

"His mother's really sick," Claire told him, and Ed nodded to show that he knew about it. "He needs to be home taking care of her."

"His mother?" Ian said, again very loudly. "Delia's his mother. Is Delia sick?"

"No, Dad," Claire said. "Scott worked for you when you were chief of police; he's not your son."

"I know that," Ian said. "I don't know why I said that."

"I forget things, too," said Ed. "All the time. It's no big deal."

"I think I'm losing my mind," Ian told Ed, and there were tears in his eyes.

Claire felt tears spring to her eyes as well.

"Oh, Dad," she said. "It's going to be alright; I promise."

"You don't need to worry," Ed reassured him. "Claire and Delia will take good care of you, and all your friends will help."

"That's good," Ian said, and was immediately cheerful again, while Claire felt like she'd been put through a wringer.

Ed smiled at her in a way that felt like a pat on the head.

"You and I need to talk," Ed said. "I guess I missed all the excitement."

"I'm not sure Sean will let me talk about it," Claire said.

"About what?" Ian said.

Claire couldn't think of a lie quick enough, but Ed didn't hesitate.

"Claire's movie star was here in town," Ed said. "I wanted to take her picture with Claire."

Claire gave Ed a grateful look, and he smiled again. She hadn't remembered how attractive he was; a little nerdy but very appealing. Maybe he was improving with age.

While her father talked to Ed, Claire studied him. Ed and Scott had been friends all their lives, had played baseball and wrestled on the same teams. Ed had been studious and always got perfect grades; Scott was more athletic and cared more about baseball cards than books. Ed had always been quiet; had always hung back or watched from the periphery of what was happening; observing, analyzing, and recording. These skills made him a natural as a reporter; he had attended one of the best journalism schools in the Northeast and worked at a Philadelphia paper after he graduated.

When his father died of a heart attack Ed came home and took over The Rose Hill Sentinel, the paper his grandfather had started. His wife Eve, whom he'd met in journalism school, had not factored a small town weekly paper into her career plans, and they broke up.

Ed started losing his hair at a young age and was now almost completely bald; what hair he did have was buzzed close to his scalp; Claire bet he did it himself with clippers; no-nonsense and cheap. He wore glasses now, the wire and black plastic ones that were a throwback to the fifties; they suited his face, which no one would call handsome, but Claire thought it was actually kind of nice. When she thought of him as a character to cast she realized he was already exactly who his character would be.

"Where were you?" Claire said. "On vacation?"

"Kind of," he said and didn't say any more, so Claire let it drop.

"Where's your young man?" Ian asked him, and Claire's curiosity was piqued.

"Tommy had to catch the bus to school," Ed said. "He goes to Pine County Consolidated."

"Rose Hill has a perfectly good school," Ian said. "You ought to send him there."

Claire started to say Rose Hill High School had been closed years ago and made into a community center, but Ed gave his head a quick shake and spoke first.

"You know these kids, Ian," he said. "They want to do what they want to do."

"Liam will go to Rose Hill High School," Ian said. "I won't stand for any of that nonsense from him."

It had happened almost every day since she came home, but it still felt like a kick to the stomach. Ed looked at her with concern, but she shook her head.

Phyllis brought Ed his breakfast: oatmeal and bacon.

"The bacon giveth the cholesterol," he explained to Claire, "and the oatmeal taketh it away."

"So it's a balanced breakfast," she said.

"Exactly," he said.

"Who's Tommy?" she asked.

"You know Tommy," Ian said. "He's Mandy's boy."

"I'm afraid to ask who Mandy is," Claire said under her breath.

"I'll tell you later," Ed said under his.

"Do I still drive the school bus?" Ian asked Ed.

"Nope," Ed said. "You're retired now."

"I am tired now," Ian said. "But Claire's making me do all the work."

Claire was puzzled by this statement, but Ed just smiled.

Phyllis set a huge plate of beige food in front of Claire. She looked at the two halves of a gigantic biscuit covered in sausage gravy and decided if it weren't for how heavenly it smelled she could convince herself not to eat it based on appearance alone.

For several years now she had subsisted on a steady diet of steamed vegetables, poached chicken breasts, and grilled white fish, with only a semi-annual chocolate cupcake cheat-a-thon to reward her. She decided one bite wouldn't hurt; she'd get back on the wagon tomorrow. Before she knew what had happened, however, the entire plate was bare, and Ed was staring at her in amusement.

"I guess I was hungrier than I thought," she said.

"Phyllis can bring more if you need it," Ed said, smiling. "I guess those five-star establishments you're used to don't dabble in the country-fried food genre."

"They do, they just call it sauce instead of gravy," she said.

"I bet it's not the same, though."

"Why does it feel so right?" Claire said. "I feel like I've been craving this food for twenty years."

At 7:45 Ian insisted they leave. Claire tried to use her credit card to pay, but it was declined.

"That can't be right," she said, embarrassed.

Ed quickly paid with cash, and said, "You can get the next one."

"I've never had a problem before," she said.

"It's probably nothing," Ed said.

But it wasn't. After dropping her dad and dog off at Uncle Curtis's service station, Claire crossed the street to unlock The Bee Hive. Once inside she called the customer service number on the back of her credit card and was informed it had been reported as stolen. When she called about her other two cards, she was told the same thing.

"Damn you, Sloan," she said and proceeded to recite all the curse words she knew, ending with the worst one she could think of.

"Excuse me," someone said, and Claire turned around to find that, to her horror, Sister Mary Margrethe was standing in the doorway of the beauty shop with a look of shocked disappointment on her face.

"Oh, Christ," Claire said, which didn't help matters.

Scott woke up spooning Maggie in his childhood twin-size bed. She was awake, reading a Hardy Boys mystery from the collection in the bookcase headboard.

"Why didn't you wake me up?" he said, as he stretched and then reached for her again.

"You only got about three hours of sleep," Maggie said. "I thought you needed a little more."

"I need a little more of this," he said and pulled her even closer.

"Stop that, I'm reading," she said. "I never knew Frank and Joe were such badass detectives."

Scott laughed and kissed her neck.

"Don't start that," Maggie said. "I'm leaving."

She put the book back on the shelf and got up.

"Where are you going?" Scott said. "It's still early. Come back to bed. I promise to behave myself."

"I've got businesses to run," Maggie said, as she put on her shoes. "Plus I don't want Sister M Squared to catch me here."

"It's Delia who's coming this morning," Scott said. "She'll be thrilled to see you here."

"Oh no," Maggie said. "Then the smug smiles will start. I don't think I can stand it."

Scott got out of bed and grabbed her by the hand before she could get away. He pulled her into an embrace.

"You can tell them all to go to hell," he said. "I don't care if you're nice to them or not, just don't let it change your mind."

"That's good to hear," Maggie said. "Cause you know I don't have a sweet bone in my body and I'm not likely to develop one this late in the game."

"Oh, I think there's some good stuff in there," he said. "You just save that for me."

Maggie kissed him and held him close for a moment. Then she smoothed his hair back from his forehead and looked into his eyes.

"I'll be back," she said.

Later that morning Scott sat at his mother's kitchen table with the referral nurse from Hospice and answered all her questions as well as he could. There was the Hospice paperwork for his mother to sign, and several other documents spread out on the table, including her insurance papers, her Medicare card, the advance directive, the medical power of attorney, and the "do not resuscitate order" that Doc Machalvie had signed. This, he reflected, was his mother's fate encompassed in paper and ink.

Exhausted, Scott could hear his sister snoring in her bedroom, and he resented it. He tried to listen to what the Hospice nurse was saying, but his attention was riveted to his mother's labored breathing in the room down the hall.

"Do you have any questions?" the nurse asked him.

"The home health aide said she didn't have much time left," Scott said. "What do you think?"

"It's hard to say," the nurse said. "Some people rally and seem much better right before they take a turn for the worse; some people steadily decline, and some people can go quite suddenly; everyone is different. You'll know when she's actively dying from the signs I described to you; I'm leaving this booklet so you can identify the stages as they happen. Anytime you have a question or a concern you can call our number and someone will answer. If it's the answering service, you'll have a call back from the on-call nurse within fifteen minutes. We can come out anytime day or night if you need us."

"Thank you," Scott said. "I had no idea how much you all actually do."

Scott saw her out and returned to his mother's room, where she was now reposing on a hospital bed with an IV pole next to it. She was attached by IV to a pain medication machine; if she felt any pain she could press a button kept near to her hand, and a dose of pain medication would be released into her IV. The nurse had assured Scott that the doses of pain medication were carefully measured and monitored; if his mother pushed the button several times, she wouldn't get more medication than was allowed during a certain time period.

The oxygen cannula was still draped around her head and clamped to her nostrils. Her arms were elevated on pillows, and the head of her bed had been raised so that she was reclining at an angle rather than laying flat on her back. The cool air in the room was being humidified by one machine and cleaned by another.

Scott had been concerned that his mother's color was not good; her face was pale, and her lips and fingertips were faintly violet. The nurse had explained that it was from the meager amount of oxygen that was reaching her lungs due to the fluid building up, and subsequently starving her heart.

"We aren't going to suction her lungs," the nurse had explained. "It's a traumatic, painful procedure, and our first priority is for her to be comfortable and pain-free."

"What can I do for her?" Scott asked.

"Give her anything she wants to eat or drink," the nurse had said. "But if she refuses don't force her. She's stated that she doesn't want a feeding tube or a respirator. Your job is just to be her son and spend quality time with her. We'll make sure she stays comfortable as we let nature take its course."

Scott sat down in a chair beside her bed and leaned back. He decided he would close his eyes for just a minute, and immediately fell asleep.

Delia woke him up when she came to take her turn at the bedside. His mom was sleeping soundly, so Scott motioned for her to come back in the kitchen with him. He made some coffee and sat at the table with her, drinking it

"How are you feeling?" Scott asked her.

"It was just a 24-hour thing," Delia said. "Doc looked me over this morning and pronounced me fit enough to sit with your mom."

"I appreciate all the help I'm getting," Scott said. "I couldn't do this without it."

"It's what we do," Delia said. "We take care of each other."

"How's Claire doing?" Scott asked. "I feel like I've been neglecting her."

"She's still trying to figure out where she belongs," Delia said. "I tried not to pressure her to stay, but it seems like she's going to."

"I thought maybe she'd stop by," Scott said. "I know she's busy at The Bee Hive ..."

"Claire never really got over Liam's death," Delia said. "I think it might be too tough for her to see your mom this way."

"I don't know how you could get over that," Scott said.

"You don't," Delia said. "It's like a permanent dark cloud you just get used to seeing out of the corner of your eye. Sometimes it's bigger than the blue sky, and sometimes the blue sky is bigger, but it never completely goes away."

The Hospice aide arrived, and Scott showed him where to go.

"I'm keeping in touch with Sarah over this hit and run investigation," Scott said when he returned. "I really think Claire's in the clear."

"I understand Ava had to vouch for Patrick," Delia said.

"That news sure traveled fast."

"Gossip always does."

"I thought maybe that was why you didn't work for her anymore," he said.

"She's like a siren," Delia said, "luring sailors to their deaths."

"You warned me," Scott said, "but I didn't listen."

"You escaped," Delia said. "Patrick won't be so lucky."

"Do you think she and Patrick will marry?"

"Only if he wins the lottery," Delia said.

"She's not that mercenary," Scott said.

Delia smiled as she shook her head.

"See," she said. "You're not out of the woods yet."

Scott smiled sheepishly.

"How's my buddy?" Scott said, in an attempt to change the subject. "I miss our breakfasts."

"He's the same," Delia said, "Which is a blessing because he's not going to get any better."

"What's the latest prognosis?"

"They just don't know," Delia said. "We'll keep him at home as long as we can."

"Then what?"

"I don't know, and I can't worry about that now," Delia said. "We'll cross that bridge when we come to it."

Sarah Albright came in the salon and Claire immediately felt sick at her stomach. She had two ladies under dryers, one in a hydraulic chair, and one in the waiting area.

"Hello Detective Albright," Claire said. "What can I do for you?"

"You can confess to killing your boyfriend," Sarah said, with an evil gleam in her eye and a smirk on her face.

The two ladies under the dryers leaned forward, the woman in the hydraulic chair turned around to look at Sarah, and the woman in the waiting area put down her magazine.

Claire was so stunned she didn't know what to say, and in that interval, something happened she didn't expect.

"Shame on you," the woman in the hydraulic chair said to Sarah. "Don't you have better things to do with your time than harass innocent people?"

"What did she say?" one of the dryer ladies said.

"She said Claire killed somebody," the other one said.

"I don't think it's legal for you to come in here and say things like that," the woman in the waiting area said. "That's harassment."

"It's slander," the first dryer lady said. "Or is it libel?"

"I'd call Scott," the second dryer lady said.

"I'd call her boss," the woman in the hydraulic chair said.

The smirk faded off Sarah's face and was replaced with a hard, angry look. Claire could tell she wanted to say something more but must have realized she would only dig herself in deeper. She turned and walked out, but before the door shut, she got to hear some last words.

"Don't let the door hit you in the ass on the way out!" the lady in the waiting area said.

"You women are fierce," Claire said, with tears glistening in her eyes. "Thank you."

"She picked the wrong town to pull that crap," the lady in the hydraulic chair said.

"Just let us know if you decide to file a complaint," the waiting room lady said. "We were all witnesses."

"I think her hand was on her gun when she said it," the first dryer lady said.

"I'd swear to it," the second one said, and then they all laughed.

Later in the morning Gail Godwin left The Bee Hive with a free haircut and blow dry after telling all the gossip she'd heard about the night Tuppy died. This left Claire wound up and anxious to follow up on what she now knew.

"Hannah," Claire said as soon as her cousin answered the phone. "We have a new lead on Tuppy's murder."

"I'll be there in a flash," Hannah said. "I just have to find my cape."

Maggie came in looking grumpy, with circles under her eyes.

"You need coffee and an ice pack," Claire said, and quickly delivered both.

"We got no sleep," Maggie said moments later, from under the ice pack she held over her eyes as she reclined in the shampoo bowl chair. "His sister Penny sawed logs down the hall while we sat next to his mother's bed and listened to every breath she took. No kidding, I thought each one would be the last."

"I bet he was so glad you came."

"Hmph," Maggie said. "I worked for my mother this morning, and I swear that woman has second sight. She kept giving me these knowing looks. You didn't tell your mom, did you?"

"No, I swear."

"It was probably that worthless Penny," Maggie said. "She probably told the first person who came to sit with her mother and that person put out an all points bulletin."

"I don't remember Penny," Claire said.

"She's insufferable," Maggie said. "She's making it all about her, like, 'poor me, how could this happen to me?' Never mind it's her mother who's dying."

"Drama queen," Claire said.

"She could give that actress of yours a run for her money."

Claire told Maggie what Sloan had done to her credit cards.

"What can you do?"

"It took me half an hour just to prove I am who I said I was. They're sending new cards; I just have to wait until they arrive."

"How can I help?"

"I need to take the rental car to Pendleton and turn it in," Claire said, "but I don't have the cash I need to pay for it. I don't have an account at Knox's bank; do you think they'll let me have some money?"

"I think Knox will give you anything you ask for right now," Maggie said. "He wouldn't dare decline you, but I have cash at the store if they say no."

Hannah came running in, saying, "Knox is on TV right now, having a press conference."

Claire turned on Denise's TV, and channel surfed until she found it.

"He's doing it from his hospital bed," Hannah said.

"Oh, my gosh," Maggie said. "He looks awful."

"The better to elicit sympathy," Claire said.

They'd missed most of it, but the news channel replayed it with commentary. Knox was wearing makeup to cover his bruises, and although one eye was swollen shut he was still lit in a flattering way. With every carefully crafted sentence he spoke, every subtle wince of pain, it seemed obvious to Claire that his performance had been as skillfully orchestrated as an award-winning scene in any classic film.

He claimed that his wife had taken a new allergy medicine and had mistaken him for a bank robber.

"He's good," Claire said when it was over and they went to commercial.

"He even made me feel sorry for him," Hannah said, "and I know what a rotten egg he is."

"Poor old Knox," Maggie said. "He has the worst luck with wives."

"It sometimes doesn't pay to be an ambitious sociopath," Claire said. "I'm relieved to know it."

Claire reported Gail Godwin's gossip to her cousins, about the students who were drag racing after Phyllis's party.

"It's just like Phyllis to be in the middle of this," Maggie said. "You know her son killed Theo Eldridge."

"Now I remember," Claire asked. "I just didn't relate the name to our Phyllis from high school."

"Billy thought Theo was his father and he'd inherit a fortune," Hannah said. "That turned out to be wishful thinking on Phyllis's part. He died in a car wreck up near the state park with the cops right on his tail."

"Do you think Phyllis will tell us anything?" Claire asked.

"She hates me," Maggie said, "and the feeling is mutual."

"She's not crazy about me, either," Hannah said.

"I guess it's up to me, then," Claire said. "I think the students in the depot this morning might have been the culprits; they were acting really weird with Phyllis."

Claire had a short break and ran down to the Mountain Laurel. The parking lot was empty, and Phyllis was sitting on the side porch smoking a cigarette.

"You wanna order something?" Phyllis asked her. "There might be some gravy left."

"No, thanks," Claire said and sat down upwind of Phyllis's cigarette. "I wanted to ask you about what happened last Friday night."

Phyllis pointed her cigarette at Claire and narrowed her eyes.

"I don't know nothin' 'bout that," she said. "I was home in bed when that happened. I got seven witnesses that'll tell anyone that's true."

Claire wondered why so many people were on hand to witness Phyllis at home in her bed but decided not to follow up on that line of questioning.

"The man that was killed was a friend of mine," Claire said. "I'm just trying to find out what happened."

"Well, I'm sorry to hear that," Phyllis said, "but like I said, it don't involve me."

"Were there some college kids at your house that night?"

"No, I was alone," Phyllis said.

Claire was no lawyer, but even she could see it would be hard to uphold Phyllis's claim of simultaneously being home alone in bed while also having seven witnesses on hand to swear to it.

"It doesn't have to involve you," Claire said. "Maybe you just heard something that would be helpful."

"I gotta get back to work."

She stood up and flicked her cigarette toward the river.

"I don't want to get you in any trouble," Claire said. "I just want to know who the boys were that were drag racing that night."

"Sorry," Phyllis said. "I got no idea."

She went inside the depot, leaving Claire frustrated and depressed. She had nothing with which to blackmail Phyllis and no junkyard dog like Stanley to do her dirty work. She went back up the hill and met Ed coming out of the newspaper office.

"Hey," he said. "You look like you could use a hug."

"Thanks," she said as she accepted one.

Claire was surprised to feel a little spark when they hugged. It temporarily flustered her, and she felt herself blush.

"What's going on?" Ed asked, seemingly oblivious to her discomfort. "What did you do to your hand?"

"Off the record, I took a swing at Knox," Claire said. "I think it hurt me more than him."

"Congratulations," Ed said. "I've wanted to do that many times."

"If you've got time now I can get you caught up on Tuppy's murder investigation," Claire said. "Scott says I'm not a suspect anymore."

They went back inside the newspaper office and sat down at the elevated work table in the middle of the room. A mock-up of the latest issue of the Sentinel was on the table, and she could see he had saved space for a piece about Tuppy's death. Ed took notes while she talked.

After she finished recounting everything she was comfortable sharing Ed looked thoughtful.

"I may be able to help," he said. "I can probably find out who the college kids were in the depot this morning."

"That would be great," Claire said. "It's a long shot, but I'm running out of suspects."

Claire went back to The Bee Hive, where her next two customers were waiting. To her delight, she managed to talk one of Denise's life-long shampoo set customers into a short, flattering haircut. The second appointment wasn't so brave, but she did let Claire schedule her for some highlights to perk up the dark brown helmet she'd been sporting for several decades.

She had two permanent waves, a color and cut, and then two walk-in customers who had seen her on the news the night before with Sloan. They were young stay-at-home moms who had been best friends since grade school. They picked their haircuts out of celebrity magazines, and fortunately neither one asked for Sloan's Tweetheart 'do. Considering that had been a wig, Claire couldn't really claim ownership of that design.

Ed came in as she finished up the second one, and he waited patiently until he was alone with Claire.

"I've got two first names," he said. "The busboy at the Depot heard Phyllis call them Kyle and Peyton. He said they've been coming in every morning for about a week."

"It's a start," Claire said. "I just have to figure out what to do with that information."

"I'll go down to the campus and see if one of the security guards knows who they are," Ed said.

Ed left, and Claire began cleaning up after her last appointment. She was mopping the floor when Hannah came in dragging a man behind her. She introduced him as "Dr. Drew Rosen." Claire shook his hand, and he smiled at her.

"It's a pleasure to meet you," Drew said. "Hannah said you had a haircut appointment available and she insists I need a trim."

"You guys have a lot in common," Hannah said.

Drew rolled his eyes, and Claire suppressed a laugh.

"Now that I've met you I feel sure we'll be married before the year is up," Claire said.

"I hope you like kosher food," Drew said, "because I could never raise children with someone outside my faith."

"Very funny," Hannah said. "Ha, ha, ha."

Claire gave Hannah the first names of the boys and Hannah said that was all she needed.

"I've got connections all over that campus," she said. "I'll track them down."

Hannah left and Drew sat in the shampoo bowl chair.

"I really could use a haircut," he said.

As Claire washed his hair, she considered his green eyes, lanky, muscular frame, and hiker attire.

"Were you a Peace Corps guy?" she asked.

"Yeah," he said. "How'd you know?"

"I'm just a good guesser," Claire said, satisfied now that she had correctly cast him as an ecological crusader in the Amazon rainforest who falls passionately in love with the beautiful but brainy microbiologist he hates for the first half of the film.

They chit-chatted as she trimmed his hair, and although he was a nice enough guy, he didn't ring any bells for her. Claire was pleasantly impressed, and that was all. As he left two more customers arrived, and she didn't give him another thought.

Scooter Scoley dropped by, but he wasn't interested in a haircut. He was still sporting the same mullet he'd worn ever since they were in the tenth grade, only now the shiny black hair was mixed with silver.

"You didn't think I was gonna let you come to town and not sing for me," he said. "We're playing at the Thorn this weekend, and I want you front and center."

"I don't know," Claire said. "I'm pretty rusty."

"Don't you give me that," Scooter said. "You get there about seven, and we'll get your pipes warmed up for the eight o'clock show."

"I can't believe you're still doing it," Claire said. "I thought you'd meet some local gal and she'd make you settle down."

"I meet local gals all the time," Scooter said. "That's one of the reasons I keep doin' it."

"You always were a ladies' man," Claire said. "You haven't changed a bit."

"We're booked up through the New Year," he said. "We'll be traveling all over the Southeast. I'd love to have you come along."

I don't think so," Claire said. "I'm thinking of settling down myself."

"You won't," Scooter said. "You're just like me; we're the restless kind."

"Tell you what," Claire said. "Anytime you're playing in the Thorn I'll join you."

"That's a deal," Scooter said. "I'm holdin' you to it."

Ed stopped in to say he'd found out the full names of the boys.

"I ran into Hannah," he said. "She knows the registrar, so she's going to take it from there."

"Thanks, Ed," she said. "Do you have a minute?"

"Sure."

"I had my head so far up my own backside this morning I forgot to ask you about Tommy."

"That's understandable," Ed said. "Being a murder suspect will do that to you."

"So who is this boy and why does he live with you?"

"His mama and I dated for awhile, and he and I got close," Ed said. "She had to go away for awhile, so he's staying with me until she gets back."

"Was this the Mandy who lived with my mom and dad for awhile; way back, like ten or fifteen years ago? The waitress?"

"One and the same," Ed said.

"I'd forgotten all about her," Claire said. "Why'd you break up?"

"Because I'm an idiot," he said. "I didn't know what I had until I lost it."

"I'm so sorry," Claire said. "Do you ever hear from Eve?"

"We e-mail once or twice a year," Ed said. "She's working for a big news organization in New York."

"She never liked me," Claire said, "but I did try."

"We all tried," Ed said. "She just didn't belong here."

"I wonder if I do," Claire said.

"Give it some time," Ed said. "You're not in any hurry are you?"

"I guess not," Claire said. "I've got no place to go or anyone waiting for me."

"Let's you and I get a beer this weekend at the Thorn," he said. "We'll get all caught up."

"It looks like I'll be singing there with the Snufftuckers on Saturday night," she said. "I'm not sure it's wise, but I'm doing it anyway."

"That's how we get to experience the best life has to offer," Ed said. "Sometimes you have to take your heart out for a spin and leave your head at home."

"You've changed," Claire said. "I always thought of you as the most sensible, cautious person I know. What happened?"

"I fell in love with a pretty young waitress," Ed said, "and then like a fool I let her get away."

"She's coming back, you said."

"She's coming back here, but not back to me."

"You're not dead yet," Claire said. "So there's still hope."

"How about Pip and you?" he said. "Is there still hope there?"

"I won't kick you for suggesting it this time," Claire said, "but don't do it again."

As Claire worked on her next customers, she was distracted by thoughts of what she would do when she did know who the students were. Why would they tell her anything? She wasn't young enough to seduce them, and she didn't have any power over the rich brats who attended Eldridge. She could threaten to blackmail them as if she knew what had happened, and hope to get them to confess. In her mind, she went back through decades of the films she'd seen looking for a plot that covered this situation, but in almost every one someone ended up getting shot.

"I know where those boys hid their car," Hannah said as she rushed in through the door to The Bee Hive at just past noon. "They just hired Hatch to tow it from a storage unit to a body shop in Pendleton."

"Phyllis must have tipped them off that I was asking about them," Claire said.

"Hatch is going to let us ride out there with him," Hannah said.

"I can't leave right now," Claire said. "I'm double-booked the rest of the day."

Claire was putting the finishing touches on an impressive up-do, more suited to 1967 than the current year, perhaps, but still an architectural marvel, nonetheless. She had another lady waiting, and expected two more people within the hour.

"We can't let them get away with it," Hannah said.

"I'm sorry," Claire said. "I promised Denise I would see this through. Call Scott."

"His mom's dying," Hannah said, "and I somehow can't see Skip and Frank pulling this off."

"Call Tiny Crimefighter," Claire said. "She lives for this stuff."

"No way," said Hannah. "I'll be back."

Claire just shook her head and went back to her customers.

A little later Gwyneth Eldridge came in to look down her nose at everyone in The Bee Hive. Her expression suggested she was the only clean person in a room full of mud wrestlers.

"Hello Gwyneth," Claire said.

"I can't believe you'd rather work here than for me at the Inn," she said.

"Sorry," Claire said. "I'm sure my mother will be back to work soon."

"She just resigned," Gwyneth said. "Now I have no one."

Hannah came in, saw Gwyneth was there and scooted around her to sit in the unoccupied second hydraulic chair. Gwyneth gave her a look that telecast just how little she thought of her, and then turned back to Claire.

"I don't understand you people," Gwyneth said. "You won't get another opportunity like I'm offering you. There is no better place to work in this godforsaken town, and I can pay more than anyone else."

"I'm not interested," Claire said. "I'm sorry if that offends you."

Gwyneth looked as if she'd like to stamp her foot. She was power-sulking like the champion pouter she was, only this time it didn't get her what she wanted.

"I'm so disappointed I don't know what to say," she finally said.

"I believe 'off with your head' is traditional," Hannah said.

Gwyneth rolled her eyes in contempt and left.

"I wonder if Mom is going back to work for Ava," Claire said.

"I doubt it," Hannah said. "And I'll tell you why later. Here comes your relief."

Denise Deluca's mother Delphina Gambini, known as Delphie, entered The Bee Hive. She was wearing a brightly colored, abstract-patterned sequined tunic over stretch pants, and her highly-teased hair was bright copper red. She looked as if she had on stage makeup, and her thinly-drawn eyebrows arched high above where her natural brows used to reside, giving her a perpetually-surprised look. Pleased to see Claire, she hugged her and kissed her cheek. Her floral perfume was overwhelming, and her stiffly lacquered hairdo scratched Claire's ear.

"Wait 'til you see my new grandbaby," she said. "He's the spittin' image of my youngest; you remember Nicky? He's got a full head of black hair and dimples in both cheeks."

"Sounds like another Gambini heartbreaker," Claire said.

"You gotta come over and see him," Delphie said. "Come for dinner tonight."

"Maybe this weekend," Claire said. "I'm still getting settled."

"I'll make you some gnocchi," Delphie said. "You have been such a blessing to Denise, taking over like this. I would have done it, but Grandpa Frankie has the sleep apnea so bad I'm afraid to leave him for very long. He could take a nap and boom! He'd be dead. My Stephie's with him this afternoon, and she'll keep an eye on him. You remember her; she's my youngest. What a klutz. She broke her ankle in two places and has to wear a cast for six weeks. She's boy crazy, but she can't cook. She's tired of cutting hair, she says. She's going to the community college to be a web developer, whatever the heck that is."

"I'm sorry we have to rush off," Claire said, remembering that you had to be rude to get away from Delphie because she never took a breath.

"You two go on, honey," Delphie said. "I'll take care of this lovely lady. Come for dinner, though, as soon as you're settled. We've always got a room full of people to feed, sweetie, so come anytime. My kitchen stove is always hot."

"Thanks again," Claire said as Hannah pulled her out the door by her arm.

"Glad to do it, honey. You girls go on," Delphie said, and then to the customer, "Hello, darling. What can Delphie do for you today? Look at this thick head of hair, you make me so jealous. Let me tell you about my new grandson ..."

Claire and Hannah ran across the street to the station, where Hatch was waiting in the wrecker.

"You're making me late," Hatch said as they climbed into the cab.

Morris Hatcher had been Hannah's boyfriend in high school. A lanky, skinny, dark-eyed country boy, he'd had to quit school when his parents died, leaving him in charge of his four younger siblings. He was now raising his nephew, the red-headed Joshie, whom everyone suspected was Brian Fitzpatrick's illegitimate son with Hatch's sister.

"What's the plan?" Claire asked Hannah.

Hannah shrugged.

"I hadn't really figured one out."

"You girls is in way over your fool heads," Hatch said. "If it were me, now, I'd call the law and let them deal with it."

"They'd have to get a search warrant," Hannah said. "It would take too long. We have to do something now before we lose the evidence."

"Like what?" Claire said.

"I'll think of something," Hannah said.

"That's what I'm worried about," Hatch said. "Like as not we'll all end up in the pokey."

The two college kids Claire recognized from the Mountain Laurel were waiting by the storage unit when they pulled up in the wrecker. The two young men were wearing khakis, polo shirts, windbreakers, and loafers with no socks. Claire instantly cast them in a coming of age film set at a resort in the summer. Having got tangled up with the local waitress, an aging seductress, they had been drawn into her tawdry world of drama and drug addiction.

Claire could almost feel sorry for them, having accidentally killed someone, now panicked and trying to cover up their crime. They hadn't intentionally killed Tuppy; it had been a terrible accident. Maybe, Claire thought, she should just let them dispose of the car. An arrest would ruin any hope they had of productive futures. They were so young, after all.

'We all do things we regret,' Claire thought.

"Took you long enough," the taller one said when Hatch rolled down the window to greet them. "You were supposed to be here a half hour ago."

"Maybe he can't tell time," the other one said. "Maybe they just teach readin' and writin' but not 'rithmatic 'round here."

Hatch just rolled his eyes and shook his head as the two boys laughed at him. Any sympathy Claire felt immediately evaporated. She and Hannah got out of the car and stood to the side as Hatch backed the wrecker up to the door of the storage unit.

"Why are you here?" the shorter one asked Hannah.

"He's just giving us a ride," Hannah said.

The two young men looked at each other, rolled their eyes and snickered at Hannah.

"Weren't you in the depot this morning?" the taller one asked Claire. "Sittin' with that crazy old guy?"

Claire felt her blood pressure rise. Hannah gripped Claire's arm, and she just pretended she didn't hear the insult.

"Hey, yeah," Claire said, breaking out her brightest smile. She wished she had on her heels and something more flattering than her mother's tennis shoes, jeans, and a t-shirt.

"I remember you two," Claire said, as Hannah stared at her in amazement. "Phyllis says you guys love to party. She said you all are hardcore."

The taller one puffed up a little and the shorter one looked Claire up and down.

"I guess," the taller one said.

"Phyllis said you were looking for some serious party supplies," Claire said. "That just happens to be my specialty."

Now they looked interested. The taller one walked over and motioned to Claire to move away from Hannah. Claire smiled, hoping her rusty frat-boy-charming skills still worked and followed his direction. The shorter one moved closer in order to hear.

"What have you got?" the taller one asked her.

Close up, she could see that his pupils were already dilated. Claire knew next to nothing about drug culture, as Sloan's vices were more mundane, limited to cigarettes, verbal abuse, and sexually punitive role-playing. She'd just have to pretend to be more knowledgeable than she was. Luckily she remembered some dialogue from the hooker movie for which Sloan had won her academy award. She hoped these two were too young to have seen it.

"I've got everything," she said. "Ecstasy, Vitamin K, smack, meth; you name it, I got it."

"You got any Oxycontin?" the shorter one said, and the taller one said, "Shut up, Peyton."

It suddenly struck Claire that Peyton was the name of Meredith's son, the one who attended Eldridge. Could it be?

"I just got back from LA," Claire said. "I've got some extra-pure blow and some killer skunk that's guaranteed to blow your socks off."

"How much are we talking?" the taller one said.

"I let good customers sample everything before they invest. How about we party together and then you can decide which ones you like best?"

"Cool!" Peyton said. "Spencer, we should totally do that."

"Where's your place?"

"Tell ya what," Claire said. "I'll give you a little something right now if you want."

"Sure," Spencer said.

Claire went over to the truck, opened the passenger side door, and leaned inside; giving the boys a good long look at her toned rear end.

"What are you doing?" Hatch asked her.

Claire reached into her purse, took out her phone, pressed the commands that caused it to start recording, and stuck it down in her bra. Then she took Hatch's small, round can of snuff off the dashboard and emptied it into a mint tin she had in her purse. When she looked up at Hatch, his eyes were wide, and his mouth hung open.

"Pay attention," Claire said. "Things might get a little crazy here in a minute."

As Claire passed Hannah, she said, "Get in the truck and wait."

Hannah did as she was told.

When she got back to where Spencer and Peyton stood, Claire said, "Hatch needs to get back to work; does he really need to tow your car right now?"

"Yeah," Spencer said. "We need it done now."

"You're not a cop, are you?" Peyton asked, and Spencer punched him in the arm.

"She's not a cop," Spencer said. "The cops in this town are more like the three stooges."

"So what's up with the car?" Claire asked.

"We had an accident last weekend," Spencer said. "We're just getting it towed to the body shop to get fixed."

"And you're worried about the cops seeing it?" Claire said. "Shouldn't you have it towed at night, then?"

"We don't have time," Peyton said, and Spencer said, "Would you just shut up, Peyton?"

"Hit and run?" Claire asked, as her heart began to beat faster.

Spencer shrugged, and Peyton looked down at the ground.

"Hey," Claire said. "I'm a drug dealer; what am I gonna do, call the cops?"

"What do you have?" Spencer asked her.

Claire took the tin full of snuff out of her pocket and opened it like she was revealing caviar.

"This, my friends," she said. "Is Jamaican turtle-hash."

"Do you smoke it?" Peyton asked.

"Yep," said Claire.

"You have any papers?" Spencer asked his friend, who pulled a small folded box of rolling papers out of his back pocket as he answered, "Of course."

Claire watched them roll up Hatch's snuff into a tight little cigarette and then tried not to wince as they lit it up and sucked in the acrid smoke it produced. They passed it between them a couple times, coughing and trying hard not to show how awful it tasted.

When they offered it to Claire, she said, "No thanks, I have to drive to Pittsburgh later to pick up a shipment; that stuff is going to knock you on your asses here in a minute."

"Cool," said Peyton as he choked.

Spencer looked a little green around the gills, and Claire had to bite her lip not to laugh.

"So this accident," Claire said. "You kill somebody?"

Peyton choked harder, and Spencer's complexion turned even greener.

"Cause I heard some guy got mowed down on Peony Street last Friday night. Was he a friend of yours or a local?"

"We didn't know him," Peyton said.

"Shut up!" Spencer said.

"The locals around here are idiots," Peyton said. "We don't party with them."

"Well, I can see how you'd want to get rid of the car," Claire said, her heart pounding in her chest. "His blood's probably all over it."

"There was no blood," Peyton said. "This hash is amazing."

Spencer ran to the side of the paved area and puked in the grass.

"He can't handle it like you can," Claire said to Peyton. "I can see who the real man is here."

"Damn straight," Peyton said. "I'm gettin' wicked messed up on this turtle-weed and Spencer's over there pukin' his guts out."

"No big loss, I guess," Claire said. "The guy you hit."

"That's what I figured," Peyton said. "But Spencer's all freaked out about it. He's afraid his mother's going to find out and cut off his money."

"What about your mom?"

"My mom's locked up in a loony bin," Peyton said. "And my stepdad doesn't have access to my trust fund. I got nothin' to worry about."

"Was Spencer driving," Claire said. "When you hit him?"

"Yeah," Peyton said, taking a long, choking drag on the snuff cigarette. "We were hauling ass, and it was way wicked foggy. We thought it was some stupid local loser, but it turns out he was from Hollywood or something. This guy just runs out in the street, right in front of us. We popped him up, man! He hit the windshield and rolled over the hood and landed on the street behind us; Spencer didn't even stop, he just kept going. We were so messed up; he kept saying 'it was a deer, it was a deer,' but I was like, 'man, that was no deer.'"

"Does anyone else know about this?"

"Just Phyllis; she hooked us up with the guy who owns this place. He doesn't care what you store here or why you store it, especially if you pay cash."

Spencer came back over, rubbing his stomach.

"That's awful," he said. "How can you smoke that?"

"I'm a real man," Peyton said. "That's how."

"You better let them haul your car now," Claire said. "Then we can go back to my place and have us a party."

"Excellent suggestion," Peyton said. "But you'll have to drive, Spencer; I'm already wasted."

Claire waved to Hatch to back up the wrecker.

Hatch backed the wrecker right up to the door. Peyton unlocked and removed the padlock, handed it to Claire, pulled up on the handle of the door, which was just like a garage door, and then lifted and rolled it back.

"Make sure the parking brake is released and the gearshift is set in neutral," Hatch called out to them. Peyton went inside the storage unit, and Spencer waited outside.

Claire craned her neck to see the car, which was parked nose-out. It was a very expensive German car, a newer model. She hadn't expected to feel as emotional as she did when she saw the dent on the front of the hood and the windshield's spider web of cracked glass. She felt like she might be sick, too.

"You're lucky there's no blood," Claire said, although her jaw was clenched. "Peyton told me all about it. He said you were driving kind of fast and the guy just stepped out in front of your car."

"Peyton's an idiot who should learn to keep his mouth shut," Spencer said.

"No need to worry," Claire said. "Telling your drug dealer's like telling a priest."

"I heard it was some homo from Hollyweird," Spencer said. "So no big loss."

"You son of a bitch," Claire said and lunged at him.

She caught him completely off guard. She shoved him into the storage unit, where he fell onto the concrete floor next to the passenger side door of the car. Claire had only a brief glimpse of the stunned face of Peyton sitting inside the car before she grabbed the strap attached to the storage unit door and pulled it down to the ground. She fumbled with the padlock but got it clasped before the boys began pounding on the door and yelling.

Claire stood back, unsure what to do next.

"Damn, woman," Hatch said as he sauntered up to the back of the wrecker and leaned on it. "Remind me never to piss you off."

"That was awesome!" Hannah said, jumping up and down next to Claire. "You knocked that snotty kid on his ass!"

Claire's heart was racing, and she was breathing hard, but she pulled her cell phone out of her bra, ended the recording, and then scrolled until she found the number she was looking for.

"This is Claire Fitzpatrick from Rose Hill. I found the car that killed my friend Tuppy and the people who were driving it," she said to the person who answered, and then gave directions to the storage unit facility. As soon as she hung up, she began to cry.

The young men were banging on the garage door, treating them to a colorful assortment of profane words. Claire couldn't seem to stop crying. Hannah put her arm around Claire on one side, and Hatch put his around her from the other side. Oddly, it felt like a safe place to fall apart.

"You were so brave!" Hannah said. "I'm gonna have to give you a cape and a comic book name."

"You done good, girl," Hatch said. "I reckon your friend's lookin' down on you from heaven. I bet he's purdy proud right now."

Claire imagined Tuppy sitting on a cloud, looking down at how she was attired, in Megamart jeans, puffy white tennis shoes, and a Fitzpatrick Bakery t-shirt, being embraced by a man in dirty coveralls which for some reason had the name "Dwayne" embroidered on the left breast pocket, and by a short woman in a ball cap, sweatshirt, jeans, and hiking boots. She thought pride wouldn't be the primary emotion Tuppy would be moved to express.

'Nice shoes,' she heard him say in her mind. 'Did Dwayne buy them for you?'

'I'm sorry you're gone,' she thought. 'You didn't deserve to die that way.'

'Homo from Hollyweird, Claire? Really?' he said. 'That's my epitaph?'

'I would say handsome, stylish man about town,' Claire thought, 'and a good friend.'

'Too good for you,' Tuppy said. 'And those two boys aren't fooling anyone, by the way. Be sure to tell them I said that.'

'Goodbye, Tuppy,' Claire thought. 'I'll miss you.'

'Don't call me, Claire,' Tuppy said. 'Don't make it weird.'

Then he was gone.

Claire could tell Sarah's warring emotions were making her extra irritable. She was thrilled to be able to arrest someone for the murder but couldn't think of a way to take credit for everything. She listened to Claire's story and the recording before she asked to see the snuff can. After she sniffed it and made a face, she said, "That's snuff, alright. What idiots."

She let Claire wait in the wrecker with Hatch and Hannah while she and her deputies removed Spencer and Peyton from the storage unit and then put them in separate county cruisers. When she finally returned to the truck, she stood at the open window looking almost jubilant.

"Do you know who that kid is?" Sarah asked. "That's Peyton Stanhope Huckle."

"I thought it might be," Claire said. "That should make things interesting."

"I'll need you to come down to the office and give me your statement," she told Claire, and to Hannah and Hatch she said, "You two can go."

"Thank you, Ms. Albright," Hannah said in her best Sunday school voice.

"That's Detective Tiny Crimefighter to you," Sarah said. "And don't you forget it."

Peony Street by Pamela Grandstaff

Chapter Eleven - Friday

Scott held Maggie's hand as the Hospice nurse gave him and his sister the latest update. They were sitting at the kitchen table with Penny, her recently-arrived husband Kyle, Doc Machalvie and Father Stephen. Sister Mary Margrethe and Claire's mother Delia were hovering nearby.

"It won't be much longer," the nurse said. "You should say what you need to say."

"They're killing her," Penny said to Scott, "and it's all your fault."

Penny fled sobbing down the hall to the bedroom with her husband right behind her. Scott felt his eyes fill with tears and his vision blurred. Maggie squeezed his hand, but he didn't look at her for fear that he might lose what composure he had left.

"I want to thank you all," he said to the room full of people, after clearing his throat and wiping his eyes, "for everything you've done for my mother, my sister, and me."

Everyone made the appropriate noises but to Scott, they sounded very far away, and he didn't really listen; he just nodded, clasped the hands that were offered, accepted the hugs and the words meant to comfort. After they left he sat there for a while, he didn't know how long, before he realized everyone was gone; everyone but Maggie.

"What time is it?" he asked her.

"It's after three," she said. "Sister M Squared is in with your mom and Delia went home to make you guys some supper. Doc said he'd be back later, and Father Stephen went to get his last rites ... kit, I guess. I don't know what they call it."

"I was ten when my dad got sick and died," Scott said. "They sent me to Ed's house to stay until the funeral was over; they didn't think I should go. Ed's mom was still around then. She said I should always picture my dad doing something I loved doing with him. We used to toss a baseball for hours in the backyard; that's how I remember him."

"Your dad was so fun," Maggie said. "He was always smiling."

"After going through this with her, I don't know how I'll remember my mom any way except how she is right now."

"It will take time," Maggie said. "My memories of Grandpa Tim are from when he was much younger, not how he was at the end."

Scott felt his mind wander, and it was some time before he felt present again.

"I've always taken for granted that we live in a town where people help each other; where, if you fall down, someone will come along and pick you up," Scott said. "I do realize how lucky I am to have all these people who are willing to help."

"It's the flip side of everyone knowing your business," Maggie said. "Assistance paid for by the loss of any kind of privacy."

"It feels worth it today," he said.

"It's what church people are supposed to do," Maggie said. "It's what friends and neighbors are supposed to do. When Grandpa Tim and Brian died lots of people were kind to our family. It even restored my faith, in a way."

"I've been wrestling with this idea of expecting God to solve my problems if only I'm good enough," Scott said. "After what I've experienced over the past few days I don't think it works that way. I think God must not be able to do anything on His own, that He can only inspire people to act on His behalf. I think God makes His presence known through the kind acts of people, and we decide whether to invite His presence or send it away through how we treat each other."

"You've been spending way too much time with these religious people," Maggie said. "I'm going to have to take you down to the Thorn to get you some perspective."

"It's not easy to do the right thing all the time," Scott said. "It's not easy to love thy neighbor."

"You're awfully good at it, though," Maggie said. "I mean, you're almost sickeningly generous and kind. Plus you're so damn helpful I can hardly stand you half the time. Hannah's comic book name for you is Nicely Super Scout."

"I find it hard to be kind to people I don't like, and people I don't approve of," Scott said. "I judge everyone all the time."

"I don't like 99.9 percent of the people I meet," Maggie said. "I can count the people I like on one hand and still have a middle finger left over to show the rest of them."

"Everyone in this town could show up here tonight to help me, and I would be grateful," Scott said, "but not as grateful as I am to be sitting here, holding hands with you."

"You know how I hate it when you get squishy," Maggie said. "It makes me want to pinch you."

"I hope you never get tired of pinching me."

"I hate to tell you this, Saint Scott of Rose Hill," Maggie said, "but I really have to pee."

"Alright," he said. "If you really have to."

Maggie got up and went down the hall just as Scott's brother-in-law Kyle came out of his sister's bedroom.

"How's she doing?" Scott asked him.

"She's resting," Kyle said. "How are you holding up?"

"It doesn't seem real," Scott said. "A week ago she had a bad cough, and now she's dying."

"Penny thinks the Hospice people are killing her."

"I know."

"I don't think that," Kyle said. "Penny's just upset."

"I know," Scott said. "It's okay."

"When Penny's upset she says awful stuff," Kyle said. "She doesn't mean to hurt you."

"I know," Scott said. "I love Penny; we'll be fine, eventually."

As Maggie walked back down the hall toward Scott he thought to himself that she was the reason he could get through this; she was why he knew he would be okay. Maggie was giving him the extra strength he needed. He couldn't imagine she needed God's inspiration to do that. She was too pigheaded to let anyone tell her what to do. No, if she was here it wasn't divine intervention, it was because she cared.

"I'm going to run over to Delia's," she said. "I'll bring your dinner back here in a little bit. Call me if something happens."

"Thank you," Scott said, rising from the table to embrace her, "for everything."

Maggie pinched him really hard on the arm, and he said, "Ow!"

"What did I tell you 'bout that?" Maggie said and then kissed his cheek.

Kyle waited until Maggie left to ask, "What did she do that for?"

"She loves me," Scott said.

When Claire stopped by Denise's house to drop off the week's deposit, Denise immediately handed her a sleeping baby swaddled in a flannel blanket.

Claire looked down at the little old man face of Dom Jr. His lips were very thin, and he had flaky, blotchy skin all over his scalp and face. It was all she could do not to whip out something with which to exfoliate the child. She didn't feel all ooey-gooey inside like she thought she would. He didn't smell very good, for one thing.

"He has cradle cap," Denise said. "I've been picking at it all morning."

"He's so big," Claire said. "It's hard to believe he was just inside your belly."

"Nine pounds eight ounces," Denise said. "Took to the bottle like a champ. I'm not nursing this one, and his two nonnas are having a fit over it. 'They're my boobs,' I told 'em. 'Not yours; so lay off.' They're relentless."

"I'm so happy for you," Claire said.

"Let me ask you something," Denise said. "I've been looking for somebody to buy the salon. What do you say?"

"I don't think so," Claire said and handed the warm bundle back to his mother. "My life is in serious disarray right now. I can't commit to anything."

"Someone called us with an offer," Denise said. "It's from a company in New York. I thought maybe you had something to do with it."

"No," Claire said, although she had a good idea who had.

As Claire was walking home from the Delucas' house, her phone rang.

"Miss Fitzpatrick," a man said. "This is Morton Devorah. I was the late Mr. Tupworth's literary agent."

Claire listened, fascinated, as Tuppy's agent outlined a publisher's six-figure offer for her to contribute additional material to Tuppy's book.

"That's a huge advance these days," he said. "Unfortunately murder and scandal make excellent bargaining tools."

"I have a confidentiality agreement," Claire said. "I can't divulge any information about Sloan."

"According to Mr. Tupworth, those documents were all lost during the transfer of Ms. Merryweather's legal files from one firm to another."

"I can't comment on that," Claire said.

"The Tupworths have expressed interest in publishing on their son's behalf," he said, "but you've known her for 20 years; that would give the book more credibility."

"Thank you, but no," Claire said. "I'm ready to leave all that behind me."

Mr. Devorah assured Claire he would try again. Claire assumed he thought she was playing hard to get in order to push the price up.

Scott was surprised to see Sarah at his mother's front door.

"Skip and Frank are on duty today," Scott said, stepping outside rather than inviting her in. "Was there something you specifically needed me for?"

"I just wanted to let you know we caught the hit-and-run driver who killed Mr. Tupworth."

"That's good news," Scott said. "Who was it?"

"A couple of college kids were drag-racing," Sarah said. "I got a tip they were attempting to move the car to another location and was able to get there before they did. The damage to the car is consistent with what we thought happened, plus I have a recorded conversation of the driver admitting he did it."

"That's certainly another feather in your cap," Scott said. "Congratulations."

"How's your mother?" she asked.

"Not well," Scott said.

"Is there anything I can do to help?" Sarah asked.

Scott must have conveyed his disbelief in her sincerity through his facial expression because she said, "I mean it; I want to help if I can."

"Thanks, Sarah," he said. "I'll let you know."

She started to leave and then turned back.

"If you got any complaints about me you'd let me know, wouldn't you? I mean before you passed them on to my supervisor?"

"What did you do?"

"Nothing," Sarah said. "I'm just reminding you that we need to have the kind of professional relationship where we watch out for each other. I make you look good, and you make me look good."

"I'll let you know if I hear anything," Scott said.

"Good," she said and left.

"I wonder what she's done now," Scott said to himself as he went back inside. "Although I'm sure I'll hear about it before the day's over."

When Delia got home, Claire was in the kitchen cutting her father's hair.

"Your hand still looks awful," Delia said, "although the swelling is down."

"It looks worse than it is," Claire said.

"What'd you do to your hand?" Ian asked, and grabbed it to take a look.

"She accidentally slammed a door on it," Delia said.

"The hell you did," Ian said. "Who'd you take a poke at?"

"Knox," Claire whispered in his ear, "but don't tell."

Ian laughed.

"I wish I'd seen that," he said. "My darlin' girl decked that insufferable bastard."

"Ian!" Delia said. "Claire would never hit someone. And don't curse in my house."

"Good for you," Ian said to Claire. "Don't let anyone give you any guff."

"Did you see your boxes arrived?" Delia asked her daughter.

"Yes," Claire said. "I've only been here a week but none of my pants fit."

"You should have seen her eating biscuits and gravy at the depot," Ian said. "She needed a shovel."

'Thanks, Dad," Claire said.

"Kay wants to know if you'll sing at church this Sunday," Delia said. "Her daughter's got a bad sore throat and doesn't think she'll be able to do it."

"What's the song?"

"The Lord's Prayer."

"I'm ashamed to admit I may not remember the words."

"I can't remember lots of things," Ian said.

"We'll practice until you do remember," Delia said. "Think how it would look if you needed to read the words to 'The Lord's Prayer.'"

"Is this going to be a thing now?" Claire asked. "Where I have to sing in church every Sunday?"

"It would be nice," Delia said, "if you thought of it as something you wanted to do and not a chore."

"Just this once," Claire said. "That's all I'm promising."

Claire's mother smiled in a way that showed she had got her way, and Claire knew this would indeed become a regular thing.

"I saw Scooter Scoley over at Curtis's station the other day," Ian said. "He said you were going to sing with him, but I don't remember where."

"That would be fun for you," Delia said.

"Tomorrow night in the Thorn," Claire said. "I'm getting butterflies just thinking about it."

"All the more reason to practice," Delia said. "I need to get our piano tuned."

"Do you remember singing at my mother's funeral?" Ian asked Claire.

"I certainly do," Claire said. "I'm surprised you do."

336

"You sang like a bird," Ian said. "It did my heart proud to hear it."

"'Abide with Me,'" Delia said. 'That's what she sang."

"There wasn't a dry eye in the house," Ian said.

"Including mine," Claire said. "How is it you can remember that?"

"He can remember the distant past much better than the recent past," Delia said. "It's something about where older memories are stored versus newer ones."

"I can't remember why I can't remember," Ian said. "Did I get hit on the head or something?"

"Might be," Delia said.

"I played a lot of football when I was in school," he said. "That was probably it."

"I'm sorry it took me so long to get to this," Claire said as she resumed cutting her father's hair.

"It's just like the plumber," he said, "but I can't remember why that is."

"How was the, um, talk with Sarah?" Delia asked her.

"It was fine," Claire said. "I'm just glad to have it over with. How's Scott?"

"Well, your cousin Maggie is over there, believe it or not," Delia said.

"Oh, I believe it," Claire said. "They belong together."

"You missed your chance," Ian said. "She must be a better kisser."

Delia looked at Claire as if to say, "What?" but Claire just shook her head.

"Everything's going to turn out like it should," Claire said. "I'm back home, Maggie and Scott are back together, and you're finally getting a haircut."

"I've got hairs in my ears," Ian said.

"Don't you worry about that," Claire said. "I've got plans for your ears, your nose, and your eyebrows."

"Claire's going to make me beautiful," Ian told Delia.

Peony Street by Pamela Grandstaff

Delia stooped down to kiss his cheek as she passed
by.

"You're always beautiful to me, Chief," she said.

There was a commotion outside, and Delia looked
out the back door window.

"Where's Mackie?" she asked Claire.

"Around here somewhere," Claire said. "Why?"

"No reason," Delia said with a smile.

"How's Scott's mom?"

"Not good," Delia said. "I'm going to take them some
dinner."

The phone rang, and Claire answered. After she hung
up, Delia asked her who it was.

"Denise," Claire said. "She asked if I would continue
to run the shop while she's on maternity leave."

"And?" Delia asked.

"I said I would," Claire said. "I'm not doing anything
else, so why not?"

"Why not, indeed," her mother said and gave her a
hug. "I think that's wonderful."

"I've got to go clothes shopping," Claire said. "I'm
about to wear out these jeans."

"I'd like to have my shoes back," Delia said.

"I have come to really appreciate these shoes," Claire
said. "I may have to get some, myself."

Hannah came in the front door.

"Has anyone seen my son?" she asked. "My mother
just called to say he's run off with that pack of wild dogs
that's raising him."

Delia pointed at the back door.

Hannah went outside, and Delia began assembling
ingredients for dinner.

Maggie came in through the front door.

"Oh, my Lord, that sister," she said. "What a selfish
witch."

"Now, now," Delia said. "Everyone grieves in a different way."

"I think Scott's having some sort of religious experience," Maggie said. "He's talking like a TV preacher."

"Maybe," Delia said, "this is strengthening his faith."

"Or he's lost his mind," Maggie said. "I don't know if I can handle four sermons a day from now on."

"It will pass," Delia said. "If it makes him feel better right now I say let him do whatever he needs to."

"I passed a kidney stone once," Ian said. "I felt much better afterward."

Maggie, Claire, and Delia all looked at one another, each suppressing a smile. Claire reflected that although the fact that he had dementia certainly wasn't funny, some of the things he said certainly were.

For the next several minutes Claire listened to Maggie carrying on about Scott's family, and Delia admonishing her to be nicer, and Ian interjecting statements that didn't make perfect sense. Dogs were barking out back, and Hannah could be heard shouting at Sammy.

Claire felt as if she'd been home for months instead of only a week. Her life with Sloan was already receding into the past, and this life was becoming the real one, the one to which she belonged. She was looking forward to the weekend ahead of her; some shopping with her mother, some breakfasts, lunches, and dinners with various family members. She'd like to go see her Uncle Fitz, and maybe call up some old friends.

She wanted to do something nice for Scott and his family. She needed to get her room in some sort of order; right now it was like sleeping in a hoarder's nest. She would start working on her parents' house, she thought, and maybe look for a place of her own nearby.

She thought to herself, 'it's so good to be home,' but she didn't dare say it out loud for fear Maggie would pretend to throw up.

Hannah came back inside and said, "Hey, Claire, do you know where your dog is?"

"She's probably back in the bedroom, sleeping," Claire said. "Why?"

"Where's my little darlin'?" Ian asked Claire. "Where's Papaw's angel?"

Claire realized she'd lost track of Mackie Pea and didn't know where she was. She didn't want to agitate her father if Mackie had run off, so she said, "You've worn her out, Dad; she's probably taking a nap."

Claire searched and called for her, but Mackie Pea was not in the house. Claire called Skip and Skip's mom, but neither of them had seen her. Much to Claire's surprise, they didn't seem too awfully worried.

"She'll show up when she's hungry," Skip's mother said. "They always do."

"She's probably chasing shrews down by the river," Skip said. "She'll find her way home eventually."

Claire tried not to worry, but she kept picturing Mackie Pea wandering around lost and afraid in her little pink and purple coat. There were so many dangers for a small dog not used to living in such a rural environment. Possums and raccoons could be terribly mean, not to mention there were actual bears in the woods beyond the town. Some people shot strays rather than rescue them. What if Mackie chased someone's chickens and they shot at her?

The more her worried thoughts raced, the more panicked she felt. Should she leave and go look for her or wait here for her to come home?

Hannah tapped on the back door window, and Claire opened the door.

"Come out here," Hannah said through the screen door.

Claire went out the back door onto the porch. Maggie and her parents followed.

"It's freezing out here," Claire said.

Sammy was sitting on the porch steps, laughing and clapping.

"What's going on?" Claire said.

"Watch," Hannah said.

Hannah's dogs Jax and Wally streaked across the yard, followed by Mackie Pea in her pink and purple coat, now caked with mud. Wally had something in his mouth that Jax was trying to take away from him, and they ended up in a tug of war with whatever it was, growling and snarling at each other.

Jax, the Siberian Husky, was no match for Wally the Border Collie; Wally could dart, double back, and turn on a dime. Mackie Pea kept trying to get a grip on whatever it was they were fighting over, but she couldn't keep up with the bigger dogs. Jax and Wally completely ignored her, but she seemed to be having the time of her life.

Claire tried to picture the pampered, spoiled princess she'd brought to Rose Hill a week ago, with her expensive, organic, grain-free dog food and Louis Vuitton pet carrier. It was hard to believe this could be the same dog, now covered in filth and jumping, snapping, and rolling in the grass with the big boys.

"What is it they're fighting over?" Claire asked.

"Me's bad guy belt," Sammy said.

Claire sighed as she recognized what was left of her baby blue Birkin bag accessory, the one she'd traded for Tuppy's book.

"Tell me again how much that fancy purse set you back," Hannah said, and Claire smacked her lightly on the arm.

"I think Mackie's going to fit in very well," Delia said as she put her arm around Claire. "Just like you."

Next door, Ed Harrison and Tommy walked outside to watch the dogs.

"There's Liam," Ian said and waved merrily at the young boy, who waved back.

"Come home for dinner," Ian shouted.

Delia gripped Claire's hand as Hannah said, "That's Tommy, Uncle Ian."

"Tommy?" Ian said. "I don't know any Tommy. I know my own son when I see him. Call him home, Delia. He needs to eat his dinner before soccer practice."

"He's going to eat with Bonnie's boys," Delia said as she took him by the arm and led him back into the house. "You know how he likes her cooking."

"She's mean, though," Ian said as they went back in the house. "Mean as a striped snake."

"That must be so awful, Claire," Maggie said. "I'm so sorry."

"Poor Tommy," Claire said. "This morning Dad knew who he was."

"Tommy just goes along with it," Hannah said. "He doesn't mind."

"He must be a nice kid," Claire said.

"He is," Maggie said. "His mother's nice, too."

"What's that story?" Claire said. "And why isn't Mom working for Ava at the B&B anymore? And why did Lily sell her farm and move? I need to be brought up to speed, girls."

Hannah covered up Sammy's ears and said, "Not now."

"Bad words," Sammy said. "Gimme you's dollars."

"I want to hear more about you skinny-dipping with Scott Gordon," Hannah said, and then let go of Sammy's ears.

"Me, too," said Maggie. "I'm going to require a much more detailed version of that incident than what I've received so far."

Ed called out "see you later," and he and Tommy went back in his house.

"Give me the scoop on Ed and the waitress first," Claire said.

"It was doomed from the start," Maggie said. "They had nothing in common."

"Ed's single now," Hannah said. "I could fix that up for you."

"Don't let her do it," Maggie said. "She's a horrible matchmaker."

"I may have failed with you and Scott," Hannah said, "but otherwise I'm actually quite successful."

"I'm pretty good myself," Claire said, with a sly glance at Maggie, who then pinched her.

"Look," Hannah said, "it's snowing."

Sure enough, small flakes of snow were falling, carried sideways by a brisk wind.

"But it's April," Claire said.

"Welcome back to Rose Hill," Maggie said. "We have eight months of winter here, remember?"

"I better go turn in my rental car before it gets bad," Claire said. "Will you guys follow me to Pendleton and then bring me home?"

"Sure," Hannah said.

"Can we's go to Megamart?" Sammy asked hopefully.

"Sure," Claire said.

"Me wants a monster truck," Sammy said. "A big one!"

"If you're very, very good," Claire said.

"Careful," Hannah said. "That's a very slippery slope."

"Me need a new gun," Sammy said. "They's never lets me plays with guns."

"No way," Claire said. "Just a truck, if you're good."

"And a video," Sammy said, "and bubbles and candy and a magic trick and a dinosaur and a fish."

"He knows exactly where those fish are and can fit several in the front pouch of his long johns," Hannah said. "He also picks pockets, so don't bring any cash with you."

"I can handle it," Claire said.

"Ha," said Maggie. "This I want to see."

"Ask him about riding in the shopping cart," Hannah said.

"Noooooooooo!" Sammy whined. "Me no riding in the buggy!"

"Maybe we'll just drive through somewhere and get a kid's meal," Claire said. "There's always a toy in there."

"Me wants a cheeseburger and a mountain moonshine slurshee!" Sammy said. "Please, please, please, please, please? We's go now!"

"Is it too late to back out?" Claire said.

"This is just a small preview of what's to come," Hannah said. "We haven't even had the car seat fight yet."

"Me no riding in the car seat!" Sammy yelled.

"That's non-negotiable, surely," Claire said.

"You would think," Hannah said. "Unfortunately it's against the law to restrain him with duct tape, and Sammy has yet to meet the child seat locking mechanism he cannot defeat."

"Maybe he could just stay with my mom, and we'll bring back something for him," Claire said.

"Now you're starting to see my side of it," Hannah said. "Hey Sammy, let's call your father and see what he's doing."

"Noooooooooo!" Sammy wailed. "Me no want Daddy; Me want Claire Bear to takes me to Megamart and buys me a monster truck and a mountain moonshine slurshee!"

Mackie Pea came running up the steps, foam dripping from her muzzle.

"Oh, my Lord," Claire said. "What's wrong with her?"

"She's just rolled in deer poop or something," Hannah said. "They foam like that when something's particularly smelly and gross."

Claire picked up the little dog, and the stench almost knocked her back.

"Her's stinky," Sammy said and held his nose.

Claire pealed the knitted coat off her back and considered what was left of it.

"Skip's mom is not going to be happy about this," she said.

"Let me ask you something, Claire," Hannah said. "Aren't you worried about what might happen to Mackie, running away like that? Wouldn't she be better off in a doggie daycare where she can play with other dogs? Why I wonder, can't you control this small dog?"

"I get it," Claire said. "I really do, and I'm sorry I was so judgy when I first got here. There's really only so much you can do, isn't there? You can't control everything all the time."

"You're coming along quite nicely; I'll have you fully grown up in no time," Hannah said. "Hey, where's my kid?"

Sammy was gone, and so were Jax and Wally.

Hannah speed-dialed her husband.

"I don't know what I did with all my time before I had that child," Hannah said, "but I wish I'd taken more naps."

Claire carried Mackie Pea into the house and down the hall to the bathroom to give her a bath, only to find a naked Sammy sitting on the toilet.

"Me pooping," he said.

"Hannah!" Claire called down the hall. "Found him!"

"You's living in Delia's house now?" Sammy asked her. "With you's daddy and you's little girl dog?"

"I am," Claire said.

"You's staying a long time?"

"I am," Claire said to Sammy. "I'm staying a long, long time."

Acknowledgments

This book is dedicated to my father, John R. Grandstaff, who taught me what it means to be a grownup. I also want to honor my brave, strong, generous mother, Betsy Grandstaff, for everything she does and is.

I'm grateful to my sister Terry Hutchison and her family, and my niece Ella Curry and her family, for their loyalty, faithful support, and practical assistance.

Many thanks to my wonderful friends Martha, Sharon, Mitzi, Harriette, Ethel, Karen, Jaimie, and Christy for their good advice, big hearts, and shared laughter.

Thanks so much to Ella Curry for her expert editing, and to Joan Turner and Mitzi Cyrus for their expert proofreading.

Thank you to Tamarack: The Best of West Virginia, for selling my paper books in your beautiful building.

I also want to thank the people who buy and read my books. Thank you so much.

Finally, I want to thank Henry for being such a good dog; I miss him so much.

If you liked this book, please leave a review on Amazon.com (Thank you!)